Watch Her Fall

Erin Kelly

Watch Her Fall

HODDER

First published in Great Britain in 2021 by Hodder & Stoughton
An Hachette UK company

This paperback edition published in 2022

1

A CIP catalogue record for this title is available from the British Library

Paperback ISBN 978 1 473 68085 2

Typeset in Sabon MT by Hewer Text UK Ltd, Edinburgh
Printed and bound in Great Britain by Clays Ltd, Elcograf S.p.A.

Hodder & Stoughton policy is to use papers that are natural, renewable
and recyclable products and made from wood grown in sustainable
forests. The logging and manufacturing processes are expected to
conform to the environmental regulations of the country of origin.

Hodder & Stoughton Ltd
Carmelite House
50 Victoria Embankment
London EC4Y 0DZ

www.hodder.co.uk

For my daughters

'A dancer dies twice – once when they stop dancing, and this first death is the more painful.'

Martha Graham

PRELUDE

Swan Lake, the eternal story of doomed love, is one of the most performed ballets in the world: a nineteenth-century Russian dance, based on a German fairytale.

Prince Siegfried must choose a wife. On his twenty-first birthday, he goes hunting by a moonlit lake, where a flock of white swans turn into young women. Prince Siegfried falls in love with their leader, Princess Odette, at first sight. She explains that the lake is made of her late mother's tears and that her stepfather, the evil sorcerer Von Rothbart, has bewitched Odette and her friends to live as swans by day. Odette can only resume her human form if a man who has never loved before promises to love her forever.

White swan.

Siegfried invites Odette to a ball at his palace the following evening. At the ball, six foreign princesses compete for Prince Siegfried's attention while he searches the ballroom for his beloved Odette. Von Rothbart arrives with his daughter Odile, dressed in black and disguised as Odette.

Black swan.

Odile and Siegfried dance together; believing her to be Odette, he asks her to marry him. Only when he glimpses Odette through a window does he realise that he has been tricked – and that he has condemned his true love to eternity as a swan.

Devastated, he rushes to the lake, where he begs Odette to forgive him, but she dies of grief in his arms, and the waves overwhelm them both.

The ballet is divided into the black acts, the scenes at court;

and the white acts, the swans by the lake. The prince is on stage for most of the ballet, but it's the swans audiences flock to see.

In early productions of *Swan Lake*, Odette and Odile were performed by two different dancers. These days, the same dancer usually plays both roles: after all, the white and black swans never meet. They are only seen briefly together at the ball, when Odette appears in the window and Siegfried realises his mistake. This second Odette can be played by anyone resembling the principal dancer.

Because of the faultless ballet technique required to master the steps, and the emotional range needed to perform both the virginal Odette and the dark, seductive Odile, this challenging dual role is one of the most coveted in all ballet.

Dancers would kill for the part.

ACT I

AVA

I

It was nine o'clock in the morning and already thirty-one degrees. London shimmered in a dirty haze. The weather reporter on the radio had said that it was hot enough to fry an egg on the pavement. Ava Kirilova thought about this as heat from the paving stones burned through the soles of her shoes, but she was not allowed to eat fried eggs, and wouldn't have known how to cook one if she were.

The stroll to work always eased out the aches of the day before, but today the sun blasted away any comfort. Sweat stung the crooks of Ava's elbows and the backs of her knees. A red bus sneezed a cloud of diesel that stuck to the sunscreen on her arms in little black globules. She had begun to crave the shower in her dressing room almost as soon as she had left the place she called home, even though the theatre was and would always be that.

The London Russian Ballet Theatre was a concrete block at the end of an avenue of thirsty plane trees. It was a palace of magic, a hothouse of excellence that looked, to the uninitiated, like a multi-storey car park. Today there was a splash of colour on its grey façade: a picture that quickened Ava's pace as well as her heart until she was standing before a poster, three metres high and two metres wide. Ava was reflected in the frame, her skin shiny as the glass. She watched her mirror twin's hand go to her mouth in happiness and disbelief.

At last, she thought.

Across the top of the poster, the red legend SWAN LAKE; underneath that, Ava herself, large as life, in costume as Odile, the sly black swan in a dress and crown of glossy black feathers. She had been lit so that her skin looked impossibly white, and behind her, entwined around her, Luca's limbs gleamed like polished wood. Their heads were turned from the camera but their bodies were as expressive as faces: sly suggestion in the slope of her shoulder; youthful energy in the curve of his calf. Beneath the portraits in tiny print was a list of the cities they would visit over the next nine months, summer 2018 to spring 2019. A huge undertaking, covering most of the globe. There would be eighty dancers on stage at once, a *Swan Lake* bigger and more daring and *darker* than anyone had done before. And, across the top of the poster, the name of the only person insane and ingenious enough to attempt it on that scale: A NEW PRODUCTION BY NIKOLAI KIRILOV. The ballet masters' ballet master, founder of the company, owner of the theatre: Nikolai Kirilov to his audiences and to the world's press, Mr K to his dancers, Nicky to a select few friends, and Papa to Ava.

He had been waiting her whole career, which was her whole life, for her to grow into the ultimate role. And now every ten-hour day, every bloodied ballet shoe, every pleasure denied, had paid off. The posters made it real in a way that the announcement and the months of rehearsal and costume fittings hadn't. The enormity of it made Ava sway, the street tilting around her. *I have to do his vision justice*, she thought, staggering as if expectation itself had reached out and shoved her. She put out her hand to steady herself, pressing against the concrete wall. It was as hot as a hob. The skin on her palm glowed, as if the building had branded her.

The main door was open, which meant it was safe for Ava to enter the theatre through the front. After ten the public were allowed in, and it wasn't worth meeting the fans because they'd invariably ask for selfies and never understand when she had to decline. She pushed the heavy glass. The atrium – fifteen metres high, the dimensions of a cathedral cast in the material of motorway bridges – was barely cooler than the street. Nicky Kirilov's theatre was five miles and a world away from the gilt and brocade of the grand West End theatres, and that was the point. Strip away the candelabras and the swags of red velvet and all you were left with was the ballet: the *work*, in all its challenging genius. Only the most dedicated balletomanes made the pilgrimage to this unfashionable corner of the city with its graph-paper office blocks, but they made that pilgrimage from all over the world.

The interior walls were lined with more *Swan Lake* posters. The engineers were in, measuring and tapping and photographing. Two men with clipboards examined a rumbling air-con unit, installed thirty years ago and unfit for this overheating century. The whole place was being dragged up to date: glass, wires and pipes ripped out and replaced. The shiny new theatre would be the version she would inherit one day, along with the company and its repertoire. Nicky's life's work would become hers. She was lucky – she would never be exiled from the ballet world – but the next stage of her career meant two of Ava's nightmares would come true: her own retirement from the stage, and her father's death. A weird mewling came out of her mouth now at the thought, drawing the attention of the one of the engineers.

'Alright, love?' He clearly had no idea who she was. To be anonymous in this building gave her a little thrill. She regained her composure to nod and smile with practised grace.

The five floors in the complex were linked by an Escheresque system of concrete stairs, balconies and galleries. High above Ava's head, an unseen door banged and voices drifted down from the gallery that circled the second floor.

'I'm boiling to actual death. Why does he even want us in this early?'

The acoustics in this atrium were as sharp as a stage but it could have been any ballerina talking. Nicky drew his dancers from all over the world and they shared the subtle accent that anyone who'd grown up in the company developed, no matter where in the world they'd spent the first half of their childhood: received pronunciation with a trace element of Eurotrash.

'Ours not to reason why,' replied her friend, then drew in her breath. 'Oh! The posters are in.' They leaned over the edge of the walkway, casting elegant silhouettes on the floor. 'Look at her. She's so beautiful. She looks *unreal*.'

Ava took a step back, pressed herself against a pillar and smiled to herself. If they came down the main staircase for a closer look, she would duck out of sight, but they seemed to prefer to judge from on high.

'Just in the nick of time, too,' said the first dancer, her voice scored with significance.

'What d'you mean?'

Yes, thought Ava, what did she mean? She was aware, of course, that she was the subject of gossip, but it was rare that she got to hear the details. Her spine throbbed against the cool concrete.

'Well, she's *thirty*.' The dancer dropped the word deliberately, left a beat to relish its echo. 'It's all a bit now-or-never, isn't it? The beginning of the end?'

Ava's feet twitched to step into the girls' view. One word from her – one *look* – and their careers would be over. She was the prima ballerina and her father's heir. But the sick need to know what came next held her still.

'As if *she* needs to worry. She'll go on forever.'

The silhouettes retreated and a door squeaked on its hinges.

'Honey, *none* of us go on forever.'

The door banged closed and the girls were gone. Ava would never know who they were, but it hardly mattered. They all thought the same way. They thought she was secure. They thought it was easy, once you were at the top. They couldn't understand that to dance at her level did not exempt you from paranoia: it stitched it to your heels as tightly as your shadow.

They had no idea what it was like to carry a show, to carry a *name*, with nothing but responsibility stretching out into the future and everyone's eyes on you, all the time.

For the second time that morning, Ava Kirilova's nerves unbalanced her. She pressed deeper into the column as though it might absorb her, and engaged the muscles of her core to steady herself. What they didn't understand – what nobody understood – was that the higher you flew, the farther you had to fall.

2

The sounds of the theatre played out around her: a drill in the far distance as the techies worked on the set; faint piano music from a studio and the fainter percussion of cutlery from the canteen. A lift chimed, doors opened and a young dancer emerged, dragging a huge suitcase in her right hand. Her left arm curled around a rustling bin-liner that obscured her face and vision: she charged directly into Ava, sending her wheeling around on her heel, almost losing her balance.

'Excuse me!' said Ava, in order to give the girl permission to speak her apology. The expected, mortified, 'I'm so *sorry*, Miss Kirilova,' didn't come; the dancer barely broke her stride towards the front door, kicked it open and stood on the pavement. Ava was so shocked by this breach of etiquette and the loss of control – the two virtues Nicky prized above all others – that it took a while for her to recognise the dancer. Not by name – at Nicky's insistence, it was a while since Ava had been on first-name terms with everyone in the company – but by role. She was the junior soloist Nicky had chosen to play Odette at the ballroom window, the moment where the white swan appears to show her prince that he has been tricked by the black swan. It was an appearance rather than a role, half a minute of heartbroken fluttering, but a big deal for a young ballerina, so why did it look as though she was leaving?

A black BMW pulled up, stopped on the double red line and a young man Ava had never seen before leapt out. He was in his late twenties, the strange soft body of the non-dancer lent structure by a suit. With the engine still running and to an angry orchestra of car horns, he loaded the girl's chaotic luggage into the boot, kissed her on her forehead and swept her into the passenger seat in one fluid movement, pausing only to give the theatre a filthy look before disappearing into the city traffic. It had all taken under a minute.

'This is unfortunate,' said a voice at her side, the nicotine growl of the spy-movie double agent. Raisa had a habit of materialising soundlessly, gliding about the theatre as though on castors. *Silent art form*, Ava heard Nicky say, as surely as if he were with them.

Raisa had been Ava's coach since she was a little girl. But not a mother figure, never that.

'What was that all about?' asked Ava.

'Your father had to let her go,' said Raisa. 'She broke a rule.'

'Oh, for goodness' sake,' said Ava. 'Is now really the time for that?' Nicky's rule book was long and arbitrary: dancers were punished for minor transgressions as well as major breaches of their complicated contract. So far this year he had sacked a junior male dancer for being in possession of a smartphone – his hatred of the devices was obsessive – and only last week he had screamed at one of the corps de ballet for eating breakfast bought from the Costa opposite the theatre rather than the company canteen. Pre-packaged food was for touring only. 'She's the second swan! Does he not realise it's only three weeks till first night?'

'Yes, of course he realises,' snapped Raisa. 'But it was a big rule. She's *pregnant*.' Raisa placed vein-roped hands in a V-shape on her narrow pelvis to illustrate her horror of childbearing. She had the attitude that a ballerina should offer up her body to the ballet, almost as one might donate one's corpse to medical science. It was a point of pride for Raisa that at the height of her career she had not menstruated for five years. These days that would have you marched straight to the doctor, but Raisa was from another generation. '*Pregnant*,' she said again, when Ava didn't react.

'Ah,' said Ava. 'Well, then.' Nicky took a dancer's pregnancy, especially one resulting from a relationship with a civilian, as a personal slight. His dancers were allowed to have children – and encouraged, in fact, to bring those children, with their long legs and elastic joints, back to him when they were thirteen – but only *after* they had retired and vanished to the suburbs. The lucky ones were kept on as coaches or transferred to a job backstage, but no one who kept a baby ever returned to the London Russian as a performer. They would quietly quit at the end of their maternity leave, knowing that the company was tough enough if you were in Mr K's good books, but that dancing in the shadow of his disapproval was a fate worse than not dancing at all.

If they were lucky, another company would take them on, but it was unlikely. Few Kirilov dancers ever defected to rival companies. People on the outside thought that the Kirilov training with its emphasis on dramatic, extended positions was too Russian, too old-fashioned, too clockwork and uncanny for modern audiences, and that the dancers, cloistered in this theatre since childhood, were too weird for the mainstream.

Ava knew the truth: Nicky taught his dancers everything but compromise. Nowhere else was good enough. His Russian ballet was as pure and exact as mathematics. When his dancers stood in first position, with their heels together and their toes turned out, the line of their feet was as straight as a minus sign. That was the attraction, and the challenge.

A familiar heavy footfall behind her told her that Jack, the company physiotherapist, had caught Raisa up. Six foot three in his Crocs, he was pink in the face above the white tunic he always wore.

'You haven't let her go?' he asked Raisa in dismay.

'She can hardly *stay*,' said Raisa. 'The boyfriend is moving her in. She's packing up her room now. We have given her three months' wages. She will not sue us.'

'Sometimes I wish one of them *would*,' said Jack. He pulled at his high collar as if to let steam escape. 'Might put an end to this bloody shabby treatment. I swear to God, Raisa, one more girl gets the heave-ho like this and I'll leave. I mean it this time.' He seemed only then to register Ava: he put a hand on her forearm, and said, 'Morning darling,' before retreating to the gym.

He wouldn't leave, and they all knew it. Jack's remit was to treat the dancers' bodies but unofficially he served as the company's conscience. It was the one job Nicky didn't seem to mind outsourcing.

'But she is *pregnant*,' Raisa called after him, as though that settled it. She glanced at Ava's flat belly and said, 'At least we don't have to worry about *you* in that respect.'

Ava didn't know whether she meant because her status as Mr K's daughter made her invincible, or because no man who knew Nicky would dare approach her. The spotlight was a shining cage, and it kept you safe or kept you lonely, depending on how you chose to look at it.

3

The stage, which had only yesterday been empty, was now occupied by the bones of a set, the interior of the palace where the ball is held in Act III of *Swan Lake*. These blank plywood structures would soon be painted, not in the fussy nineteenth-century marble effects of a Tsarist palace but in the company colours, the only three shades Nicky would allow on stage. Revolution-red, the wedding-night purity of white, and the unseeing of black. The colours of bones, blood and night. He allowed the occasional accent of gold; he was a rich man, after all.

Nicky stood at the foot of the staircase and frowned up at the ballroom window. Ava winced at the sight of him. He had never been a young father, but now he seemed to age a year every day, arthritis and osteoporosis taking over his body like dry rot, the delayed legacies of childhood summers spent dancing indoors. He still wore the uniform he had adopted at the height of his fame in the 1970s, a loose polo-neck and slacks that – ironically for a dancer who valued precision above all else – evoked the formless sounds and shapes of the 1930s jazz era. But where once his clothes had fallen elegantly against the plumbline of his belly, now they hung loosely on a body fast losing mass. His thick silver hair had thinned and turned almost completely white in a matter of months. The cane he leaned on was elegant – lacquered black wood, a swan's head for a handle – but it was still a walking stick.

'Hi, Papa,' she said with a brightness she didn't feel. 'The set looks fabulous.'

The sound of her voice softened his face. He spread his free arm out to her and she jumped on to the stage. The sprung floor bounced a welcome to its brightest star.

'Odette, my darling.' He always called the dancers by their roles once a show was cast, even his own daughter. 'How you like palace?' Nicky's Russian accent had not mellowed over the decades and he ignored the rules of English grammar, discarding words that slowed him down. Ava privately thought that if the whim took him he could come out with a perfectly constructed sentence and the enunciation of a Shakespearean actor, but where was the mystique in that?

'You hear about my second swan?' He nodded at the empty window. 'Now who I find?'

'There must be a spare soloist?'

He flicked his hand to shoo away her suggestion. 'Cast is *arranged*. Military precision. All soloists already cover two parts.'

She sighed. Of course it had been engineered so that all his dancers were accounted for at every second, and the only spares would be in the corps de ballet, the dancers whose grand title 'Artist of the Company' belied their status as foot-soldiers. This was the price of a small company staging such an ambitious production. This was the gamble. He had given himself almost no margin of error. He was not allowing for illness or accident. He was not allowing for his dancers to be human. It was not (yet) Ava's place to contribute ideas of any kind, but Raisa had told him this, Felicity and Jack had said it, and even reliable yes-man Boyko had broken the habit of a lifetime to point it out. But the London Russian Ballet Company was not a democracy.

The politics of casting and the brain-ache of logistics were two more reasons Ava was in no rush to swap her *pointe* shoes for schedules and spreadsheets.

'Just get anyone to do it,' she said. 'Any one of the white girls, anyway. It's only twenty seconds, and the audience will all be looking at Odile and Siegfried.'

His mood darkened again. 'I teach you nothing? *Not* anyone can do it. *Best* dancer only. Twenty-one days.'

'Twenty-one days is a long time,' she said, knowing it would feel like longer. Raisa could spend three hours drilling a five-second movement into a dancer. Whoever they ripped from the ranks this time was in for an intensive three weeks of ice baths and screaming muscles.

'Enough of stage,' said Nicky irritably, as though it were Ava's fault that they were there at all. 'We take tea in my room.'

Even with Ava supporting his arm, he grimaced with every step. He walked gingerly; it was all too easy to imagine his hips grinding away to powder.

'Oh, Papa. This operation can't come fast enough.'

A couple of days after the first night of *Swan Lake*, Nicky was booked for a double hip replacement, followed by six months of rehab at some place in the country he'd bought to recuperate, overseen by Raisa and an army of carers.

'Is nothing,' he said, but as she guided him backstage he leaned on her hard. He should have had the surgery a year ago. '*Swan Lake* first,' he'd said when she'd tried to cajole him into bringing it forward. 'What is little pain to dancer?' But it was no little pain he was in now. It had affected his personality as well as his body, trimmed his already short fuse to a fizzing stub. Working with Nicky Kirilov was not so much like treading on eggshells as dancing on splintered ice. You never knew where the next crack would appear.

They made agonising progress through the warm, soupy air of the corridor. This was their world – this building. Nicky owned it all, having spent so much time with high-net-worth individuals that he was on the verge of becoming one himself. He had a gift of asking the right people for the right things. The magnetism he'd been known for on stage was just as powerful across a dinner table or, when it was necessary, the space between two pillows. Nicky had done very well out of property bequests. By his fiftieth birthday he'd had a housing portfolio to rival any London landlord, owned the freehold on the theatre complex, and had the kind of financial freedom other ballet masters could only dream of. No grants to chase, few sponsors to appease, and those who did donate did so on the understanding that they were not to interfere with the purity of his vision. He had no one to rein in his maniacal desire for perfection. Raisa was there to carry out his orders (in a bold moment, Luca had once said she was Goebbels to Nicky's Hitler). Jack was a lone voice of restraint, but he tended to pick up the pieces once the damage was already done.

The grey maze was brightened by red fire extinguishers and signs saying NO MOBILE PHONES. There were more of these backstage than there were in the atrium. Nicky thought that smartphones were a fatal distraction, that they encouraged the wrong kind of narcissism. Kirilov dancers had a relationship with the mirror, not the screen. Nicky alone controlled their image in public. Woe betide the dancer who let an unauthorised photograph leak into the public domain.

Ava's skin, which seemed to be permanently damp at the moment, sprang with fresh sweat. 'Please tell me you're spending a *million pounds* on air-con.'

'I make it Moscow in January for you.'

'That's more like it.'

'Siberia!' He splayed his fingers like Jack Frost. '*Icicles*.'

'We'll dance in furs,' she said.

He giggled like a child. 'At *last* you think like Russian.'

Their laughter echoed along the concrete corridor. In that moment, they might have been the only two people in the building. They might have been a couple of dancers on a stage, so lost in their work that they barely registered the audience at all.

4

The backstage lifts were reserved for senior dancers and management and there was no question of Nicky reaching the second floor any other way. The steel doors protested as they drew together. Once moving, a series of irregular bangs and rumbles made it disconcertingly easy to picture both the workings and the potential failings of the ageing machinery inside. Ava tried to resist the comparison to her father's body and failed every time. When the lift lurched to a stop at the second floor, the jolt made Nicky gasp with pain.

In the corridor were a dozen little girls from the ballet school in their regulation red tracksuits over black leotards. They were first years, twelve and thirteen years old. *I need girl by thirteenth birthday*, Nicky liked to say, *and I make her dancer. She sleep and eat and dance and learn and live under my roof and I will* create *her.*

These girls were babies, still young enough for stuffed toys and crying for their mothers (a word Ava had schooled herself firstly not to think about without a pang, and then not to think about at all). They wore their long hair not in traditional ballerina buns but in the style Ava herself often wore, a long plait wound around the top of the head in a coronet. She knew that they helped each other do it in the dorms, inexpertly jabbing hairpins into each other's scalps to get the style perfect, which was as good a metaphor for the co-operation and rivalry of being a ballerina that Ava could think of. Friendships even among the youngest dancers were hard work, freighted with competition and neuroses.

For all that, she was nostalgic about her own stint in the corps, six months of in-jokes and illicit cigarettes before she had been promoted out and the girls she had been sharing a dressing room with were forced to address her as *Miss Kirilova*. Watching these students, with everything yet to come, Ava couldn't help a twinge of envy, followed by the lurch of altitude sickness that sometimes assailed her when she thought about the distance between her and the rest of the company.

When the girls saw Nicky and Ava they stopped and curtseyed low in accordance with ballet school protocol.

'How do my smallest creatures?' asked Nicky.

The girls mostly addressed their reedy chorus of 'Verygood-thankyouMrK,' to their slippers.

'Good!' He clapped his hands. 'You dance extra perfect for me today, yes?'

'I *wish* you wouldn't call them that,' said Ava, as the girls funnelled into a studio.

'*Ty moyo luchsheye tvoreniye*,' he said and immediately translated for her, 'You best creation of all,' but then his attention snagged on the last girl, a few inches taller than the others and deeper into puberty, thicker at the thighs and fuller in the breast. 'She gets hips,' he said, his tone that of an executioner, and Ava wondered if he had made his second cull of the day.

Who had it worse? The dancer who had her dreams crushed before her fourteenth birthday? Or the dancer who had been with him for fifteen years, her career ending on the street outside the theatre, a baby in her belly and her ballet shoes in a bin bag?

She double-checked that all the girls were gone, then craned her neck in the other direction before turning left. The concrete maze backstage had only one dead end. Ava and Nicky stopped at a door marked CLEANING CUPBOARD. She punched in a key code and the door clicked open to reveal not mops and buckets but blackness. She felt for the switch and striplights overhead relayed into action, pointing the way down a thin corridor.

Ava was one of only a dozen people and certainly the only working ballerina in the company who knew about this place. When, as part of the building's overhaul, the place got CCTV, this was one location where cameras wouldn't be installed.

As they walked, Nicky's grunts of pain alternated with little hums of satisfaction. He was obsessed with secret passages and corridors. It was through a backstage rat-run like this that he had made his escape from Soviet Russia to the West. Desperate to escape the constraints of Russian ballet – he was allowed to dance only the same few state-approved ballets on repeat – he had defected in 1971, smuggled by fellow dancers through the warren of a Parisian theatre and into a waiting car, knowing he would never be able to return to Russia again. All he'd had with him were the clothes he stood up in – the velvet doublet and white tights of Don Quixote – and his once-in-a-generation talent. This narrow space was packed tight with meaning, and Ava could never tread its floor without feeling grateful for all that he had risked, and all that she had been handed.

At the end of the passage, another door gave on to Nicky's room. They called it his room but it was more than that: it was a time capsule, a recreation of old Russia. It was his lair; it was the beating heart of the theatre, of the company itself. In here, rich colour ran riot: greens and golds and the dark burgundy leather of wingback chairs with crocheted antimacassars and a Russian rug, coloured wool hand-knotted in geometric patterns. Ava boiled water for tea in the silver samovar, the urn that was the only way for a true Russian to make his tea.

'Oof,' said Nicky as he sank into his chair, and settled in front of the room's most remarkable feature. One wall was a floor-to-ceiling window that looked on to the cavernous Studio 1, its scuffed floor and its whitewashed walls and the barres, waist-height railings, around the edges and in the centre. It was a two-way mirror but the dancers did not know that. As they checked their position and preened, they had no idea that they were being observed from the other side of the glass. At that moment only the pianist was there, fingertips dancing up and down the keyboard.

'You should've let me help you,' frowned Ava.

'I can sit in fucking chair,' he snapped back.

'How's the new house?' she asked, sensing the need for a gear change. 'Have I got time to come and see it, before the tour?'

'Is good. I make special room for you! But you no have time to leave studio before tour,' he said. 'I *chain* you to barre.'

'Ha!' she said. 'Point taken. But have you got the place how you like it?'

He shrugged. 'I no see yet. I move in after operation. Is *countryside*.' He shuddered theatrically. He felt about the countryside the way Raisa felt about motherhood. He was a committed Londoner in the way that only those born elsewhere could be. He had pioneered a kind of cosmopolitan diversity before he'd known the meaning of either word, trawling inner-city comprehensives as well as the Home Counties ballet schools for promising students. He had even Anglicised his nickname, shunning the Russian diminutive Kolya in favour of Nicky.

'You can hardly get better here with all the pollution and the mess,' she said. 'People have recovered from operations in the countryside since time immemorial. The quicker you mend, the sooner you can join us on tour.'

The snort he gave was the closest he ever came to admitting that someone else might be right.

Steam from the samovar layered a gauze over the pictures on the walls: a black and white shot of the thirteen-year-old Nikolai Kirilov at the Vaganova Ballet Academy in Moscow. Shorts, vest, knee socks, suspended in a *grand jeté*, his split legs as straight as a spirit level. Below it, a shot of Ava in the same position at the same age, in London of course, in this theatre. The backgrounds were different and so were their bodies but they shared a distinctive tilt of the chin, an impossible extension of the limbs, a gaze trained on another world.

Stage photography showed Nicky leaping through the last half of the twentieth century, from the sixties to the nineties, from the Soviet Union to London and beyond. In all the iconic roles – Romeo, Don Quixote, and, of course, Prince Siegfried – he had partnered Raisa. Decline was inevitable, it was built into the career, but Raisa had managed hers as gracefully as any dancer could hope to, dancing at the highest level alongside Nicky into her forties, before taking her place behind the scenes, at his side. Ava had long ago resolved that she would match Raisa's record and best it. She would dance longer than any prima ballerina had done before.

Under these images hung a picture of the first time Nicky and Ava had danced together, a two-hander created by him, for them. *Frankenstein's Creature*, with Nicky as Frankenstein and Ava as his monster. She had been seventeen and he sixty. It had launched her career, and the reviews had been raves, but some of the press had been so personal and intrusive that Nicky had banned profile interviews from then on. Far from impeding Ava's rise, it had been a master stroke, adding to the London Russian's mystique and freeing everyone to focus on the work, unfettered by hawking and preening. His creatures must exist only as dancers.

Their last onstage collaboration – *Zeus and Athena*, about the Greek god and the daughter born full-grown from her father's head – had been Nicky's final appearance on stage. It was hard to square the dancer in the picture, compact with muscle, with the shrunken man in the chair beneath it.

Ava laid out a spoon and a saucer and unscrewed the lid from a jar of strawberry jam. Glancing down, she noted with alarm how many empty blister packs of co-codamol littered the floor. She would talk to Jack about that later.

'You choose,' he said, waving a hand at the empty studio.

'I choose what?' she asked.

'You choose replacement swan. *You* try at casting.'

Ava froze. To take part in the casting process was to inch closer to the day when she must select her own replacement. The morning's gossip replayed in her mind. Was this the beginning of her end? And, if it was, how did those girls know what she didn't?

Nicky, as ever, read her thoughts so well she wondered if she'd spoken aloud. He had done so much to shape her mind that he could wander its corridors without her permission.

'You have long, long time left. I no retire you tomorrow! But one day decline begins and you no dance principal role *one day* after you pass prime. Is my reputation on line.'

Sometimes he treated her more like one of his own limbs than a separate person. But she knew better than to argue.

'Come on, then,' she said. 'Let's do it.'

5

'Raisa rehearse *danse des cygnes,*' said Nicky – as roughshod with French pronunciation as he was with English – as Raisa entered the studio, followed by eight ballerinas. All the girls had creamy skin and the exquisite and rare proportion that turned heads in the street but were the baseline inside the London Russian: narrow hips, small head, long neck, and delicate, blank-canvas features. In short, they all looked like Ava. Nicky even had a preferred leg length, so that onstage their tutus appeared to float like lilies on a pond. Their pink faces and diadems of sweat at the hairline showed that they had already warmed up. He must have dragged them from their beds as soon as the second swan had delivered her news. Two of these, then, must be the girls she had heard in the atrium that morning. A wave of something dark washed through her.

One girl, unaware she was being watched, pulled her leotard away from her crotch, while another sniffed under her underarms and winced. Ava turned away to give them some privacy, poured black tea into a glass and spooned a dollop of jam into it.

'These swans we can spare,' he said. 'Enough time to change, dance second swan, change back.'

'So.' She was pleased to hear that her voice held steady. 'Do *you* have one of them in mind, for the second swan?' She set the tea glass down at his arm and licked her thumb for the trace of jam.

'*Spasibo,*' he said: *thank you.* When Nicky answered a question with a *non sequitur* it meant the discussion was locked down. When he spoke in Russian, that indicated he was throwing away the key. It was clear that it was up to her. He wasn't going to hold her hand.

His rare trust sent a flush of pleasure through her.

'*Right.*' She turned back to the mirror. Nicky's room was soundproofed but as the pianist struck up the music the bass notes seeped through the wall, their progression so familiar, so ingrained in Ava, that her mind's ear easily layered on the rest of the orchestra. The dancers were, of course, excellent. All perfectly on the music and moving in the military unison that Nicky drilled into his creatures.

Ava had always thought that the *danse des petits cygnes,* the dance of the baby swans, sounded as though it should be danced by children, but this was no beginner's dance. It wasn't about adorable waddling. The routine was some of the most precise footwork in any ballet, and Nicky had them so well-schooled that even their eyes were downcast at the same angle. These dancers were the cream of the corps de ballet. *Corps* meant body, and these dancers were as interdependent as heart and lungs. Even the most ambitious dancers had to blend in: if a dancer in the corps was doing her job properly, no one would notice her at all. And that was the problem right now. Kirilov dancers had had their personality drummed out of them: or rather, they'd had Nicky's instilled, just as Ava herself had.

She raised her forefinger and let it hover along the line. The crook of Nicky's walking cane shot up, the black swan's head hooking down her wrist.

'No guess! *Look.*'

Faced with a row of world-class athletes each pitted against other world-class athletes, Ava decided to look for something beyond precision. Since they had begun working on *Swan Lake*, she had started to feel that the magic happened not with the faultless execution of technical steps but when she was on the inside edge of control. Odette and Odile had brought something out in Ava that thrilled and frightened her in equal measure. There were moments when a wild, animalistic dancer seemed to occupy her skin, as likely to make herself known through the face as the feet, touching a different kind of truth.

'Who you like?' prompted Nicky. The cygnets moved sideways *en pointe*, arms rising and falling, no idea they were auditioning. 'One is star!' he said incredulously. 'You no see?'

A pale redhead at the end of the line had something about her: a plasticity that extended to her face, a sense that she was giving this rehearsal her all rather than marking steps. Beautiful, natural turnout gave her a little more liberty than the other dancers, made them seem like mere machines, pistons and cogs of muscle and bone. Now Ava had seen it, she couldn't unsee it. Surely this was what Nicky meant by star, that sweet spot between storytelling and technique.

'I think *she's* got something about her?'

Nicky's grunt was unreadable, but he never gave anything away if he could help it. 'Come. I show you. Come.'

They began the agonising journey back down the corridor, his walking stick clacking an echo. I think I could lift him, thought Ava, fingers almost encircling his withered forearm. I could hold my father above my head as Luca holds me.

The creaking door announced their arrival. All eight dancers stood a little taller. Even the pianist straightened her back.

'You no see Mr K,' Nicky said. 'He is no here.'

It was a joke, of course. His presence changed the very air in the room.

Raisa came to stand next to him and they began to mutter in Russian. Their partnership had progressed from stage to bedroom and come out the other side into something forged in both but more enduring than either. Now they were like two gnarled old trees that had grown around each other.

'From beginning!' Nicky clapped his hands twice, the music began and they started the sequence, their hands crossed and held in front of them, their legs forming moving patterns as intricate as basketwork. Even though Ava wasn't dressed to dance, she automatically held her feet in B-plus, the ballerina's resting position, one foot behind the other, knee slightly bent, and her hands in a loose bowl in front of her hips.

'Stop, stop, STOP!' Nicky cut through the music. 'You!' he tipped his cane towards the redhead and Ava's heart performed a *jeté* of elation. 'Again.' Five seconds in, however, Nicky banged his cane on the floor in fury, not approval. 'Enough.' His tone brought back to Ava every correction he had ever given her and her heart took a dive. She had been wrong to favour expressiveness over artifice. She and her father were not on the same page after all. They were not even reading the same book.

'You know Shakespeare?'

The redhead looked to her fellow swans in panic, but they all lowered their eyes. 'A little bit?' There was a drop of French in her accent. Even in the grip of discomfort, Ava couldn't help but compare it to the girls she'd overheard that morning. She could have recited their words, but not identified their voices.

'You see actors ad-lib *Macbeth*? Think they know better? They decide *rap,* in middle of play?' A spray of spittle flew from Nicky's mouth and landed on the girl's shoulder. She didn't dare brush it away, merely shook her head. Only Ava knew that at least half this tirade was not for the dancer but for Ava herself for choosing badly.

'Then why you think you improve my steps?' He threw back his shoulders and shimmied in an unfair exaggeration of the ballerina's movement. 'This *classical ballet*. There is right way, precise way, every turn, every jump, every step.' He banged his cane again, so hard that the piano let out a faint hum. 'Ballet non-negotiable. This *Swan Lake*. Same steps, great ballet masters Petipa and Ivanov choreograph in 1895. Only person embellish is me. Is *me*.'

The redhead was on the verge of tears. Please don't cry, Ava willed. We'll be here all day if you cry. A stone formed in her throat and she realised that she was instructing herself.

'*You!*'

Nicky's cane pointed at the next dancer in the line. This girl was – well, it was ridiculous to describe her as nondescript, but in the context of this line-up she was. He beckoned her with an upward nod. Clearly thinking she too had been singled out for criticism, she stepped out of the formation on trembling legs.

'Do again, only you,' he said. The company pianist played the score by heart, taking his cue from steps, not sheet music, knowing exactly which bar to come in on when Nicky said, 'Pick up at *pas de chat*.'

As the music began, the girl's nerves seemed to evaporate. Perfectly on the notes, she executed a 'cat step' that took her sideways across the floor as smoothly as though she were gliding on a rail. Her arms became fluid and boneless while her feet executed the steps to a hair's breadth, but there was an imitative quality that Ava couldn't quite define. Nerves, perhaps, making her brittle.

When she was done, her chest rose and fell exaggeratedly as she braced for her ballet master's punishment. Nicky picked up her hand and held it up.

'See little finger here?' He was talking to Ava but everyone nodded. 'This!' He shouted in triumph. 'This *perfect*. Look. She *is* baby swan! *You*.' He took her whole head in his hands, one hand cupping her chin, the other cradling the back of her skull. Ava knew that feeling: it felt like a blessing, like being cured of an illness by a storybook king.

The girl blinked up at Nicky, eyes brimming, and Ava felt a rare barb of jealousy. She wobbled slightly, as though someone had kicked her perch.

'She know arms come from back, not from hands. *This* where wings begin.' He thumbed her between her shoulder blades.

It's true, thought Ava. That's exactly what I do.

'Our second swan is gone,' he announced. 'So we need another to fill window. And here she is. *You* dance Odette at ball.' The young dancer's own smile was muted – ooh, she's good, thought Ava, admiring her control. Her overspill of pleasure showed in a blush that lit her cheeks and blotched her chest and neck. He would love that, she thought: surface control but just enough emotion leaking through to know he'd got to her.

'You are *perfect* creature,' he said, before letting her go.

This was how he did it: this was how he got the best out of his dancers. He gave out just enough love to make you want it for the rest of your life, whether it was a moment's eye contact or twenty seconds in the spotlight. And it would inspire not just the girl who had received it but those around her. The other cygnets disguised their envy as delight, patting her on the shoulder, smiling gritted stage smiles.

'Ava, we go,' said Nicky. He held out his arm to her as though he was offering to support her, but when she crooked her elbow she subtly slid it under his.

She looked over her shoulder as they left the room. The chosen dancer looked at Ava with defiance, something approaching a smirk. She even seemed to have reversed her blush, as though she could call blood to skin in a performance for Nicky's benefit. Ava felt herself blanch. Self-control was one thing, she thought, but that was unnatural.

6

'From *first*, now let's go and *front* and lower and *point* and back, and *front* and lower and *back* to first.' Nicky's voice was precise as a metronome over the pianist's medley of show tunes and ballet scores. 'Arms!'

Eighty pairs of arms moved slowly one way and then the other, with the lazy accord of a reedbed in summer. Ava rested her right hand on the barre and bent her knees in time with seventy-nine other dancers. Eighty left feet swished on the dusty floor. Eighty necks glistened with sweat. Eighty pairs of calves burned with lactic acid. Seventy-nine people watched Ava, at the very front of the class, positioned there to lead by example.

Ava, still unsettled from the whispers and wrong guesses of the day before, lost herself in the comforting, familiar movements. Foot in, foot out. Point toes, flex toes. Arm up, arm down. Company class was the same every day whether performing, touring, rehearsing or resting. Class was one of the few places in ballet where the movements were more or less the same for men – who never had to dance *en pointe* – as for women, who did. Class mapped the company hierarchy. Rank, as important in the London Russian as in any army, was demarcated by dancers' placement at the barres: principals in the front left corner, with the luxury or punishment of two mirrors; first soloists behind the principals, soloists behind them, junior soloists to the back and right; and the character artists and the corps at the less sturdy centre barres. Despite yesterday's little promotion, the second swan had not presumed to migrate from the centre barre. Ava took a petty comfort from that.

'Left heel rotate *in*, right heel *down*.'

Class kept decline at bay, as evidenced by Boyko and Felicity, the character dancers in their fifties at the front of the centre barre. They'd graduated from princes and princesses to kings and queens, no longer superhuman on stage but still beating time with their bodies every morning. They worked as coaches and deputised for Nicky and Raisa. They both looked decades younger than they were from a distance, but Boyko's waist was starting to thicken in a way that must be anathema to him. And as Felicity bent sideways in a backless leotard, the flesh between her shoulder blades crêped. Jack was treating her for some kind of ankle strain, but, given that Felicity's roles now were more mime than dance, she had nothing to worry about. The 'sudden death' injuries that every dancer dreaded were actually vanishingly rare. You heard about Achilles tendons tearing on stage, the grisly pop of breaking ligament being heard at the back of the stalls, but such injuries were seldom spontaneous and usually due to an inexperienced dancer deluding themselves that the tingle or cramp would go away on its own.

Denial took many, many forms in ballet.

'Coming into *six* through *feet*, stretch *toes*, *demi-plié*, *demi-pointe!*'

Class was about muscle memory. Ava's foot swished against the floor as if there were a groove worn in it just for her. She moved through the stretches and shuffles, the bends and the flexes that were the repetitive, production-line movements that remade her a ballerina every day. Odette and Odile's routines were made of the same steps, just as the music they danced to was composed of the same twelve notes. Odette's music was gentle and flowing, and so were Ava's movements. When she took the stage as Odile, the musicians attacked their instruments and her body responded in kind.

To Ava's left, Luca moved in perfect time with her. Behind them, Sakurako and Tomasin completed the formation. Professional monogamy was discouraged in other ballet companies, but once Mr K liked a partnership, the couple were stuck together for the rest of their careers. Sakurako and Tomasin had taken this to its logical conclusion and had been married for six years. They were Ava and Luca's ghosts, their understudies, their safety net. Sakurako's refinement – even now, as she sank into a *plié* in scruffy warm-ups – never let you forget that ballet was a nineteenth-century art form. However, she was five years older than Ava and this, combined with Ava's status as a Kirilov, levelled the ground between them.

Ava's eyes followed Nicky. His gaze kept returning to the back of the room, where his second swan pointed and lifted and stretched. Ava held her back a little straighter, turned her toes out until they looked as if they might swivel a full three hundred and sixty degrees.

'Front, toes, toes, lower and close inside,' Nicky intoned hypnotically, then banged his stick on the floor. '*Inside*, Odette!'

Seventy-nine pairs of eyes bored into Ava's neck. Her cheeks, already flushed from exertion, now flared with shame. There had been *nothing wrong* with the positioning of her feet. Had there?

Luca looked a question at her in the mirror: everything alright? She nodded her reply: *later*. That glass wall that kept Ava apart from the other dancers . . . in Luca's case it was made of something else, transparent jelly, flexible and soft.

The class went on. The movements became more dynamic: those who had come in wearing layers shed the last of them as they moved on to centre work, crossing the room in great bounds that, done right, made it look as though they were suspended on wires.

At the end of the class they observed a quaint little ritual known as the *reverence*, with each dancer bowing or curtseying to the teacher. The second swan sank low into her curtsey for Nicky; Ava made hers an inch deeper and a second longer, then immediately thought, *pathetic*.

No one was allowed to leave until Nicky had gone. In the agonising wait for him to cross the room, glistening backs were discreetly turned on him and low chatter filled the room.

Ava bent forward, rolling her spine one vertebra at a time until she was folded in half. A pair of shoes appeared upside-down in her eyeline. She straightened up to find herself face to face with the eager, shiny face of the second swan.

'Did you hear?' she said. 'We're exactly the same!'

The remaining dancers turned to see who was addressing Miss Kirilova in such an informal way.

'I'm *sorry*?' said Ava.

'Wardrobe measured me? Our bodies are the same, literally inch for inch? They don't have to adjust your costumes at all for my scene at the window? It's like they were made for me!'

'Those costumes were made for *me*.'

Ava's voice reverberated, silencing the chatter. The girl's blush this time was a lava-surge of humiliation. 'No. Of course, Miss Kirilova. I wasn't getting ideas.'

Ava swept out of the studio and turned left, for the lift to the principals' dressing rooms. Luca caught her up as the doors opened. He spread his arm to let her go first.

'That was a bit much,' he said gently as the doors closed.

'I *know*!' said Ava, relieved. 'Who does she think she is?'

He addressed his reply to the lift floor. 'I didn't mean her.'

7

Luca's lips moved as he punched in the six-digit code for the principals' corridor. The only time he could retain numbers was when he was counting steps.

Tomasin and Sakurako were checking their pigeonholes. Ava made a show of friendliness to make up for her diva turn in the studio.

'Anything exciting?' she asked Sakurako, who was reading a letter.

'One from a little girl in Osaka wanting an autograph, and one from a man in Cardiff who wants me to send him a pair of used tights.'

'Standard postbag, then,' said Luca, whose own pigeonhole was empty.

'Does anyone fancy a coffee in my room?' asked Ava, who hadn't finished being magnanimous and knew they wouldn't say no. They filed into her dressing room, the biggest in the theatre, the size of a small studio, with room for a daybed and a sofa as well as a dressing table. There was no samovar here but a Nespresso machine and a water cooler, and an ice machine whose cubes were not for cooling drinks but for filling a bucket with, to soothe aching feet. 'I'll be mother,' Luca said, clicking a pod into the coffee machine, then he turned to Ava. 'I didn't mean—'

'Jeez, Luca, it's not a swear word,' she said. The word was not banned but it was a trapdoor it *was* best not to tread upon. Even Luca had trained himself to avoid using it around Ava. It was just easier that way. 'Black, no sugar,' she said.

Luca saluted her. 'Sir, yes, sir!'

She straightened the photo on her dressing table of herself aged, what, fifteen? In it, Nicky held her in a fish dive, her body arched backwards in a crescent, her feet higher than his head and her arms outstretched. The photograph was a rare accent in a room that was otherwise tidy to the point of sterility.

Luca fired up the machine. 'I see you're still keeping the *domovoi* at bay,' he said. *Domovoi* were little spirits of Russian superstition who haunted dirty houses: Nicky had instilled a fear of them into his students in an effort to uphold the Kirilovan virtue of cleanliness.

'They're all having a party in your hovel, that's why,' said Ava.

'The poster looks stunning,' said Sakurako, gesturing to the scaled-down version that Nicky had hung on her wall without asking, replacing a painting she'd chosen herself. 'It already feels like a classic.'

'Surely this image confirms us as the most iconic partnership in the history of all ballet,' said Luca.

'More than Fonteyn and Nureyev?' suggested Tomasin.

'Never heard of them.' Luca stood before the poster and ran his finger down the list of cities. 'Tallinn,' he said. 'Berlin. Helsinki. Bogotá! *Havana*.' He rubbed his thighs.

'He wants someone to ask him what's so special about these places,' Ava told the others. 'Please do not give him the satisfaction.'

'It's not *you* I want to satisfy me. I'm just making a list of where the best men are. While these two stay up late knitting or doing Sudoku or whatever it is married couples get up to in hotel rooms, *we're* going hunting.' He mimed the drawing of an arrow in a bow.

Ava smiled at the memories: while Nicky and Raisa had long dinners with foreign sponsors and patrons and critics and ballet masters, the dancers were let off the leash. There were parties with other dance companies and broken-English flirtations. Nightclubs! Neon lights and sticky dance floors where she could unlock her hips and let the beat be her instructor. Men outside the dance world, men who tasted of beer and wine and cigarettes and their eagerness to know if it was true that ballerinas could tuck their feet behind their ears the way other girls could tuck a stray hair.

'Not this time,' she said ruefully. 'I'm deputising for Papa. I'll be wining and dining with Boyko and Felicity.'

'But this is terrible news,' said Luca, sinking on to the sofa.

'Boyko and Felicity aren't *that* bad.'

'It's terrible news for *me*.'

Steam puffed from the coffee machine and made clouds on the windowpane. Luca leapt up again. 'It's like a bloody *greenhouse* in here.' He forced the rusty, single-glazed window farther open. The topmost branches of London plane trees tickled the glass. While the principals, here on the top floor (connected by a lift that delivered them to the side of the stage), got the leaves, the soloists, sharing smaller rooms a storey below, got the branches, and had to access the stage via the stairs. The corps de ballet, on the cramped first floor, looked out on to trunks. Wardrobe and props were in the rat-run of the basement. And outside, the street: smartphones and earbuds and Ubers, eight-hundred-calorie take-out coffees and beer in plastic glasses on the pavement. Ava thought, not for the first time, that they might as well live in a moated castle for all that they were connected to the city.

Beyond the trees was the Gulag, the tower block joined to the theatre by a glass walkway, where all the corps lived, and the schoolchildren. It got its unaffectionate nickname from the bleak Soviet prisons that featured in her father's nightmares and more than one of his ballets. Curtains billowed around the edges of windows that were fitted with catches that prevented them open-ing all the way; there'd been a jumper a few years ago, a fading soloist who'd mistaken tough love for personal rejection.

The theatre was self-contained, a city state. Laundry was done in the basement. The canteen provided three meals a day, with the right balance of macro-nutrients depending on whether you were rehearsing or performing. Dancers were paid in cash, no banking to deal with, no bills or expenses: everything that might distract from training (or require a dancer to leave the complex) was taken care of.

'The heroic effort of making this coffee has made me too hot to drink it,' said Luca, handing the cups around. He sat cross-legged on the daybed, then punched the seat. 'I can't believe we haven't discussed Jennifer yet.'

Jennifer. That was the pregnant dancer's name. Ava had known that, somewhere.

'Not to mention poor Janine,' Luca went on. 'Talk about a baptism by fire.'

'Who's Janine?'

'His new second swan. Janine, Jeanette, Lynette.' Luca waved his hand. 'Something in that name family.'

Half the ballerinas were called things like that. It was easier just to think of her as the second swan. The *second* second swan.

'I can't believe it about Jennifer,' said Sakurako. 'Do you think she'll come back?'

'I mean,' said Tomasin, 'the guy's not a dancer. He does something in finance.'

'So she'll have money, at least,' said Sakurako. 'But I guess it lessens the chances of Mr K keeping her in the fold.'

'Yeah, it's not like she'll come back in thirteen years with a pure-bred ballerina,' agreed Luca. 'He's *such* a eugenicist.'

'*Luca!*' said Tomasin, but he was looking at Ava. Luca was the official court jester of the company, able to speak the truth disguised as a joke, but he had stepped across more than one line here. There was Ava's own lineage, for a start.

'He *is*, though,' said Luca.

Ava laughed despite herself. 'He has a type,' she conceded, knowing that, despite everything, she was the living embodiment of it.

A thought occurred to her, so obvious she couldn't believe it was only landing now. She turned to Sakurako. 'Hang on, are *you* planning a baby?'

Sakurako glanced at Tomasin, checking it was OK to breach the marital confessional. At his nod, she said, 'It's not on our agenda, no.'

'So why retire? You're still at the top of your game.'

Sakurako blew on her coffee. 'If I'm honest, I do feel I have another two or three years in me. But I'd rather go out on a high. And, you know, we'll both stay on as coaches, so it's not as if we're *leaving* leaving. But for the past few shows, if there's even a tiny twinge, I lie awake, paranoid that it's something serious. And that's what I *couldn't* bear. To have it cut short in a way that's out of my control.'

Sakurako had named the only fate worse than decline. These days most injuries could be rehabilitated, but you could be out of the game for months, even years, and during that time you weren't getting any younger. When a dancer was beyond rehab, Nicky gave some of them jobs – the props department, for example, was stuffed with former dancers – but he couldn't employ them all.

One day Ava would have to concern herself with these things too. Money. Letting dancers go. Budgets, repairs. Since yesterday, thoughts of the future, once vague shapes that would flit across her mind, had begun to nest. Now the thought of responsibility, far away as it was, seemed to lower the ceiling in the room.

She pushed her coffee away from her.

'Well,' said Luca, sensing the dip in mood, '*you're* never allowed to retire.' There was a pause while they waited for the gag. 'You're my meal ticket and don't you forget it.'

But no one laughed. He had voiced an uncomfortable truth: shattered the illusion that the four of them sitting around sharing coffee were equals.

The jester only keeps his post by permission of the king.

As, in a way, does the princess.

8

Two weeks before the first night, Ava and Luca had their first rehearsal on stage. As they exited the lift, she clipped a rehearsal tutu around her waist. This plain ruff looked nothing like the real thing but it changed the space she took up, shifted her centre of gravity and altered her balance, tipping her closer to swanhood.

Luca was already centre stage. When he saw Ava he extended his hand and they caught each other by the wrists: theirs was a joining of flesh as smooth as sculpture, closer than sex.

'Can we quickly run our first *pas de deux*?' he asked her.

'Good idea. I feel like the lift . . .' She didn't need to say any more.

'Da, da-da-da-dah . . .' he sang. The first note alone summoned the orchestra in the empty pit below them, the second conjured the lights on the moonlight lake, and by the third she had become the shy, quivering swan maiden Odette and Luca was a prince, assuming a virgin gawkiness he'd never had in real life. In the first steps of this *pas de deux*, without knowing anything about each other, Odette and Siegfried recognise what has already begun between them. It's a slow, hesitant seduction. Luca spun Ava between his hands as though she were clay on a potter's wheel.

'You're perfect!' said Ava.

'You're right, I *am*. Just wanted to check you appreciated me.'

'I keep a gratitude diary and literally all I do is write your name in it every night.'

Partnering was as much art as science, but frame and proportion came into it: Luca was the right height and weight for Ava, taller than her when she stood *en pointe*, but not so tall he dwarfed her on stage. His arms were the right length to swoop her towards the floor in a fish dive or hold her high overhead. More than that, Luca had best internalised Nicky's philosophy that the minute a male dancer becomes a partner he is there to serve his ballerina, not control her. In this sense, Luca embodied the ideal Kirilovan male.

The click-click-click of Nicky's cane announced his arrival. The clicks grew farther apart every day, like an old clock slowly winding down. He wore a scowl that made Ava's neck prickle.

'Morning, Papa.' She kissed his cheek. He barely acknowledged her. She girded herself for harsh corrections later and reassured herself that some of it, at least, would be the pain talking.

Boyko trailed behind him, so used to operating according to Nicky's instructions that he had slowed down his own walk and even altered his posture to fall into step with him.

'Miss Kirilova,' said Boyko, bowing to Ava.

'Boyko.' She reciprocated with the lightest flex of her knee, while behind him Luca flourished elaborately to mock the over-the-top deference. Ava's relationship with Boyko was a strange one. He was the more experienced dancer, he was often her coach and he knew more about the mysteries of managing the company than anyone except Nicky and Raisa. His Eastern bloc upbringing meant he shared Nicky's philosophy and training. His hands were one of the few pairs – along with Nicky, Jack, Luca, Raisa – that knew Ava's body intimately, that would have been able to pick out her hips or her shoulders blindfold. Yet on stage he was a satellite to her star. And one distant day she would own the company that employed him. Their relative status could shift three times in the same minute.

The recent announcement that Boyko would stand in for Nicky as creative director on first part of the tour had given him a temporary edge right now, or was that Ava's paranoia talking?

The company pianist scuttled into the orchestra pit and unlocked the grand piano. Nicky clapped his hands. 'Act Three, *entrée* and *adage*. You are warm?' Nicky ran his finger along Ava's clavicle and examined the sweat on his thumb before turning to the empty seats. 'Marks, where fuck are marks? You want every-one fall to death into orchestra? My swans murder cellists?'

An unseen stage manager flicked a switch and red strips of light were beamed on to the edge of the stage, theatrical cats' eyes, glow-in-the-day safety measures to stop the dancers, half-blinded by the spots, falling off the edge of the stage. A single red light, a marksman's dot on the back wall, gave spinning dancers some-thing to focus on to counteract dizziness. Beneath it, a rectangle of light expanded and collapsed as two people crept into the stalls. Two pairs of eyes glittered in the dark, then faded. The old seats were shabby, but the theatre's acoustics were as sharp as they had been the day the ribbon had been cut. The voices were young, female, taut with the restraint of gossip. Their whispers travelled as far as the stage.

Ava looked to see if Nicky could hear them. His eyes were as sharp as a young man's but his ears, like his hips, betrayed his age. The words were barely intelligible even to Ava until one of them broke out of her whisper.

'But is it actually official?'

'Not *yet*.'

They *sounded* like the girls from the other morning, but so did they all.

'Why don't you just ask him?'

'You can't *ask* him, Céline. You have to wait for him to offer. Have you even *met* him?'

'Shhh!' The stage manager silenced them before Ava could find out who had promised what to whom. They were probably talk-ing about whether some male dancer was going to ask one of them out, she told herself. But the inner voice that carried her through the longest rehearsals, the most challenging moves, suddenly lacked conviction.

She flexed the legendary Kirilovan ability to compartmentalise and found that that, at least, remained intact. She forced the discomfort to a dark corner of her brain and pulled her focus back to the moment.

'We go,' shouted Nicky to the pianist in the orchestra pit, and the familiar notes began. It was a *pas de trois*, Siegfried and Odile partnering while Von Rothbart lurked in the background, controlling his disguised daughter from a distance. From the moment she stood *en pointe*, it was not Ava spinning but Odile. As quickly as she had inhabited Odette, she was now the black swan, her father's creation, triumphantly stealing another woman's prince. The bare stage became a ballroom. Sometimes it frightened her, how easily she could become someone else; how much more real she felt playing an impossible enchanted creature. How her heavy stage costumes and *pointe* shoes felt more comfortable, more *right*, than the dress and sandals she'd walked to work in. Von Rothbart's moves were more *t'ai chi* than ballet as his hands pulled Odile's invisible strings; in character, Ava and Boyko achieved the closeness that eluded them as colleagues.

Nicky clapped his hands and the palace in which she had been dancing dissolved to nothing.

'What's wrong?' asked Ava.

'Tell me,' said Nicky, his eyes flashing dangerously, 'in this variation, what Odile want?'

'She wants to seduce the prince.' Ava knew she was correct. The unease in her chest told her she had also somehow made a mistake.

'So close to first night and still you no understand.' Nicky thumped his cane on the floor. 'Is not *Come to bed, Siegfried*. Is *Look at me, Daddy*. Why no you know this by now?' Ava sensed Luca cringing on her behalf. 'She dance for Rothbart, no one else. Tell me now, what Odile want?'

'She wants to make her father happy?'

'And what Odile thinks? As she spins?'

'Look at me, Daddy,' Ava parroted. It was so obvious now: Odile had no agency, no desire of her own. This wasn't about two lovers, but a controlling father and his daughter. And he had sprung the revelation on her at the last minute, knowing it would fire her up. You bastard, she thought. You *genius*.

'I get it,' she said. They repeated the variation and Ava danced with a deeper understanding. Look at me, Daddy, she thought, searching out her father's eyes. *Look at me, Daddy.*

Nicky's scowl loosened its grip on his face. 'Is not shit,' he praised. 'We go to *coda.*'

Ava's pulse danced a jig. Every ballet, no matter how powerful its story, how beautiful its design, has its money shot, a technical feat the audience await with bated breath. In *Swan Lake* this takes place in Act III, with the infamous thirty-two *fouettés*. Odile, a vamp in black lace, knowing she's got her man and doomed her rival to an eternity as a swan, spins on the spot in spiteful triumph in a speeded-up, turbocharged version of the music-box ballerina's elegant rotation.

Luca began with a series of energetic pirouettes and then it was Ava's turn. It was as though he had handed her not a baton so much as a lit stick of dynamite. She whirled seamlessly into the thirty-two *fouettés*, the leg on the ground pointing and flexing. No need to count; the music was her guide. She spotted off the red light on the back wall and completed the set without a single misstep – the last turn was even a double *fouetté*, meaning she whipped all the way around without her heel touching the floor – then turned, panting, to Nicky. A double! She stood, chest heaving, calves on fire, and waited for his praise. There was a beat of silence instead, broken only by the wink and creak of the auditorium door opening and closing as their private audience left. 'Why have you the wanderlust?' Nicky swept his arm wide, as though she had traversed the entire stage.

'I'm only, what, a metre from where I started?' But she knew it was bad, not just because she had strayed from her mark but because she hadn't felt herself do it in the moment.

'Metre is mile on stage.'

'The thing is, Papa, isn't it more about expression? Will anyone notice from the audience? I'm acting – isn't that what they'll respond to?'

She began to regret her words while she was still speaking them. Nicky's expression was the same one he'd worn when she'd suggested the redhead for second swan. And was Boyko *smirking?*

'They respond to *perfection*. I see it done properly now.'

Ava resumed her starting position.

'Not by *you*.'

In the wings was the ancient public address system. Nicky leaned into the microphone, pressed a switch, and his voice was broadcast with a sibilant pop: 'Second Siegfried, second Odile, stage, now.'

Beside her, Luca placed a hand on her back, rubbing his thumb over the calluses she had formed, like the stubs of wings, by his repeated lifting of her. 'He doesn't mean it,' he said unconvincingly.

Sakurako and Tomasin were there in less than a minute, flushed and glowing after the sprint from studio to stage.

'*Coda*,' ordered Nicky. 'You show this one how is done.'

Sakurako blinked an apology Ava's way before they began. With Luca's hand on her shoulder, Ava watched Sakurako. Sakurako's Odette was a performance Ava had learned from: she embodied the white swan's brittle hesitancy perfectly. But Odile? There was no sexy, triumphant, I'm-stealing-your-boyfriend attitude in Sakurako's turns, let alone *look at me, Daddy*. Sakurako turned thirty-two perfect *fouettés*, staying on her mark as though she were screwed into the floor but her face was immobile. She wasn't *acting*. She was an instrument playing Nicky's tune, not her own, and certainly not Odile's.

Ava knew better, now, than to point that out.

'There,' he said, when Sakurako stood panting with her hands on her thighs. 'It. Can. Be. Done.'

'That was gorgeous,' said Ava, mainly for Sakurako's benefit. 'But isn't there room for her to do it her way and me to do it my way?'

'*Your* way?' Nicky breathed in and out very slowly as though he were doing a Pilates exercise, trying to control some deep inner muscle. When he spoke again, his voice barely breached a whisper. 'Who is star of company?'

It was a trick question but she still had to answer it. 'I mean – well – obviously, I'm the principal.'

He banged his cane on the floor so hard Ava felt it in the soles of her feet.

'Star is *me*!' He was shouting now. '*My* work. *My* dancing. Crowds no come for Ava Kirilova! Crowds come for Nicky Kirilov ballet. Old way. Best way. *Russian* way. You get *fouettés* perfect or I give first night to her.' He nodded his head backwards in Sakurako's direction. Ava felt the floor tilt beneath her feet. 'Ballet is precision. Not millimetre wrong. Not *millimetre*.'

He left the stage as fast as his bad hip would allow. The pianist cracked her knuckles into the ensuing silence. Ava heard Tomasin swallow.

'He won't put me on,' said Sakurako, a delicate hand on Ava's arm. 'He's just nervous. The fans *absolutely* come for you and he knows it. He *said* it, last week. And what else is that poster all about?

'Thank you,' said Ava, exhaling at last. 'Thanks for saying that.'

'He's in a lot of pain,' said Tomasin. 'And he's stressed about not coming on tour. He wouldn't do that to you.'

'He wouldn't do that to *me*, either,' said Luca. 'We all know I'm his real favourite.' The others laughed, relieved that Luca had broken the tension. 'Come on,' he said. 'Let's get the fuck outta this joint. By which I mean a nice cup of tea and a sit-down upstairs. I might even have a handful of almonds.'

'Whoa!' said Tomasin.

'I know, I can't be tamed.'

Ava smiled, but said, 'Give me a minute.'

The other three left the stage; she felt the faint vibration as the lift carried them to their dressing rooms.

Alone on her stage, she resolved to execute it Nicky's way. I've got the rest of my life to chase my own ambitions, she thought, and then felt a strange lurch, as if the front of her body was trying to run away from the back. This was the first time she had pushed the door open on the idea that she had her own ambitions at all: that her work might one day take her beyond preserving her father's work, like a thing embalmed.

The guilt shouldered its way into this new space as soon as it was created. She mentally taped her thoughts down, as she would cover a blister. The first night was weeks away and all that mattered was the performance.

She fixed on the floor, dusted with rosin from Sakurako's turns, before shaking herself back into action. Staring at the spot wouldn't help her adhere to it; only practice would do that. She clapped her hands at the pianist in the pit, just as her father had.

'Again,' she commanded. Once more Odile possessed her; once more she kept on the music. Once more, she ended up a *jeté* away from where she'd started. She kicked at the air in frustration and shouted 'Fuck!' so loudly that it bounced back at her from the gods.

The stalls door blinked opened again then banged shut. Who had witnessed that?

'House lights!' shouted Ava, and the auditorium flipped from grey to red. She shielded her eyes from the spotlight and stared into the back row, but there was nobody there.

9

In her dressing room, Ava towelled sweat from her neck and face. She unwound bloodied padding from her toes to reveal the crime scene of her feet. The bruise on her right big toenail bloomed black. She pulled the padding from between her first and second toes, rolled up the red rags and tossed them in the wastebin. *Goal*.

The thing was, Nicky sometimes made an example of her even when she was right, just to dispel the inevitable notions of favouritism in the ranks. But he hadn't been doing that this time, because the theatre had been all but empty. Apart from that lurker in the stalls. Which must mean it was her performance, her lack of control, that had offended him.

When, exactly, had her way and Nicky's way stopped being one and the same? It felt like something that had started with *Swan Lake*, but now she wondered if it had been going on for months, maybe even years? Whatever: the fact remained that she had given him her best, she had shown him her *self*, and he had thrown it back at her like a dirty rag.

She massaged her feet, placing fingers between each of her toes and pulling them from side to side, hearing the click of metatarsal bones, matchsticks under the skin, as they were restored to their natural state. He wouldn't do that to her. Not when they had worked towards this for so long. No matter how stressed he was, no matter how much pain he was in, he wouldn't do that to her. Would he?

She took a shower, pipes groaning as they dribbled lukewarm water from the rusted fitting. When she was clean and dry, she still had no idea what had happened, and what *would* happen. Perched on the edge of the daybed, she suddenly wanted nothing more than to lie flat, pull the thin sheet over her head and sleep the clock round. The mental fatigue of a life second-guessing her father could be more overwhelming than physical exhaustion.

'Knock, knock!' a pure treble sang outside the door. 'It's me, Delia!'

'And Raisa,' boomed the bass.

She eyed the daybed longingly, but replied, 'It's open!'

Two dressmakers' dummies slid into the room on wheels, one dress in black, one in white. Behind them were Delia, the wardrobe mistress, and Raisa.

'Final fitting!' grinned Delia. Years of talking through a mouthful of pins meant that she gritted her teeth even when she was happy.

Ava desperately tried to read Raisa's body language. Did those folded arms say, 'I have come to inspect the costumes,' or, 'Your father has just told me that Sakurako will dance the first night.'?

She couldn't bring herself to ask outright. If it was true – if she really had been demoted – it was better that the rest of the company find out via the noticeboard than the wardrobe department rumour mill.

Felicity walked past the door, caught sight of the costumes then doubled back on herself. 'Ooh, hello!' she said. 'Can I have a sneak peek?'

Ava groaned inwardly. Felicity's default mood was one of permanent delight – or rather she wore a permanent expression of delight to cover all her moods, meaning you never knew where you stood, what she was really thinking. She had a tendency to overfill silences, unable to suppress a stream of *wonderfuls* and *how lovelys* that left you unable to link from one thought to the next. She opened her mouth to say no but then caught something rare and human and longing in Felicity's expression. Felicity had been about thirty when it had been decided that the London Russian would save their *Swan Lake* for Ava. A week ago this would not have moved Ava, but now, with the second swan pecking at her heels, she felt an unexpected swell of sympathy. 'Sure,' she said. 'I'd love your take on it.'

Once they were all in, and the door was closed, Delia cracked her knuckles. 'Let's have you in Odette, shall we?'

The white dress that Delia held up had, like the set, begun life as a sketch from Nicky's pen. The feathers were real, of course, and, because this was a Kirilov production and *twee* was a dirty word, the costumes also featured, in their skirts, real bird bones, glued into stiff patterns as tiny and intricate as lace. Ava had worn a prototype version of Odile's costume for the poster, but that had been held together with pins and prayers, nothing anyone could really move in. This was the real thing. Climbing into it felt like a homecoming.

As Delia fastened the dress at the back, Ava marvelled at its comfort. It was one thing to design a dress that looked spectacular, quite another to make that same dress easy to dance in. The fabric of the bodice flowed over her like water. She marked the steps of Odette's first variation.

'Delia, you're a genius,' she said. 'I can't feel the bones at all.'

'No disrespect to Mr K,' said Delia, adjusting a feather at Ava's waist, 'but those bloody bones! He's had me make some weird stuff over the years but going to restaurants and asking for quail skeletons was something else. Not that you'll be able to see them beyond the third row.'

The bones were not really *for* the audience. They were for Ava, to remind her that Kirilovs did things differently. That pretty fairytales were for babies. 'Oh, my goodness, oh, look at that,' gushed Felicity. 'Look at the detailing. Oh, Delia, you are clever. Isn't she *clever*?'

'She is,' said Ava enjoying Delia's glow, tasting a drop of Nicky's power to please. 'This is exactly what he wanted.'

Raisa nodded her approval and said, 'Headdress.'

Ava turned to the mirror. The crown framed her face. The downy white feathers' tips were rimed in violet shimmer, the better to catch the lights on stage. When Delia placed it on Ava's head, disguising her, transforming her, all four women gasped.

'How lovely!' said Felicity. 'Amazing.'

Raisa's hand went to her scrawny breastbone. 'It's like seeing you on your wedding day, Ava.' Her tone had regained its usual neutrality by the end of the sentence but this was still the greatest outpouring of emotion Ava had ever seen from her. 'You are part of the chain.'

She knew then that if Nicky was going to demote her he hadn't told Raisa about it yet, which gave her hope. The *chain* Raisa referred to was the line of ballerinas who had danced the swans across the centuries. Even with written notation and video available, learning a role was a hands-on thing, passed down from artist to artist, through words and demonstration. Raisa had learned her Odette from someone who had danced it, and that dancer from another who had gone before *her*, a chain extending back to the ballerina Pierina Legnani – even thinking her name made Ava feel as though someone was tracing a feather down her spine – who, in 1895, had been the very first person to perform Odette and Odile in the version of *Swan Lake* on which all modern productions had been based.

Ava felt no desire to extend this chain; she wanted greedily to hug the role for herself, to dance it forever, for this to be the last *Swan Lake* ever staged. To let her performance hold all the others inside it, like the last in a series of Russian dolls. With the right performance in the right role, a ballerina could become immortal.

She raised her hands above her head, felt the dress move with her like another skin. If he takes my tour away from me, it will kill me, she thought.

'I'll tell your father the costume fitting is a success,' said Raisa.

'So absolutely lovely, just delectable,' said Felicity, backing out of the room with a haste that betrayed a grief at the skipped generation, the broken chain. 'Really completely amazing.'

When she had gone, Ava was left alone with Delia. She climbed unselfconsciously out of her dress and crossed her dressing room in her underwear, throwing a sundress over her head while Delia carefully manoeuvred Odette's costume on to the dummy. Ava watched the white feathers tremble.

'I have a favour to ask you, Delia,' she ventured.

'Of course, Miss Kirilova.'

'Can I keep them in here. With me?' She gestured to the two mannequins, the inanimate swans. It was a big thing to ask of Delia: costumes were strictly kept under lock and key in Wardrobe in the bowels of the theatre.

'Oh . . .' Delia looked about her as if the room might be bugged. 'I'm not sure.'

'I won't tell him,' Ava said. 'I just feel . . . I need some time alone with them. I need to become *my* version of them. Not Raisa's, not some dancer from a hundred years ago. I need to break them in, mould them to *me*. And I need to do that alone.'

Delia was an artist too; she understood. 'Well, I wouldn't do it for anyone else,' she said and then, nervous now that she had committed to it, 'But what if he finds out?'

'We'll say I threatened you at knifepoint,' she said. Delia laughed.

'Go on, then. Just for a few days, and then they're back under lock and key.' On the way out, she stopped, her fingers resting on the doorknob. '*Ah*. I've just remembered. I did say Sakurako could try yours on. I'm not even starting her fitting for another week.'

Ava frowned. 'What for? We're not the same size.'

'Well – the same reason as you,' said Delia. 'To get into character. Feel the thing.'

Ava felt a fresh surge of possessiveness, and asserted her status. 'Sakurako can wait.'

Delia blinked, but said, 'No problem.'

When she had gone, Ava slipped into Odile's dress and felt a dangerous current buzz through her. The sleek black feathers trembled as she rose on *demi-pointe*. She didn't look like a bride any more, but someone at a funeral, dressed to steal the spotlight from the corpse.

10

By class the next morning Ava still hadn't heard from Nicky, and the flame of hope she'd felt during the costume fitting had guttered overnight. She shouldered the door of Studio 1 in a state of hyper-vigilance. Whose dropped eyes would betray the dancer who'd overheard Nicky's reprimand? But, inside, Ava barely made a ripple. All eyes were on Felicity, who stood in Nicky's place at the front of the room.

Ava's stomach tightened. It wasn't unusual for Felicity or Boyko to lead company class but she always, always knew about it beforehand, and she always knew why. She found herself scanning the barres and mirrors for the second swan, and when she couldn't find her in the sea of lookalike ballerinas she leapt to the conclusion that they must be together. The only dancer Nicky ever skipped class to focus on was Ava.

She made straight for Felicity. 'What's going on?'

'Nothing to worry about,' said Felicity brightly. 'Mr K's got a meeting this morning. Some last-minute legal thing. Raisa and Boyko are in it as well. Didn't he tell you?'

Pride handed her the oldest excuse in the book. 'Of course,' she said. 'I forgot.'

'Pre-production brain,' said Felicity, with what might have been pity. 'We've all got it.'

Ava set her bottle and bag at the base of the barre. When she straightened up, she saw that the second swan was a knight's move away, one metre to the right and two metres behind her. Ava had been the last one in; she must have been there all along. She was staring at Ava, a nervous smile on its starting blocks, but then the music began and Ava broke eye contact.

Felicity's class was hard, fast, exacting, so rigorous that, as the sweat began to smart in her eyes, Ava wished she'd done a warm-up to prepare for the warm-up. The demands of instructing filleted Felicity's usual niceties and for forty-five blistering minutes the steely dancer at her core was exposed. *There* you are, thought Ava. It was a reminder that no matter how long you had been dancing, no matter what your position, everyone had something to prove and something to mask. It was as exhausting as it was reassuring.

When she opened her dressing room door, something slithered sideways across the floor. Ava shrieked and performed a spontaneous *sauté*, landing on the daybed. If the cockroaches from the Gulag had migrated to the theatre she didn't think she could take it.

The creature didn't move. Ava summoned the courage to inspect it and saw that it wasn't a cockroach or a living thing at all but a single black feather, the span of Ava's hand, a rime of purple glitter on its tip. Her relief was short-lived. Odile's costume was locked in the mirrored wardrobe. Had someone been in there?

She took the key from her dressing-table drawer and opened the wardrobe door. The mannequins stood side by side but an asymmetry on Odile's neckline made it clear where the feather had come from; in fact there were a few missing, a bald patch on the fabric. This happened, feathers came loose all the time, and, while a gap under the wardrobe door accounted for its presence on her floor, where were the rest of them? She crawled on all fours but there was no sign.

Sakurako knew the costumes were here, and she was only next door, and the four principals locked their dressing-table drawers but not their doors. You never knew when you might run out of padding or tape. Delia had said that Sakurako wanted to try the dresses on for the same reasons Ava did. Could she have damaged the dress, accidentally or – the thought brushed Ava's mind like a feather riding a breeze – out of spite, or some kind of deliberate sabotage? It was the kind of thing you heard about, but there was the small matter of it being the most out-of-character thing Sakurako could do. Nicky's paranoia was infecting her. It must have been me, thought Ava. I must have dislodged them and the cleaners, not realising that every feather was hand-painted, must have swept them up.

She was tired, she was sore and she was, she realised as her belly imploded, ravenous. From the fruit bowl she took a banana – ninety calories but worth every one of them, with fibre, Vitamin B6 and potassium for muscle recovery – and peeled it. Purple glitter – that stuff got everywhere – left a faint smear on the yellow skin. She caught sight of herself in the mirror. The banana looked like a tree going into a woodchipper. When there was a rap on the door she said, 'It's open,' through a mouthful of simple carbohydrate.

'Is only us.' Nicky's voice stepped her nerves up a gear. He must be here to confirm, or deny, her demotion. The first night was Sakurako's, or it was hers.

He loves me, he loves me not.

As the door handle turned, she prepared to arrange her features to reflect his mood, in the hope that she could bring about a last-minute reprieve if there was one going, but when he creaked into the room there was nothing to bounce off. On his face, pain had painted out all other feeling. Raisa's expression gave no more clue. Ava felt her earlier defiance change shape inside her, and the impulse to apologise rise up, but Nicky spoke before she could.

'You have interview day after tomorrow,' he said. 'Important journalist. Sunday broadsheet.'

Surprise overtook relief and Ava swallowed the rest of her banana whole. Of course the press reviewed their shows in the dance pages, but Nicky had always behaved as though he actively wanted *not* to be known outside the dance circles, as though the dinner-and-a-show brigade couldn't understand his work and didn't deserve it. He had always said that the only reason to court the papers was to fill the box office, and what did that matter when his capital and his shadowy oligarch patrons would bank-roll any show?

'Why now?' she said, when the banana had finished its painful progress. Her next thought nearly brought it back up. 'Are you – are we running out of money?'

There had always been money, and she had been brought up to assume that there always would.

'Nooo.' He laughed to dismiss the idea, pitching her from panic back into relief so quickly she felt a kind of seasickness. 'Is because I am *proud* of you.'

It was as if her blood itself halted. She drew the deepest breath she had taken all day. 'So you aren't giving the first night to Sakurako, then?'

'Pff!' He threw his hands up in the air. 'You take things so serious.'

Her blood flowed again, hotter than before; anger pushed it through her veins at a rolling boil. It had not been a joke at the time and they both knew it.

'Right.' Raisa, to his right, gave the slightest of eye-rolls. Ava found herself wondering what would happen if someone were to follow her around all day measuring the adrenaline levels in her blood. She pictured the tight zigzag it would make on a graph. She wondered what that did to a body, over time. She wondered what it did to a mind.

'What if they ask me about—' She was afraid to say *my mother* but Nicky knew what she meant. Their father-daughter telepathy had its uses away from the stage. He shook his head.

'They won't. Or money. Is condition of giving interview. Is *coup.*'

'That's hardly a word a Russian uses lightly,' said Raisa, and Nicky roared with laughter.

'OK,' Ava said. 'It'll be interesting, I'll look forward to it.'

'*Moya lyubimaya devushka,*' he said, *my most, beloved girl,* which often meant that a present was coming, and sure enough his hand went into his pocket and pulled out a purple roll of notes. 'This is prize for surviving. Go to Bond Street. Get something nice for first night. Red, white, black only.'

'Thank you, Papa.' Ava's hand closed around the slim roll. She could measure cash with a bank-teller's expertise: there were three hundred pounds here at least.

Raisa clicked her tongue. 'Always with the cash.' Ava swallowed the reply that Raisa hadn't thought cash wasn't so vulgar when he'd put her up in a flat near the theatre, or when he'd bought her a little *dacha* for her holidays on the Black Sea. 'You know I don't like the girls carrying that much money around London. It makes them vulnerable.'

Whenever Raisa displayed flashes of almost maternal concern, she always countered it with a gesture of disapproval. Now, she ran her finger over Ava's dressing-table mirror to inspect for dust.

'But I *like* cash,' said Ava. 'You can see it disappearing.'

Nicky laughed, and Ava felt the internal glow that only came on the rare occasions she got to side with him against Raisa. 'Cash teach value,' he said. 'You no overspend what you no have. Raisa, you should understand that.'

Raisa said something in Russian that Ava thought was *I guess so*. Like Nicky, she had grown up in poverty – empty-belly, icicles-inside-the-house poverty – in Soviet Russia. He had been born under Stalin, for goodness' sake. With a childhood like that, who could blame him for hoarding cash? When the only bank was run by the state that was also your jailer, was it any wonder he didn't trust financial institutions?

'I'll be careful,' said Ava, and kissed him. A rasp against her cheek drew her attention to a little white triangle of stubble where he'd missed a bit shaving.

'I know you are always in and out of each other's rooms but if you are going to have all that cash lying around, you *must* lock the door,' said Raisa on the way out. 'I walked past earlier and it was wide open. I had to close it myself.'

So someone *had* been in. Ava's eyes went to the black feather on the dressing table, then darted away in case she betrayed Delia's breach of protocol. 'The locks are going, that's the problem,' she said. 'The magnet on Luca's door hasn't worked for weeks.'

'Only insane person go in Luca's bloody pigsty anyway,' said Nicky. 'New locking system will be state-of-art. Face scan. Like airport security.'

It took a while for the seasick feeling to subside when they had gone.

Ava counted the cash. Five hundred; she was losing her touch. She set eighty aside. She would do what she always did: pick up something from Zara, knowing that her dancer's body made off-the-peg look bespoke. The remaining money she would add to what she called, when she allowed herself to think about it, her fund. Ava's fund amounted to tens of thousands of pounds – she had never counted it all – skimmed off her father's gifts over many years. Whenever she locked money away like this, in a drawer here, in the safe at home, she would ask herself what she was doing, have a moment of revulsion as she thought about the good it could do for charity, or compared her income to the low wages of the junior dancers in her own company. Yet she was as power-less to spend the money as she was to stop herself hoarding it.

Was it for running away? She couldn't have said. Sometimes, at night, on the threshold of dreaming, her fund punched its way out of her subconscious, shocking her awake, and for a brief moment she would understand with perfect clarity that *the secret was the point*, and that she had chosen money rather than drinking or drugs or starving or purging or cutting because it didn't impact her performance. The fund was privacy; the fund was control. But then that understanding would be swallowed by sleep, and the following morning it had always gone again.

Ava opened her dressing-table drawer, added the four hundred and twenty pounds to the rolls and wads already there, and experienced a hot wave of banana-flavoured nausea which subsided when she locked the drawer and returned the key to its hiding place above the window ledge. It was only when she looked down at her hands and found that she was counting on her fingers that she realised she was mentally listing all the people who might want to unseat her. *Swan Lake* had obviously reopened old wounds in Felicity. Boyko would do anything to make Nicky love him. This tour was Sakurako's last chance to shine and, while she was incapable of duplicity, Tomasin would do anything for his wife.

Not to mention that bloody second swan.

A breeze struggled in through the window. In the mirror, Ava watched the black feather on the dressing table float slowly upwards, then tumble to the floor.

11

Ava sat cross-legged on the floor of Studio 3, holding a cigarette lighter to singe the toes of her shoes – hand-made on lasts moulded to her feet by Freed of London, and embossed with her initials – so they wouldn't slip or make too much noise on the stage. In heat like this the last thing she wanted was to be near a naked flame, but this was the way she broke in her shoes. Everyone had their own method: some girls cracked the shank in half or scored the soles. Sakurako, in a habit at odds with her dainty exterior, liked to slam her shoes repeatedly in a door; a dull repetitive thump told Ava she was currently making use of the heavy fire door in the corridor outside. Years ago, a dancer whose method involved tearing out her insoles and then supergluing them back in had accidentally stuck herself to the floor of Studio 2. She had lost a role as a result.

A CD player in the corner of the room played the *Swan Lake* score: Act IV, the scene from the lake – the moment where Odette says her anguished goodbye to her prince, accompanied by yearning violins. Ava paused for a second to feel the music. Heartbreak was so deep in the DNA of this melody that surely anyone who didn't know the story would be able to divine it through the melody alone?

She moved on to sewing on her ribbons with unwaxed dental floss. Her fingertips were calloused with the effort of gripping the needle. No part of the body was immune from the ravages of ballet. She pushed the needle through the fabric binding that encased the drawstring. She would miss these rituals when at last she hung up her *pointe* shoes, when they were prised from her clawed hands. She felt a wave of pre-emptive grief for her life beyond the stage. The needle slipped, digging into her nail bed and making her cry out. What was *wrong* with her at the moment? Usually preparing her shoes was a kind of meditation for Ava, but today her mind would not stay in the moment. She wondered, secretly, traitorously, if they had waited, not until she was ready for *Swan Lake*, but too long. Five, even three years ago, Ava would have been satisfied – proud, ecstatic! – to dance the role exactly to Nicky's specifications.

But that wasn't it. It was only *since* dancing Odette and Odile that the feelings of rebellion had risen inside her. It was only since being given the roles that she had started to doubt what kind of dancer she really was.

The music reached its conclusion, the whole orchestra seeming to weep. Ava closed her eyes, lost herself not in the task in her lap but in the ballet itself, mentally marking the steps, feeling phantom hands on her waist, surrendering to Odette's grief. When the final chord sounded, she found herself breathless.

In the silence that followed, she became aware of her surroundings again. The floor came into focus first, followed by the mirrors and the walls. When she looked at the open door to see the second swan framed between the jambs, Ava found that she had been somehow expecting her. The girl had been dancing: her coronet was coming loose, she'd sweated salty drifts on to her black leotard, and dark patches circled the underarms of her cropped sweatshirt. She had a black and red canvas LRB tote bag slung across her body.

'D'you want to borrow this?' She brandished a little silver hammer, a tool from a folk tale. 'It's really good for cracking the soles. Or, if not, *I* could do your shoes for you? So you can relax, ahead of the dress rehearsal. Or I could do your ribbons?' She pulled a sewing kit from her bag.

Ava looked around to see if there were any witnesses to this extraordinary suggestion. Whoever you were, even – *especially* – if you were the director's daughter, with all the example-setting that entailed, you always did your own shoes. No one knew better than a ballerina exactly where to sew the ribbons in a way that best supported her feet, and no one knew better than a ballerina how much damage a weak or misplaced stitch could do.

'Thank you. But I prefer to do it myself. It sets me up for going onstage. Even if it's just a rehearsal.'

'Oh, my *God*, me *too*,' said the second swan, as if this were a million-to-one chance. She seemed to realise she'd overdone it and abruptly began to examine her fingers as though they were stained with something she couldn't wash off, or maybe it was just a way of avoiding eye contact. 'But,' she addressed her hands, 'it's just – the way I do it, I put a bit of wax on the toe, *then* singe it? It just provides that extra bit of grip. For turns. Like, if you travel during *fouettés*.'

She held met Ava's gaze now and held it, letting her know that she had been the one at the back of the stalls. She had witnessed Ava's dressing-down and now here she was, on an ego trip because she'd been singled out by the ballet master, trying to tell Ava what to do? Ava drew in her breath.

'Thank you. But no.'

The girl tapped her silver hammer against her palm. Why was she still here?

'Can I maybe get you a coffee or something instead?'

Oh, for God's sake. '*No*.'

'Alright, no need to snap.' The girl's voice was clogged with hurt. 'Just trying to make things easier for you. I understand the pressure you're under, now I'm in the spotlight too.'

Ava didn't know whether to laugh at her or scream at her. As if anyone else had the first *idea*. She was about to put the girl in her place when—

'I think Miss Kirilova needs some time to herself.' Sakurako was in the corridor outside. No stranger to being the object of a crush herself, she had clearly misdivined the situation. 'I'm sure you understand.'

'I mean I only – but yeah. Whatever,' said the second swan.

'Thank you,' mouthed Ava to Sakurako, who put her hand on the small of the second swan's back and steered her away from the studio. Sakurako was wearing a pale lilac wraparound cardigan with a hood. In it nestled a single black feather whose glittering tip caught the light as she pulled the door closed behind her.

So it *had* been Sakurako in her room. Ava didn't know which was more unsettling: Delia breaching their confidence about where the dresses were hidden, or Sakurako trying them on behind her back. But no: it had only been Nicky Delia had promised not to tell, and in Sakurako's shoes, she would probably have done the same. She was letting petty things distract her when all her focus was needed for the ballet. Don't worry, she told herself, and was surprised to hear herself say it out loud. 'Don't worry, don't worry, don't worry.'

She sat alone on the studio floor, muttering the phrase over and over, as though, if she said it often enough, she would be able to obey her own command.

12

Ava's breakfast – two hard-boiled eggs and a few leaves of spinach from the canteen – sweated in their plastic bowl. Ian Bayer was a Serious Critic from a Serious Newspaper and it was a mark of importance that he had been permitted to bring into the theatre not just a phone but an iPad as well. He placed his glassy devices on the boardroom table next to his Leon takeout coffee, then frowned at the ceiling.

'I'm sorry, Miss Kirilova, we'll need to turn that off.'

Ava stretched to turn the air-con unit off and immediately the temperature rose by ten degrees.

Bayer was middle-aged, with a sandy beard and tortoiseshell glasses and just about the worst posture Ava had ever seen: shoulders up around his ears even as he extended his hand to her. He needed a good six months of Reformer Pilates to sort that back out; she had half a mind to send him Jack's way to work on his Spanish-Inquisition machines with their racks and pulleys. Ava struggled to summon respect. The problem was that Ian had never been a dancer. That his job should be to judge others' dancing deeply offended her. It was the sort of job you should do after ten years of training, after toenails that peeled off like stickers, shin splints and torn shoulders, no friends outside the company. For a civilian to just *decide* to be a dance critic, without training as a dancer? It should be *illegal*.

Bayer hit a red icon on a black screen. 'That should pick up nicely now.' At his words, a white line spiked, like a heart monitor or a lie detector. 'Shall we begin?'

Ava nodded her consent then assumed the ballerina version of a resting face, a light smile held by cheek muscles as strong and supple as any dancer's calves. Ian Bayer leaned forward, fingers steepled.

'So. *Swan Lake*. What can we expect? The London Russian hasn't done a canonical ballet for a few years now. Is this, if you'll forgive the pun, his swan song? Can we expect a surprise announcement on the first night?'

Ava laughed at the thought of Nicky retiring. 'Come on. You know what he's like. You should be thinking in terms of a rebirth rather than a winding-down.'

Bayer didn't look convinced. 'So it's a crowd-pleaser, bums on seats? You must need money for the renovation job?'

Nice try, thought Ava. Her smile didn't slip. 'No, he's financing that through his other assets,' she said, hoping her delivery was confident enough that he wouldn't ask her to explain what that meant. 'And you know we don't do crowd-pleasers. I doubt my father knows the word *compromise* in any language. Our *Swan Lake*'s more horror film than fairytale. Think about it: you've got shapeshifters, a creepy mother, a doomed virgin in a white dress. When you think about it like that, it's hard to see how else you can play it.'

The heat continued to rise. Wet patches tie-dyed the underarms of Bayer's pale blue shirt. 'So I've been looking at the logistics of this tour. They're – well, the word that comes to mind is insane. Eighty swans on stage every night! Not to mention the other characters. With respect, what was your father thinking?'

Ava recalled the words Luca had said to her the previous evening: no one ever built a statue of a critic. Hold that thought, she told herself. Hold it tight and hold your temper tighter.

'He's still as ambitious as ever. We've been able to book the biggest venues in the world, and sold most of them out.'

'The same cast for every performance, though. No B-cast to back you up if things go wrong. Who does that?'

Ava suppressed the doubt she had about that. That *everyone* had about that.

'Nikolai Kirilov does that.' Ava had not been taught the steps for this conversational dance but she found she could do it anyway. She kept her voice calm, measuring her control in the even waves her answers made on Ian's screen. 'Of course we have understudies. And Sakurako Sato will be dancing one in four shows. But yes, not rotating the cast is unconventional. That's why he's factored in so much rest for us. That's why we're staying on the road for so long. Well, that and the fact that we're *de facto* homeless until the theatre is done and my father has recovered from his operation.'

Perhaps she *had* been trained for this: after all, what was being a ballerina about if not making the demanding look effortless? She felt the accustomed pleasure at doing something difficult and doing it well.

'So. Who do you prefer to dance, Odette or Odile?'

This was more like it. 'I mean, I love them both for different reasons. With Odette I get to be very sweet, very vulnerable in a way that most of us are scared to be in real life. And then with Odile, well, I would never steal someone's boyfriend in reality so it's fun to try on that side of my personality.'

'And I suppose the plot of the ballet has resonance for you and your father.'

Ava tilted her head in query.

'Von Rothbart is a single father too. His relationship with Odile revisits the territory you explored in *Zeus and Athena*. Your *Frankenstein*, too. All these fathers as, as . . .' The word he wasn't allowed to say might as well have been displayed on his screen, but he settled for ' . . . *begetters* of their girls.'

Her smile stiffened while her heart banged a drum. Swerve the question, whip away from it, dance out of its way.

'I would hardly compare my father to Count Von Rothbart,' she managed.

'Why not? Nicky Kirilov makes puppets of young women, including his own daughter. Isn't that exactly what Von Rothbart does with Odile?'

Oh my God, she thought, it is. How could she be this close to first night and still only just be understanding the ballet? You could uncover a new layer for a year and still never get to the heart of it. But at least they *were* talking about the ballet now.

'Well, we lean into that, though,' she improvised. 'Von Rothbart isn't just waving his hands in the background, he's really there with Odile, positioning her arms, controlling her like a dummy. We have fun with it.'

'I'm sure you do,' said Ian. The heat crept up another degree, as though someone were turning the dial on an oven. 'And what will it be like for you on tour without your father?'

'He's only having a hip replacement. He's not retiring.'

'But he won't be going on the road with you. You'll be dancing without his protection.'

'His protection! It's not the mafia!' *Isn't it?* Bayer's smirk suggested. 'Look, he rehearses us so thoroughly it's like he's in the room even when he isn't. Every dancer in this company has internalised my father's method, his steps, his *voice*.'

The rest of the questions Ava could answer on autopilot; she barely knew what she said. When the interview was over, she saw Bayer into the lift and stood on the balcony that overlooked the atrium while the lift cranked down.

He looked tiny, insignificant. Yet his closing words rang in her ears. He had named her fears. Not the digs about money – she had faith in that – but travelling without Nicky. How would she cope on tour with him bedridden on the other side of the planet? So much about the company's daily operations depended on Mr K's physical presence, on his ability even now to materialise in the studio just at the moment doubt set in and set everything back on its axis with one simple correction, or on the way the prospect of being on the receiving end of one of his outbursts kept them all at the top of their game. Bayer's words were an echo of whispers that chased her through the corridors. Jealous rumours from the corps de ballet, girls who felt they deserved what she had. Girls who thought that, without her father, Ava would no longer be the sorcerer's daughter but just another ballerina.

13

'Afternoon, Miss Kirilova.'

'Not long now, Miss Kirilova.'

'Isn't it *hot*, Miss Kirilova?'

In the days before a first night, it could take Ava ten minutes to walk a ten-metre corridor. A secret passage that could get her from one side of the complex to the other without interruption – now *that* she would really appreciate. She should have asked her father to design one into the refurbishment of the theatre.

She edged past a fibreglass rock. The ballet was a work in progress right up until opening night and so was the set. A box of plastic goblets for the ball scene waited in the corridor; in the hangar behind the stage, the last brushstrokes were being applied to the towering red pillars that formed the palace gates.

Delia hurried by with an armful of cygnets' costumes, their soft feathers the same warm grey as her hair.

The stage itself was occupied by the ballroom set and Ava intended to mark the steps of the *coda* one last time. Dancers were strictly forbidden from going on the stage without a stage manager present, but it would be a bold member of staff who told tales on Ava Kirilova. She dipped her toe in the rosin box at the side of the stage, enjoying the crunch of satin on the sticky powder. White dust billowed around her foot.

Stepping out of the wings, she realised that someone else had had the same idea. The second swan was in her position at the window, pale blue leotard and stiff white tutu, repeatedly going over the steps. Ava watched transfixed, not just at the girl's daring – being here alone was a sackable offence – but at her talent. *Now* she saw it. She was good: the liquid sweep of her arms now came from even deeper in the back. Raisa was a good coach but Ava had never seen her cajole an improvement like that from anyone, and certainly not in under three weeks.

The second swan came to the end of her variation, then asked a question to the shadows below the window. 'More like that?'

'Exactly this,' came the voice from below. 'Exactly this on stage.'

Of *course*. Only Nicky could get these results from his dancers. But what was he thinking, wasting spare time he didn't have on this? He needed to rest, not work harder. All this fuss for twenty seconds on stage?

She beamed. 'Oh, Mr K, thank you. I've been working very hard.'

'*Da*. Hard work, good results. You stay like this, you dance both swans one day, maybe, yes? Future. Long away *future*.'

'Omigod yes. Yes,' breathed the second swan. Ava clutched at the black drapes. He had all but promised the girl her crown and she felt the urge to stamp her foot and say, but that's *mine*, even knowing she couldn't wear it forever.

'But I'm not thinking about the future,' the girl said earnestly. 'Today is what matters. The performance. I know it's only a moment but I want to get it *perfect*.'

Nicky banged his cane on the floor. Ava had come to know its tones as well as she knew his voice: the tap signified approval, not anger. 'What is Kirilov ballet but series of perfect moments? *Moya lyubimaya devushka*.'

Moya lyubimaya devushka.

Only Ava's grip on the curtain kept her upright. That he was giving this girl private lessons was one thing. But to call another dancer his most beloved girl? She felt as though she'd caught her lover in bed with another woman.

'You OK there, darling?' A warm, dry hand was on her shoulder. She turned to see Jack, who looked all wrong in a linen shirt where his tunic should be. She often thought of him as an action figure whose clothes couldn't be changed.

'How long have you been lurking?'

'I'd have said that was more of a skulk than a lurk,' said Jack. 'I've come to escort His Nibs to hospital for a last once-over before the big op. Blood pressure and so forth. Wish me luck.' He squeezed her shoulder, cleared his throat and stepped out of the wings. 'Our taxi's here, Nicky.'

The second swan assumed B-plus, framed in the window, her chest rising and falling. Nicky blinked at Jack with that confused, irritated look he always got when real life intruded on the ballet.

'Your consultation,' said Jack. 'The last one. Before surgery.'

Ava wondered whether Jack mightn't have been a better choice than Raisa to nurse Nicky back to health after his surgery. He was as unflappable as Nicky was irascible, and he understood dancers' bodies in disrepair better than anyone she knew. Raisa was hardly Florence Nightingale.

'Fuck bloody *sake*!' Nicky shouted at Jack, as though he were personally and solely responsible for his needing the surgery at all, then clicked his way off stage. 'You keep doing! Do better!' he shouted up at the ballroom window, his anger now directed at the second swan. If she took it personally, there was no sign of it. She blinked twice, said, 'Yes, Mr K,' and curtseyed.

She's playing him like a violin, thought Ava.

Jack led Nicky off stage left. Ava remained where she was, hidden in the wings, her eyes on the second swan. She was watching for a little smirk of triumph, or for her to look out over theatre, her face giving away – what, exactly? Ambition? Every dancer in this company was ferociously ambitious; you didn't get here, much less stay here, otherwise. But, as she watched, the second swan simply danced, in silence, repeating the same intricate steps again and again, nodding and muttering to herself at the end of each round, then starting again. She became Odette for half a minute at a time, and, in the moments between, she became her own coach. Talent and determination, thought Ava, but the admiration was swiftly eclipsed by dismay as the other dancer descended the staircase and, without music, began to move through another set of steps. A different role, a mirror role. A role

Ava knew because she'd been rehearsing it for half a year, preparing for it for half her life. The second swan became the black swan, dancing Odile's first variation, moving with such conviction that Ava heard the music in her head and became swept up in the performance.

Then, abruptly, she stopped, bent to knead the muscles around her left knee and looked up and into the wings, straight into Ava's eyes. She paled under the spotlight.

'*Jesus!*' she said, and then, hastily, 'Miss Kirilova. It's not, I don't . . . I'm just trying it out for fun.' She began to babble nervously. 'I've got a little . . .' she waved her hand over her knee '. . . sort of twinge thing. Can't seem to stretch it out. Jack says ice and rest. And I will, if it gets too much. But I'm on top of it.'

Ava meant to say, *should* have said, something like, 'If Jack tells you to rest, then you should rest,' but instead she heard herself say – heard it at a remove, like watching a recording of herself – 'Well, I mean, pain is a part of the process. We're all dancing through something.'

The girl nodded, as though Ava had endorsed her resolve. 'Don't worry about me,' she said in a voice shot through with granite. 'I'm not afraid of pain.'

14

The orchestra buzzed like a giant bee in the pit. Through a crack in the curtain, Ava watched the audience file in. To this dress rehearsal, Nicky had invited not only his own pupils from the London Russian Ballet Academy – the first three rows were a sea of coronet plaits – but also a select audience of ballet students from all over the UK. It was a mark of his standing in the art that many of them would have been rejected for his own ballet academy but still jumped at the chance to watch the LRB rehearse.

Was there a better sight than seats filling up? All the aches and pains of the past few days' rehearsals seemed to melt away, replaced with a surge of energy. If you could bottle the analgesic effects of an audience, Ava thought, you could sell it to Big Pharma and make your fortune. An excited crowd gave you life when you thought you were so tired you couldn't stand, and then afterwards made you feel as if you could do it all over again. Never mind mimicking flight through dance; at that moment, Ava felt capable of flight itself.

Swan Lake. The big one. This was it.

The word 'future', which had lately reared up to frighten her, was now reduced to this performance.

The PA system crackled into life, faint from the depths of the building, so that Raisa's voice, when it came, sounded like a whisper from the stage. 'Ladies and gentlemen of the London Russian Ballet Company, five minutes to curtain.'

'Back in a minute,' she said, and escaped backstage.

'Miss Kirilova!' The stage manager waved his clipboard after her. 'You're supposed to be in the wings.'

'Sorry,' said Ava. 'I just need to wish the others luck.' She was using her privilege to flout the rules for good reason. Her father had whipped the company, particularly the corps, into a state beyond the energy needed to perform. She could relate to that. She knew that a word, a nod, a smile from her would bolster them all.

In the corridor, dancers dressed in red lined the walls.

'*Merde.*' Ava blew kisses down the line. 'Let's show them how it's done.'

Merde, French for 'shit': the ballet dancer's version of *break a leg*, dating back to ballet's origins, when the more horse muck there was on the street outside the Paris Opera House, the more carriages, and the larger the audience.

'That goes double for you,' said Ava, to Luca, kissing him on the lips. 'That goes *triple* for you.'

'Triple *merde*,' said Luca. 'I'll be knee-deep in it.'

In Studio 1, the sixty-seven swans and cygnets who wouldn't be needed until Act II were preparing, triple-checking ribbons and dusting white powder on each other's arms and backs for a uniform skin tone. Feathered caps covered their hair and eyes and it was impossible to tell them apart. It was hard to believe that in such a short time they would be so elegant on stage, or that they would be able to remain still during the lovers' first *pas de deux*. Ava sometimes thought, as she watched shaking limbs hold awkward poses for minutes on end, that they had the harder job.

Seeing Ava, they stood to attention.

'*Merde,*' she called.

'Places!' Raisa's voice came over the PA.

The show began with Ava and Boyko alone on stage by the lake, a two-minute prologue showing Von Rothbart putting his curse on Odette. As Ava went through the last of her stretches, he lurched into view, his owlish costume wide and heavy. Large bones clacked softly in his cape. Ava didn't want to think about what Delia had had to do to get those. She spared a thought for him in his heavy clothes under the lights.

'God, Boyko,' she said. 'Rather you than me in that on a day like today.'

He gestured to a two-litre bottle of water at the side of the stage. They exchanged grins, their power struggle momentarily forgotten.

There was exquisite satisfaction in knowing that every member of the company was where they ought to be, from the corps members to Nicky himself, standing where he always did, in the box, at the stage-left tip of the circle. In its black cocoon he looked like a floating face and hands, silent, expressionless.

The house lights dimmed and the curtain rose. The oboe played, a plaintive B-flat that was almost a minor chord in itself, and the ballet began.

15

By Act III, Ava wasn't thinking about her second self, fluttering in the window. She was Odile, lost in her own triumph, carried by the music, executing the *fouettés* perfectly, even turning a double on the last rotation. *Look at me, Daddy*.

In the interval before the finale, it took half a bottle of water and a costume change to go from bad to good, black swan to white, seductress to virgin. If the *fouettés* are *Swan Lake*'s money shot, then Act IV is the tearjerker. Prince Siegfried, understanding that he has been tricked into pledging his love to Odile, returns to the moonlit lake to beg for his white swan's forgiveness. Heartbroken, Odette jumps to her death from a rock, swiftly followed by Siegfried. In some versions of the ballet the remaining swans dance out their grief. In Nicky Kirilov's, they tore Von Rothbart wing from wing, the stage a blur of feathers and red scarves, and, when they had finished, Siegfried emerged from the lake, his lover's drenched and lifeless body returned to human form in his arms.

In practice, this involved Ava climbing a two-metre fibreglass rock and jumping on to a bank of foam mattresses. There, Delia would swap Ava's tutu for a diaphanous gown and her headdress for a long wig, both wringing wet so that, as Luca carried her to the front of the stage, the water caught the light and her body itself appeared to weep.

Ava relished the seconds before the drop: she could feel the audience, pregnant with applause, a wall of adoration at her back. The stepping off and the rollercoaster swoop of the belly on the way down was a moment of liberation after the discipline of the past two hours, the past six months, the past twenty years.

She hit the mattresses and rolled over. A tiny white feather wafted slowly down into the tub of lukewarm water where Delia kept the costumes and trembled on the surface. As her tutu was unfastened and her headdress peeled by unseen hands, Luca jumped from the rock, a black shadow in flight, and landed in a crouch.

'We smashed it,' he whispered, taking her hand as the dripping wig was placed on to her head. 'Your *fouettés*! You were a tornado!'

'Did you see the last—'

A scream tore through the music, a high, piercing note that seemed to last longer than human lungs could sustain.

The orchestra stuttered to a halt, a single violin trailing off into a yowl. Ava threw off the wet wig; she and Luca dashed around the edge of the set to see all the swans huddled centre stage.

'Jack?' Raisa's voice silenced the murmuring house. '*Jack!*'

He shot from the wings. 'Let me see her.' The swans parted to admit him to their huddle, and he dropped awkwardly to his knees. Ava saw a white-stockinged leg sticking out at a grotesque angle. Beside her, Luca gasped.

Boyko removed his Von Rothbart headdress and stepped to the front of the stage. His words carried to the gods without the PA system. 'As you can see, we have an emergency on stage. Please, make your own way out. House lights?' he shouted to the lighting desk and then, over his shoulder, 'And *curtain*, for goodness' sake!'

The house lights illuminated a hundred shocked faces before the curtain dropped.

'Who is it?' asked Luca. 'They're all the same with their masks on.'

'I don't know,' said Ava. One of the swans ran off retching, revealing the girl's leg up to the thigh. It was swelling before their eyes, as though someone had stuck a bicycle pump in her calf and was inflating her knee. Ava had seen career-ending injuries before, and this looked up there with the worst of them. Everyone knew the quote about a dancer dying twice, the first time being when they stopped dancing, and here it was playing out in front of her. This was not an injury but a death.

The girl pushed her mask off her face to reveal the wet dark eyes of the second swan. In the breath between two screams, she stared an accusation at Ava. *You told me to dance through it,* her eyes said. *You.* Then Ava blinked and realised that the girl was blind with pain: she was staring not at Ava but through her, at the onrush of that dark horizon every dancer feared.

Two techies were back with a stretcher; under Jack's supervision she was taken offstage. The remaining swans dispersed in weeping clusters, arms that had convinced as wings only minutes earlier becoming human flesh again, wrapped tight around friends' shoulders for comfort.

Jack dashed back on to the set, his brow as damp as the dancers'.

'The ambulance should be here in five,' he said. 'I'll go with her. Fuckitty *fuck.*'

Nicky emerged from the wings. 'What she has done?'

'Knee. I can't tell for sure just by eyeballing but it looks like the meniscus has gone. Apparently you could hear the pop.'

'Oh, hell,' Luca whispered to Ava. 'No tour for her.'

Pain is part of the process. We're all dancing through something. I'm not afraid of pain.

Ava thought she might vomit.

'*Oh, hell* isn't the half of it,' said Jack, overhearing Luca. 'Apparently she'd been having twinges for a couple of months, but you know how the young ones are.'

Everyone all but assumed the brace position. The silence expanded until even Jack realised the significance of what he'd said. 'Obviously I can't be sure that—'

'She *know* she has injury?'

'She can't have realised the extent of—'

'Too bad,' said Mr K. 'Give her usual three month cash and send away.'

Jack's jaw dropped. 'Nicky, have a bit of compassion: she—'

'You are still talking? I have one day to bring new cover! She dance on injury, she fuck up opening night! Get rid! Send home to *Mummy*.' He spat the word as if it was another weakness. 'I go now, find replacement for my replacement. Fuck bloody sake.' His cane echoed as he left the stage. Everyone remaining held their positions, like a tableau, until he was gone and the slam of a distant door released them.

Raisa turned on Jack. 'What did you tell him that for?'

Jack's eruption, coming from the mildest-mannered man Ava knew, was almost more terrifying than Nicky's. 'Why do you think they keep going on broken legs, Raisa? They're *terrified* of him, they're half in love with him, they need his permission to *breathe*. This culture of fear needs to change, and someone needs to tell him.'

Oh, Jack, thought Ava. All these years with the company and you've still missed the point. He *knows* about the culture of fear, he created it on purpose. That's how he gets results. You don't get to be the best without being the worst.

'Jack! Ambulance is here.' Boyko's voice came down the corridor.

'One bloody minute, Boyko!' Jack turned back to Raisa, his face darkening to purple. 'I'm going with her. I only hope they say it's minor. And *you*, Raisa – you can bloody well take your duty of care seriously this time. I have stood by for *thirty years* watching him throw dancers away like dirty tissues, giving girls a carrier bag of money and dumping them in some bloody high-rise flat until their time's up. Will you look after this one properly, given that the whole company will be on tour and the aftercare, such as it ever was, will be completely lacking? Will you for once do the right thing? Because I have *had enough*.'

Raisa spread her hands. 'What are you suggesting I do? You know Nicky has a procedure for easing out dancers.'

'*Easing out*,' snorted Jack. 'I don't bloody know the ins and outs, Raisa – just be a human about it.' He turned on his heel and followed the screams.

Raisa clapped her hands. 'Everyone has too much emotion as the show gets closer. Jack will calm down.'

Luca shook his head at her coolness, but Ava knew what Raisa meant. There was only one way to cope with other dancers' misfortunes and that was to harden your heart against them.

So why did hers feel as though an invisible hand was squeezing and twisting it?

In the dark of her dressing room, Ava sat with her feet in a bucket of ice, enjoying the loss of sensation in her toes and wishing there were an equivalent treatment for the mind. Outside, the plane trees were strung with lights that made the green leaves glow: laughter and cigarette smoke floated up from the pavement below. Somewhere in the building, Nicky and Raisa were deciding upon a replacement for the replacement. Ava noted that, this time, he had not asked her to help him choose. She pitied the girl who got the gig. There was no time to rehearse another dancer to Kirilov standard.

There was a gnawing in the pit of Ava's belly. She had told the girl to dance through the pain. If she were to look at it logically, it was clear that she couldn't take responsibility for another dancer's choices, no matter how disastrous the outcome. She was not a ballet mistress, let alone a physiotherapist. She had given no instruction. But then, she had to admit, she was being disingenuous. She spoke so rarely to the lower-ranking dancers that, when she did, her words carried weight. This feeling came from somewhere more primal than logic.

Odile towered above her from the tour poster. *She* wouldn't give a shit, thought Ava. She wouldn't tie herself in knots over some careless kid. And yet the feeling persisted. Ava held two opposing thoughts in her head: the knowledge that this wasn't her fault, coupled with the need to atone for it.

The list of cities glowed white on black: places the second swan would not visit, certainly not this time around, maybe not ever as a dancer. Jack had talked about housing her somewhere decent.

Perhaps Ava could offer her *her* place? Who wouldn't want to live in her carefully curated home, with its clean white sheets and its beautiful artwork that Nicky had paid for but she had chosen? It even had a barre the girl could use for rehab.

As soon as she had the idea she felt reluctant, and it was this reluctance that softened the ache in her belly. She didn't want to do it: it was costing Ava her comfort, and that must be what they meant by atonement. She would find Raisa and tell her later. She imagined Luca's face when she told him how generous she had been. Problem solved. Guilt absolved.

Ava stepped out of the ice bucket, felt her feet spread, and then throb, on the warm linoleum floor. She tilted her fan to her face. The whirring blades absorbed the noise from the street below, where, outside pubs and restaurants, glasses were clinked and selfies were taken and cigarettes were smoked. Even at night, London held tight to the day's dirty heat as if the city might run out of sun. She prayed that the temperature would drop by the first night. This summer was beginning to feel impossible, like something they would all be lucky to survive.

JULIET

16

In that space between sleep and reality I think the sound – an old-fashioned, mechanical trill – is a backstage bell. Ten minutes to curtain: time to check my make-up, secure my headdress, tame stray feathers, breathe in, breathe out. I am not napping in a dressing room at the London Russian or on a bunk in the Gulag; and that bell will never sound for me again.

I am in Ava Kirilova's big white bed, sweating all over her tight white sheets, and the noise is her doorbell.

'I'm coming!'

My voice echoes in the too-big space. In this bungalow, the bedrooms are at the front of the house and the front door is close by. Still, the journey when I contemplate it feels ten times longer. Gingerly I raise myself to sitting; carefully I grip the crutches that have stood sentry while I slept. The pain in my knee is not the wonderful ache every dancer knows but the burn of injury and the cramp of disuse. I pick my leg up by the thigh so that my foot doesn't jar when it hits the floor, and begin my slow shuffle.

The front door itself is solid bronze, more suited to the entrance of a museum than a private house. Either side of the door are glass panels the texture of bark, and through one of these I see a shifting pastel shape. Sliding back the bolt and turning the key is a balancing act. The door swings inwards; heat hits me as though I've opened an oven. The shape reveals itself to be a huge bouquet of flowers, fat pink peonies and heralding lilies, supported by tanned bare legs in hideous gold gladiator sandals. My heart soars in my chest. I may be injured out but I haven't been forgotten after all; they've—

85

'Flowers for Ava Kirilova,' says the voice behind the bouquet, and my cheeks burn, not with disappointment but with shame that I'd thought they might be for me.

'Oh, sorry. I'm Juliet.'

'Right.' There's impatience in the florist's voice; she doesn't care who I am. 'It's just that we tried to deliver these yesterday and if no one takes them they'll have to be destroyed.'

'Fine, fine. I'll take them.'

The florist thrusts the bouquet into my arms, nearly knocking me off balance. Her eyes widen when she sees my face. I must be sleep-stained and oily, fallen far below the standards Mr K expects from his dancers.

'Thanks, then.' Her gold shoes flash in the sun as she climbs into her van. 'The main gate's not working, by the way. Anyone could come in.'

At the end of the long driveway, a red Royal Mail van sails past. Behind that, a black hybrid car crawls in slow-mo silence, the driver's dark glasses just visible through tinted windows. Lettering on the side says FORCE PATROL. Its logo is two yellow eyes in a yellow-edged black hexagon. Black and yellow, the colours of wasps or the sign for nuclear waste. This is the private security firm that babysits the empty houses here. And whose job it is to make sure the gate works.

Oh, well. Not my problem. Not my house. Not my stuff.

I try to balance the bouquet on one arm. The lilies are already browning at the edges and the peonies are imploding, a sour note of decay under the sweetness. My bones are shards of glass deep in the jelly of my knee. From the bedrooms at the front, a long corridor of white walls and original art leads to the open-plan kitchen and living area at the back. The ceilings are too high; the proportions cruelly mock those of a stage.

On the chic mid-twentieth-century hallway table with its stacked teak drawers and hairpin legs, the sleek black telephone rests silently in its holster. I do not expect phone calls. My parents died when I was a child – it's fine, it was all a long time ago – and the company became my family. But once someone leaves the London Russian, the remaining dancers act as though she never existed.

I know this because I did it to other girls.

Karma's a bitch.

My progress along the corridor is lumbering and inelegant. Mr K teaches us to land gracefully, silently. I travel noisily now: thud *thunk*, thud *thunk*, each step a betrayal of his values. He teaches us to leap as high as our heads and still land soundlessly. People come to see ballerinas, not to hear them. *Silent art form*, he says, sometimes with a twinkle in his eye and sometimes with ice in his voice. Missing him, missing working with him, is going to be the hardest part of all. Thinking about him buckles some vital supporting wall inside me. It's better if I don't.

Thud *thunk*, past Ava Kirilova's home studio (of course she has a home studio: of *course* she does), where the acrid pine tang of rosin hangs in the air around the door. All the internal doors here have locks and she has shut me out of this one, either from kindness (doubtful) or so I don't sully it with my presence (far more on-brand). Her haughtiness is all part of the mythology, I get that: just like Mr K, she likes the mere mortals to think she breathes a different air from the rest of us. She doesn't exactly have a reputation for compassion, but only I know how spiteful she can be. My knee throbs as if to underline the thought.

I make the flower-arranging last because after that there's nothing to do. My life has been timetabled by the pursuit of perfection for as long as I can remember. I don't know what to do with an unstructured day.

There are so *many* things I don't know how to do.

Cook for myself.

Operate a washing machine.

Use a computer to do anything beyond a cursory search.

Drive a car.

Pay a bill.

Get a job.

Have a conversation with someone outside the ballet world.

Most of all, I don't know how to come to terms with the loss of my vocation. Career isn't a strong enough word for it. Career is a suit and an office and a pension. Vocation means calling: a voice offstage summoning you to do one thing and one thing only. Unanswered, it only cries louder. It's kind of screaming right now.

I take a step back to admire my flower-arranging and white lightning pain zips from my foot to my knee. The meniscus is the ligament that holds the knee in place and mine is torn in two. There are two types of tear. A lateral tear will see you out of performance for a year, but ultimately a good surgeon can fix you. A radial tear drops a curtain on your career for good. Guess which one I have?

I don't remember the moment my life divided into a before and after.

Mr Sandhu, the expensive orthopaedic surgeon the company hired to determine whether I was worth their continued investment, and who broke the news that I wasn't, said that this often happens. It's a way of the brain protecting itself. He told me that ninety per cent of the patients he treats after road traffic accidents blank out not just the impact but the hours, days or even weeks either side of it. Sometimes the memory never comes back. That's been my experience too: snatches of my old life, of the rehearsals leading up to it. I remember the thrill of being laced into Odette's costume at last, the nudge of impostor syndrome instantly calmed by how well the silk sat against my skin. I remember Mr K giving me private instruction; I remember his hands on my face and his eyes on mine. I wish now I had treasured that moment but I took it for granted, thinking I had years of his attention left. But the performance itself? The moment of injury? There's nothing there, and long may it stay that way. Even the good memories are too painful to bear, so Christ knows what the bad ones would do to me.

I am grateful they have housed me here. Of course I am. Living on one level makes the constant negotiation of life on crutches easier. But I can't make myself *like* the place. It's like living in a magazine, and my presence feels like one giant greasy fingerprint. In the living room, the angled wood and curved leather second-hand furniture is the kind that costs ten times the price of new stuff. A huge dark blue painting, a moonlit lake of tears, dominates the living area. There's very little technology: a radio, a flat television set discreetly on a wall, and a lone telephone in the hall. The glasses are hand-blown, the plates hand-thrown. Ava Kirilova lives in beautiful accordance with her father's principles of minimalism and grace. Mr K insists that we do everything – not just dance, but eat, speak, walk, dress, *live* – with poise.

The only vulgarity is the poster for our *Swan Lake* tour, framed but not yet hung. It leans against the wall, the dancers' perfect bodies and the tour dates taunting me. It's stupid: I know it's only a poster but I can't help thinking of it as *her*. She's still looking down at me, with her face hidden, as though even her reproduction is too high and mighty to regard me at the same level. I am in your house, I can't help thinking. The least you could do is say hello. As I said: stupid. But was it too much to ask that she put it somewhere else or at least turn it to face the wall? It is lemon juice in a cut that will never heal.

A long, tall window in the kitchen gives on to the boundary of the house next door. Huge patio doors stretch from the kitchen area to the living room and overlook a garden that's pure Hockney, more LA than London with its oversized tropical plants in hard landscaping; there's a swimming pool whose cover I can't open because it would involve kneeling down. The grass behind the pool is yellowing already after a week of baking sun; by the back wall there's an arc of emerald in one corner where next door's sprinkler overshoots the fence. I turn the key and slide the huge glass doors into a recess in the wall. The flagstone terrace is too hot to tread on in bare feet.

But this is home for the next nine months, until the sainted Miss Kirilova comes home from tour and I go . . . where? They paid me off with three thousand pounds in cash, currently resting on the hall table. It sounds like a lot but it's all I have to retrain, to find something else to do with my life.

The obvious thing for me to do is teach but I can't do that at a high level, not just because I won't be able to demonstrate the steps but because to be so close to the talent, the potential of young dancers, is almost worse than nothing. Herding five-year-olds around a church hall would be even worse.

Whatever form my new life takes, I'm going to start by buying a smartphone. You seem to need one to survive outside the London Russian. Perhaps I'll try somehow to trace some of the other girls who dropped out and we can form some kind of survivors' group. It feels like sacrilege, but I don't need to keep my mind uncluttered for dances I will never now learn.

17

I open the fridge then close it again. I've been living off Alpen and milk (skimmed, obviously). Long-term, I don't know what I'm going to do about food. Ready meals, I suppose, although they don't come cheap. Lack of money is a new way to *maintain length*, which is ballet-speak for stay thin.

I go through the exercises the hospital physiotherapist gave me but it's ten o'clock, time for company class, and this old habit refuses to die. Using the long kitchen counter as a barre, I attempt a *port de bras*, the carriage of the arms, the fluid sweep through all the basic positions I've been doing since I was tiny. Only when I instinctively check the opposite wall to see how I'm holding myself, and stare instead into the dark blue painting, do I remember that, apart from a little square of glass over the bathroom sink, there are no mirrors in this house. I had a complex relationship with my reflection, but I miss her now she's gone. The exercise is agony – even my arms feel heavy and useless – and I'm glad when the telephone rings because it gives me an excuse to drop the pretence that I'm still a ballerina.

I should know better than to hope it's someone calling for me, but it would be so good to hear from someone from the company. The thing is, after I fell I was rushed into this place straight from the hospital with no time for goodbyes. The only way the others could have got this number is if someone senior passed it on, and *that's* not going to happen. I can just hear Raisa saying, 'It is a shame for Juliet but we move on. The show is everything.'

Hope, however, sneaks in like water through a crack, and I can't help but wish that there's friendship, gossip, a voice from my old life, on the line.

'Hello?' My voice is already rusty with disuse.

'Hello, lovely, it's Lizanne!' She says her name with the grating brightness of a nursery-school teacher, and as if I should know who she is.

'I'm sorry, can you remind me . . .'

If a second's silence can contain a sulk, hers does, before resuming its professional chirpiness. 'I'm in the theatre today and I just thought I'd call in, check up, see if you need anything.'

My disappointment is a swoop from breastbone to belly. Not a friend, just the temp who's manning the phones. It's amazing how a voice can contain a whole personality: I picture a mumsy woman, doing a bit of admin between school runs, straining the stripes of a Breton T-shirt. The kind of person who stands too close to you in conversation.

'Are you all set for your physio appointment?'

There's a month-to-view calendar on the hall table with just the one appointment on it. I touch the red-ringed date. 'Thank you, yes.' The LRB are clever about aftercare, providing just enough that former dancers don't sue them for neglect. As if we could sue anyone on the money they leave us! And as if anyone who has trained under Mr K would dare to challenge him in court! Stockholm Syndrome keeps his creatures captive long, long after the door is thrown open.

'Have you got all the details, lovely?'

I rifle through the unopened fan mail on the table. 'Actually, if you could remind me . . .'

I find a pen and jot down the time and place on the first page of an empty notebook – a plain, mint-green leather-bound notebook that probably cost more than a pair of *pointe* shoes. I go to hang up, but Lizanne hasn't finished.

'Shall I come with you, lovely? Bit of moral support? There isn't much for me to do here, to be honest.'

I imagine someone who only dances at weddings sitting in on my consultation. 'I'd rather go on my own. Thanks.'

I don't know what she's saying as I hang up on her, but I think

I catch the word *understand* as I end the call. As if she could even begin to.

I study the handset for a moment, its unfamiliar interface. There are half a dozen buttons I don't understand. One looks like a pair of binoculars. It makes me feel watched, like the logo on the side of the Force Patrol cars. I glance up and down the empty corridor before setting the phone back in its dock.

Breathe in, breathe out, reset.

The notebook's blank pages and their back-to-school potential are just what I need to plot the rest of my life. I thumb the pages as I think. A to-do list, once I have decided what needs doing. Two-thirds of the way through, though, I realise it's not brand new after all. There's a sentence in elegant handwriting: *For the safe*. What safe? Then there's row after row of tallies, four lines and a strike, the kind prisoners scratch into walls in old-fashioned films, but the numbers underneath suggest, not days in captivity, but multiples of thousands of pounds. £18,900, says one. £7,900. The next set of tallies haven't been summed up, but if each strike represents a hundred pounds then it means there's something like another nine thousand. I know Mr K likes to deal in cash but he always said it was for us to learn discipline, to understand that sooner or later the money will always run out. I didn't expect Ava Kirilova to be on our hardscrabble wages but nor did I realise she spent on this scale.

For the safe. What safe? Where? I look around, but all I see is painting after painting after – of course. It'll be hidden behind some work of art. I lurch down the hall, examining every huge painting. Most are nailed, not hung: to deter thieves, perhaps? Those that are hung hide nothing more exciting than more white walls. Perhaps the safe is in her studio.

I leave the lake painting in the living room until last. It seems at first touch to be nailed to the wall like the others, and I'm about to give up when I accidentally push instead of pull. A catch is released; the canvas is on a hinge. A dark blue door creaks open to reveal a little safe: a steel rectangle, set into the wall like a pizza oven. There's a keycode pad and a little sticker underneath, those yellow eyes in their hexagon. The text underneath reads: *Supported by Force Patrol. For assistance call 0330 330 3330.*

I lean away from it. The absolute last thing I want is an alarm being triggered, and some security guy storming in. It'll get back to that Lizanne in the office, and what if they decide to throw me out? They've done that before: promised to look after former dancers and then evicted them on some pretext. I push the painting flush against the wall so it clicks back into place.

The movement makes the tour poster slide an inch down the wall. I want to hate but I can only admire. The lovely flat bone of her patella: the heart shape of her calf, the avian sweep of her arm. The list of tour dates, dances yet undanced in Prague, Colombo, Kolkata, Kyoto, Moscow. Envy is a physical force; it's a dirty drug that gives me hot shivers. It's not about the money, not really. I just want to dance, and no amount of money will buy that back.

18

Today's mission – to buy a second-hand smartphone – gives me a transgressive thrill and a much-needed sense of occasion. I slide my battered feet into Birkenstocks, and put on a red sundress which is already a little snug around the waist despite the heat taking away my appetite, but which covers the worst of my knee. To the untrained eye this is still a dancer's body, but I feel my muscles wasting already. Dancers don't just look a certain way: we *are* a certain way. We get called wraiths and waifs and ethereal, and various other words that make it sound as though we're made of tissue paper and light. The ballerina body is superhuman strength disguised as weakness. There is more power packed into our tiny frames than you'd find in men twice our size.

I rap a hard thigh and wonder how long I have left before I have to talk about dancers in terms of *they* rather than *we*. Until the atrophy softens me all over, I'll cling to the present tense.

Ready for my expedition, I open the door and there's a ballet dancer on the doorstep, finger poised over the bell. I'm so surprised to see her that I scream. It's not long, but it's loud. No one comes: it's as though the hot air has swallowed sound itself. So much for Force Patrol and their all-seeing eyes.

The dancer is about my age and wearing full stage make-up: winged eyeshadow and sculpted cheekbones. Her dark hair is pulled back in a bun. Her brows must be tattooed on to maintain those corners in a heatwave. It's a face you could see at the back of the stalls, up in the gods.

'God, sorry. I wasn't expecting anyone.'

She isn't fazed. Now that I've got my breath back, I can see that she isn't a dancer at all: she's too tall, her shoulders too wide, her hips too broad and her thighs too thick and her breasts too large and low. The kind of curves men love and women pay to surgeons to create, but which dancers have to starve out.

'Hyellow,' she says. Eastern European. I knew she wasn't English, not just because no English woman would do her face like that before dark, but because English women tend not to have faces like that in the first place: the nose so delicate, the eyes so wide, the lips so full and the parts arranged in such perfect symmetry that she looks almost computer-generated. And those cheekbones aren't make-up at all, just young skin stretched tight over a beautiful skull.

'Excuse please. I give you beauty.' Well; it is certainly hers to bestow. She gestures to a little wheeled case at her feet. First the florist, then her: so much for the secure community. 'Manicure, facial, waxing. You want?' She looks down at my feet and to her credit says, 'Pedicure?' without wincing. Dancers' feet are famously ugly. Mine will always look as though someone took a hammer to them but, after a few days without dancing, the skin on the knuckles of my big toes has healed and faded to the shiny satin of a slipper and my left toenail is starting to grow back, a little yellow rind forming at the base of the nail bed. But for now there is nothing to paint, and it's hardly the best use of my time, let alone my money. 'Massage?' she says.

This *does* tempt me. Everything hurts and it would be so lovely to be touched. But I must be disciplined.

'You want?' she repeats.

'I wish I could afford it.'

She can't disguise the flash of disappointment in her eyes. I wonder how long she's been walking. I wonder how much money she hoped she might make out of me.

'Is not a problem . . .' she begins, but then her eyes land on the pile of cash which I did not, I now realise, put away. She can't help herself: her pupils flare, with a greed I can't judge her for and, I guess, with contempt for me, the 'rich' woman who has so much money she leaves great sums of it lying around the house. 'Hev a good day.'

I don't know why the look she gives me is so unsettling. This house literally has its own private police force. There's no way she's going to be able to steal from me.

'Thanks,' I say. 'You too.'

She turns to go and there's something in the way she raises her arm like a wing to scratch her head that unsteadies me and for a crazy second I expect to see – I am almost convinced I see – a black feather fall away from her, the way a feather might fall from Odile's costume. My heart races the way it used to in the wings before a show.

Then I blink, and she's just some door-to-door beautician in a nylon tunic.

But the connection has been made, the door to memory has been opened. Music from *Swan Lake* plays, every note as clear as if the orchestra were in the house with me. Of course the piece I hear is from Act III, everyone in the ballroom, Odette fluttering vainly in the window. I put my hands over my ears, even though I know it's all in my head.

'Whose side are you on?' I say out loud to my subconscious.

It didn't take long for me to start talking to myself.

The interaction has completely drained me. I can't go out today; I can't face anything more demanding than daytime TV. I'll try again tomorrow.

19

Next morning I try again. I dress in the same red sundress, weave my hair into a plait, wind it around the crown of my head, and apply sun lotion sparingly to the nape of my neck: without protection, my pale skin bubbles and burns, but there are only another two or three applications left, and the good stuff is a tenner a bottle. Another expense I used to take for granted. I can't balance a handbag on my shoulder with the crutches, the straps are too short, but I have one of those reusable tote bags from the London Russian Ballet theatre gift shop, the logo block-printed red on black. I can sling that over a shoulder, loop it through a crutch so I can dip in and out of it.

As I set the burglar alarm, my eyes are drawn down that long gallery of a corridor, to the living room and the safe on the wall. If only I could store my money in there. It's ridiculous to contemplate breaking *into* it to make a deposit rather than take possession of its contents. Not being a master criminal, though, I'll have to do what normal people do and put my money in the bank. I'm pretty sure there's a Halifax on the little high street outside the gates. I'll have to set myself up at some stage, so why not today? I drop the brick of cash into my bag, punch in the burglar alarm code and leave the house.

The sun seems twice its usual size, bouncing more white light off the sculpture on the front lawn. It's a tangle of bent steel girders, abstract at first glance, but viewed from a certain angle they make the form of a dancer, frozen in a gunmetal arabesque. That's a very Kirilovan touch: you don't get it and you don't get it until all of a sudden you do and it's beautiful.

I'm the only person on the pavement, the thud *thunk* of my crutches the only sound. Unusually for London, there are no diggers or cranes. I suppose that's because when the houses are this big they don't need extending, and most of them already have pools. The house next door is a hideous new-money hangar with fake Greek columns and a huge stone pediment. The mock-Tudor mansion on the other side hides behind a bank of tall pines. I think they're both empty, as is the Art Deco place opposite. Lumbering down the hill, I feel like the only human left alive after a disaster. Where is everybody? As far as I can see it's just me and an emaciated woman who drives a Range Rover with a yoga mat on the passenger seat. Who owns these places? Premier league footballers away for the summer? Foreign oligarchs who use the places as investments? The crutches are rubbing the skin under my arms raw. Next time I'll do this journey in a T-shirt, not a strappy dress.

The florist was right: the pedestrian gate that's supposed to keep the plebs out is jammed ajar. It makes a mockery of the expensive private security, but it's not my home and I'm not going to go to the trouble of dragging it closed.

Gabriel's Hill is such a nice neighbourhood that I wonder why Ava Kirilova is so keen to be locked away from it, unless it's to signify privilege within privilege, which now I come to think of it sums up her life. It's one of those London suburbs so gentrified it's almost in a time warp. There's a toy shop selling wooden trains, a little bookshop, a candle *emporium* if you please, a wine merchant and even a cheesemonger's. Café Rouge, Cath Kidston. The supermarket is a Marks & Spencer Simply Food. The pharmacy window looks more like the Selfridges beauty hall than somewhere you'd get your Band-Aids and paracetamol. (Not that paracetamol would touch the sides for me: my hardcore pain meds will be delivered to the door.)

But there are traces of a different London among the blow-dried ladies smoking at pavement cafés and the good-looking dads with their babies in carriers. A tired-looking woman wearing a tabard over cheap sports gear picks litter from the gutter. Two teenage girls, their skin patchworked with sunburn, pout into a phone at a bus stop. A pasty, hollow-eyed teenage boy on a bike, far too old to be cycling on the pavement, weaves in and out of pedestrians. I'm standing back, judging them, until I realise that I probably look like one of the poor people too.

Everyone looks half-dead of summer. The heatwave has, in a way, made dancers of everyone: civilians are experiencing what it is to drag discomfort around with you, to not be allowed to forget your flesh.

I keep going past the White Company, Gail's Bakery, Sweaty Betty. There's only one down-at-heel-looking place on the whole street, and that's the shop that sells used phones and vapes. I optimistically peel off three twenty-pound notes from the bundle in my bag, and go inside. The guy behind the counter tells me that if I want one that won't be out of date within the year I'll need to spend at least three hundred pounds just for the handset, and that doesn't even include paying for the data. (He also has to explain to me what data is, which is embarrassing.) Three hundred pounds is one tenth of all the money I have left until who knows when, and I lose my nerve.

'I'll think about it.' I lurch out of the shop as the kid on the bike flies past, knocking one of the crutches out from under me. It's only thanks to my ballet dancer's core (still got it) that I don't land next to it on the ground. He wheels back, at least.

'My bad,' he says, 'I weren't looking.' I watch, impressed, as he leans sideways to retrieve the crutch without leaving his saddle. When he hands it back to me, his fingers brush my arm and the shock of human contact ambushes me with longing.

'Thank you.' I feel bad for having judged him.

The bank is two doors down. I don't think I've been in one since I was a very young child, paying in a birthday cheque maybe, and it's a lot more modern than the wood-panelled, red-carpeted place I was expecting. It's modern and bright with screens everywhere, on the wall, at ceiling height, machines blinking in corners. While I'm queueing, I count them. Seventeen, if you include the ones the clerks are tapping at behind their screens. When it's my turn, I stand before a clerk with blue hair and a nose ring. Another surprise.

'I'd like to open a bank account,' I say.

'Savings or current?'

Oh, crap. I don't know. 'Can you remind me of the difference, please?'

'Well, will you be paying a wage in every month?'

'Eventually, yes. I think? I will get a job, one day. Most jobs pay into the bank, don't they? I think the way we do things, with cash, is pretty unusual.'

She blinks twice, as if she doesn't know what to make of that. 'Well, let's see your ID, get you set up.'

'ID?'

'Driver's licence or passport, plus a recent utility bill and proof of address.'

A hot blush climbs my neck. I'm so used to having everything done for me that it hadn't occurred to me I'd need ID, but of *course* I do. Sometimes it's almost as though Mr K doesn't *want* us to function outside the company. Actually, that's not fair. That sounds as if he's deliberately out to spite us. It's simply that he stops caring once we can't dance any more. We might as well stop existing the day we leave the LRB.

Thinking like this makes my nose fizz with tears and my next words sound thick and nasal. 'I haven't got any with me. Just some money.'

'Tell you what,' she says gently, 'you go home and get some ID, and we'll sort you out. Something simple, a passbook account. Yeah?'

I'm getting to recognise the expression on her face: it's pity.

'Ok,' I say. 'Thanks. Before I go – will I need ID to buy a phone, do you think?'

'From him next door? I doubt it. Not if you get a pay-as-you-go SIM.'

'Right. Thank you.'

I leave the bank very carefully in case my friend on the bicycle is up to his old tricks again but he's nowhere to be seen. It's only on the threshold of the phone shop, when I put my hand in my bag to peel three hundred pounds from my block of cash and my fingers find nothing but my house keys and a bottle of water, that I realise why he was so eager to help me.

20

Fear and shock propel me across the petrol haze of the high street. The pedestrian gate to the estate is closed now, and I punch in the code with shaking fingers. That little sod. I just can't *believe* anyone would steal from a person so obviously vulnerable. But I also can't believe how irresponsible I was, walking around with all the cash the LRB gave me in a gaping cloth bag. This is *exactly* the kind of carelessness that makes Mr K throw lightning bolts.

What am I going to do?

What the hell am I going to *do*?

The hill leading back up to the house might as well be a mountain. The skin under my right arm burns, preparing to break then bleed. I try to put all my weight on the left crutch and carry the right one, but it's hopeless, and the bag only becomes more entangled. I'm having a fight with sticks and straps when an electric car rolls silently by. Force Patrol: yellow on black, an electric wasp. It's going slowly enough that I can safely step out in front of it, forcing it to stop.

The window slips down to reveal an unsmiling man in his early thirties. 'Can I help you, madam?' His accent is Polish, I think. He has sharp features, a one-day shadow of dark hair dusting his head and jaw.

I hold up Ava's house key, with its Force Patrol key fob. 'Number 36. I don't suppose you could drive me up the hill?' Funny how some vestige of pride remains. I'm saying I don't suppose you could when what I mean is, I'm desperate, please help me.

'I am not allowed to have clients in the car,' he says in a jobsworth's monotone.

'Oh, but I'm—' I catch myself just in time. I was going to say that technically, of course, I'm not his client, but then he'll have me down as a trespasser. 'Please. Surely they wouldn't begrudge you helping me out. Please.' I feel knives behind my eyes. I mustn't cry in front of him. I am trained not to show pain. Pain makes you ugly; it drives people away when you need them most.

'Protocols,' he says gruffly. 'Insurance.'

To my shame, a couple of tears spill out. Shaking his head, he gets out of the car and motions me round to the passenger side.

'*Thank* you,' I say, landing in the seat with an involuntary *aah*. He lays my crutches across the back seat.

I'm close enough to smell the chewing gum on his breath. His face is drawn and weathered. His frown lines are deep. The grooves between from his mouth to his nose suggest someone who smiles a lot but his eyes – the kind of blue usually accompanied by a siren – are cold.

'This is so nice,' I say. 'I've had a terrible day. I was mugged. Lost all my money.'

He grimaces, probably assuming that this is simply a case of me cancelling my gold credit card and having a tough few days while I work out how to keep myself in caviar. I haven't got the energy to put him right. I just want to get into the house and lie down.

'You don't call the police?'

The *police*. I'd been so worried about what Mr K and everyone would think, that didn't even occur to me. The thought of it is exhausting, though, and it's not as if it'll bring my money back. 'I'll do it in a bit,' I lie.

As he feeds the steering wheel through his hands, I read his lanyard: Maxim Shevchenko. I don't think *chenko* is a Polish suffix. Russian, maybe? My education is patchy, but one thing ballerinas are good at is international names.

'Where are you from, then?' I ask him. Six deserted-looking houses slide by.

'Ukraine,' he says, as if I've forced it out of him at gunpoint.

'Ooh, which part?' I say, as though that means anything to me: all I can come up with is chicken Kiev and that things are bit of a mess in . . . I want to say Crimea? I wonder if I could even locate it on a map.

'The contact line,' he says eventually, which still tells me nothing. 'The danger zone.'

The car's dashboard is like the flight deck of a spaceship, little screens playing CCTV, a digitised map, a removable tablet with a feed of names and addresses.

'I could stay in this car all day. Just for the air-con,' I say, and then, when I see the alarm on his face, 'It's OK, it was only a joke. Thank you. You've been very kind.'

He shrugs. 'It's nothing.'

He drops me at the door of 36. I stumble inelegantly out of the car. The engine doesn't start up again immediately, and I can feel him watching me. I used to feel men's eyes on me with desire: now they stare at me with pity.

It's a relief to shut the door behind me.

When I get back the phone is ringing.

'How are you doing, lovely?' Lizanne sing-songs. 'I'm actually organising the delivery of your next few days' worth of meds. Shall I pop them over myself? It's no bother.'

What is *wrong* with this woman's concept of personal space? 'I'm fine,' I say, then hear myself blurt, 'Lizanne, I don't suppose you know of any jobs?' The catch in her breath contains a world of judgement, but I've started now. 'I mean, I know I don't have any skills apart from ballet but how hard can it be to—'

'*You?* A job?' The scorn in her voice takes me by surprise. 'Surely Mr K – surely you're being well looked-after? If you've run out of money *already* I can try to get in touch with Raisa and see what she says?'

It must be panic that prompts my next suggestion. 'Or we could ask Mr K?'

I know it's ridiculous as soon as I've said it. No one ever goes direct to Mr K for anything.

'But – that's not – I don't—' I can tell by her voice that I've put her in an awkward position and my conscience flexes gently inside me. Knowing the LRB, she's probably being paid minimum wage in cash herself. I doubt she has any more access to their money than I do. I doubt she's ever even *met* Mr K.

'Forget it,' I say hurriedly.

Lizanne sighs, deep and long. 'I *really* think I should pop over and check up on you. I can bring you Starbucks?'

'I've got coffee here,' I say.

'If you're sure,' she huffs. 'But the offer still stands.'

The sun hits the back of the house in the afternoon, and walking into the kitchen/living area is like stepping into an oven. I open the patio door. The pool is trapped under its blue cover. The grass has yellowed even more since this morning: it is a carpet of tinder, one carelessly abandoned glass or tossed cigarette away from catching fire. The golf-course-green corner at the back looks vulgar: I suppose all of the lawn next door is like that, kept verdant for an owner who never sets foot in the place. What a waste of water. What a waste of land.

I pop a dozen cubes from the ice tray, wrap them in a tea towel and hold it to my knee, where they melt before they've had a chance to bring down the pain. I'm down to the dusty dregs of my Alpen and half a pint of milk. All those years existing on the brink of hunger; I never thought I would be starving through poverty. Tears that have been balled in my belly for days flash-flood my face. I give myself over to uncontrolled wailing, the occasional swear word giving things shape. At the London Russian you got used to crying in the toilets after a casting didn't go your way, or Mr K gave you harsh corrections. This might be the first time in my adult life I've ever let go like this.

It's ironic: now that I can drink alcohol, now that I'm no longer training my body for perfection, I can't afford to. In lieu of liquid oblivion, I crack open my non-steroidal anti-inflammatories, then neck a double dose of paracetamol with a tramadol chaser.

I flop on the leather sofa, eyes resting on the big painting until it seems to ripple and I wouldn't be surprised to see a swan swim across the canvas. Outside, the sun sinks until the sky is the same starless dark blue. At night, with the lights on, the huge glass door becomes a mirror. The girl in the glass is ragged and blotchy, swollen and ugly.

My last thought before I float into sleep on a chemical cloud is of the money in the safe ten feet away from me. Water, water, everywhere, nor any drop to drink. I don't want to steal from Ava Kirilova but if I could *borrow* it somehow, it would save my life.

It's the *least* she could do for me.

Stupid idea. A fantasy. My eyelids grow heavy. Money worries dissolve as I fade away to a place where the music plays. I dance in my dreams, and I live again.

21

Ballet dancers learn early on that the trick with hunger pangs is to count to ninety and they will pass, for the moment at least. I have needed that discipline today, hanging around the M&S Simply Food until six o'clock when the staff put yellow discount stickers on the out-of-date food. By the time the little potted salads drop to affordability, I am faint with hunger. I'm so ravenous, in fact, that my navel is grazing my spine, and as I get in the gate I wonder if I'll make it back to the house without collapsing. There's a tree with a wraparound bench at the bottom of the hill. I sit on the far side, hidden from the street and bloody Force Patrol and their cameras because I can't be bothered with another altercation, and eat a pesto and pasta salad with my fingers, then swallow six or seven peppery, garlicky squid rings without chewing them.

Back inside, I wipe the oil from my chin and clean flecks of basil from my teeth. I take my glass of tap water outside. The evening sky is shot through with strands of saffron: even Ava Kirilova's horizon is expensive. I devote a few therapeutic seconds to resenting everything she owns and everything she stands for.

A man coughs, close and loud, and fear shoots an arrow straight through me. It pins me to the spot. He clears his throat again. He's in the garden next door, on the other side of a thick laurel hedge. When people talk about isolation being frightening, it's not the isolation that scares them but its loss: it's the stranger in the empty space.

Through thick leaves I hear the shuffle of feet on stone and the noise of a long zip being undone. The grass silences the thud of my crutches as I approach the fence, water slopping over the rim of my glass. I come to a stop at the stone path that rings the garden. It seems insane, given the level of protection these unoccupied houses have, that there's very little to divide this property from its neighbour: here dense shrubbery hides nothing more than a waist-high wire-link fence. Perhaps they presume honour among the fellow rich.

I pull back a laurel branch and almost laugh with relief to see that it's only that Ukrainian security guard, Maxim Shevchenko, doing his rounds. It hadn't occurred to me that Force Patrol's remit would go this far but of course it makes sense that they would carry out checks on empty houses. The guard isn't inspecting the grounds: rather, he's checking the CCTV camera on the wall above him. The garden is exactly what you'd expect given the exterior of the house, an absolute *nouveau riche* horror. Faux-classical marble statues nestle in among lurid cerise roses. The lush lawn is criss-crossed with the hosepipes that keep it that way. Right in front of me, there's a double shower built into the wall: the taps are gold, the showerhead a hideous gold Medusa head.

He walks crabwise with his back to the wall as though he's allergic to bad gardening. It's only after he looks intently at one of the cameras then ducks out of its way that I realise that he isn't making sure they're working. He's making sure they haven't picked him up. He's being furtive, not thorough. It doesn't make sense.

Before I can form a theory, he does something I couldn't have predicted if I'd been given a thousand guesses. He begins to undress. He thumbs open each button on his short-sleeved black shirt before peeling it off damp skin. A life surrounded by dancers' bodies gives you an abnormal standard of beauty but I suppose he's passable, for a civilian. A T-shirt tan: good arms. On his chest, two muddy boot-prints of hair above slack abs. As he goes for his buckle, I look away. On the grass there's an oversized holdall, unzipped to reveal what looks like more black clothes. A sleeping bag is laid out. Next to it is an iPhone with a cracked screen, and a bottle of water.

My eyes are drawn back to him – naked now, under the water, and clutching a bar of soap, but facing away, thank God – as he raises his arms above his head and lets out a long, baritone moan. I can hear in his voice the release of a hard day's work. My cheeks have their own pulse. You'd never think, from this outbreak of prudishness, that I was used to being around male bodies, working with them, having them lift me, watching them get changed.

I shift on my crutches in order to turn my back on him and in doing so let slip the glass in my hand. It smashes on the path.

He ducks, reaches for a T-shirt to cover himself, steps out of the jet still covered in soap suds and starts to pull his underpants on, but they stick on his wet skin. Mortified on his behalf as well as mine, I turn a clumsy half-circle, wondering how long I should give him to dress.

'*Please.*' His voice goes straight to begging, as if it's the fourth time of asking. I twist around slowly. One thud, one *thunk*. He's dressed again and framed by dark green foliage. His eyes have doubled in size and locked on to mine, but his shoulders have rounded in a cower that tells me that, for whatever reason, the balance of power is in my favour. '*Please* don't tell anyone.'

I follow the direction of his gaze and it becomes clear that he's not talking about the time I got in his car. He's looking at the sleeping bag, the phone and now, I see, clothes and a towel in the gaping holdall.

I know a life packed tight when I see it, I've been on tour enough times.

He isn't looking after this garden. He's sleeping in it.

'You're *living* here!' I cry. His face darkens with shame as he buttons up his shirt. The poor bastard, I think, and then, as it hits me that he will have been able to hear me crying and raging for nights on end, 'Oh, my *God*.'

'It's just for a little while,' he says. 'I am . . .' He searches for the right phrase, fails to find it. 'Money.'

In his shrug, I see a man's pride roll over and die. A job like his should be a living but something has gone very wrong in this man's life. As, of course, it has in mine. He can't be here illegally, though. Security can hardly be an industry you can enter without references and paperwork.

'Debts?' I try.

He nods quickly: I think he's grateful I said it for him. 'They will sack me if they know about this. I *need* my job.'

I wonder what it would take to change his life. A thousand pounds? Two? Same as mine, probably. Enough for a deposit somewhere and a few weeks' living expenses.

Then I think about the safe in the wall, where a rich woman's spare change sleeps.

Supported by Force Patrol. For assistance call 0330 330 3330.

Mr K once said that when he was making an original ballet the whole story suggested itself at once; the steps came with the narrative. That's how I feel now: as though a plan has arrived in my head fully formed. This guy can get me into the safe behind the painting. It wouldn't be stealing – just borrowing, until I can get back on my feet. Just three thousand pounds. She can spare it.

I can't.

Can I?

'Don't worry,' I hear myself say. 'Your secret's safe with me. You stay there as long as you like.' I reach my arm through the leaves. His hand is large, warm and dry. 'I'm Juliet, by the way. It's nice to meet you.'

He frowns as he repeats my name. '*Jyulyit.*' Something about the way he says it is familiar, like an echo of a variation I used to love, used to dance to. 'But the client is . . .' He casts his eyes right, for remembrance. 'Ava Kirilova, no?'

Fuck, fuck, *fuck*. I should have let him think I was Ava Kirilova, then we could have opened the safe no problem. I hook on my stage smile.

'I'm looking after her house while she's travelling.'

He frowns. 'It's not on the system. I would have remembered.'

'Ah. I'm sorry, I thought she would have—' What if I get Ava Kirilova into trouble with Force Patrol, flagging some breach or causing some problem that I have to tell Lizanne about: a chain of events that lead to Ava Kirilova being interrupted, on *tour*, by something as banal as security arrangements. The thought of it chills me. 'Well – you know I have the keys. From the other day. And – you probably don't want them to know we've been chatting, do you?'

My smile holds fast. We make that pact. He doesn't know what's coming.

Borrowing. I'm just borrowing.

A queasiness churns inside me at the thought of exploiting a desperate man, but I am desperate too.

22

The Marks & Spencer Simply Food is so cold it was worth braving the blistering sun for. Crutches and a wire basket might not make for the most elegant progress through the aisles but they're good for clearing a path. I use my right crutch to halt the path of a well-heeled woman whose trolley is full of prosecco and ready-made trifles. If you can afford to do your big shop in M&S then you don't need the reduced aisle. That belongs to those of us with thirty quid to our names. It's rich pickings tonight, even better than yesterday: some of the salads are just 20p.

I *cannot* stop thinking about that safe. I was awake all last night, pinging between logistics and morality. Surely even someone as bricked into her ivory tower as Ava Kirilova couldn't begrudge an injured dancer a few meals. Would someone as wealthy as her even *notice* a few thousand pounds missing? It's as if all the energy I used to channel into dancing has found a new home. I see now that I miss ballet not only for its own sake but for the sense of purpose it gave me. The idea of borrowing cash from the safe is not just a plan for my survival: it's somewhere to put my thoughts. And, unlike ballet, it doesn't feel too tender to touch.

In the household goods aisle, a woman not much older than me wheels past a cage of toilet paper. I could apply for a job like this if I were able to stand up for more than thirty seconds without these bloody sticks. I could work in an office if they had taught me how to turn on a computer as well as how to hold an arabesque. My lack of options stops me feeling guilty about borrowing from the safe and makes me feel kind of . . . *righteous*. This is what they owe me, and not just me. There was a point last night where it felt almost like my duty: as though taking her money is something I need to do on behalf of every dancer the LRB have left destitute over the years.

If I could do it on my own I wouldn't hesitate, but of course I can't. I need Maxim Shevchenko. I have something to hold over him now, but I can't work out how to get from that to the small matter of asking him to help me crack his client's safe.

If it means him putting his job on the line, I can't ask him to do it.

In the queue for the till I fondle the coins in my pocket as though that will make them multiply. It's all theoretical until I can persuade him to explain how the system works. Once I know that, I'll know whether I'm asking him to lend me his time or to risk his job. The man's homeless: he will need money and I will give him a cut, like commission.

I dump the little yellow-stickered boxes of wheatberry and pomegranate on to the conveyer belt. He has no reason to trust me, apart from the matter of my not telling his employers he's living on borrowed time, on borrowed ground. I shake my head. I should be worrying, not about him trusting me, but about *me* trusting *him*. If we open the safe, what's to say he won't take the lot? I don't know him from Adam. He could be an escaped murderer for all I know.

It's not worth the risk. It's a stupid idea and I need to put it out of my mind.

By the time my shopping sails up to the cashier, I've changed my mind again. I'm going to at least *try*. Seduction, that's the most obvious way to get him on-side. He's not my type but I *am* a performer, after all. Once upon a time – less than three weeks ago – getting him into bed would have been easy. Men outside the industry, and some within it, you can see the word *ballerina* flick a switch in them, draining blood away from their brains. I don't have that capital any more. I—

Bang! I'm jolted from my thoughts as, with a pop and a fizz, the overhead lights go out. There's an eerie groaning sound as all the fridges and freezers power down simultaneously. Everyone blinks in the unexpected darkness, the sun through the window throwing the cashiers into chiaroscuro.

'You are *shitting* me,' says a man holding a single pint of milk, as staff emerge from a back room and a sales assistant pulls a shutter over the wine aisle.

'Sorry, ladies and gents, we need to close,' says a mountainous security guard. 'We've had an outage.'

'But my shopping!' protests the woman with the trolley full of puddings.

'I'm sorry, madam. We can't ring it up if the tills aren't working. We really must ask you to leave.'

'But my barbecue is *today*.' She asks if she can pay in cash, wilfully misunderstanding their patient explanations. The cashiers take over the evacuation, gently guiding an elderly lady and her shopping trolley towards the exit while the rest of the staff crowd around the barbecue woman, whose temper is rising with the heat in the shop. 'You don't understand, I've got family coming. Get me the manager. Get me the *regional* manager, on the phone. I'm not going anywhere.'

A daring thought soars inside me. If there's no power, then there are no cameras and no alarms. The woman in front of me had bagged up most of her shopping before the transaction could be finished, and she's already vanished. Two sturdy totes are waiting at the end of the conveyor. Without stopping to investigate what's in them, I dump them in a lone trolley, place my crutches over the top in an X, then stroll out of the shop as though I have already paid, passing through the dead arch of the security gates in silence.

I thrust the trolley across the road, through the gates and up the hill, sweat-slicked hands sliding over the handle, my good leg burning with the effort. I don't suppose Gabriel's Hill sees many red-faced, lame ballerinas pushing loaded shopping trolleys along its leafy pavements, but today there are no skinny women in Range Rovers, no cleaners' cars or gardeners' vans, no roaming beauticians; even Force Patrol are nowhere to be seen. I have broken the law. I should feel terrible but I don't: I feel excited, alive in a way that I've only ever known when I'm dancing.

It seems that I had a visitor while I was out shopping. There's a note pinned to a bag on the doorstep. Holding on to the trolley for balance, I bend to pick it up in a clumsy arabesque. She's written in ballpoint, childish print on an LRB compliments slip.

Hope ur ok, got ur painkillers and some letters to drop off. I'll call u later. xLx

The combination of text-speak and the twee sign-off stoke my dislike for her. She has left another week's worth of my medication, which is welcome, and some fan mail for Ava Kirilova, which is fantastically tactless. I throw it into the trolley with the bags.

As I turn the key in the lock, I notice fingerprints on the letterbox and an oily nose-print on one of the front windows. It seems that Lizanne's had a good old look at the house. Nosiness, or part of her job? Only the LRB would abandon me *and* check up on me at the same time.

Stepping into the hallway, I am struck again by the simplicity, the taste, the *money*. That's when it hits me. It's not me Lizanne is checking up on. It's Ava Kirilova's house. This place is an asset, just as I once was but will never be again.

23

At last the oversized fridge is full. Much of my haul is veg that needs to be eaten soon and won't freeze, but there's also fresh tuna, smoked salmon, vodka – I remove the security cuffs around its neck with a little mother-of-pearl-handled paring knife – tonic water. Lamb pasanda with pilau rice, fresh sourdough, Pink Lady apples, Greek yoghurt with honey, brie, celery, two boxes of figs and three bottles of sparkling wine. If the way to a man's heart is through his stomach then that must go double for someone who is effectively living on the streets.

When night makes the window a mirror, I stand before it and take stock. It's not great, but it could be worse. My skin, which looks shiny during the day, takes on a kind of glow after dark. The hair I've twisted up in a braid all day falls down in waves. I have barely eaten but I'm barely moving either and the extra five pounds I've spent my whole professional life fighting can't believe its luck. If things carry on in this direction, I'm going to need a bra – another expense I can't afford. A little weight, I'm finding, looks good on my face: I look more rested, less pinched. I look younger, despite feeling a thousand years old. My knee still looks as if there's a grapefruit under the skin, though, and the less said about my feet the better. I wish I'd said yes to that pedicure girl. The money's gone anyway. I might as well have spent some of it on looking good. I'd rather it had gone to an honest worker than that thieving little bastard on the bike.

I take a drink out into the garden. Under the chink of ice cubes, I hear a noise from next door. I peer through the hedge and see a familiar figure backing away from the house. His lanyard swings from his hand and he's still in his black uniform. Does he even have any other clothes? I clear my throat before calling across the fence.

'Maxim?'

At the sound of my voice he halts, turns to face me and all but salutes. 'Yes?' he says, formal and wary.

'It's nothing to worry about. I've got more food than I can eat, and I wondered if you'd like to share my dinner?'

'I could not possibly accept,' he says, in that metallic tone – something deeper and more controlled than just an accent – that makes it hard to guess what he's thinking.

I persist. 'I said I wouldn't say anything about you staying here, and I haven't.' I lace my words with just a hint of threat. 'Are you sure you're not hungry?'

There's an unreadable beat of silence before his stomach grumbles an answer.

It's not the fence's height that's the problem but the rose bushes on his side: they tear at his face, and then at the arms he raises in protection. After some awkward scrambling, he decides to approach in reverse, so that the thorns bounce off his belt and his back, but perforate a line under his elbow.

'There's a lamb curry in the oven, and there's vodka in the fridge.'

Maxim fills two tumblers to the brim with ice cubes from the little tray in the freezer, then pours generous measures of neat vodka over the top. One scouring sip tells me that at least I don't have to worry about pacing myself; it's too sharp to guzzle.

Small talk must pave the way for the big questions I need to ask him, but as we face each other across the dinner table I realise I have none. Since I was a child, I've socialised exclusively with dancers, exclusively with dancers from the same company in fact, and you never needed small talk at the LRB because every conversation revolved around the most interesting, all-consuming thing in the world.

'Another hot one,' I say, both mortified and bewildered by how I will get from weather chat to *by the way will you just open that safe for me?*

'Yes,' he says. 'Very hot.'

'What are summers like in Ukraine?'

'They are hot.'

A *femme fatale* I am not.

I unload the oven, but he brings the food to the table: the cutlery echoes and clinks in the awkward silence. The click of my own jaw is amplified. Maxim is a considered, careful eater but clearly neither of us are used to having full stomachs because we both admit early defeat.

'It breaks my heart to waste food,' he says. 'You want to save?'

'Please,' I say. He covers the serving dishes in kitchen foil and stacks them in the fridge while I peck at the rim of my glass. How does anyone drink this stuff without a mixer? His eyes are staring over my shoulder at the *Swan Lake* poster. I presume he's admiring Ava Kirilova's body: the slender arm that hides her face, the marble of her thighs. Instead he gives a sardonic laugh.

'What's funny?' I ask.

'I'll tell you a Ukrainian joke. *Swan Lake*'s on TV. Who died?'

Me, I think, but I say, 'I don't get it.'

'When I was born, Ukraine was still part of the Soviet Union. Growing up, there was one car for every twenty people. Different problems from the ones we have now. Whenever something dramatic happened, like one of the leaders dying, the government took away all the normal programming and showed only *Swan Lake* on a loop.' During this, his longest speech yet, his voice grows less cool and more human, like an engine that needs a certain amount of words to warm up.

'I *did* know that,' I say. The memory was mothballed somewhere, that aching part of me where the ballet lives.

'They did this in 1991 when the government fell,' says Max. 'They had *Swan Lake* on all day and all night. One of my earliest memories. I was maybe two years old. Walking past the electrical store and every television of every channel, the same ballerinas doing the same moves.'

He hums the famous refrain and I react like one of Pavlov's dogs. The urge to dance pulsates in me, as strong as it has ever been, but with nowhere to go it feels like fists beating at my skin.

'*Don't!*' I shield my face with my arms, as though the music is attacking me. 'Don't, I can't bear it!'

He stops, confused and appalled. 'What is the matter?'

I drop my hands. 'I'm – I *was* – a ballet dancer.' The past tense is a humiliation but at least I haven't cried.

He looks to the poster. 'That is *you?*' He can't disguise the horror in his voice: the contrast between the otherworldly perfection of the photograph and the grotesque opposite him.

'I wish.' Bitterness embrittles my voice. '*That* is Ava Kirilova.'

He looks from the poster to me and back again, and nods as though my being here has fallen into place for him. 'Well. It will be you in that black dress one day maybe? When you are fixed?'

I feel the tickle of Odette's costume; Odile floats out of reach like a feather on a breeze. The tears I thought I had mastered bring a new heat underneath my eyes. 'No. It's over. And ballet was everything I had. Everything I *was*.'

He won't get it. He'll offer platitudes, he'll tell me that it's OK, I can teach ballet instead.

'It is extremely shit.' His blunt sympathy is disarming.

'It *is* extremely shit, yes. *Thank* you.'

He considers for a moment, then asks, 'What else are you qualified to do?'

'Nothing. Mr K didn't care about academic things.'

'Ah. Academic qualifications are not a ticket to success,' he says with feeling. 'The people who win in life have different skills.'

'I'm still screwed, then,' I say. 'Eight hours' dancing a day doesn't leave much time for life skills. That's the deal. That's what it takes. This is what it's like, being one of Mr K's creatures: you—'

'One of his *what?*' He lets out the kind of laugh that signals disbelief rather than amusement.

'Oh, it was just a term of endearment,' I say, instinctively defensive. 'It's a special thing, being a Kirilov dancer. It was a point of pride.'

'*Creatures*,' he repeats, shaking his head. 'Now I have heard it all.'

I've spent long, empty afternoons raging at the way the LRB discards its dancers, but to hear someone *else* criticise Mr K stirs the old loyalty. My anger must show, because his voice sheds the last of its robotic tone.

'But I can see it would hurt to lose it. Dance is the missing piece of you?'

'It wasn't the missing piece.' The pressure in my sinuses eases as the dam breaks. I drop my head, so that the tears join at the bridge of my nose. I catch them with the side of my hand as they run off the tip. 'Dance was the jigsaw,' I say. '*I'm* a missing piece. I don't know where I fit.'

'Oh,' he says, so softly it might be a breath, not a word. 'I can understand that very well.' The yearning in his voice halts my tears and when I look up, there's a moment of connection. 'To be an immigrant. You never quite fit.' The intimacy that opens up between us is an awkward, prickly thing, and I'm relieved when he deflects with, 'Why are you living *here*?'

'Well, it's a bungalow, so . . .' I wave at my crutches.

'No, I mean – you have no family to look after you?'

'No.' State the fact, move on quickly. 'You live like a family with other dancers, though.'

'And this is their way of looking after you.'

'Could be worse,' I say, looking out at the garden and the lights that stud the edge of the pool. I take back the wheel of the conversation. 'What about you? What's your story? I mean, what was your job?'

He refills his own glass before mine. 'Teaching. English, to adults. For business, that kind of thing.'

'That explains why your English is so good.' He tilts his drink at me to say thank you. 'Did you come here for a better life?'

'Yes,' he scoffs. 'Since I am a little boy I always dream of sleeping in someone else's garden.'

Now I feel terrible. 'I wasn't taking the piss!'

'No, I know.' He twitches a half-smile. 'It's fine. The Donbass – it's not somewhere you want to stay, if you can help it. The whole of eastern Ukraine is a war zone. All young men have to do national service; we have conscription. Once he has been trained, any man under sixty can be called to fight at any time.'

'And were you?'

Do I imagine a second's hesitation? 'Luckily I came here before my number came up. I am legal. Look, Jyulyit.' There it is again, the sensation that him saying my name will unzip me and my insides will fall out. 'I need you to see something.' He reaches into his pocket for a black wallet. He flips it open and lays before me a plastic driving licence and his Force Patrol payslip and a P45 from an old job in Peterborough that's marked with a little coffee stain in the shape of a sickle. 'I have had some bad luck with housing. With many things. But I am here legally, I pay tax.'

He is at pains to show me that he does things by the rules. And it is his job, after all, to do the right thing. To report crime, not to commit it.

This isn't going to work, is it? Because borrowing, when you don't ask first, just looks like theft.

24

'I bring you Pluffman's.' Max vaults the fence through the gap he's made in the shrubs, then hands me a sandwich in a curling cardboard carton. It cost him 79p, down from £2.49.

'Thank you.' White bread, cheese and pickle. I can already feel the paste it'll form inside my stomach but I'll eat it anyway. It's the third day running he's brought me 'dinner'. I have a feeling the food he brings me is his way of keeping me on-side. That he still expects me to report him to his bosses at any time. He only knows about the dwindling food in the fridge, not the stash in the freezer. And at the rate I'm going even that will be gone before I broach the subject of the safe.

I am down to my last twenty pounds. One ten, two fives, four ones and a handful of silver.

Every day I push a little more. There have been a couple of tiny inroads into friendship, if not yet flirtation. I called him Max as an experiment and he didn't correct me. Mainly, I've been hearing about his working patterns. Force Patrol don't just look after this neighbourhood, they have clients all over London. On the nights Max isn't here, he's crashing somewhere else. The chav Acropolis next door is far from the only place in London paying thousands for security guards for a house they don't even live in. Apparently in some parts of London it's the norm for more houses to be vacant than occupied. Max is disgusted: he thinks they should be taken over by squatters. I see this as a good sign. He is angered by wealth inequality, and what is the disparity between me and Ava Kirilova if not that? Maybe, in the right circumstances, he could be a bit of a rule-breaker after all.

He works nearly every day, taking overtime whenever it is offered. There's another gated estate, as far away as you can go and still be in London, called Millbrook Green, where he works – and sleeps – on the days he's not here. He's found a secluded spot behind an electricity substation, of all things.

What do I know about *him*, though? He always carries a book: thrillers or true crime or pop psychology. They're always from charity shops. He always closes the book and sets it aside when he sees me coming.

I think I might be the only person he speaks to outside work. He doesn't seem to have any friends. No family as far as I can tell. He isn't glued to his phone the way everyone else seems to be. I've only heard it ring once, and that was work, rearranging his shifts. The wallpaper, as far as I can tell through the cracked screen, is an impersonal photograph of a footballer holding up a trophy. He likes to give the impression that he's an island but loneliness comes off him in waves, like heat shimmering above hot tarmac; it's nothing you can touch, but it distorts everything.

We eat our sandwiches in the relative cool of the kitchen, washing them down with tap water. 'By the way,' I say. 'It's pronounced Plow-man's.' Max colours a little: he prides himself on his English, but I see him mouth the correct pronunciation to himself. Then I ask him, fake-casually, 'So what power do you actually have as a Force Patrol employee?'

'Flight, invisibility . . .' He counts them on his fingers. 'I am working hard for the X-ray vision.'

When I laugh, it's stiff, like a muscle that I haven't used in a while.

'Can you get on to these properties? I mean, you're a key holder.'

'That does not mean I can come and go as I please. The tablet I carry when I'm working, it knows everywhere I go and how long I spend there.' He shrugs. 'But I give it to the next guy at the end of the shift; we hand over the car at the gates. Once I am out of the car I am untraceable. Otherwise they would know about . . .' He glances across the fence. 'I come in through a blind spot around the side, you know. When the camera is fixed, I can't sleep here any more. I should report it, but . . .'

'What about break-ins? Safe breaks?' I'd hoped it would be smoother than that, but if the swerve puzzles him he doesn't show it.

'The safes are . . . well, they are safe.'

'D'you keep a record of the codes?'

'There's back-up, but you have to make a formal request and you need the client with you.'

And there's my answer. He'd have to request it, but he *could* find out the code. But there's no elation. It's fear, not excitement that grips me.

Unaware of the significance of what he's just said, he carries on talking. 'If someone is determined to get into a property, they will do. Doesn't mean they'll get away with it. There was a break-in in Millbrook Green a few days ago. We locked all the outside doors remotely but the burglars unscrewed the lock from the kitchen window. They were climbing out just as we arrived.' He chuckles to himself at the memory. When he smiles his eyes disappear. It's as abrupt and disconcerting as a light switch being flicked.

'Did you arrest them?'

'No. If a crime is committed we call the police.'

I look pointedly at next-door's garden to remind him that he is committing a crime and that I have never said a word. It's a pretty subtle way to remind him of my trustworthiness and, if he registers it, he doesn't show it.

'Why do you want to know?' he asks.

'No reason.' I leave it a beat. 'Is the swimming pool alarmed, as far as you know?'

He gives me a wry look. 'No. They are quite hard to steal, swimming pools.'

'You're funny. I mean, could it be opened without an alarm going off?' He has that blank, slightly fearful look again. He must know what I mean but he's going to make me spell it out. 'Could you open it for me?'

'Did she say you couldn't? Or did she just not say you could.'

I deliberately don't answer. 'It would change my life if I could get into the water. There's a million keys in the hall table, if you want to look.'

Of course I want to get into the water. I've wanted to get into the water every day that I've been here. But this is also a test. I want to see what he'll do if I ask nicely. I want to see what matters more: what I want, or what his client wants.

It is a test that he passes. I stand over him as he wrestles with the padlock. He's sweated a dragonfly on to the back of his grey T-shirt; his triceps squirm like live things under his skin. After five minutes, the cover rolls back with a clatter; chlorine rises like teargas.

'*Ow.*' I step back, eyes watering. Maxim pulls up his T-shirt and uses it as a gas mask.

'It has been cooking under the cover for weeks. We should leave it overnight.' He gets to his knees and dips a hand in the water. 'It's hot as a bath.'

A single black feather floats on the surface. I recoil from it, jarring my knee. It is as visceral a reaction as though it were a whole dead bird. My breath comes in ragged gasps.

'Are you OK?'

An unwelcome melody plays in my head: Act III, the palace. *Odile*. Not again. Just like last time I heard the music, it grows louder in my head.

'Can you get that feather out?' I'm shouting as though the music were real and I need to make myself heard over it. At least I think that's why I'm shouting.

'It won't have germs on it. Smell that chlorine.'

The orchestra in my mind loses its place: Tchaikovsky's perfect notes play out of sequence and in discord. 'It's not that. Please, can you get rid of it?' I fight the urge to put my hands over my ears.

'It's a phobia?'

'Something like that,' I say, because it's not a phobia. A reminder of Odile's costume is not something I'm afraid of, it's something I want so much it hurts to be near.

He bends and reaches, fishes it out of the water. 'There is a recycling bin in the front garden. I will put it there.'

Alone by the pool, I stare at the water until it stills and the cacophony in my head dies down. Is it oil from the feather or the light on the water or my overactive imagination that slicks the surface with a trace of violet shimmer?

The pool is still as glass when he returns empty-handed.

'This fear of feathers is a problem, when you are dancing a swan?'

'It's only the black ones I don't like.'

I wait for him to tell me I'm being stupid or childish, but he only says, 'The mind is a mysterious thing. In another life maybe I am a psychologist. I like to read about the extremes of the human brain. The places it can go. Have you read *The Man Who Mistook His Wife for a Hat*?'

I shake my head.

'It's very interesting. I'd give you my copy but I took it back to the charity shop and swapped it for a John Le Carré.'

'Where do you find the time to read all these books?' I wonder.

'I am always alone.' He states it as a fact, stripped of self-pity, but it sets vulnerability – his and mine – in the hot air between us, where it can't be ignored. He rises from his seat and stretches as if to shrug the moment from his shoulders. 'Jyulyit. Please can I ask you a favour?'

'Sure.'

He pulls out his mobile phone: the splintered screen is black apart from a few glowing pixels in the bottom left-hand corner. 'I can't make calls any more. I need to check my shifts. Please can I borrow your telephone?'

'What's wrong with your mobile?'

He shows me a shattered screen. 'I dropped it on the pavement. I can answer calls but I can't see the keypad to make outgoing ones.'

'Can you get a new glass thingy for the front?'

He rolls his eyes. 'Yes, with all my disposable income.'

'Money!' I say. 'If only there were a way of magically getting our hands on some cash.'

I study his reaction for potential corruption. I am expecting his eyes to go to the safe: if they do that, I will know he will come with me. But he just repeats his request.

'It's OK to use the telephone?'

'Sure.' I tell him where it is and leave him to it.

When he returns, his face is ashen. 'I'm so sorry, Jyulyit. I erased your voicemails. I am so sorry. It's easy to hit the wrong button on a strange telephone.'

My brain scrambles to process all this information. 'That phone doesn't even have an answer machine.'

'Not an external machine. It is – how can I explain – embedded in the phone. It has a little icon. Like a tape.' He draws a shape in the air like a pair of binoculars, and understanding dawns.

'Did you hear the messages?' I can hear the neediness in my voice.

'I didn't mean to spy,' he says, clearly mortified. 'There were only two. They were very short. I tried to save them and that's when I erased them.'

'Who from?' I don't know why my heart is beating so fast. It's only going to be Lizanne.

'Two men,' he says. 'Someone called Jack wanted to see how you were getting on with Lizanne.' I can't stop the smile spreading across my face. Dear, lovely Jack. 'He left a number. I am so sorry. And the other guy was harder to understand – it was a bad connection – he just said, "It's me," and I didn't get the rest.'

'Did he have an accent?' I ask, daring to hope it was Mr K even though I know it will have been one of the boys from the corps.

'It was a *really* bad connection. And I find it hard to tune into accents, in English. Sorry. I'm an idiot.'

'It's done now,' I say, and while I would have loved to call Jack back, to hear that kind familiar voice, I find that I'm not angry.

I'm something else, an emotion that's the ghost of happy. The others haven't forgotten me after all. 'Honestly. It can't be helped.'

'You are being very gracious,' he says. 'Well. I hope they will call you back. Thank you for another nice evening. Sorry it ended this way.'

It feels as though the night has been snatched away from us just as I was getting somewhere. I take a deep breath. 'You know there's a spare room? You could always sleep here?'

He checks his recoil, but I've already seen it. 'I could not. It would not be right. And I like it under the stars. It is cooler.'

'Fine.'

I feel an unexpected crash of disappointment as he disappears through the leaves. On the way into the bedroom, I pass the telephone. I hope he's right, and that it will ring again for me soon.

25

I wake up with the dawn, around five o'clock. As a pre-emptive strike, I call Lizanne and leave a message, safe in the knowledge that even she won't be at her desk at this hour. 'Just checking in to say that everything's fine. No need for you to do anything or bring anything for a few days. Bye, then.'

That should buy me today and tomorrow, at least.

I drink water straight from the kitchen tap, one eye on the garden next door, then go back to bed. All day, while Max drives his quiet car past empty mansions, I drift in and out of sleep and dream about water.

Clearly I've spent too much time immersed in impossible fairy-tales, because I keep thinking of my plan as a spell I must cast upon him. The classical texts ballets are based on are sprinkled with potions and royalty and magic, with enchanted juice streaked upon sleeping eyes and gods playing with mortals' hearts. I need Max in my thrall; I need him close enough and soft and stupid enough to take a huge risk on my behalf.

In a ballet this would be called love, but we all know that was just what they had to call it in the days before they were allowed to talk about sex.

Max executes a perfect dive into the deep end. I scull in the shallows, staring up at bright stars. The house glows behind us. The little kitchen radio turned out to be portable, and I've set it on the flagstones that circle the pool. The lateness of the hour silvers the tinny pop music. Under the black sky, the pool is an enchanted lake, the water is magic. The spell I meant to cast on him has worked on me. Instead of Max? As well?

Our wine glasses are still full: I'm drunk with the relief of weightlessness, and the forbidden thrill of trespass and the other-country heat of midnight. For the first time, this summer and my confinement here feel like a miracle rather than a punishment. I could easily forget the real point of tonight.

'I should get out.' I hold up pruned fingertips.

'Let me help you.' He swims the length of the pool in clean easy strokes, shoves himself up on to the side. One of the candles collapses into its bottle with a fizz.

'You look completely different,' he says as he helps me negotiate the steps. 'Your face has changed.'

I squeeze a pint of water out of my hair. We don't bother with towels; even at this hour with no cloud cover, the air wraps me like a blanket. I test my knee: it bends, just a little.

'It's just so lovely to move freely,' I say. 'It felt almost like dancing.'

My words are pointed hands, poised over the surface of the water.

'I wish I had seen you dance,' he says, carelessly, almost to himself, and then his voice intensifies. 'I wish it so much.'

That's my cue to dive.

'Dance with me now,' I say.

In the dim light I see his shoulders square, as though he's readying himself for a fight.

'I can't dance on my own. I need someone to hold me up.'

My heart is hammering as he turns slowly to face me. A bulge at his throat comes and goes. 'I don't want to hurt you,' he says, but he closes the gap between us.

'Do it this way,' I say. 'I can balance on your feet. Like this, look.'

I place my feet over his; they fit perfectly. I hook one arm around his waist, reach the other around his neck and draw him in, so that his hips are locked against mine. To my astonishment – to a joy I don't fight – Max knows the steps of a waltz and what's more he can partner, bearing my weight on his feet so that nothing jars. Of course our clumsy waltz is to real dancing what my splashing in the pool was to Olympic swimming. My leg is a dead weight. Just staying upright is sweaty, slip-and-side work, accompanied by the slap of skin on skin.

But it's enough.

Max buries his face in my damp hair. The desire I thought I would have to manufacture rises in me, and I can feel it rising in him, too. I tilt my face to his and taste salt in his kiss.

26

High noon. I stand in front of the safe, my fingers splayed upon the cold steel of its door. What happens now?

Max was gone when I woke up this morning and I don't know what to make of that. He'll either be back tonight or I'll never see him again. I know he has another place he can sleep; I know there are other security guards he could swap shifts with. Will I have to ask Lizanne for money after all? The thought drops through me like a stone.

I replay last night's *pas de deux* on the big white bed. Keen to make him think *he* was taking advantage of *me*, I let him take the lead. He didn't speak, so neither did I: silent art form. My leg ruled out acrobatics but I still have a dancer's pelvic floor. Max treated me like a bubble he was scared to pop but that was a good thing: the forced restraint became tenderness. The usual moves, done at half speed. The memory lights a fire in my face. I lean my cheek against the safe and let the cool metal carry the heat away.

When the doorbell rings, I slam the painting shut over the safe as if I've been caught stuffing diamonds into a hessian sack with SWAG stencilled on it. I shuffle the length of the corridor and wrench open the front door.

Max is on the step, black cap in his hand. 'Delivery for Jyulyit!' A smile lifts his sunglasses high on his cheeks. A silver car is parked across the road, engine idling. At his feet are two huge transparent bags of ice. He holds them at arm's length. 'Some for the freezer,' he says. 'Some for the bath. To calm down your knee, without medicines.'

I think the fizz in my belly is happiness, although whether it's knowing I may not have to go cap-in-hand to the company or just at the sight of him, I honestly couldn't say.

In the kitchen, he stuffs the cubes into the empty drawers of the freezer. In the bathroom, he tips half a sack into the tub and then runs the cold tap.

'Where did you get it all?'

'Ice machine in a pub. Can we—' Whatever he was going to say is interrupted by an alarm shrieking from his tablet. 'I have to go, Jyulyit. Big Brother is watching me. I will be late tonight. I will try to bring you a *Plow*-mans.' In the bathroom, ice cubes snap-crackle-pop in the running water. 'Got to get back to the car before they notice.'

'Are you in the middle of a shift?' I say, following him to the front door.

'Of course. Why?'

'I thought you took a cab. That silver car.' I point over the road, but it's gone.

'What silver car? I left my car outside Number 38.'

'Doesn't matter,' I say to his retreating back, but it does. He took a risk. He left his post. Force Patrol might question him about the discrepancy on his route, but he did that for me.

In the bathroom, I lower myself into the water, making sure it only comes up to my hips. With an ice bath, you want as little of the spinal cord submerged as possible, to avoid your core temperature plummeting dangerously. Even with only my legs covered, it's intense. Five seconds has me fighting for breath; ten gives me the skin of a freshly plucked swan. The pain in my knee is white-hot, not cold, but I know that if I tough it out for just five minutes my body will thank me for the rest of the day. When the water drains, my knee is close to a normal size and there's an almost post-coital rush of wellbeing.

I think we can say the spell worked.

27

The two of us have been moving in a triangle between the pool, the living room and the bed for five nights now. We chase the shade: mornings are for the garden, but from noon the sun is on the back of the house and only the bedroom is bearable.

Max was on an early shift today so we were in bed by two o'clock. During that time my ulterior motive dissolved and is only patchily re-forming now. I watch him fighting a nap, wondering how he knows what I need: who taught him that.

'Have you slept with a lot of women?' I nudge him awake.

'Many, many thousands,' he says without opening his eyes. My laughter reflex is supple now. 'But you are my first ballerina.'

My knee twinges, as if to correct him. 'Hardly a ballerina any more.'

'It still counts.' Eyes still closed, he mimes ticking off a list. 'Just need a nurse now.'

'There you go, I can retrain as a nurse.'

'Or just dress up as one.'

We go quiet for a bit. I realise he hasn't answered my question.

'Have you, though? Slept with a lot of women.'

'Honestly? Not so many.' He shrugs. 'You can count them on one hand.'

I think I would feel better about all this if he needed both hands, at least. A different ratio would feel like a mitigating factor.

He takes a sharp in-breath, as though he's about to speak, then closes his mouth. I think he's wrestling with the impulse to ask me what *my* number is. I get the feeling we're pretty well matched. 'Aren't you—' I begin, but I'm interrupted by the doorbell ringing long and hard, drilling into my skull like an alarm. Then fists pound on the door, one-two-three-four-five.

Max rolls off the bed and into a crouch on the floor in a swift duck-and-cover movement that's the first sign I've seen of his military training. I sit up too quickly, jarring my knee. The wave of pain would have me roaring in agony if it hadn't first stolen my breath. The blind is down but the window's open so the visitor will be able to hear me. I pant through the pain until I have enough control to ask, 'Who is it?'

'It's Liz*anne,*' she says, her tone implying: who else would it be?

'Whatever you've got, just leave it on the doorstep.'

She sighs. 'I haven't brought anything. I just want to talk to you face to face.'

'About what?'

I've stumped her there. 'Just – to check you're OK? I mean obviously not OK, how could you be, but . . . look, I'm no good to you standing on the doorstep. Let me in. Please, lovely. Let me make you a cup of tea.'

If she comes in she will *know*. His clothes are everywhere. The house must reek of sex. The sheets need changing. There's a two-person mess in the kitchen.

'I just don't really want to see anyone, Lizanne. It's nothing personal.' I reach for my crutch but knock it down. Without thinking, I whisper to Max, 'Can you get that?' but my voice must be louder than I thought.

'Are you on your own in there?' Lizanne asks sharply.

Max's horror reflects mine.

'Of course I am.' As soon as the lie is out I realise how many things could give us away. Has he left his boots on the doorstep? The other day, he hung his black cap on the sculpture in the front garden to make me laugh. Did he do that again?

'It's just that you didn't turn up for your physio.'

My eyes go to the calendar on the hall table. One appointment. I had one appointment and I missed it. I was in bed with Max when I should have been learning how to walk again.

'I'm so sorry.' I don't just mean it because I need the rehab. If I'd gone in, Lizanne wouldn't be here now.

She sounds resigned when she answers. 'OK, well, I'll try to rearrange, but it might take a while. I won't actually be in the office for the next few days. I'll leave you my mobile number, OK? I'm putting it through the door now.'

The letterbox hinges open, but doesn't clap shut.

'I know you're going through hell,' she says, and for the first time her voice is sad, not grating. 'You think I don't get it, but I really do.'

The letterbox, at last, falls shut with a decisive clang.

We both stay very still until we're sure Lizanne has gone.

When I turn to Max, he's sitting with his knees pulled up underneath his chin. His skin beneath the suntan is drained of colour and, although the lines in his face appear to have deepened, a new wideness to his blue eyes and the protrusion of his bottom lip makes him look like a little boy.

This is primal fear, surely of something bigger than me being caught with a house guest.

'Max?'

'I am not so good with knocking on the door,' he says to his knees. 'I have not given you all of the truth, Jyulyit.'

I have no right to judge or care this deeply, seeing as our whole time together is based on a deception, but I do. My hands tighten around the bedsheets.

'I told you that the Ukraine army didn't call me up. It isn't true. I was asked to fight and instead I ran.'

'And that's what you thought the knock was? That they'd come after you here?'

'No.' He gives a bitter laugh. 'That is the crazy thing. It's one of those things you fear even when you know it is nonsense, like you and your black feather. But sometimes the panic takes me over. The size of my problem. I can't go home again. Not even for a holiday. Maybe they do not extradite a draft-dodger but I am a wanted man even so. They like to make examples of men like me.

I touch down, I'm off to prison, and Ukrainian prisons are . . .'
He does a full-body shiver. I don't think I've ever seen goosebumps
under a sheen of sweat before.

'Do you *want* to go home?'

He shakes his head. 'I was very homesick for a long while. Even
though, the whole year before I left, I slept in my clothes so that if
my apartment was shelled I might have dignity when my body
was pulled from the rubble.' He climbs on to the bed beside me.
'There. Now you know. You are sleeping with a coward.' He
screws up his face, trapping shadows there. It takes a brave man
to be this vulnerable.

'I don't think you're a coward,' I say. 'You came here on your
own, made a new life from scratch. That takes guts.'

He is right that my view of him has shifted, but not in the way
he thinks. He is less mercenary than I thought, but he has broken
the law before, and they always say that, having done it once, the
second time is easier.

'Sorry, Jyulyit. That's not how I meant to tell you but it feels so
much better to be honest with you.' He takes my hand and kisses
it. 'Before, I had a reason not to go home. Now I have a reason to
stay.'

His sense of home is shifting, settling on me. As, I realise, is
mine on him, which is not what I meant to happen. This is not
what I meant to happen at all. And yet I should have expected it.
Ballets might be full of charms and curses but they don't always
go to plan. Where's the drama in that?

The next morning, Max bends to the doormat to collect the mobile
number Lizanne scrawled on the back of an old Boots receipt.

'This is falling apart,' he says, and goes to write it down in the
same mint-green notebook where Ava Kirilova's riches are listed.
Two leaves further into the notebook are those other numbers,
the strings of figures that gave me this idea in the first place. If he
flips the pages and asks me what they mean, I'll tell him. I'll ask
him to help me take a little money out of the safe.

I am as sure as I will ever get that the answer will be yes.

But he doesn't turn the page. Instead he pauses with the pen mid-air as something occurs to him.

'Yesterday, why didn't you let her in? Sorry. We got sidetracked by my own stupid overreaction and . . . all that stuff.' His ears turn pink as he remembers his confession.

'Honestly, I'm glad you told me. The thing with that Lizanne is that if she found out you were staying, and it got back to the company, I'd be out on my ear.'

He touches his ear in puzzlement and repeats, 'Out on your ear?'

'It means they'd throw me out. Evict me.'

'*Evict* you? When you have no work? And you have been with them since you were – what was it – twelve? And all this and the way they call you a *creature*.' He curls his lip. 'It seems to me these people make you feel like you are worthless unless you are on the stage, a perfect ballerina. They do not treat you like a human.'

I should have known he was too good to be true. I'm a fool for expecting a civilian to understand.

'How many times? It *has* to be like that. Everyone in ballet has to be ruthless. You can't hold two ideas in your head at the same time. You can't devote your every waking hour to the discipline and also think, hey ho, if it doesn't work out, no big deal.'

He cups my face in his hands. 'Jyulyit. I *do* know what ballet meant to you. I can see how hard you worked. I can see your hurt when you talk about it. That's not what I'm saying. I'm saying these people, they have given you this house but they have kept you ignorant, if you do not mind me saying, and they have made you helpless. And now they abandon you. It is like a cult.' He shakes his head. 'I am sorry, but this Mr K you like so much, he is a bad bastard.'

He knows nothing about dance. Nothing. How *dare* he? In that searing, furious second, not only does my guilt at exploiting Max evaporate, I'm actually glad I'm doing it. It's only his access to that safe that stops me throwing him out of the house.

Instead I remain very quiet and very still as he drinks coffee and gets ready for work. Rage cyclones silently through me as I watch him lace his boots and put on his cap and then leave, a black figure striding past the elusive dancer in the front garden.

I try to slam the door but it's too heavy and I'm too weak. I can only push it to a slow, controlled close. I stand in the hallway, Max's words churning up everything I don't want to think about. I don't know if I'm so angry because he's got it wrong, or because he's got it right.

28

I have never had angry sex before; it was surprisingly enjoyable, even if the release of fury does seem to have sailed clear over Max's head. He seems unaware that I'm still cross with him the next morning as he lies on his front on Ava Kirilova's pure cotton sheets and traces his finger from my clavicle to my belly button. For my part, guilt has been replaced by a new determination. I'm going to ask him now, while he's post-coital and relaxed. It was on *Loose Women* the other day that men's IQ drops dramatically in the moments leading up to and immediately after sex. They'll say yes to anything, apparently. You've got maybe a ten-minute window before the blood flows back to the brain.

I draw breath to ask the question, but Max intercepts it.

'I know you all over now, every centimetre,' he says idly. 'I can't believe I mistook you for someone else that time.'

'What time?' I try not to sound impatient.

'The first day we met.' He holds up a finger to correct himself. 'No, the second. The day I had the shower. I would never have done it if I'd thought you were in. I thought you were out. I thought I'd seen you going through the gates in a big car. Gas-eater?'

Oh, for goodness' sake, where's he going with this? 'Gas-guzzler.'

'That's the one. She had the same long neck, like you, with her hair . . .' He whirls his hand around the top of his head to indicate a bun.

'Not me,' I say. 'I'd already lost all my money by then. Listen, there's something I want to—'

'These estates Force Patrol looks after,' he says. 'They're all full of skinny women who don't drive themselves. They take a taxi to

140

the gym across the street. They take a taxi to drink coffee with their friend next door.'

He continues to list the many places lazy rich people will take taxis until he realises that I'm not listening.

'You are quiet. You worry about something?' he says.

I see my opening and put one toe into it.

'Oh, you know. Just. Money, again.' He nods: me too. 'How long did you say it was until you've paid off all your debts?' I ask.

'I think two years,' he says.

I shift a little closer to him and trace my thumb along his eyebrow. 'You know how you said, if a client forgot the keycode, then Force Patrol have to come and reset it?'

He catches my thumb between his teeth. 'Uh-huh?'

I pull it away. 'Would the record show which guard was on the scene?'

'Of course, Jyulyit.' Why *does* the way he says my name feel like a hook in my heart? 'They know where I am at all times. I stop for a piss, it is recorded.' He laughs. 'Why, are you planning a heist?'

I answer him with a question. 'Can you do me a favour? In the hallway, the table where the phone is. That green notebook. Can you bring it to me?'

He returns, mildly intrigued, flexing it between his fingers. I find the relevant page and lay it open in front of him. 'This is what's in the safe and I'm just thinking we could borrow some of it. Three, four thousand, maybe?' My voice climbs without my permission. 'Force Patrol don't know I'm not Ava Kirilova. You could say the client called you out, and I could pretend to be her?'

Max suddenly seems to be wearing a mask of his own face. His eyes are hard blue stones.

'We would share it, obviously,' I go on. 'You pay off your debts; I take enough to tide me over, till I decide what to do next. She wouldn't notice; we'd have paid her back before she even knew, if we could reset the combination. You can say, I don't know . . . the system went down and it was changed automatically? She's so careless with money, she doesn't even know how much she's *got*.'

He shakes his head. 'This is against the *law*. If they found out you were not the client, I could lose my job. They call the police on me, things are serious.' He's up, dressing with his back to me: his accent is stronger in distress: *sings are serious*. Then he freezes as he's doing up his jeans, his shoulder blades folded like wings. 'My God, Jyulyit. *This* is why you wanted me. This was always your plan?'

'No!' I cry. Although it was, the hurt on his face is enough to convince me otherwise: that I am not the sort of person who could be this manipulative. 'Hear me out—' I begin, but he's gone, slamming the bedroom door behind him so hard the art on the wall shakes. In the time it takes me to get up, dress, find my crutches, he has gone.

'Max?' My voice bounces along the empty corridor. I drag myself from room to room looking for him. A movement at the end of the garden snags my vision; I shield my eyes and screw my face up against the sun until I can make him out, pacing up and down the patch of green grass. He might be talking to himself. He presses his hands into the small of his back, as though he's been carrying an unbearable weight for years and he hasn't got much left in him.

Guilt sinks its teeth into my heart. My certainty that this is harmless, for the best, no big deal, wavers, then topples.

I need the money, but I need him more.

The contents of Ava Kirilova's safe are not worth losing Max over. Why did I have to hurt him to see that?

I give myself time for everything in my head to percolate and settle. I'll wait for him to calm down and when he comes back I'll apologise. I will lie through my teeth, say it was a spur-of-the-moment idea, a bad joke.

It feels like an hour until he walks back to the house, a three-dimensional shadow emerging from the low-slung sun. With the light behind him, I can't see his expression. His steps are slow and hesitant, as though he still hasn't made up his mind. When he's close enough to touch, my hand flutters towards his chest; when he shrinks away, it falls like a dead weight.

'Instead of this crazy idea of breaking open the safe, why don't you *ask* her to lend you the money?' he says. 'Would she not want to help you? One dancer to another? You bypass your strict Mr K and just ask her?'

I think of Ava Kirilova, isolating herself in her dressing room, refusing to make eye contact with anyone lower than the rank of soloist. Pulling up the ladder behind her. I could almost laugh at the idea. 'Yes,' I lie. 'Yes, I think she would lend me the money. If she knew what trouble we were in. But, as I said, she's on tour. You can't disturb a dancer on tour. It's not as if I'm going to fritter it on designer shoes. I need to get a flat, I need to get a job, and I can't do either on an empty stomach.'

His hand goes to his own belly; he's thinking about it.

'You are asking a big thing,' he says. 'We don't know each other.'

'An hour ago, you said you knew me all over.'

He winces at the reminder of this morning's intimacy. 'We don't know each other out of that bed. We have never left this house together. And you ask me to risk my job, my status, for a game of Bonnie and Clyde?'

'It's not a game. We both need money. In some ways you need it more than me.' He knows what I mean: I have nothing, but he has debt. I lace my fingers through his. He resists, then slackens. I am so close. 'And you should move in. Properly,' I decide out loud. 'Live here with me, for as long as I'm here.'

I find that I mean it, and it also seems that I am the incentive, because everything about him loosens and opens, as though a pin that's been holding him rigid has been pulled out.

'Give me time to think of any extra risks that maybe do not come to me yet.'

'There *is* a risk,' I say, to hasten his decision as well as for full disclosure. 'There might not *be* any money in the safe. We don't know when she wrote those numbers down; we've got no proof there's anything even *in* there.' We both look at the blue painting. 'Then we've got nothing, we're back to square one.'

His smile is bittersweet. 'Whatever else happens, I don't think we can ever go back to square one, you and me.'

'So – is that a yes?' It's just as well I can't drop to my knees, because I might.

'I said give me time to think,' he says, but gently. He sinks on to the sofa, picks up the paperback he left splayed across the arm and starts to read, shutting down the discussion.

An hour later, he closes the book without having turned a single page.

'Jyulyit. I think I have a way.'

My belly is pulled in two different directions: as if I am rising and falling at the same time.

'When?' It takes all my composure not to cheer. 'Tonight?'

'No. My next shift here isn't for another two days. I'm at Millbrook Green tomorrow. I can't change my shift pattern, just in case.'

'Just in case?'

'I *think* it is foolproof. But in case it is not – it looks suspicious if I ask to work in Gabriel's Hill, and then I am found near an open safe.'

The night seems to hold its breath, as though I'm being given one last chance to release him. But we have come so far, now: and we have arrived here together. Whatever happens on the other side of tonight, good or bad, I will make sure it happens to both of us.

'Thank you,' I say. 'You don't know what it means.'

My eyes are drawn suddenly to Ava Kirilova's poster, almost as if she has moved in my peripheral vision, lifted her head, or shaken a feather. Of course she hasn't; it's just a picture, perfection preserved in black and white while the flesh-and-blood dancer twirls around the globe. I appeal to it anyway, as though praying to an icon. Let me have this, Ava Kirilova. You have so much. You have everything I ever wanted. You can spare me this.

29

The front door is open wide. The air outside is black and hot and the dancer on the lawn is a dull pewter in the dark. I hover on the threshold, waiting for Max to drive past. It's the end of the late shift. In ten minutes he will take his car to the gate and hand it over to a colleague.

The ceiling lights in the hallway are halogen and it's too hot to have them on. A single lamp glows on the telephone table, casting concentric circles of light and shade on the floor and walls. I tap Force Patrol's number, all zeroes and threes, into the phone and let it ring out. Sweat from my hairline slides down my brow, slips sideways into a tear duct.

'Good evening, Force Patrol?' The woman has the kind of voice you only ever hear on the telephone. She reminds me of Lizanne.

'Hello, hi. This is Ava Kirilova at Number 36 Gabriel's Hill.' I take a breath, give her a chance to challenge me.

'Thank you, Ms Kirilova. I can see that you're calling from the house. How can I help you this evening?'

Only a tug in my chest prompts me to breathe. 'I need to access the safe but I can't remember the combination. You know how it is. Written it down somewhere so secure I can't even find it myself. Please can you send someone round to reset it?'

'I'll just see if we've got someone local.' I hear long fingernails click against computer keys. 'You know what, you're in luck, he's virtually on top of you,' she says. Max is already here, headlights blinding as the car pulls up outside the front door. 'Obviously he'll need to see some ID from yourself,' she continues. I see him take her call before slamming the car door behind him.

'He's here now, thank you so much,' I say.

Changing the code is the work of a moment: some back-and-forth on his hand-held tablet, some kind of master code sent back.

'I'm scared to open it,' I confess.

'Me too.' He moves quickly, as though he's trying to overtake the thinking part of himself. He pulls the handle and we squint inside.

It's a tiny recess, a fraction of the size of the door. A bulging black box file takes up most of the space. Wedged beside it are three fat envelopes to match the three sets of tallies in the notebook. I can tell as Max piles them in my arms that they contain money.

He sets the file on the floor.

'Choose a new combination,' he says.

My mind goes blank. I'm so stressed, I couldn't tell you my own birth date. 'I don't know,' I say. 'You choose.'

He shrugs, searches the air in front of his eyes before coming up with, '959595.'

'What's it mean?'

'It doesn't mean anything. It is just easy to remember.'

He enters the code again to confirm it, then takes the Force Patrol car keys out of his pocket and jitters them in his hand. 'I go and hand over the car.'

'I'll make a start on these.' I nod at the envelopes in my hand. 'Better shut that back door.'

'Sure.' He pulls the door closed and turns the key so a wall of glass seals us off from the garden. We see fear and disbelief in our reflections' eyes. It's not too late, I tell myself. We can back out of this right up until the moment we spend the first penny of this cash.

All we have done so far is change the code on a safe. That's all we have done.

'And can you shut the front door behind you when you go?' I say.

He turns away from my reflection to me. He looks hurt – the pinched brow, the way he leans back from me – and it takes me a moment to understand why. If I was using him, as he is right and also wrong to fear, of course I'd want him locked out of the house. He still doesn't trust me completely.

'Take the key?' I say, and instantly he is reassured.

'I will be five minutes.'

With all the exits sealed, the heat builds. There's no breeze to displace the piles of money I make here. Each envelope contains notes in various denominations. In the first cache alone, there is at least twenty thousand in sterling and more in euros. It's all loose, new and used notes tossed together, but dozens and dozens of them are fifties. I'm looking at far more than the thirty-five thousand totted up in the notebook.

A weird sound spins up and out of my throat. I find that I'm scared of it, all this money, the chaos it's in, the possibilities this blows open. What the hell, Ava Kirilova? How can one person have this much cash swilling around? How can Mr K pay his dancers minimum wage while his daughter stuffs money in a safe? The three thousand pounds they gave me is nothing to them.

Five minutes pass and, just as it occurs to me to get nervous about Max returning, he's here again, flushed and breathless as if he ran all the way back. Is the glow on his face exercise, or relief that I'm still here?

He drops to his knees beside me. He smells of himself and the lemon soap he uses. 'Is there as much as it said in the book?' he asks.

'There's more. There's tens of thousands more. It's a mess. I don't think she can know how much is even here.'

'*Khuy.*' He exhales his favourite swear word. 'Is she making tax fraud? Trust me, I work in security. No one has this amount of paper money unless it is dirty.' He leans forward very slightly, as though he is on the brink of something, then tips out his next words. 'You can't report something stolen if you weren't supposed to have it.'

I recognise the coded dare. 'So are we still talking about *borrowing* from her, or . . . ?'

The look that passes between us: I will if you will.

Outside, the moon climbs. I swear I can hear his heart beating.

'Maybe there's a paper trail in here that explains all the money?' He lifts the black file on to the kitchen island, starts digging through the compartments. 'But I do not think it is right that you should struggle, after everything you gave to your ballet company. I think they owe you a better living than they have given you.'

I start to sort the money but my hands are shaking and I seem to have forgotten how to add up. I pause to watch Max work his way through documents, smoothing them, putting them down in different piles. I imagine myself doing the reverse, scanning effortlessly through documents in the Cyrillic alphabet, and feel a flutter of admiration for him.

The paperwork keeps on coming.

'Is there any more cash in there?'

He shakes his head.

'What are you even looking for?' I ask him.

'I don't know,' he confesses. Under the spotlight, he looks different: older, darker. His hair and beard are growing out, the hairline – not receding, as I'd assumed – visible for the first time. He skim-reads papers then sets them down. He takes out a silver key, turns it over in his hands then lets it go. It hits the marble worktop with a flat chime.

I scale back my task, concentrating on arranging the notes into denominations rather than counting.

Outside, the water is still as glass. Occasionally a bird caws in the garden. The only other sounds are shuffling paper, my breath and his.

Max gasps, so loud and so sharp I swear his breath has a Ukrainian accent. His hands are hidden behind the box file, but whatever he's holding in them has made his face fold in on itself.

'What've you got?'

'It's a passport.' He looks at me, at the passport, at me again. 'It's Ava Kirilova's passport.'

'An old passport. So what?' But I stop stacking the money. A cold dread starts at my toes and creeps up my body, like lowering myself into an ice bath.

'No,' he says flatly. 'It's not expired, it's only two years old.' He holds it out: the maroon cover with the gold lion and unicorn on the front. 'When it is finished they cut the corner off. There are visas in here for India, Cuba, China; they are all in date. And look, Jyulyit. What can you tell me about this?'

His brow creases deeper than ever as he hands me a printout from a computer. It's an airline ticket, mailed to an address at the London Russian Ballet Company, in Ava Kirilova's name, for a flight to Madrid that left weeks ago.

'Why would she change her flight?' I say, and then, my brain ticking faster, 'Also, if her passport's here, where's she?'

He makes the same face he did when I asked him to open the safe. Incomprehension, hurt, anger. He is searching my face. I'm as in the dark as he is.

'Do not *lie* to me.' He is shaking, as though resisting some primal reflex. 'Especially not after everything I have just done for you!'

What? 'Max, don't be weird. You're *scaring* me. Let me see it.'

My arms strain as I push myself up to standing. As I step towards him a breeze strokes my back; it's coming down the corridor, which means it must be coming from— 'Didn't you lock the door behind you?' I ask Max. His hands go to his hip pocket, where the key should be. 'For God's sake, of all the times to leave it in the door,' I begin, but he barely hears me. His blue eyes are wide and his mouth is a perfect circle of fear as he looks not at me but over my shoulder. In the window, I see my reflection.

Not my reflection.

For the woman in the glass is moving while I remain perfectly still. The kind of play-dead stillness born of terror: some deep animal part of me that knows that something is very, very wrong.

'Jyulyit!' he cries, but before I can answer him there's an explosion in my head. Something hard rams the back of my skull, sending me face-first into the sofa. I scream Max's name into the leather as what feels like a baseball bat hits my legs and back again and again. There's screaming behind me, two voices in a panicked, rapid-fire foreign language.

The blows stop as abruptly as they began. As I roll slowly and painfully on to my back, the voices cease.

Max towers above me. Next to him, holding his wrist in one hand and gripping one of my crutches in the other, is someone I've seen before. The kind of face you don't forget. A ballerina at first glance, but no, she's too tall, too curvy. She is the illusion created by a face made up for the stage: the pedicure girl.

30

They are standing close enough to kiss. I press my bruised back against the sofa as Max and the pedicure girl resume screaming at each other in Ukrainian. You have to know someone very well to argue that way. He shouts something that makes her turn slowly and look at me, then she places her hand, with its long purple fingernails, on his fly and cups his balls. He's mine, says the gesture, and her narrowed eyes add: he was never yours. As if he ever could be.

You don't have to understand something for it to hurt. My head thuds like a bass drum.

'Max?' I don't realise until I speak that my lip is split. Melted pennies flood my mouth. 'What's happening? Who is this?'

She removes her hand from his crotch but her focus stays on his face. As though at some unseen signal, they both start shouting again, streams of foreign words tumbling over rocks of my confusion. Only one word stands out: her name. Katya, he repeats, Katya, *Katya*!

He can't meet my eye. His hand is in his back pocket, mockingly casual. He says something to her, clearly an instruction; she trains my crutches on me like a double-barrelled shotgun.

'Max!' I use the full force of my voice but still he doesn't look at me. Am I going mad? Can anyone even *hear* me? For a crazy second I wonder if I am dead. 'Show me that passport and tell me who the hell this person is!'

The woman tells me to shut up. Max doesn't even turn his head my way. They talk over each other, their voices rising and falling passionately. *Heathrow*, I pick out, and *Kirilova*. 'Please, talk to me,' I beg Max, but he only has eyes for the money. He picks up a bundle of euros from the floor and shoves them in Katya's face, then nods at the rest of the scattered cash. There's a flash of confusion, where she seems not to understand his instruction, but then she's off: gathering money, stuffing it into the black bag. It's as though they're in a cheap game show, trying to catch as much cash as they can within their time limit.

I was wrong, it seems, when I told Max it was impossible to hold two conflicting thoughts in your head the same time. I know that money doesn't belong to me and I also know that it is mine and I deserve it. He wouldn't know about it if not for me. It comes from my ballet company. I *need* it.

I pull myself up on a chair and reach for the bag in Katya's hand. I move quickly but she is faster: before my arm is straight, the rubber end of my crutches hits the bone between my breast, shoving me back to sitting. A hot pink circle throbs on my sternum. Katya uses the crutch to slide the bag beyond my grasp. It spins on its base and in a side pocket I see – I'm sure I see – I think I see – a single black feather with violet glitter on its tip.

Max and Katya continue to bicker but their voices are replaced by a high-pitched nothing in my head, like the ringing silence after an alarm or a siren stops.

Max looks at his watch and barks what sounds like a final command at Katya. She scoops up the bag: now it appears to contain nothing but money.

Katya. Ava. Cash. Feather. Passport. Max. The part of me that connects one event to another has broken down; my grasp of cause and effect has been knocked out of me. There are two of them and only one of me. They know what's happening; I don't. I can't walk; they can run.

They leave together, taking the bag, the box file and my crutches. By the time I reach the living room door, they have locked me in. I turn the handle, then rattle it and rattle it and rattle it.

'Max!' My voice chases him down the corridor. 'You lying bastard! How could you do this to me?'

His answer is the slam of the front door: the tumble of the lock.

INTERVAL

The London Russian Ballet
Director, Founder and Founder Choreographer
Nikolai Kirilov

SWAN LAKE
A Ballet in Four Acts

Choreography Marius Petipa and Lev Ivanov
Additional Choreography Nikolai Kirilov
Music Pyotr Ilyich Tchaikovsky
Production Nikolai Kirilov
Design Nikolai Kirilov and William Bell
Lighting Design Nikolai Kirilov and Adeola Musa
Staging Nikolai Kirilov

Cast

Odette/Odile	~~Ava Kirilova~~ Sakurako Sato
Prince Siegfried	~~Luca Alighieri~~ Tomasin Martinez
The Queen, Siegfried's mother	Felicity Christian
Von Rothbart, the Sorcerer	Boyko Andriev
Benno, Siegfried's friend	~~Vadim Abramov~~ Luca Alighieri

All other roles danced by Artists of the London Russian Ballet

ACT II

ROMAN

31

The car wash where Roman Pavluk was employed was on the forecourt of a derelict garage. From the concrete rose a haze of hosepipe spray, ozone and petrol fumes. He worked with a T-shirt around his nose and mouth as a crude filter and tolerated his colleagues' broken-English mockery. The detergent they used to clean the cars' paintwork was bad enough – if that stuff got into your eyes, you were blind for the rest of the day – but if the hydrochloric acid they used for the alloy wheels got into your lungs, you were done for. You would need a doctor. And neither Roman nor any of his colleagues was registered with a doctor.

A black Range Rover with tinted windows glided to a halt at Roman's side and a tinted window slid down to reveal a trim blonde: Gucci sunglasses and Chanel earrings, shiny hair.

'I'd like the full valet service.' She handed him her keys. 'We'll be in Starbucks.'

The back doors opened and a boy and a girl of about nine or ten, dressed in the kind of crisp old-fashioned uniform that signified private education, hopped out. Before the blonde led her children away to the coffee shop across the road, her eyes flicked over Roman in a way he still couldn't get used to. Their gaze always traced the same pattern on his body: head, toe, belt, where they lingered a beat, shoulder to shoulder and finally back to his face. He considered the irony: he was in the best shape of his life. The little gut that Veronika had said matched her own post-baby belly – that was gone, stripped of fluid too now in this heat, so he was sinew and bone, his face leaner than it had been since he was a boy. He was unrecognisable since he had shaved his head. Not a disguise, as such, because if they caught up with you they caught up with you, but because that was how most of the others looked, and Roman wanted to blend in.

They worked on the car with vacuums and leather and sponges. In the Starbucks over the road the kids drank buckets of milk with whipped cream, pencils hovering over workbooks. Roman had a maths problem for them. If you pay ten men five pounds to wash your car, a job which takes twenty minutes, how does that work out? Where is the money going? How are they supposed to fucking eat?

When the car was showroom-standard, Roman got behind the wheel, noted the full tank of petrol and briefly considered what it would be like to keep driving this car until he reached the sea and then throw himself into the water fully clothed and keep swimming until his body made the choice his mind was too weak for. He settled for the ten-second drive to Starbucks.

Inside, harsh air-con froze his damp T-shirt to his skin. The children's homework was not maths but English; some kind of grammar exercise.

'Madam,' he said. 'Your key.'

She held out a slippery ten-pound note in exchange: Roman's filthy fist closed around it.

'Thank you, so much,' he said.

Light travels faster than sound but he heard the sirens before he saw the blue lights and knew without turning around who they were here for. The little boy in his shorts and blazer knelt on his chair, nose against the window.

'An actual raid. *Sick*!' he said, but his sister started to cry, a sound that wrung the air from Roman's lungs.

'It's OK,' said their mother, but she was looking at Roman. 'It's OK, they're not going to get you.'

She means me, thought Roman. She's telling me I'm OK, that she won't tell. A good-hearted woman underneath the frosty London bitch act. He put out his hand to thank her again. She wrinkled her nose. 'Get the fuck away from my kids, you *cockroach*.'

He shunted backwards as though she'd kicked him in the gut. Given a few more seconds he would have told her who she was talking to. That he could speak three languages. That he was a *teacher*. That he had read Jane Austen and George Orwell and even Shakespeare in the original. That he had a degree in English and that her little thug of a son did not know how to use the possessive apostrophe.

Summoning a calm he did not feel, Roman pushed the fire door at the back of the shop. Without his permission his legs broke into a run. The ten-pound note wasn't looking so crisp now that it was all he had to show for his week's work. He spent five pounds on a six-pack of beer from the Polish corner shop, levered the cap off the first bottle on the shop door, and street-drank on the long walk back to the Jester.

Here he was again.

The car wash had been his fourth job since his status had shifted from teacher to tourist to illegal immigrant. Each job had been worse than the one that preceded it. And now he had to find another. Roman was not yet thirty but he felt like an old man. He was built to think, not lift. He wanted, more than anything, a job that required papers, that would let him integrate into this country and contribute to it.

Going home was not an option. They would be waiting for him at the airport and the only home soil his feet would touch as a free man would be runway tarmac. It was time for Roman to press the red button: to use Zlata's money. That he had saved and then ring-fenced that money was a lone star of pride in the night sky of shame that was his life. To spend it would be like losing her all over again.

32

Veronika fell in love with Roman because of a book. A second-hand English-language paperback bought at a market, pages worn to velvet even before he picked it up. In the final year of high school he had not so much carried the book as worn it, kept it ostentatiously poking out of his jacket pocket, hoping some girl, sick of the *obvious* guys, would bend to decipher the Western alphabet and he'd be able to say, you've never read Dorothy L Sayers? Let me tell you all about her. Over coffee, maybe? That girl had been Veronika. She was impressed not because she was a reader but because she wasn't. She didn't read for pleasure, not even in Ukrainian, let alone English, but she liked the idea of a man who did.

That romantic idea carried them along the usual channels: engagement, marriage, two-bed flat – not in the Old Town with its globe street-lamps and its cream-cake houses, but further out, where the view from their balcony was a potholed road and a decommissioned coke factory. Roman had wanted to teach English at a school or university, but corporate work paid more, so he taught English to businessmen. When Zlata was born – and by God she was perfect, so much more than the sum of her parents' parts – she made everything worth it.

Until the war.

It turned out that a lifetime spent reading about ingeniously plotted murder did not equip a man to commit it on behalf of the state. Roman tried to tell Veronika how it was, the cold and the dirt and the ill-fitting shoes that stank of another man's sweat. The second-hand guns and ammunition from other nations' armies. The things that were done in the name of practical jokes: piss in a man's coffee cup, shit in his food. The whoring and the bragging and the vodka that tasted like battery acid but was the only way to make it through the night. He hated this life more than he had thought it possible to hate anything, and yet he still burned with shame that he couldn't rise to its challenges. The weight of a rifle on his shoulder, which other men felt somehow reinforced them, added to their muscle, weakened Roman.

'You have no bloodlust,' Veronika said one night, as though bloodlust were an attractive quality and not something to be ashamed of. 'Suck it up. Be a *man*.' And then, 'You've been promising to fix the fire escape for *three years* now and you're still sat on your lazy backside reading.'

He'd been about to set down his book, but now he lifted it to make a barrier between them. If she wanted some dumb guy with a tool belt, she should have married one.

The marital bed got colder by the night.

He survived the training, somehow, but the threat of active service sent him mad. He knew that one day as a soldier would break him and they wouldn't send him to hospital but to one of the correctional colonies for cowards and deserters, gulags in all but name. Days on end in a windowless concrete cell where the only entertainment was your daily beating? That would kill him faster than the fighting.

First, he applied for jobs teaching English in schools. Schoolteachers were frontline workers and exempt from conscription. For this very reason, however, existing teachers clung to their positions, and there were a hundred applications for each post. Roman's back-up plan needed a back-up plan.

More realistically, someone with his language skills and experience could become a recruiter or a mortgage broker in Britan. One of his colleagues had got a job in a bank in London: they'd arranged her visa *and* given her a basic salary of twenty-five thousand pounds a year. Twenty-five thousand pounds! Roman and his family could live like *kings*.

He applied for international passports and tourist visas, which he was granted on the basis of a working holiday. He kept them locked in his desk at work. This was itself almost a crime. If a man was called up he must surrender his international passport at once; the army would seize it the day you got the letter. Not keeping your passport at home was tantamount to pinning a sign on the front door declaring yourself a flight risk. He found a farmer in Romania he could bribe to let them cross the border.

The travel documents were four weeks from expiry when Veronika opened the letter from the army and rang him at work. Now that it was real, she was frightened, which Roman took as a sign that there was still some vestige of love after all. But not enough love to listen to his plan. Not enough love to come to England with him.

He got in the car, still in his suit, and drove to the airport, knowing that if he left he could never go home again. He didn't say goodbye to Zlata because he knew if he saw her he would stay and it would kill him or worse. One day he would make her understand that it was better for her to lose him like this, to have him still thriving and in contact and sending money and waiting for Veronika to bring her to England, than it was to have a father broken and dribbling in an institution.

London was a different kind of war zone but Roman was confident, charming his way through to the second round of interviews for one of the fabled mortgage broker jobs. He was on the steps of the office block when his phone lit up with a Ukrainian number and Veronika's brother told him that their apartment block had been shelled in the night. It was smoke that killed them, not the blast: they should have been able to climb to safety, but it looked as though Veronika hadn't been able to open the fire escape.

Roman cut the call, went upstairs to the job interview, walked out halfway through, bought a litre of caustic Russian vodka on the way back to his two-star hotel room and drank it, staring blindly through a grimy window at bare branches. By the time he came up for air, the blossom had been and gone, and he was ten kilos and a thousand pounds lighter. He was haunted every night by Veronika and Zlata and by another ghost too: a version of himself who had stayed in Donetsk, who had fought, who had fixed the fire escape, who had been a *man*.

33

On Roman's walk back to the Jester, he got through five of the six beers in the pack. He passed the landmarks of his neighbourhood: the letting agent, the jeweller-slash-pawnbroker on the corner with the thick steel shutters where they turned gold to cash and cash to gold.

Even in a good mood this was an uninspiring walk, and now, when he was unemployed again, it corroded what was left of his soul. Roman had grown up with a very specific idea of London, gleaned from classic English fiction: Dickens of course and Conan Doyle and Agatha Christie. His imagined London was mist-shrouded Victorian cobbles and mansion flats with Bentleys parked outside. The London he had found himself in went betting shop, vape shop, barbershop, nail bar, repeat to fade. It was in its way as uniform as any Soviet street, rows of red roofs, bay windows, gables all slathered in shingle. The pebbledashing took him by surprise. Growing up, Roman had always assumed the ugly weatherproofing *hal'kovyy* that coated the identikit apartment blocks in Donetsk was something peculiar to Ukraine. The Jester was covered in the stuff, although it was coming away in chunks.

At first glance the Jester looked like a serving pub, but the empty hanging baskets, the plywood behind the stained-glass windows and the car park full of dirty vans and bikes gave it away. A sign outside warned: *This property is protected by Guardians.* Over the door was a little brass plaque declaring that the proprietor was licensed to sell intoxicating liquors on these premises although these days the air itself was intoxicating, a fug of marijuana smoke hanging about the place.

He twisted his key, a copy of a copy of a copy, in the front door, and hoped for a clear path to his cubicle. Saleem, the British guy who ran the place by default of being the sole contracted tenant, had got some of the construction workers to put up stud walls in the old saloon bar to make little boxes for the 'internationals' to sleep in.

The locker-room smell of ten men living together turned Roman's stomach as it always did upon entry. It was ironic that after so many years loving women, living with women, losing women, Roman now spent his days and nights in almost exclusively male company. Saleem didn't sublet rooms to women, but of course there was a constant stream of pick-ups and one-night stands. There was a ban on long-term girlfriends but no woman would want to live here anyway. The plasterboard walls didn't reach to the ceiling so there was no sound privacy. Most evenings music or group chat or sport were played out loud on phones and his immediate neighbour, Sergey, streamed noisy porn as if it were a bedtime story. When someone brought a girl back, that was the worst, especially if she'd drunk enough to drop her inhibitions. Sometimes you could smell them, perfume and shampoo and then sex itself through the walls, and Roman would be tortured by involuntary arousal which no amount of visualising Sergey's spotty backside could dampen. Sometimes the memory of sex, the knowledge that he had touched Veronika for the last time, would wind Roman. Once he'd even cried out in anguish and someone had shouted, 'Nice wank?' to cheers from the others and it had been days before he'd lived it down.

Tonight, Roman's path was not clear: in the corner of the bar they used as a communal area, Saleem lounged on the sofa in a cloud of blueberry vape gas, a paper carrier bag at his side.

'Roman, bro! Catch!' Roman raised an arm and caught the sandwich sailing towards him in a graceful arc. Crayfish and rocket, not bad. Saleem's day job in Pret meant he often fed the whole house. At night he was a DJ; Roman had no idea when he slept. Most of the British guys worked what they called a 'bread job' to fund something creative. The internationals were not expected to have any kind of ambition or inner life.

He took his sandwich into his cubicle, two metres by two of relative privacy. The light travelled through the stained-glass windows through the day and acted as a kind of sundial, so you could loosely tell the time by where the yellow and gold refracted light fell on the plasterboard walls. Its position now told Roman it was around eight pm. Usually he would now collapse into sleep, but what was the point when there would be no work tomorrow? He lay on his back. The front door banged a few times; Saleem threw more sandwiches; the sweet smell of weed overlaid the base note of socks and then an even sweeter temptation beckoned: the sound of spoken Ukrainian. Sergey, Roman's only compatriot, who oversaw a cannabis farm a few streets away, evidently had a friend over. Roman suddenly craved conversation in his mother tongue the way he habitually craved a bowl of *kasha*.

He revised his opinion as he rounded the bar – Sergey's swarthy companion was shaped like a hand grenade and gave off the same energy – but they had all seen him.

'Roman!' Sergey's eyes were even more bloodshot than usual. 'Come and have a smoke with our fellow countryman. This is Ardem, it's his last week in London. Lucky bastard's made enough money to retire home.'

Roman took the joint Ardem proffered by way of greeting and tried to make a shallow inhalation appear deep.

'You wanna buy?' Ardem pulled at the mouth of an Aldi bag-for-life with a picture of English countryside fields laid out in the shape of the Union flag. Inside were a hundred transparent sachets of pills, weed and powder, dozens of blank credit cards, and a bunch of loose documents in a clear folder.

'Lost a job today,' said Roman. 'So thanks, but no.' But curiosity drew him as ever to the written word: he squinted at the papers, trying to make out their contents.

Ardem saw him. 'If you can't afford a bit of weed, you can't afford that. That's a life in there.'

'He's got some fake British passport he's trying to sell,' explained Sergey dismissively.

'I am selling it, but it's not fake and it's not British. Ukrainian guy with leave to remain in UK. Maxim Shevchenko.'

'Joe Bloggs,' said Roman in English.

'He's a blogger?' Every once in a while, Sergey showed a flash of perception that made you wonder what he'd be like without the weed. 'Like, a political blogger? That how he got leave?'

'Joe Bloggs.' Roman switched back to Ukrainian. 'It's kind of an Everyman name. Like John Smith.' That went over Sergey's head too.

'Like John Doe that they call unidentified dead bodies in American movies,' said Ardem with unnerving relish. This, Sergey understood.

'How did Shevchenko get leave to remain?' asked Roman.

'Asylum. He grassed up a friend, back home.' Ardem relished his own dramatic pause. 'That's also how he died.'

Roman's blood ran cold as he understood how Ardem had come by his wares. The only way to get your hands on a dead man's documents was to be the man who killed him. 'Anyway,' said Ardem matter-of-factly, 'you ever meet an Eastern European guy with five grand to spare for a new life, you come to me.'

Roman's heart began to beat faster, even as Sergey stroked his chin in mock thoughtfulness. 'What shall I sell, the Porsche or the Lexus?' The laughter broke the tension. Sergey blew a smoke ring, and asked, 'What happened with the job?'

'Car wash got raided.'

'Bastards.' It wasn't clear whether Sergey was talking about the police or the owners. 'They'll spring up again somewhere else.'

Ardem clapped and the watch on his wrist caught the light: a chunky rose-gold bracelet, dials within dials, a Bond-villain flash to it. He caught Roman staring, grinned and asked, 'What's the function of this watch?'

Roman recognised the tone: it was the school bully posing a riddle to which every possible answer means humiliation.

'To tell the time?' Roman offered up the answer, which was *correct* but bound to be somehow *wrong*, straight away, to get the ridicule over with.

'No, my friend! This is a device for rinsing money clean.' Ardem flexed his arm and made a fist, the better to display the watch. 'When you work the way I do, there's only one good way to get cash through customs and that's to wear it,' he said. 'This watch can buy four, five apartments in our country. The jeweller guy on the corner sorted me out. He's a good guy. Discreet. If you ever have a hundred grand you don't want the bank to know about, go see him, tell him Ardem sent you.'

A hundred thousand pounds for a watch! No wonder the jeweller kept the grille on his front window all day long.

'Good to know, man.' Roman let the joint sail around the sofa, this new information spinning in his mind. When the air got too thick, he took a glass of water out to the beer garden. If Ardem was going home, he would no more want to carry a dead man's documents through customs than a bag full of cash. Surely Roman could drive a bargain. The English expression he was looking for was *don't look a gift horse in the mouth*. He was sure he could talk his way into something that at least paid for a proper flat-share. To put more money by.

When Ardem got up for a piss, Roman saw his moment. He followed the guy into the gents' toilets and stood next to him at the filthy urinal. He thought about the downward spiral he'd been in since he got the bad news on the office steps and knew it had to end, by any means necessary.

He cleared his throat and looked Ardem in the eye. 'I have money.'

34

A beeping icon on Roman's tablet told him that an alarm had been triggered on Gabriel's Hill. After a month on the job, he was familiar with some of the properties. No. 38 was the ugliest house on the street, done up like a Greek temple: silent alarm and a note on the system to say the owners would be away all summer. Despite its pastiche exterior, 38 was a Smart House, everything controlled by timers and apps, all well and good until the wifi went down for a nanosecond and then the silent alarms went off.

The house's CCTV feed, playing on the tablet that also monitored his every move, showed no signs of burglary, but Roman put his foot down anyway. Driving to an incident, Force Patrol guards were allowed to move fast. The lanyard around Roman's neck on a black and yellow cord displayed his face but Maxim Shevchenko's name. As he turned into the tree-lined street, he had the notion that Shevchenko's spirit was somehow beside him in the passenger seat, not just forgiving Roman but actively giving him his blessing. Roman coped with what he had done by thinking of Shevchenko as a kind of victim-benefactor, rather like an organ donor. He felt relatively little guilt about stepping into the dead man's shoes, and his fear at being found out was at last beginning to subside. And, if Sergey wondered why Roman had gone from cash-in-hand work to a job that required papers and references, he was too smart, or simply too stoned, to make anything of it.

He pointed his key fob at the steel gates and they parted to let him into the Gabriel's Hill estate. If anything disturbed him, it was how easily he had made peace with spending money he'd set aside for his daughter. Zlata's money he had spent and then some, maxing out a credit card taken out in Shevchenko's name. Ardem's original price hadn't included the doctoring of Maxim's passport or his fake P45 or the references from his last job, a nightclub called Secrets in Peterborough. (Ardem had a gift for euphemism: when describing the manner of Shevchenko's death he'd said, Let's just say there were some yuppie flats being built along the waterfront in Peterborough whose foundations were part organic.) Roman was going to have to ask Saleem for a couple of weeks' grace for the next rent payment. Force Patrol paid decent money, but it would still be a good year before Roman had anything like the kind of financial cushion he needed to move out of the Jester.

The fob got Roman through the gate of No. 38. Only half the CCTV cameras swerved to observe him; there was a loose connection on the side of the house that bordered the mid-century bungalow at No. 36. Roman made a mental note to add that to his report.

Inside, Ancient Greece had been abandoned in favour of something resembling an airport hotel. The place was all marble and chrome: a chandelier the size of a small car hung from the ceiling. The staircase had a long, curved banister that Zlata would have loved to slide down. Roman tried to shut the thought down. When would it end? Not thinking about his family wasn't working. Why did his mind allow the memories in when they caused so much pain? Perhaps he should stop fighting them and try to schedule them: set aside five minutes a day for the pain, like a punishing meditation.

He looked at his watch – 3.31pm – and let himself return to Donetsk, to their old school gymnasium after hours. He and Veronika were newly engaged and taking dancing lessons from a private teacher for their wedding. Climbing frames pushed to one side of the wall; trophies and ribbons in a bookcase. Veronika in her office clothes, her hair falling out of her ponytail, both of them laughing as they tried to master the *one* two three, *one* two three of the waltz, counting the numbers in neat English syllables. He checked his watch. 3.33. Three more minutes to go. He closed his eyes again. Years later, when the marriage was going to shit, this dance, the only one he knew, was how he got out of trouble with Veronika. He would dance with her in the kitchen, sometimes with Zlata on one hip, bringing her back to the early days. In the last couple of months, when she heard his key in the lock, Zlata would come bowling into the hall of their flat and throw her little arms around his knees. 'Dance me on your feet!' she would say, and he would take off his socks so that the arch of her little feet fit perfectly across the top of his, and he would perform the steps of a waltz, dancing her into the kitchen, where Veronika would roll her eyes and laugh.

His tablet beeped an alert, releasing him early from the memory, forcing him back into work mode. He tapped a message to his digital overlords. *Property secured. Interior inspection commencing at 3.35.*

Roman patrolled the perimeter of the house, straightened out a kink in the hosepipe that was flooding into the garden next door – water wastage was not his problem – and tapped the report on to his screen. He forgot to log the broken cameras.

On starting the engine, he noticed that the water level was dangerously low. The last thing he wanted was to burn out in this heat, so he uncapped the bottle of Evian he'd been refilling with tap water for the past fortnight, and flipped the bonnet. God, these hybrid vehicles – he didn't know where to start. Roman leaned deep into the car, only his back and legs visible, and didn't hear the girl approaching until she spoke.

'Is it really you?' she said in Ukrainian. 'Oh, Max, I've missed you so much!'

35

The girl – and she really was a girl, she couldn't have been more than twenty – was as tall as him. Her beauty was unnerving: obvious, irresistibly, arousingly vulgar. She must be an immigration official, thought Roman, some kind of police honey trap. It's over, he thought. I lived as Shevchenko for a month, and then I was busted. He all but held his arms out for the cuffs.

'You are not Maxim Shevchenko.' Roman saw hope pass through disappointment on its way to anger; her bottom lip was shaking. 'Who are you?'

Roman held up his lanyard, got the strap caught in nervous fingers, and tried to bluff. 'There must be loads of Maxim Shevchenkos, even in the UK. There were two in my year at school.'

She studied it for a moment, then flicked it back against his chest.

'There cannot be two men with the same name in this same firm.' She shook her head. 'When he didn't call me, I went to Secrets. The other doormen hadn't heard from him either. That's how I *knew* he hadn't left me – something had happened to keep him away. I kept going back though and eventually someone mentioned that a company called Force Patrol had been asking about him. It's taken me days to track him – you – down, so *don't* tell me you're Maxim Shevchenko and don't take the *piss*.' She slammed a fist into the car's roof: the cameras mounted there shook. 'What happened to my fiancé and who the hell are *you*?'

Fiancé? Horror rose through Roman. Ardem had sworn blind that Shevchenko had no one to miss him. The girl's anger now gave way to tears. Roman was grateful that no one twitched their curtains on Gabriel's Hill, grateful too that she was doing all this out of the sight of the cameras on his car, and acutely aware that if he didn't start moving soon his tablet would bleep. He needed to get her away from here, and fast.

'I'm really sorry,' he said. 'My name is Roman. Maxim's dead. I've – I've taken over his identity.' Better to bludgeon her with the truth than enter into a tangle of lies.

'No. I checked. No death reported.' But she looked unsure.

'I'm sorry,' he said again, and steeled himself for fury when she made the connection. Instead, he saw only relief.

'I knew he wouldn't have left me,' she said, putting her hand to her collarbone. 'Everyone said he had, but I knew it.' Then misunderstanding rose, and she staggered backwards. 'What did you do to him?' she said.

Before he could answer, she lunged at him. He grappled with her in the street, doing a mental inventory of all the cameras on the houses: if this was being recorded anywhere then it was goodbye Force Patrol.

'You killed him!' she shouted, and then in English, 'Murder!' She looked up and down Gabriel's Hill, as though she expected a crowd to come running. For fuck's sake! Roman took the girl by the elbows and guided her, *one* two three, *one* two three, into a corner away from the cameras.

'I'm not a murderer! Shit, woman, calm down,' he said, his own panic coming out as aggression. It hadn't occurred to him that he might be considered *responsible* for Shevchenko's death. Trying to keep the girl at arm's length wasn't working – her arms were as long as his, and she was nearly as strong. In films you slapped a hysterical woman to calm her down, but that would hardly persuade her he wasn't a violent man.

'I swear, if you knew me you'd know I . . . Look, I didn't kill him but I can give you some answers. Come here.'

She swiped at him, and on impulse he drew her into an embrace that was more for restraint than comfort. It was as if he was squeezing the truth into her.

'I can't believe I'm never going to see him again! What am I going to do without him?' She cried into his shirt, smearing apricot make-up on the black cotton.

'What's your name, sweetheart?' he said, when the tears had soaked through to his skin.

'Katya,' she sniffled.

'OK, Katya. You've had a shock. We both have. Look, my shift is nearly over. I need to hand over my car but then I'll tell you everything I know. OK?'

She shook her head. Roman's tablet started to beep. He'd been stationary for too long.

'Please don't be scared. There's no need to be scared, not of me. Look, I don't know what else to say apart from you deserve some answers. I can't give you all of them but I can tell you what I know. We can sit down and have a drink, somewhere public.'

She didn't threaten to call the police, and that told him something about her own relationship with the law.

'Come on, Katya.' He held the back door open for her. Up close, he saw the red filaments in the whites of her eyes. Her toenails were polished to glossy scarlet ceramic but there were blisters between her toes where she'd walked a long way in plastic flip-flops, and as she slid into the seat he caught the gamey smell of a woman who'd spent a long, hot day in synthetic clothes. She sniffed deep and long, snot and tears rattling in her head.

Roman noted on the way out that the pedestrian gate was jammed ajar. He added that to the list in his head.

There was an upmarket pub called the Wheatsheaf just outside the Gabriel's Hill estate. Roman pulled up outside it, gave Katya a ten-pound note and told her to buy herself a large drink and wait for him in there while he handed the car keys and the tablet over to another man in the same black uniform as him.

The Wheatsheaf was dark inside, with a welcome churchy coldness, wood panelling and velvet seats. Unlike Roman's neighbourhood, Gabriel's Hill was the kind of area that could accommodate what the British called a gastropub. Katya sat in front of two empty glasses – she'd made fast work of his money – in the darkest nook, make-up and perfume reapplied. There was a part of Roman, a lonely, tragic part, that, even in the grip of panic, enjoyed the buzz of being seen out with a girl like this.

She didn't bother with small talk. 'You say you didn't kill him. So tell me, how do you have his things?'

Over more drinks than he could count and certainly more than he could afford, Roman gave her everything he knew about Shevchenko and as much of his own background as he dared. Veronika and Zlata he kept to himself, as was his duty, as was his burden.

He found that Katya had been expecting Shevchenko's death: that it was the false hope of 'finding' him she was coming down from, rather than shock. She didn't know Ardem by name but she knew that Maxim had been involved with some 'high-risk men'.

'I mean – are you thinking of reporting Ardem?' asked Roman nervously. 'He's gone home now. All I have is a first name.'

'Ardem wouldn't have been his real name!' Her laughter was contemptuous. 'Max said this little island wasn't big enough to hide in. He *said* they would catch up with him.' For a moment she got a romantic, glazed look in her eyes and Roman wondered if the dangerous company Max kept had been part of the attraction. 'He did it for me, you know. For us. Said it was worth the risk to buy us our first place together. Said that once you owned a little piece of England, you'd made it. *Christ*. The things men do for their women.'

'The things we do,' said Roman, thinking only *the things we don't do. The things we should have done*. 'I'm sorry he's dead, and I'm sorry that you got your hopes up again because of me. Have you got work?'

She splayed her beautiful hands with clear pride: long, pale pink nails filed to a tip. 'I'm a nail artist. Spend all day filing and polishing lazy English bitches who talk over my head like I'm not there, for a boss who would work me 24/7 if he could get away with it.' She noticed him staring at her left hand. 'I sold my ring to pay for the Eurobus.'

With a sense of millstone obligation, Roman listened to Katya's story. She and Maxim had worked together back in Kyiv. Always ambitious, always keen to make something of himself, he'd got in too deep with a local gang, fled to England where the authorities had taken him in. Once he was settled, Katya had come to Peterborough on a coach, four days in a hard seat next to a man eating hard-boiled eggs, but she hadn't cared, because he would be waiting for her. Maxim didn't want her to work, but she wanted everything to be just right, so she'd got herself a little job in a nail bar, cash in hand, to save up for a dress, hand-made in China, *encrusted* with crystals, a fifth of the price you'd pay in a London boutique. She'd already measured herself for it. She showed him the website, the order sitting in her basket waiting for the click to confirm. Once they were married her job would have been to care for Maxim. He'd been going to find a way around her lack of papers; he was a clever man, Maxim – not book-clever but money-clever. He knew people who could made fake credit cards from real ones and by the time the banks worked out what was going on you'd spent ten thousand pounds. They'd been going to buy a little flat, Katya went on: there were some new-build waterfront flats in Peterborough; they'd been going to have a balcony.

Roman didn't tell her what he knew about their foundations.

Then one day Maxim hadn't come home from work. Katya had been evicted from the room they shared; now she was working in London, painting nails for slave wages and sharing a room with eight other girls, stacked like spices in a rack in teetering IKEA bunk beds.

Roman drank steadily, miserably, tuning in and out of her monologue, only snapping back to reality when her leg slid between his.

'Take me home with you.' Her breath sparkled with sugary wine; her lips looked soft as a bed. 'I've been so lonely.' Loneliness: an ugly state only the very beautiful could admit to. Her bare foot worked its way up Roman's thigh to his groin; she felt him stiffen against the sole and smiled. 'Please. I just want to be close to someone.'

The lounge bar at the Jester was like a sauna. Laughter coasted on hot air from the beer garden out the back. Katya followed Roman to his cubicle and stripped without ceremony, talons clicking against the buttons on her dress. The sun burned through the leaded lights and cast shadows, red, gold and green, tulips and trumpets on her perfect skin. Roman tried not to think about the way Veronika's flesh had always yielded its welcome. The last time he'd been with a woman, they had both had the sponginess of parents. Maybe that's for the best, he thought, as his shaking hand found its way on to Katya's breast. I am not the same man as I was at home.

She made all the right noises, all the right moves, but she kept her eyes closed throughout, only opening them as he neared his finish. When she looked at him, she flashed first horror and then disappointment, and her eyes filled with tears. She was pretending I was him, Roman realised. He tried to withdraw – he couldn't keep fucking a crying woman – but he was past the point of no return. After he was done, she rolled from under him and turned to face the wall, leaving Roman with a bitter aftertaste and the feeling that some kind of terrible contract, the terms of which he did not yet understand, had just been signed.

—

36

The hours had crawled by as Roman lay awake on the edge of his single mattress, Katya's body clammy beside him. He'd escaped a couple of times in the night, to piss and to drink water from the communal kitchen tap. Both times on his return she had been sleep-slack and naked, her perfect form sour and oily on top of the sheet. Roman crouched on the floor, torn between wanting her again simply because she was there, and wanting her gone. He had heard men talk about the way you want a woman to leave after sex, but that had never been his experience until now. He wanted to see Katya and her grief get on a train and never come back. Instead of desire, he felt a sickening weight settle on him. What if she wanted a relationship with him? He knew it was groundless, but he felt that by taking on Shevchenko's identity he had somehow absorbed the man's responsibilities. There was an equally illogical sense that, having let down Veronika and Zlata, he couldn't let this girl down too.

Katya woke up at five and, to Roman's relief, covered herself with the sheet.

'The Tubes start running in ten minutes,' he said. 'I'll walk you to the station.'

She'd told him that she lived and worked five postcodes away, in a part of London Force Patrol didn't cover, so once she was gone he need never see her again.

They had the street to themselves, the only other human a driver helming an empty bus, who craned his neck to get a better view of Katya and had to swerve to avoid a traffic island.

'I won't be able to see you again until Saturday,' said Katya, as the Underground came into view. Roman's stride faltered but she didn't notice. 'I only get one and a half days off a week. We can talk about what to do then.'

What the fuck? 'What do you mean, what to do?'

She turned her almond eyes to his. 'I can't stay in that crappy job, sleeping in that crappy room with all the other girls. I need to get my life back on track and I can't do that without your help.'

At the station, staff unlocked the grilles for the first commuters of the day. Roman touched his card on to the barrier, trying not to think about the cost, and followed her down to the platform.

'There's nobody for me at home and God knows there's no money. But here – it was supposed to be the dream. I was supposed to be in a nice flat now.' Her lower lip wobbled. 'I was supposed to be a *wife*.'

He felt a wave of pity for her that was quickly overlaid by horror at what he thought she might be suggesting.

'I can't – we can't – I can't *marry* you, Katya.' He was going to tell her he was already married; even though death had released him from that contract, he was still willing to use Veronika to get out of this. Then he remembered that of course Roman Pavluk might already be married but Maxim Shevchenko wasn't.

'Oh, no. I don't want *you*.' She said it with anger rather than scorn. 'It's not like men are interchangeable, is it? No offence, but with you it wasn't exactly . . .' Wasn't exactly what? The flare of paranoia momentarily distracted Roman. 'But you know people, don't you, who can help me stay here? You clearly know the kind of person who can get a fake ID. That's what I want. A name. A life.'

The wind that blew through the tunnels was as hot as air from a hairdryer. Christ. Did she really think that he moved in the same circles as her ex? That he could hold his own in a world of night-club bouncers and dodgy dealers? Could she not tell from talking to him, from *sleeping* with him, that he was not that kind of man?

'Katya, no, listen, that was a one-off. I wouldn't know where to begin with something like that. I'm not a criminal, I just . . .' He was about to say I just got lucky but realised in time how that would sound: as though Shevchenko's death had been nothing more than a happy accident for him. 'It was just a one-in-a-million chance that I met the guy who set this up. He's gone home; he's not in London any more. Look, I'm sorry.' His voice betrayed the weakness she had clearly recognised in him at first sight. 'For everything you've lost. I wish I could help you. But I'm barely surviving myself.'

One metre behind and two metres below her, the tracks buzzed dangerously.

'Please.' She made Bambi eyes at him. 'I really feel like you owe me?'

So she too thought he had a duty towards her. He could almost feel Shevchenko's elbow on his ribs, nudging him to do the right thing.

'I mean, I'll do what I can,' he said, 'but what *can* I do?'

'*Thank* you,' said Katya, but it was the cold, exhausted thanks of someone who has at last persuaded their unreasonable opponent to see their point of view. 'You know, I feel like maybe in a way he sent you to me, sort of from above? Almost like a guardian angel?'

The fact that Roman had thought something similar didn't stop him realising how stupid it sounded, spoken aloud.

'All Maxim could get me into was shitty nightclubs. You can get me into rich people's houses.'

Again he was a few beats behind her. 'Why would you want to get into—' he began, and then her words took their meaning. 'Do you want to *steal from my clients*? How's that going to change your life, except for getting us both arrested and deported?'

'But I can't live like this any more.' Her voice carried; the other passengers' heads swivelled their way. 'You said you would *help* me.'

'I meant I would . . .' He trailed off. He didn't know what he had meant. He had just been saying words to calm a hysterical woman down.

'Not stealing money,' she said. 'That wouldn't be right. But I was awake all night.'

You were? thought Roman. He must have slept after all.

'I was thinking about how you got the documentation to stay and I didn't, and I was thinking there must be a way I can do this. Not money. A name. A life. You can do it with credit cards. All you need is the numbers. This was Maxim's plan for me, Roman. Find some woman who could stay here and then I could *become* her; we could've got married without any hassle.' She unlocked her phone and showed him a report she'd found on the *Kyiv Globe* website about identity fraud. 'This is what Maxim did. You just make yourself a clone of someone who already exists. How hard can it be? And I told you yesterday, the banks give people compensation for it. So your precious clients would be safe.'

Roman didn't see how that could work; surely the 'clone' was traceable, and what if at some point the victim and the impostor met? And also, in this case, there was the question of the deception itself.

'It won't work, Katya.' He found he was using the gentle voice he used to adopt in the early stages of negotiation with Zlata about a second ice-cream or an extended bedtime. 'You have an accent. Won't it look a bit suspicious, you living as Sarah Smith or whatever? *And* they'd need to be white. This is London; those properties are owned by families from all over the world. You're hardly going to convince as a Patel or an Abdullah.'

'There must be a way.' She all but stamped her foot. 'I *have* to.'

The indicator overhead told them the train was due. In sixty seconds she would be carried to the other side of London, and knowing that made it easier for him to give her a categorical no.

'I can't do it, Katya. I wish you well. I'm sorry.'

The hot breeze ran cooler as the train approached. Her face mirrored the regret he felt.

'No, *I'm* sorry,' she said. The train slid sideways behind her and the doors opened. 'I wanted you to help me because you wanted to, not because you *had* to.'

Fuck her, trying to guilt-trip him. His patience and sympathy expired. 'I'm sorry about your fiancé. I really am. But I don't *have* to do anything for you.'

'I'll meet you in the Wheatsheaf on Saturday at 9pm.'

'No. I won't be there.'

Katya stepped backwards on to the train. 'I think you will.'

As the doors slid closed in front of her, she drew from her handbag Roman's yellow wallet that contained his Ukrainian passport and driving licence. It also contained, tucked into a slit in the lining, the only physical photograph he had of Zlata and Veronika, and it was this, rather than the blackmail implicit in Katya's possession of his papers, that had him banging his on the dirty scratched glass of the train door as it pulled away. Roman watched it disappear, the tail-lights swallowed by the tunnel.

He could resist a guilt-trip, but hard evidence of his crime? That was different. He felt hotter than he had since the heatwave began, the sweltering, suffocating feeling of being trapped in another man's skin.

37

At the bleep of the Force Patrol key fob, the iron gates slid open and the baked black tar of Gabriel's Hill rose between banks of yellowing trees. Katya sat beside Roman in the passenger seat, out of sight of the cameras, ready for her house-to-house sales calls in her work uniform, a black nylon tunic worn over cropped trousers. A little wheeled case packed with the tiny bottles of her trade clinked in the back seat. She tapped constantly at her phone, which he suspected probably held photographs of his Maxim Shevchenko ID as well as the contents of his yellow wallet: same face, different names. She had all the dirt she would ever need on him. Her phone was a loaded gun. He'd worked out the code from glancing in the rear-view mirror; 959595. Roman would go through the phone if he could, see just what she had on him, but she never put the bloody thing down.

At the top of the hill she said, 'Drop me here.'

Her case rolled over the smooth paving stones. Roman drove ahead, keeping her in his rear-view mirror rather than driving along behind her where the camera might pick her up. His plan, inasmuch as he had one, was to humour her for a couple of days. Katya was bright but unschooled. Her grasp of the Western alphabet was shaky. Her little scam would never get off the ground.

She stood now before the vast gates of one of the mock-Tudor houses, finger on the buzzer. To his surprise the gates parted to let her in. He made three slow circuits of the estate, turning things over in his mind. If he hadn't bought Maxim Shevchenko's identity, Katya never would have found him. The British said that ignorance was bliss but Katya had hardly been in bliss before she'd found him, more a state of great agitation, stalking and waiting and asking, fixating on the life she had lost to ease the pain of the love she had lost.

He understood it, in a way. Anyone who had lived on the contact line in Ukraine knew that grief made you mad, made you cling desperately to the wreckage of your before. There was a widow everyone called Baba Sofia on the ground floor of their old block in Donetsk who'd lost her only son in a shelling but still set the table for him every night. If you saw Baba Sofia in the supermarket she'd show you the basket full of beetroot and sorrel she'd got in to make her son *borsch* just the way he liked it: he was working hard, he needed a good hot meal to come home to. Roman had always wondered what happened to Baba Sofia when she went home. Did she have a conversation with an empty place setting? Scrape the uneaten food into the bin? Veronika had tried to help her, showing her the newspaper reports of her son's death, but she seemed to think the story was commending him for bravery, as though the letters themselves were reforming to confirm the story she was telling herself. Zlata, only four at the time, had said, 'Why don't you just pretend with her, if she's happy?' and that was what they had all done.

And now Katya was channelling her grief for her fiancé into creating the life they had been due to live together. Roman was merely the enabler, indulging her fantasy.

On his fourth circuit, Roman saw Katya sitting on a low front wall, rubbing her feet. He parked facing the Greek Temple's gates but out of the sightlines of its cameras. Katya popped the boot herself and threw in her case: a hundred tiny bottles of nail polish clinked. Sunburn was rosy on her forearm, but her face remained a flawless vellum and her eyebrows held their shape, perfect corners sharp as knives. She was all smiles as she sank into the seat next to him and pressed her face into the air-con vent.

'The only people who answer the doors round here are servants,' she said. 'I made thirty pounds, though. Gave a shape-and-polish to some housekeeper around the corner.' She looked more than thirty pounds' worth of happy, and he soon found out why.

'Anyway, I got one lead. That one there.' She pointed to the house that crouched low in the landscape, No. 36. 'Single woman, a cripple, all bent over on walking sticks. And she was mean as hell: she stood on her doorstep and said she couldn't afford a pedicure but she had cash lying around the house. There must have been a thousand pounds. Also, she's lazy or mad or something. She hasn't opened her mail for God knows how long; there was this giant pile of letters. You could take half her post and she still wouldn't notice.'

Roman felt the hairs on his arms rise in warning. *Was* this grief? It looked a lot like greed.

'And the best thing about her is her name. Look her up, find out how many people live there.'

She leaned forward in the passenger seat, turned up the air-conditioning as high as it would go while Roman tapped the address '36 Gabriel's Hill' into his tablet.

'Ava Kirilova,' he read aloud. 'She's registered as sole occupant.' The client had, Roman noted, purchased the Basic Protection package, not yet upgraded to a Smart House. There was a Union flag next to her name.

'What does this mean?' said Katya, pointing to it.

'Means the client's a British national,' he said without think-ing. 'So many of our properties are owned by foreign nationals that we—'

'She is British?' Katya's voice leapt an octave. 'Then this is a *gift*!'

'I don't see the significance.'

'*Ava. Kirilova*,' she said, putting on a Russian accent. 'You're right, I couldn't pass as an English girl. But I could be Ava Kirilova, I could go out in the world as Ava Kirilova, looking and sounding the way I do. No one would question that.'

'Kirilova is a Russian name,' he said automatically, ever the teacher.

She sighed, long and low. 'Do you really think these people round here know the difference between Russian and Ukrainian? Do you know how many countries I've been told to fuck off back home to since I've been here? Poland, Lithuania, Albania, Romania?'

Get the fuck away from my kids, you cockroach.

He felt a brief unwelcome kinship with Katya.

'Yes,' he said. 'I know.'

'Did I tell you that this morning there was mouse shit in my shoes? This is not the life my Maxim promised me. And look, this woman is worth millions of pounds. Even if the bank didn't pick up the tab for this kind of fraud, people like that can buy themselves out of any little trouble. All it needs is someone to get inside, pick up some of that mail, and bring it back to me.'

The storm had passed; she was calm again, rational even. Roman pictured some old divorcee or widow wondering how to spend her millions. It was horrible, but, as Katya said, if they were going to target someone it should at least be a person who could afford it.

The freezing air was drying out his throat. He turned down the dial on the air-conditioning. 'But you said she didn't even let you in the house,' he reminded her.

'That's true. I'm a very good judge of character, I can tell when someone doesn't trust me. And why should she? Some Eastern European beautician turning up on her doorstep in cheap shitty clothes.'

Roman kept his eyes on the road, licked his parched lips. It was 5pm, and away from the enclave of Gabriel's Hill the roads were clogged with rush-hour traffic.

'You know what else I can tell about her? She's lonely. I recognise *that* when I see it.' She let that hang in the air for a moment. 'I tell you who she *would* trust. Someone in a proper uniform, someone she thinks is there to look after her. She would let *you* in.'

38

Roman tried to talk himself into it.

Ava Kirilova was an old woman. The guys at the Jester said that old people in this country were the richest of all and none of them had even had to work for it. The guys at Force Patrol said that by the time you got rich enough to afford their services, you could afford to be burgled. Still, the idea sickened him.

He drove past No. 36 Gabriel's Hill extra slowly the following morning. A young woman left the house, swinging between two crutches, a black and red bag bouncing on her hip. Katya had made it sound as if Ava Kirilova were a crone shuffling towards the grave. She wore her hair the way the Ukrainian women did for May Day parades, a long plait wound in a coronet around the top of her head. A memory assailed him, jolting his focus away from the street: Veronika trying to braid a three-year-old Zlata's wispy hair, laughing and saying, 'Her hair's like smoke! I can barely touch it!' and all three of them laughing as the braid fell apart in her hands. He automatically looked at the clock: 9.30am. He set his hands on the wheel and allowed himself to spend five minutes with his little girl. When he opened his eyes, they were dry, but he'd gripped the wheel so tightly his knuckles had turned to pearls.

Ava Kirilova was long gone.

He drove on, thinking hard. If his target, for want of a better word, was out for the day, he could not knock on her door on some spurious pretext, enter the house and leave empty-handed. It was a charade he had to go through so that he could convincingly lie to Katya that he had tried and failed. Besides, she might be watching him: the previous evening she had turned up unannounced in Millbrook Green to 'check on his progress'. Katya kept a closer watch on him than even his employers.

An hour later, and no closer to knowing what to do, he saw Ava Kirilova dragging herself up the hill. The muscles on the backs of her skinny arms pumped and her toned back rippled. She might be injured but she was in shape, a specific London rich-woman yoga shape. At the car wash they had called them the yoga bunnies and, if they could get away with it, charged them a few pounds extra and pocketed the difference. There was a studio near the Jester that charged £30 a class.

The woman he was looking at now didn't look rich, with her grimy skin and her shabby tote bag, but when she spoke it was to demand a favour of him, as if he was her personal chauffeur.

'I don't suppose you could drive me a hundred metres up the hill?' she asked, and, when he protested, 'Surely they wouldn't begrudge you helping me out. *Please.*'

Her accent threw him as much as the request. He'd been expecting a Russian inflection but Ava Kirilova's voice was from a BBC costume drama, clipped and precise and slightly superior. Just the kind of person he had always been desperate to impress – and the kind of person who in this new context despised him.

He relented and let her into his car. Up close she was pinched and pert. Her face didn't fit magazine-beauty standards like Katya's and she had none of Veronika's welcoming dimples.

'This is so nice,' she said. 'I've had a terrible day. I was mugged. Lost all my money . . .' even as her bag fell open on her lap to display a bottle of water, a tube of sunscreen and at least three loose twenty-pound notes, each one a day's wages at the car wash or a single cocktail at the Wheatsheaf. It was true, then: she had money floating around. Contempt surged inside Roman for this sheltered woman who couldn't even get herself home without her phone and her credit card.

You could tell she had grown up in huge privilege: there was a helpless quality you saw in women who had had everything go their way since childhood. The kind of woman it was easy to take advantage of, who would think nothing of letting a man in uniform in to check the locks, re-set the alarm.

She had taken him by surprise, that was the problem. He drove so slowly that the car almost slid back down the hill, and then they were at her front door. Offer to help her into the house, he thought, but he was paralysed in his seat, even as she struggled with the key, even as she got the door open and he saw the piled-up post on the hallway table. No matter how heartbroken Katya was, no matter what trouble she was in financially because of her bereavement, Roman could not bring himself to steal from a private home. Katya would—

Roman touched his forehead to the steering wheel. He had to get out of this mindset, thinking of Katya as though she were a criminal mastermind. She was grieving and alone and he knew the desperate places *that* could take you. But really, she had only ever brushed up against organised crime. She was as clueless as he was. What harm would it do to slip in after Ava Kirilova now, to sleight-of-hand a gas bill and give it to Katya? He might as well write a poem on a blank sheet for all that she would be able to do with it.

Roman unclicked his seatbelt and killed the engine. But the huge front door had swung shut, and his opportunity had gone.

39

Two days had passed since Roman had given Ava Kirilova a lift. He was drinking more, heading straight for the pub to spend money he didn't have, money he owed other men, after every shift. He had stuff to do – today was laundry day, for example, and he'd rolled up his fusty sleeping bag and packed all his clothes in a holdall this morning, to drop at the launderette halfway between Gabriel's Hill and the Jester on the way home from his day shift – but the Wheatsheaf had thrown open the doors and the beer pumps glistened in the dark interior, beckoning him towards them. A single pint would cost the same as a service wash but he was helpless against the siren call of a cold beer.

He sat in the shade at a pavement table, wanting his beer to last but losing his thirst as it warmed up. His phone buzzed in his pocket: Katya. *Any luck with the skinny bitch?*

'Fuck's sake,' he muttered in English. Anyone else would have realised by now that this was a fruitless endeavour but Katya was only becoming more fixated. He went to delete the text but his phone slipped in his sweaty hand and hit the pavement. A black hole like a cigarette burn appeared in one corner of the screen. That was *all* he needed. He frowned, put the phone back in his pocket and wondered how long he could stall her. A hundred metres away, the familiar sound of the gates opening drew his eyes. A huge black people-carrier emerged, Addison Lee sticker on the window, driver in a suit and tie. Alone in the back, in a fuel-hungry vehicle big enough for seven people, rode Ava Kirilova, clearly returned to her old lifestyle after having been mugged the other day. She was silhouetted against tinted windows and look-ing in the other direction, but she was familiar to him already, the way she carried her small head on her long neck with a dancer's poise; the way she wore her hair, twisted on top of her head like a girl in a May Day parade. The car idled for a while at the junction then turned left towards central London.

She must be going out for the night. So much for her being destitute after her mugging. Perhaps she was one of those people who thought 'poor' meant 'just the one holiday this year'. People in this part of London had no fucking idea.

Roman took another sip and mindlessly slid some icons around his phone to test the screen. There were only four numbers stored: Force Patrol head office, two drivers, and now Katya. He deliberately kept his screensaver impersonal. It would be torture to see Veronika and Zlata every time he needed to answer a message. He checked the weather app, appalled to see that the temperature was set to climb again the following day.

What should he tell Katya? He could go there now, while the house was empty, and get – what? Proof that he *couldn't* get into the house? Photographic evidence? It almost didn't matter. He had started to wonder if what Katya really wanted was just reassurance that he was doing something. She didn't want him to commit a crime so much as to pay her back for Shevchenko's murder.

I'm going there now, he wrote back. He had to tap the cracked screen hard to send the message, and the black hole expanded. He gave himself an hour – the length of, say, a facial or a massage – to finish his drink, taking just a millimetre off with every sip. If Ava Kirilova hadn't returned by the bottom of the glass, it meant she was out for the night and the house would be his to explore.

Beer dispatched, he threw his bag over his shoulder and let himself in to Gabriel's Hill through the pedestrian gate. Sweat streamed off him as he climbed the hill, sticking his shirt to his back. As he passed the Greek Temple, something on the pavement caught his eye: a black feather, something from a child's Hallowe'en costume. I'll save that for Zlata, he thought, and he'd tucked it into the side pocket of his holdall before he remembered. He stumbled but didn't fall.

As far as he could see, No. 36 was empty. The huge front lawn was easy to access but the rear of the property was walled off and the side gate was locked. He took advantage of the blind spot on the near side of No. 38, and slipped through the fence and along the side of the house, witnessed only by the statues: the sea god Poseidon with his trident, Artemis the huntress with her bow pointing straight at him. Medusa, with her writhing head of snakes, was there too, in the form of an elaborate bronze shower-head built into one wall of the house. Suddenly the heat and stickiness overwhelmed Roman and clean skin became the most desirable thing in the world. He threw his sleeping bag on to the ground, where it unfurled, and dropped his holdall beside it.

He stripped completely, skin finally able to breathe after ten hours in his uniform. There was a weird violet glitter all over his hands from the feather: he soaped it away. Ironically, given that he was in the open air, he had a greater sense of privacy than he had felt in months. A sense of absolute solitude.

An illusion which vanished with the smashing of glass on stone.

Whoever he had seen in the taxi, it had not been Ava Kirilova, because here she was now, peering through roses and laurel leaves, the whites of her eyes ringing flared pupils. How could he have been so stupid? Just another yoga bunny, that was who he'd seen. *Khuy.*

He gathered up his trousers to cover himself, hoping that if he was quick enough at least she wouldn't be able to record the evidence of his indecent exposure before she called the police. But she didn't produce a phone to call the police or Force Patrol, just looked from him to his bag and back again.

'You're *living* here!' Panic sluiced his veins with ice. He trawled his mental library for a comeback, a criminal mastermind's cover story, but drew blank after blank. She brought her hand to her breastbone. 'Oh, my *God*,' she said, but with compassion: someone was speaking to him like a human being for the first time since he came to this country. There was an understanding in her misunderstanding: a connection that cast a line out to his heart.

'Money,' he said. 'They will sack me if they know about this. I *need* my job.'

Dammit. That made him sound more dangerous, more desperate. Still she didn't scream or threaten. Instead, she introduced herself as Juliet. She was not the client after all, only a house-sitter. When she had said she'd lost all her money, she had meant it.

Juliet. It suited her better than Ava.

Only after she went back into the house did Roman realise how coolly clever she had been. She was biding her time, until she could lock the door behind her and then call the police. He grabbed his things and, crossing and re-crossing the road to avoid the cameras, he ran down the hill. The gradient gave him so much extra momentum that when he reached the gates he felt he could have smashed his way right through them.

40

He kept running until the heat broke his stride. He caught sight of himself in a shop window and recoiled from the angry stranger in the glass: red in the face and pouring with sweat, he looked every inch the escaped convict. He might as well be wearing an orange jumpsuit as his black uniform.

Khuy. *Khuy.*

The bus he caught to the Jester was packed and smelly, bodies obstructing the feeble breeze, but Roman, drenched and deranged, got two seats to himself. What a vehicle for his last ride as a free man. Most of the passengers were on their phones, conversations in half a dozen languages from every continent. He surveyed them to see if anyone looked like they might understand Ukrainian – he didn't know how, but he could spot a countryman at a glance – and when he was satisfied that he wouldn't be understood, he called Katya. He had to be creative, turning the smashed-up phone on its side to make the call.

'What did you get?' she greeted him.

Roman drew a fortifying breath. 'We can't do it. It won't work.'

'But it *has* to work.' He knew the face that would be accompanying her voice as it cracked, the smooth skin puckering around the chin. 'Roman. I'll never have an opportunity like this again. She's the perfect target.'

The bus idled at a red light and instantly became a mobile sauna. 'No, hear me out. The reason it's not going to work is because it's not her house. That woman you saw, the one with the walking sticks – she isn't the client. It's not her property. She's just some poor English girl house-sitting. She's barely got any more money than us.'

'But the actual client, Ava Kirilova, is British too.' She breathed reverence into the word, all Shevchenko's promises wrapped up in it. 'She has a British passport. She doesn't have to work for slave wages. She can *stay*.'

Roman thought about the British Deliveroo boys who sometimes crashed in the Jester for a week or two, sleeping on the sofas for a few pounds a night. To be British was no guarantee of untold riches, but he knew what Katya meant, and knew too that she treasured the delusion because it was all she had left of her fiancé.

'The point is,' he said, 'it's not the victimless crime you thought it was. This girl would get the blame; she might get prosecuted. It's not fair. She's not rich.' (Of course he couldn't add that he needed to keep Juliet sweet: she could still report him for trespass and worse.) 'Come *on*, Katya. Just leave it. Move on.'

'And do *what*?'

He wanted to scream at her: *it's not my fucking problem!* But the kompromat Katya had on him made Juliet's leverage fade to nothing.

He couldn't read the silence on the line until Katya's tears bubbled up.

'I'm sorry, it's just that I'm going *crazy*. I don't *want* to steal, I don't want it to happen this way. I just can't stand it any more in here, Roman. I can't sleep in that room with all those other girls; there's no air. When I think about the life I was supposed to have with my Maxim . . . It breaks my heart, it actually hurts my chest. It's in my lungs – I can't *breathe*.'

'I'm sorry.'

He said it automatically – it was just what you said when someone was distressed or bereaved – but Katya said, '*Thank* you,' the same way she had before, as though she was accepting his apology for the whole situation. 'Please try one more time.'

'If I rush into something stupid I'll get sacked, and then I'll be no use to you.' For all he knew, he had only hours left in his job anyway. Force Patrol had his address at the Jester; there might be a police car waiting on the forecourt to arrest him for indecent exposure. 'Give me time.'

Katya cut the call. Roman wondered how long *give me time* would work. The bus passed a bookmaker's. Roman wished he could predict the future: what little money he had, he would place on a horse, give his winnings to Katya, ease his conscience and get her out of his life, two birds with one stone. Surely there must be a sum that would be worth more to her than a new name. Surely there was a number that would get her off his back. Everyone had their price.

There was no marked car waiting outside the Jester. Perhaps Juliet was waiting until she was sure he was far away before calling the police. Perhaps the police were only now on the phone to Force Patrol. With shaking hands, Roman washed his clothes in the scum-rimmed sink before hanging them out to dry over the old Schweppes crates that littered the beer garden. A new resident who didn't appear to speak English offered him a joint as a greeting. They smoked it in companionable silence. When they were dry, he folded the trousers and shirts into squares and set them out on the floor in his airless cubicle. He lay on the mattress, braced for the sirens, for the knock on the door.

Morning painted the Jester in stained-glass colours. Roman had not been arrested or – he checked his shattered phone – sacked. Juliet had, it seemed, kept her word and her silence. She would have let me in on any pretext, thought Roman, as he dressed in his black uniform. I could have taken what Katya wanted and she wouldn't have noticed. Gratitude quickly turned to frustration and concern at her naïvete. She shouldn't have done that, he thought on the bus to Millbrook Green. She shouldn't trust me, he thought as he took the car keys from a colleague.

All the more reason to take advantage of Juliet.

All the more reason not to.

He turned the situation over and over in his mind as he drove the bland, new-build streets of Millbrook Green. His remit was to watch the houses, look out for intruders, but after half an hour Roman couldn't have told you which streets he had driven along or what he had seen. At the end of his shift, the guard he handed the card to said, 'Where's your lanyard, mate? They'll come down on you like a ton of bricks if they know you've forgotten it.'

Even as he felt for it around his neck, his mind's eye showed it to him, swinging from the shower where he'd left it, evidence of the sackable offence of his trespass.

It took ninety minutes and three buses to cross London. In the Greek Temple garden, the sprinklers rained down on lush green grass. Roman tiptoed through them to retrieve the lanyard. He wound the strap around the card and pocketed it. He was edging back to freedom when he saw her, smiling across the fence.

'Maxim?'

He should have nodded and walked away. But she was the first person to see him in so long, and he was so hungry that his belly growled an answer that made her smile. What harm could it do to join her for a meal?

41

'I should get to sleep,' he said, astonished to find it was gone midnight. His belly was distended with the strange, mismatched food that Juliet had served him. Curry and vodka, a smoothie with a straw in it. It was like something a child would assemble from a buffet. For someone with no money, Juliet had strange shopping habits: expensive pre-prepared meals that Veronika would have made for a fraction of the price. She regarded the oven as she might the flight deck of a spaceship.

'I'll see you out,' she said, heaving herself on to her crutches with the strong arms that now made sense.

'Thank you for the lovely food,' he said with a straight face.

At night, the huge palms and yuccas were lit up like a Hollywood film set. Roman could see that the lighting had been carefully designed to bounce off the rippling surface of the pool. As it was, it made pale splodges on the blue tarpaulin that covered it. Why doesn't she swim? he thought, and only then understood quite how helpless she was with that bad leg.

'Safe journey home,' she said, and for a moment he wondered how she knew he'd missed the last direct bus back to the Jester, but then he caught her smile and realised that of course she didn't know, she was making a joke about his brief journey over the fence.

'Thank you. I think I will find my way. Goodnight, Juliet.'

'Goodnight,' she said. He felt self-conscious and clumsy as he climbed through the shrubbery and then vaulted the fence.

He sat in the statuary until he was sure she had gone to bed. It would be a long walk back to the Jester now and he was back on shift here at Gabriel's Hill at nine, only eight hours away. He might as well sleep in the garden for real. His sleeping bag was at the Jester, but the grass was soft enough. Actually? It was alright here. Quieter than the Jester and, with the roses, and the jasmine coiling from a nearby urn, far more fragrant.

What an odd, interesting person Juliet was, and in a very different way from his first impressions. All his presumptions from that time in the car were now recast. Then, he had thought her a spoiled rich girl. As she'd talked about her life as a dancer this evening, he'd seen the same qualities but viewed them differently. She had been stunted rather than spoiled, kept helpless since girlhood by her school and then her dance company. He respected dancers' training and dedication, of course he did, but the stories in ballet were hard to grasp and boring, and the performances seemed designed to exclude anyone who didn't already know the background. Give him a thriller any day. As for this Mr K guy, calling his dancers *creatures* . . . he sounded more like a cult leader than a ballet teacher.

Too wired to sleep, he tried to look up the London Russian Ballet Company on his phone, but the dead pixels had spread like spilt ink behind the spiderwebbed glass. Only the home button worked. A new screen would be a hundred pounds, and he had less than that to last the fortnight to the next payday.

He didn't need to be an expert on ballet to see what it had meant to her: her voice changed when she spoke about what she had lost, as though someone had their hands around her throat.

'*I'm* a missing piece,' she had said, echoing the way he had felt his whole life.

Something in Juliet's vulnerability held the door open for his.

A text from Katya with its signature beep landed on his screen. He couldn't read it or reply and there was relief in that. He set his phone face-down and lay on his back. It was a cloudless night. Light pollution dulled the stars but he liked knowing that they were there, even if he couldn't see them. The full moon glowed, strange pinks and golds: a peach, ripe for the picking.

42

After three evenings eating cut-price sandwiches along with left-overs with Juliet, and four nights sleeping under the watchful eyes of Poseidon and Artemis, Roman returned to the Jester to pick up a change of clothes and run his electric razor over his head.

On the bus, he had space to think about Katya. She was now rapid-cycling between heartbroken and calculating, the only consistency her conviction that they must throw Juliet to the wolves and press on with stealing Ava Kirilova's identity. If she knew he was spending this time here, that he had been in the house, walked past stacks of unopened post on the way to the bathroom and not touched any of it, she would lose her temper; she might make that call to the police and he would be on the first flight back to Ukraine.

And Juliet: it would break her.

Their strange friendship was based on a lie that was based on a lie. But there was a deeper connection there, something about her that he recognised: a reserve, a sadness, a burden too heavy to share. It was grief, of course; they had both lost the most important thing in their lives. But there was a dark current flowing below the grief, specific yet intangible.

He couldn't get her laugh out of his head. They had been eating reduced petrol-station baguettes and he'd made a stupid joke about superpowers. Laughter changed Juliet's face. It was like watching dust sheets shaken off the statues in a shuttered mansion. It changed her from plain to beautiful. I did that, he thought, as the bus disgorged him on to the foul pavement outside the Jester. His heart sank at the thought of the smelly men inside. Do I miss her? he wondered. He knew only that he wanted to *talk* to Juliet, to tell her about Veronika and Zlata. The words were always crouched and ready to go on his tongue: I had a family, Juliet. I had a wife and child in Ukraine and because of my haste and my cowardice they are dead. I am not the man you think I am, in any sense.

Better to let Juliet get to know him as Max Shevchenko. Roman Pavluk didn't deserve her. Better still, forget thinking in these terms at all. Forget thinking in terms of this being an actual friendship you can pursue. She is someone whose life has briefly crossed yours, he thought, and, once you've got Katya off your back, you need never see her again.

He was entirely unconvincing, even to himself.

The Jester stank of unemptied bins and body odour. Saleem was in the lounge bar, reading a three-day-old *Evening Standard* in only his shorts.

He looked up. 'Roman! You're a dark horse, brother.'

For a moment, Roman couldn't remember what dark horse meant – whether it was as sinister as it sounded or a term of endearment. 'Oh, yes?' he hedged.

'Your bird's here. She's fit. Like, *porno* fit.' Saleem described an hourglass with his hands while his face expressed utter bewilderment that such a woman should seek out Roman.

Roman only knew one woman that shape. Christ! He had not anticipated that she would come after him, but of course she would have.

'Thanks, mate.' On his way back to his cubicle, he noticed that Sergey's was empty: just a bare mattress in a cell. He stopped in his tracks, looked a question over his shoulder at Saleem and prayed the answer had nothing to do with Ardem.

'They raided the weed farm,' said Saleem. 'He was arrested and banged up. Poor fucker.'

Poor fucker indeed. But the link between him and Ardem had gone. Now the only person in the whole of the UK who could blow his secret was Katya.

She lay on the bed with her legs resting up on the wall. When she saw him, she narrowed her eyes. 'You stopped answering my texts.'

He showed her his broken phone. 'I'll get it fixed.'

'I've been thinking. If you can't get anything from the Kirilova house, I'll have another try.'

'Katya, no. That girl, she's *vulnerable*. Not just because of her injury. She's got no one in the world.'

Katya swivelled her head towards him like an owl sensing prey; Roman felt the heat flood his face. His passion would have given him away even if the information hadn't.

'How come you know so much about her?'

The air around Roman seemed to chill a little. 'It's literally my job to look at these people and notice things. She's never had a visitor.' He finished the sentence in his head: apart from me, every day.

Katya drummed her nails – an iridescent beetle's-back greeny-blue today – on the screen of her phone. 'If she is all alone in the world, that's a *good* thing for us.' She raised an eyebrow at Roman. 'She could get an infection. Maybe she's in so much pain she forgets how many pills she's taken? That tramadol she's on is pretty dangerous stuff.'

'Katya, that's not funny,' he said. His muscles knotted a warning across the nape of his neck. 'How do you know what medication she's taking?'

'I went through the bins,' she said. 'It's all empty pill packets and luxury food. And she really gets through the vodka. I thought you said she was poor?'

'You've been back to Gabriel's Hill?'

'Of course I have. Since you're doing such a lousy job.' She might have been an employer giving a lazy worker a dressing-down. She had stopped blowing hot and cold in favour of a consistent icy blast.

The thought of Katya so close to Juliet aroused an atavistic male protectiveness he hadn't felt since Zlata was born. 'How did you even get in?' It was an effort to keep his voice even.

She shrugged. 'The Ocado guy.'

'Of course.' There probably wasn't a driver in London immune to the batting of her eyelashes. He sank on to his heels. 'Well, it's in pretty poor taste, Katya, but you obviously don't mean it.'

'Don't I?' Her voice was poisoned honey. The knot of muscle extended across Roman's shoulders and down his arms, so tightly that for a moment he wondered if he was having a heart attack.

'You're talking about *murder*, Katya. You of all people should know how horrible it sounds.'

He waited for her to say that of course she was joking, that he was a fool to have fallen for it, but instead she said, 'Have you got a better proposal?'

'I have, actually. Forget the whole stupid idea. Leave Juliet alone.'

His voice cracked on her name, and *alone* was freighted with more emotion than even he had known he felt.

'*Juliet.*' She pursed her lips. 'What are you, her best friend or something?'

She seemed to vibrate with an anger that gave Roman a fore-taste of what she might do if her desire to steal a life was coupled with the knowledge of how he'd been spending his evenings. He didn't delude himself that Katya wanted him – he had worked that out while he was still inside her – but she wanted him to do her bidding, to replace the life, if not the man, she had lost.

He wanted more than anything to protect Juliet but he under-stood, with a lurch, that he must do that at a distance. As a guard patrolling the estate. The best way to protect Juliet was to end their friendship. It was the only good thing in his life, but the way to save her was to give her up.

43

Knowing that the evening meant goodbye gave the day a horrible charge for Roman, as if he was carrying around a bolt of lightning in his pocket.

He planned to tell her that he'd lost his job, that he was being transferred to another city, that he was going back to Ukraine – anything that got him out of her life and so freed her from the threat of Katya. Force Patrol covered enough sites in London, and enough colleagues owed him enough favours, that he could ensure he didn't work a shift at Gabriel's Hill for a good couple of months.

He rehearsed his lines all day. 'It's all very last-minute . . .' he practised on the Tube. 'The security industry is like that . . .' he said under his breath as he trudged past the Wheatsheaf. As he approached the gates, he alternated unconvincingly between, 'It was nice knowing you,' and, 'I won't forget you.' 'This is my last day in London,' he tried out as he let himself into the garden, and then, as he edged past Zeus and Athena, 'No, I don't know where I'll be working next.'

But then she was on her back in the water, two glasses by the side of the pool, the radio playing soft music and he told himself that a swim would clear his head. He would find the right words in the water.

After an hour, when the glasses had been drained and refilled twice and their fingers were pruning, he helped her up the steps and out of the water. She looked like a nymph from a fairytale: huge sunken eyes, darkened hair in dripping rats' tails over gleaming shoulders, and Roman's excuses deserted him.

He cleared his throat, ready to tell her that he was moving on, but instead heard himself say, 'I wish I had seen you dance.'

Idiot. *Idiot.* It was the wine, it was the water, it was a year of loneliness suddenly manifesting itself in the imperative to *know* a woman again.

'Dance with me now.' Light words in a heavy voice, spoken as though her life depended on this.

'I don't want to hurt you,' he said.

She thought he meant her leg, and she laughed and said, 'If we do it this way . . .'

As the arch of her foot closed over the bridge of his, he was helpless against an inpouring of memory: another pair of feet, another dance, another girl, who called him by a name no one else had ever been able to use. Tears pounded behind Roman's eyes as he held Juliet tight around the waist and took her through the only dance steps he knew. *One*-two-three, *one*-two-three, *one*-two-three. It was mercifully different from dancing with Zlata, nothing like partnering Veronika. Even with one shattered leg Juliet moved like magic, guiding him into grace, and laughed with delight to find how well they fitted together. With every step she was pulling his heart out through his ribs. He had never wanted anyone as much in his life, not even at the beginning with Veronika; and as for Katya: *this* showed *that* up as nothing more than an itch to scratch.

Abruptly, mercifully, the song finished and the dance was over. Juliet gently stepped off his feet and Roman congratulated himself on his self-restraint. Then she raised her face to his and his heart made a jailbreak. Her flesh was cool and dry but her mouth was hot and wet. The world was reduced to her skin and control evaporated like water on hot stone.

44

He didn't know what to call it. Five days and six nights in, and he had no idea what it was.

A love affair? All the signs were there: the loss of appetite, the preoccupation, the profound wrongness of time spent apart from her. But even a relationship begun in honesty couldn't really be called that after less than a week, could it?

Lust? Well, *yes*. But without the abandon he'd associated with the word. In bed with Juliet, her injury meant exercising the same restraint he had to in conversation. Far from being frustrating, it was addictive. The enforced stillness, the slowness, the delayed gratification was new to him, and the way she opened up, the fever she transmitted through her skin, made him question every time he'd been with Veronika.

If there was a right word, it was *subterfuge*. He was certainly on high alert for Katya. He'd been seeing phantom Katyas in his peripheral vision everywhere he went, in the back seat of his patrol car, in shadowy corners of the house, behind lampposts and trees and bins, so when the knock on the door came his brain leapfrogged the evidence to presume that it was her. He'd rolled off the bed and cowered like a kid on the carpet, his heart thumping his breastbone like a mallet long after he realised his mistake.

Unable to hide his panic and knowing he'd need a good explanation for it, he'd groped for the next secret along and blurted out that he'd run away from home so he didn't have to serve in the army. As the confession unspooled he had felt a lightness that bordered on ecstasy. It was the relief of saying something *true* to her for the first time. Of sharing who he really was. He had begun to regret it by the time he finished. How would she respect him, knowing that?

But the contempt he braced himself for did not come.

Juliet was no Veronika.

The next morning, he dressed for work in the clothes he'd left on the floor the night before and left Juliet sleeping. Passing the telephone, Roman picked it up and checked the handset. The message icon was dark. It looked as though her old colleagues had forgotten about her after all.

When they were together the threat of Katya seemed to recede, only to rear up again with twice the force afterwards. A couple of days later Roman was thinking about Katya – her potential to blow his cover now, to have him exiled from these sheets, as well as the harm she meant – when Juliet asked him to fetch the notebook from the hall table. He was only half listening as she said, 'This is what's in the safe,' with a quiver in her voice and showed him the page with its prison-wall tallies and its telephone-number figures. It took a few beats for what Juliet was asking to hit him and, when it did, hurt catapulted Roman out of his own deception and on to the moral high ground.

'*This* is what you were up to. You have been using me the whole time!' He was on his feet and dressing, shouting at her for the risk she was asking him to take, reminding her that he had more to lose than she did and then slamming the door behind him to delay her, marching to the end of the garden knowing how long it would take her to catch up. The grass was green and cool underfoot down here where the sprinkler overshot the fence.

He paced up and down on the spongy ground until his anger assumed its true form of hurt. He felt it like a kick in the balls. Of the three women he had slept with, two of them had been using him. Katya hadn't even bothered to do it convincingly, but Juliet . . .

To still his whirring mind, he forced himself to think about the logistics. With Juliet posing as Ava it would be easy. It depended only on mutual trust. What a huge word that seemed right now.

Could they trust each other? She shouldn't trust him, and yet in asking this favour of him she had trusted him with everything she had left. Emotion barged back in, clouding his thoughts.

He sought refuge in another practicality: this time, profit. Juliet was talking about borrowing a few thousand. Ava Kirilova did not have an inventory of the contents of her safe but those clients who did often kept valuables worth six- or even seven-figure sums. He turned to the house. The low evening sun bounced off the plate-glass doors, turning the back wall into a great gold ingot. How much was in that safe? He pictured a million pounds in cash. He pictured a treasure chest overspilling with rubies. Enough that they could take what he and Juliet needed for survival, give the rest to Katya and face the consequences further down the line.

And if it was empty? The thought of a hollow black box broke a fresh sweat on his skin.

There was only one way to find out.

'Max?' Juliet's voice floated down the garden.

Of course it was a yes.

It could only ever have been a yes, for her.

He wouldn't tell her straight away. He would pretend to turn it over in his mind for another hour or two. The more she thought she was manipulating him, the better. He could not bear for her to know it was really the other way around.

45

It was a week past midsummer. Dawn came so early that after a while it was easy to doubt there was any such thing as true dark. Roman crouched in his cubicle, folding his London life away into his black holdall. In the side pocket, the black feather he'd found in the street had grown matted and ragged, glitter congealing at the tip. In just a few hours he and Juliet would open the safe at No. 36 Gabriel's Hill. He was light-headed with hunger and exhaustion and his own daring. He folded black socks, black underpants, a black shirt. By tomorrow, the uncertainties that were robbing him of sleep and appetite would be gone.

Outside, the heat had softened the tarmac and there was an acrid, burning-rubber smell in the air. The bus shelter offered scant shade: when Roman leaned on the glass, it burned his skin through his shirt. He stood under the merciless sun, closed his eyes under dark glasses, and listened to the sounds of the city in meltdown. The stop-start rumble of traffic, an argument between two children that floated from some high window. Music competed from shops, cafés and at least three different phones.

The rumble of plastic wheels on paving stones.

Before he even opened his eyes, Roman *knew*.

Katya had two cases with her: the little rolling one she usually carried, and a larger, more battered bag on wheels. She had packed up her things, which meant she'd left her home, which meant—

'You've lost your job.'

'I told you, the boss is a prick. Can I leave these in your room? They're very heavy.'

213

Reluctantly he let her into the Jester. He felt as though he had a plastic bag over his head. He felt like *putting* a plastic bag over his head.

'It's very bare in here,' she said, looking around his cell. 'Where are you planning to go?'

'It's bare because I don't bloody *own* anything.'

Katya stiffened for a second, like a machine switching between two modes. He wondered who he would get: cool, cunning Katya or poor little heartbroken Katya. As she turned brimming eyes on him, he found himself wistful for the schemer.

'How is it fair that *she* has a house she doesn't even live in, and I have to sleep on your dirty mattress?'

'We'll find you somewhere,' he said automatically.

'With what? I've got no money. That bastard kept back my wages. I should be sleeping somewhere like Gabriel's Hill. That's what Max would have wanted for me.' Her eyes suddenly narrowed: *here* was the true Katya. 'I think we should just get the cripple out of the way. You said that Ava Kirilova herself won't be around for months; no one would notice if that girl was gone.'

At first he took the tingling in his hands for a side-effect of the heat. Until he looked down and saw that they had formed fists without his permission. How had he come to a place in his life where the only way to stay safe was to do ever more dangerous things? He shook his fingers loose. 'Actually, they *would* notice. There's someone checking up on the house, dropping off her medication. You couldn't just disappear her.'

'Bullshit!' Katya threw back at him. 'We could sell that house, cash buyer, and be gone. We could go anywhere, with money like that.'

'Even if you could "get the cripple out of the way", as you so horribly put it, without anyone noticing, you can't just sell a house as if it's a second-hand car. You need identification and references; a bank account in Ava Kirilova's name, for a start, and her passport, and that's off with her, somewhere in Europe. Katya.

You've got to stop thinking like this. It would be prison for both of us, if we were caught. And we *would* be caught.'

It repulsed him to touch her now but he took her by the hands. 'The thing is, Katya, I've been keeping something from you.'

'I knew it!' Her face was a picture of triumph.

'I might have found another way to get a bit of cash.' He thought as fast as he could, threw the trail up and over London. 'A footballer, over in Millbrook Green. Premier League. He's just a kid earning insane money and he's really lax, you wouldn't believe the stuff he leaves lying around.' Ardem unexpectedly came to mind, saving him for the second time. 'I think I could get a watch and sell it for cash; you wouldn't have to work for a year. You could become ten different women with the kind of money I'm talking about. You could easily find someone to sort you out with the right paperwork, take the risk for you. It might even be enough to put you up in a little flat for a year. You could meet a nice man, maybe even an Englishman. They'll be queuing up to look after a girl like you, give you the life Maxim wanted you to have.'

Her eyebrows drew together like the blades of scissors. 'Why has this watch suddenly appeared *now*?'

Fresh sweat seemed to spring from each of Roman's pores at once. 'He's a new client,' he invented. 'Only just moved in.'

'Maybe,' she said. 'Maybe this would do for a *while*.'

But he knew, now, when she was being an actress: her lips twitched with the effort of repressing a smile. He could have cried with relief.

'Look, I'm late for work,' he said. 'Just wait here, OK? Stay in this room, and let me see if I can bring you something back.'

'Don't mess it up,' she said. 'I can't live like this forever.'

Nor can I, he thought.

He would go for broke: clear the safe. And if that didn't work he would be forced into, into . . . the English phrase *drastic action* came to mind. He was unable to voice even to himself what he meant by that; he only knew that he needed Katya out of his life for good. He thought this first with despair, and then with a kind of exhausted resignation, as though this was merely the final step on the path on which he had set off when he had hidden his passport in his desk at work.

Since leaving Donetsk, Roman's moral compass had gradually lost its true north. Given what he was now contemplating, stealing from Juliet's hostess was now the least of his worries. It no longer even seemed like a crime but something necessary – right, even. Didn't that company owe Juliet a better future, after she had given them most of her life? Ava Kirilova had money and property and unlike poor Juliet she still had the ballet. If she lost a little cash, it would be the only thing that had ever gone wrong in her charmed life.

AVA

46

The week before she died, Ava Kirilova danced the dual roles of Odette and Odile in *Swan Lake* to the greatest acclaim of her career. In his double-page-spread interview for *The Sunday Times* – headlined, with dreary inevitability, 'Swan Song' – Ian Bayer had posited that they were pulling out all the stops because this would be the last great ballet Nicky Kirilov ever choreographed, and that he was falling back on the failsafe classic because he was all out of ideas. Nicky had gathered the company on stage and dismissed Bayer's theory by holding up a copy of the paper and snarling, 'Is bullshit.'

The rumours turned out to be true, but not for the reasons Bayer had predicted.

The production opened on a flaming June evening. The day had marked the boiling point of a record-breaking heatwave and the thin, tacky layer of grime that coated London was starting to feel permanent. Outside the theatre, the poster – the iconic shot of the black swan and her helpless dupe of a prince – was sliced through with a diagonal banner proclaiming *TONIGHT*. A white van flashed its hazard lights on the kerb as a delivery driver pushed clinking crates of champagne and glasses towards the side entrance. Delia took delivery of three huge bags of just-in-case feathers. In just a few hours the foyer would be thronged with press, patrons and the most dedicated dance fans in London – no, the world. Balletomanes had travelled from as far as Canada, Serbia, Finland, South Africa, too impatient to wait for a new London Russian production to reach their part of the globe.

Ava Kirilova leaned out of her dressing-room window and watched the guests arrive and mingle. The trick was to convert the pressure they brought with them into energy on the stage. With no more time to worry or try to make it better, a kind of freedom approached. Guests from the ballet world outnumbered the critics and the overwhelming spirit was goodwill, not judgement. You could taste it, like petrol in the tired air.

On her dressing table were her *merde* gifts: bouquets of lilies and vases of orchids from fans. Peonies from her shoemakers, freesias from her leotard-makers and, from Luca, a dozen red roses.

Felicity knocked on the door.

'He wants you.' Stress clipped her voice. They were all Mr K now, using as few words as possible, delivering the necessary information and little more.

'Where is he on the Richter scale today?'

'Off the scale. He wants you to coach the new second swan. The third second swan? I've lost track.'

'I'm not a coach! I'm the principal and I'm on stage in two hours! Why aren't you doing it?'

'He says it needs to be someone who's danced Odette.'

'Sakurako, then, or Raisa?'

Felicity inhaled and pinched the bridge of her nose. 'I'm just the messenger. Could you demonstrate it once, and I'll take over?'

Ava saw the impossible position Felicity was in and relented, winding and tying her ribbons so fast her hands blurred, swapping the lift for the stairs and dropping into a few *pliés* to warm up.

The corridor was busy, preparations not just for the show but for the reception afterwards: sets and musicians and catering and wardrobe and the useless air-con units that seemed in that moment actually to generate heat. Sounds collided to become white noise.

Nicky's voice carried backstage. 'From *back*!' he was shouting as they entered the wings. 'Arms move from back, fuck bloody sake!' His knuckles were white around the head of his cane. His other hand was on the small of his bent back and Ava understood that his tantrum was as much to do with the pain he was in as the pressure of training up another second swan at a few days' notice. 'Lazy little *bitch*,' he screamed.

The silence that followed was charged with enough energy to power a spotlight. Even in his most furious moments, he had never resorted to name-calling. The dancer covered her eyes with her forearm but her shoulders shook.

Ava rosined up and emerged stage right.

'Odette!' said Nicky, as though she had missed a long-standing appointment. 'Where you been? Baby swan here needs to grow up.'

'I'm here,' she soothed. 'I'm here.'

The new girl looked to Ava for reassurance. Ava knew what they wanted: a smile, a nod, the love that Nicky could not give today. Sometimes the responsibility and power of her presence in a room exhausted her: she felt like God's representative on earth. But the best way to deal with this was to remain professional, be a cool counterweight to her father's fever. She led by example, not emotion.

'Like this,' she said, and spread her wings wide.

47

The ballet unfolded like a dream. Luca's puppy-dog Prince Siegfried did not fall in love so much as plunge head-first into it. The corps de ballet managed to be both a grand machine and a piece of poetry. Ava let not just Odette but also Nicky dance through her. Her turnout was impossible, her extension super-human. She embodied the flesh-and-bone geometry of the true Kirilovan ballerina.

Act III, the ballroom scene, and the *coda* approached. Ava was Odile – *Look at me, Daddy!* – as she danced her way to the thirty-two *fouettés*. When she pushed up *en pointe* for the first turn and fixed her eyes on the red light at the back of the stalls, she was aware that every eye in the house was on her, every heart willing her to get it right. Ava rose to meet their expectation, knee locking for a second too long perhaps on the second turn but then she found her rhythm, repeating the words *up, up, up,* in her head, to propel herself around. She knew, as the variation built to its crescendo, that she had executed every one of them flawlessly. This stage, this role, these people, this moment was the centre of the world and she was its perfectly spinning axis. She was her father's invention. She was his precision missile. Here was the perfection Ava had spent her whole life chasing: the ideal dancer that she had seen only in fleeting glimpses in the mirror had finally been made flesh. Eighteen years of company class every morning, thousands of hours of barre, every glass of wine undrunk, every party unattended were poured into one minute. Here was the Kirilov Odile, a lifetime in the making. She made a double turn, then a triple. A triple! The audience began stamping and cheering. *Look at me, Daddy!* Spontaneously, Odile – you could not have said it was Ava – dipped her head, grinned and winked at the audience, breaking the fourth wall and bringing delighted laughter in on the tail of the applause. Odile, speaking through Ava, had said that she might have bewitched the prince at her father's behest but there was something about the seduction that was all hers.

After the last turn, she had a split-second to glance at the floor and there was the evidence that she had hardly moved from her mark: a little curly line, tight as an old-fashioned telephone wire, already disappearing on the shiny stage floor.

The third second swan fluttered facelessly in the window. When Siegfried saw her and realised his mistake, fireworks exploded on stage, and Act III ended in sparks and a standing ovation.

In the interval, Ava was divested of Odile's costume. 'You kept *that* to yourself,' said the dresser, up to her wrists in the glossy black plumage. 'I knew you were good but I never saw you do a triple before. Where did that come from?'

'It just *happened*,' said Ava. 'It was like I was *possessed* by Odile.'

'Yeah, she has that effect,' said the dresser. She held out the white bodice. 'Anyway, the audience loved it. I haven't seen a reaction like that for a long time. You'll have to do that every night for the rest of the year. No pressure!' Ava stood, arms outstretched, while the dresser fastened her tutu and fixed her headdress. 'Nearly done now, Miss Kirilova. *Merde.*'

If Odile had possessed Ava in Act III, Odette and her reliable heartbreak took over for the finale. There was no improvisation here, just silent sorrow. After the jump into the lake, after another quick-change from swan to mortal, the wet dress cooling her boiling body, she shared a moment with Luca behind the rock. While the swans tore Von Rothbart limb from wing, Odette and Siegfried – who were and also were not Ava and Luca – locked eyes and knew they had given the performance of their lives.

When he picked her up she went limp in his arms and her head lolled back, her sopping dress and hair trailing along the floor. At the front of the stage he dropped to his knees as the orchestra crested the final strains.

The crowd got to their feet as though the move had been choreographed. Single roses rained from the gods. Sweat finally broke through the barrier of white make-up on Ava's face; when she curtsied, she dripped a milky daisy on the stage floor.

Eventually the clapping changed, becoming slower and more rhythmic as the audience exhausted their admiration for the dancers and summoned the ballet master himself. When Nicky appeared from the wings, in his slacks and roll-neck, Ava finally understood the meaning of 'raise the roof'. The applause was hot air, a dangerous volatile gas, expanding in excess of the space that could contain it.

'Speech,' called the audience. 'Speech!'

In front of this crowd, his people, Nicky seemed to grow an inch, and his cane to endow elegance, not diminish it. His eyes shone as he looked into the auditorium. He spoke without a microphone, trusting the acoustics.

'I am becoming old man,' he said. 'And my theatre, she grows old with me. You hear her breathe,' he said in a nod to the wheezing air-con. The audience laughed. 'So. I dedicate *Swan Lake* first night to my theatre, for the past she gives me and the future we have together when she is reborn. And I dedicate this show to fathers of Russian dance, Petipa and Ivanov, and of course to great Tchaikovsky. I dedicate to my beautiful creatures, my dancers, who do everything so perfect.'

She waited for him to single her out: his brightest creature, his best love, his daughter, his Odette, his Odile, his life's work. And although he lifted her hand and raised it with his as they took their bows together, he did not say her name. Her heart contracted painfully. The audience didn't seem to have picked up on her humiliation, but surely they would whisper about it over champagne and blinis later.

Nicky's grip was as strong as Luca's: his thumb a steel rod of pressure in the palm of her hand. It was a deliberate antidote to the drug of adoration. He was putting her in her place. Fear was an electric shock from her heart to the tips of her fingers and the soles of her feet. What could he possibly be angry about? she fretted. *I was perfect. The audience loved me.*

It couldn't be because of that wink, could it? It was only her face, and she knew it had been done in the context of technical perfection. She had thought *Look at me, Daddy* all the way through, and that was the result.

She had only done what she was told.

When the last bows had been taken and the house began to empty into the atrium, Nicky dropped Ava's hand and was borne away on a crowd of white feathers. He didn't look back at her.

The arm Luca draped over Ava's shoulder felt heavier than usual.

'There are five hundred people in that foyer,' he said, 'And all of them are in love with you.'

She wanted to ask Luca if he had noticed the slight but if he said yes that would make it real, and she had the party to get through yet.

'With *us*,' she corrected him.

'I don't delude myself that I am anything other than your bitch.'

'Absolutely.' Ava laughed, then grew serious. 'I couldn't do it without you, Luca.'

'And you'll never have to.' He kissed the top of her head. 'Come on, let's get into our party dresses.'

They were the last to leave the stage. The overhead lights blinked on and the techies in their mime-artist black began to roll back the scenery. With the spotlights off and the music gone, the moonlit lake was no longer a place of magic and tragedy. It was just a stage set, nothing but plywood and paint.

48

Ava faced Odette in a proscenium arch of lightbulbs and wiped the white swan's face on to a cotton pad. The heavy eye make-up never quite came off completely, its remnants ringing her eyes with a fine line of kohl. She set her shower to freezing and was dry in seconds with no need of a towel. She unwound her hair from its bun and stuck the nozzle of the hairdryer into her roots so it bloomed thick and wild around her face. The red dress reached her ankles but she felt naked in it, the slinky fabric insubstantial after her stage clothes; she missed the comforting tension between skin and cloth. The mirror in her dressing room was a glossy magazine and she was the cover girl, but perfection in stillness was easy; it only counted in motion. She winced as she slid her feet into a pair of low silver heels. Wearing dress shoes was like walking with tiny needles in her skin. Ava found it easier to dance *en pointe* than to walk in three-inch heels. She caressed the head of a pink peony; petals rained down like feathers.

A rap on the door made Ava jump. 'Are you decent?' asked Luca. In black tie and with wet hair slicked back, he looked like an advertisement for an expensive watch.

'Two more minutes,' she said, rummaging in her drawer for plasters. 'I need to sort my corns out. These shoes are like bloody razors.'

'It's the heady glamour of ballet that keeps us all dancing,' said Luca. 'I'll see you down there.' When he'd gone, she wished she'd asked him to send a glass of champagne to her room, cold bubbles that would go efficiently to her head on an empty stomach.

Her silver shoes pinched like glass slippers. Keen to tackle as few steps as possible, she took the lift, hitting 2 for the second floor. Nicky had choreographed her entrance: she was to emerge on the balcony, pause for a count of five to let the applause build, and sweep down the staircase into the atrium. The scent of the lift oil overpowered her perfume; the old machinery clanked on the descent. She flexed her fingers. A bruise was already forming between two metacarpal bones, a splash of dirty water from a dark lake.

When the doors slid open, her father was standing in the second-floor corridor, leaning on his stick, his eyes black vortexes of fury. At the end of the passage, a fire door gave on to the balcony and chatter from the party drifted from the atrium, but Nicky's expression made Ava want to scuttle back to the safety of her dressing room. It took all her courage to step out of the lift.

'Hello, Papa,' she said in the little-girl voice she hadn't needed to use for years. 'I did the triple! Did you see?'

'I see,' he said. He drummed his fingers on the top of his cane, tapping on the black swan's beak. 'Ten minutes I wait! There is making entrance,' he looked pointedly at his watch, then waved his free arm towards the staircase, 'and there is taking piss.'

'I'm here now.' Downstairs, a glass broke and guests applauded. 'Sounds like it's going well?'

He didn't answer, just held time still with his stare.

The lift doors closed behind them.

Ava held out her arm to him, only realising as she did so that he had gone off-script. 'Hang on, you can't do those stairs. You were supposed to wait for me down below. What are you even doing up here?'

When he spoke again, his voice was so low that Ava had to lean in to hear it. 'Do I look like comedian?'

'What?'

'Is easy. Do I look like comedian?' He pointed to himself, then drew a circle in the air with his forefinger. 'Is this face of clown?'

Where was he going with this? 'No?'

'Then why you turn my ballet into comedy? The *looking*, like this.' He mimicked her nod to the audience. 'Your job is not do your own thing. Your job is follow my instruction *exactly*. What is tonight? Fucking improv? Fucking *jazz*?'

Right. OK. He thought she had done it to prove a point rather than from a place of pure immersion, but that was easy to set right. 'Papa! You've got the wrong idea. It was just, I knew I was doing my best ever work – *your* best work – and in that space Odile sort of took over. I didn't *plan* it.'

Whatever gains she might have made with the flattery she immediately lost. His lips went white, his only tell. To act spontaneously, to lose control, was unforgivable.

'Sakurako does not change my ballet,' he said. 'For rest of tour, she is swan. This time I mean it.'

She should have backed down then, but no precedent for an argument between them meant there was no template for it, and she was still running high and reckless on the adrenaline of the performance.

'In, what, eighteen years, I put one drop of myself into a perfect performance – which the audience loved, by the way – and you're acting like I started pole-dancing in the middle of the stage. Give me a break.'

Something rippled across his face, too fast for her to read.

'If you sack me,' she said, 'everyone'll say you've lost the plot. It'll undermine you. They'll all think Ian Bayer was right.'

Surely even he couldn't argue with that. She waited to watch him debate this internally but all she saw was the rock-face consistency of a man incapable of compromise.

'No,' he said. 'It make me look strong. Man who sack own daughter. It show he is in charge. That work is everything. Creator is more important than creature.'

'*I am not your fucking creature!*' It flew out of her like a bird that had been caged its whole life. The heresy reverberated along the corridor. The party noises down below took on an unreal quality: the voices were the rhubarb-rhubarb of actors playing a crowd scene, the clinking glass a sound effect from a radiophonic workshop.

Nicky closed his eyes, slowly and deliberately, as though he was bringing down the shutters on the way things had been. When he opened them again, his expression made her skin shrink.

'Oh yes you are,' he said. 'Everything you have, I give. Everything you are, I make. I can take away like *that*.' He snapped his fingers, then said, 'I put Boyko in charge,' in a tone so casual Ava wondered if she'd jumped a minute in time and missed some vital bridge in the conversation.

'Yes,' she said, carefully. 'As a caretaker, until you can come out.'

'No,' said Nicky. 'I give him job. Creative director. When I go. I change will. We talk about it, in meeting last week, but we don't decide. Now I see it. You will bring too much your ideas. Boyko carries on my work.'

'I . . .' she began, but couldn't finish the sentence as her brain scurried to process what her ears were hearing. Some legal meeting, Felicity had said, the day she had taken class. He had been plotting Ava's exit since then, and with a wink on a stage she had unwittingly erased her own future.

This is *Swan Lake*'s fault, she thought. The ballet had uncovered something. It had been a mistake for them to wait until she had matured as a dancer. He should have made the dance on her when she was still young, before she had had a chance to outgrow his work and begin to fledge her own.

'Don't do this,' she said eventually, wondering whether it would help or hinder her cause if she obeyed the instinct to drop to her knees.

'I have decided, Ava.' Ava, not Odette, or Odile. He could not have made it clearer that she had lost the role if he had ripped off her headdress on-stage. He nodded towards the atrium. 'Lawyer is at party. Paperwork in my room. I make official now. While I see truth so clear.'

Nicky reached for the DOWN button, but his reflexes had slowed with age while hers were at their peak. She intercepted and hit UP and the doors opened. You couldn't override an instruction on this old thing. *While I see truth so clear* meant that in time he might change his mind. Before he could go back to the party, the lift would have a wasted journey to the principals' floor, and that would buy them half a minute longer.

She put her hands to her breastbone in a prayer position, a balletic mime of supplication.

'Papa, please. Don't take everything away from me. It will kill me. This is my home. It's my life. You *made* it my life. You can't choose between me and the company, it's a false choice. There's no future without me. Boyko hasn't got an original idea in his head. He'll run it into the ground.'

'Boyko carries on *my* work,' Nicky repeated and Ava understood the size of his ego for the first time. It was six storeys high, it was cast in concrete, it was bigger than anything else, including his love for her. She felt a burning behind her eyes as the tears formed.

'You're making a mistake,' she said.

The lift doors closed.

Nicky's eyes began to swim and she wondered, with a mixture of horror and hope, if he might cry too, but when he shook his head no tears dislodged. 'Maybe mistake was recreate myself in you. Maybe experiment fail.'

The words were arrows, shooting through the heart of what they were to each other. Who she *was*. The shock of it dried her eyes, stripped the saliva from her mouth so her next words were croaked, not spoken.

'You don't mean that.'

Nicky shrugged. 'Is shame. Is big shame of my life.'

He turned towards the lift and used the swan's beak on the head of his cane to depress the DOWN button.

'Papa, you can't.' The doors opened and Ava jumped in front of the lift to stop him getting in but her silver shoes threw off her balance and she caught her heel on the base of his cane. It clattered to the ground and he toppled sideways, clutching for a second at the air before hitting the wall and slipping down it, landing on the floor with an audible snap. His left leg was twisted to the side in a monstrous exaggeration of the impossible turnout he had displayed as a young man.

He looked five years old, and then a hundred.

Ava dropped to her knees. 'Papa!' she said. 'Papa, oh my God. Can you hear me? Are you OK?'

His eyes were open and his chest rose and fell, but he could only grunt in reply.

49

'I'm going to get help.' Ava leapt into the waiting lift and held the button marked S for stage. 'I'll find Jack, it'll be all right.'

The doors closed and Nicky disappeared from view. This was not how she had planned to enter the party, dashing from the stage to the atrium, wild with fear and screaming for Jack, but the party no longer mattered and gossip no longer mattered and even *Swan Lake* no longer mattered. The world was reduced to her task. She braced for the swoop of descent, but the lift knocked its way upwards.

In the steel box, Ava screamed at the realisation that she had sent it that way just a minute or two ago as a delaying tactic. The doors opened, in agonising slow motion, on to the empty principals' corridor. Ava hit the doors-closing button so ferociously that she snapped a fingernail. The lift shaft was a kind of sound vent, the conversation of the unwitting party guests as loud up here as it had been on the second floor. A door banged somewhere below. At last, the lift doors closed. How much time had she lost? Thirty seconds? A full minute?

As the lift lurched downwards, the second-floor button lit up and Ava's heart gave a corresponding leap. He was on his feet already; he was making his own way downstairs. But the doors drew apart to show Nicky still supine on the floor, Raisa and Jack kneeling over him.

Raisa was whispering to him in Russian, calling him Kolya.

'Ava!' Jack was on the phone, a tinny ringtone audible. With his free hand he beckoned her out of the lift, his calm capability instantly reassuring. 'Thank God we caught you, Ava. It looks like he's had a fall.'

Ava parted her lips to tell them what had happened but the look on Raisa's face stoppered her mouth.

'He went looking for *you*,' she said, her voice caustic. 'If you had been on time . . .'

'Raisa, it's not helpful to apportion blame,' said Jack briskly. 'It's clearly an accident.'

'It was . . .' began Ava, but Raisa's focus was on Nicky and Jack's was on his phone. Now wasn't the time to explain. Nicky would tell it his way, on the other side of the abyss that was all this. She kicked off her silver shoes, sank in a full *plié*, took the hand that Raisa wasn't holding. Nicky's eyes were closed but he was breathing easily.

'Is it OK that he's not talking?' she turned to ask Jack, but his call had connected. 'Yes, ambulance, please,' he said, and gave the address. 'My name is Jack Charlton, I'm the senior physiotherapist here. Left leg shortened and externally rotated. Possible concussion? Yes, yes, he is, in and out. He's, er, he's seventy-nine.' There was a pause. 'Osteoarthritis and advanced osteoporosis. Thank you. Thank you, yes, we will.'

He cut the call, then looked between the two women. 'Ava – no, Raisa,' he decided. 'Go downstairs and find Boyko. Tell him to close the party with our apologies. Get security to evacuate the building and make sure the paramedics have a clear route up here.'

As the lift bore Raisa down, the word *concussion* finally registered and sent Ava's fingertips to Nicky's skull. His hair was baby-fine, his scalp as smooth as paper. 'Hey, Papa,' she whispered. 'The paramedics are on their way. You're going to be fine.' His eyelids fluttered at the sound of her voice and his lips twitched in – was that a smile? Were things alright between them again? You never could tell. Maybe – she was ashamed of the thought even as it passed through her mind – *maybe*, a little concussion would act as a reset button and everything would continue to glide on the right rails.

'Don't move him, Ava,' warned Jack.

'I'm just holding his hand.' Jack inspected her position and nodded his approval. 'Is he going to be alright?'

'Well, his surgery's certainly been brought forward by a few days. Oh, *Nicky*. If you'd had the operation when I told you to, but no, you had to stay on for first night, you stubborn old bastard.' His words were harsh but his tone was even and unpanicked. 'I've known cases where the fall is almost spontaneous,' he continued. 'The hip breaks to cause the fall rather than the other way around. I wouldn't be surprised if that's what's happened here.' He crossed to the fire door, pressed his nose against the cross-wired glass in the window. 'Party's in full bloody swing as well.'

Ava repeated the stroking motion on Nicky's head. This time she brought a scarlet smear on to his temple.

'Jack!' she screamed. 'He's bleeding!'

She'd never seen Jack move so fast. She'd never seen his face that colour.

'Oh, Jesus Christ, *Nicky*!'

As Jack creaked to a kneeling position, Ava whispered a desperate plea in Nicky's ear. 'Come on, Papa. Wake up for me now. If you wake up, I'll dance the way you want me to for the rest of my life. No more winking, no more losing control. We'll do things the Kirilov way forever and ever if you just wake up.' She understood that she was making a bargain not just with Nicky but with God, the Universe, any force that had the power to undo this. 'You can call me your creature every day but please wake up.'

Nicky's eyes flew open and settled for a moment on Ava's face. His smile was love, it was peace, it was forgiveness and pride. For the briefest of moments it looked like triumph but it couldn't be. Not even Nicky Kirilov could sustain a power struggle now.

'*Moya lyubimaya devushka.*' He squeezed Ava's hand to seal the deal. He fixed his eyes on hers, and Ava watched them turn to glass.

'Oh, Christ, Nicky, no,' said Jack.

'Papa?' said Ava, as Nicky released his grip on her hand. 'Papa! Papa!'

Downstairs, the news – which was old news already – was bad air blowing through the building. The murmurs of the guests fell silent for a second and then the voices broke into thunder.

50

The funeral parlour was in an old Victorian terrace a block away from the theatre. Bloodless classical music was piped in with the cool air. In a large tank, a shoal of electric-blue fish chased each other through waving green fronds as Raisa spoke with the undertaker.

'We will do all of this the *Russian* way,' she insisted.

It was the afternoon following Nicky's death. Neither Raisa nor Ava had had any sleep and plenty had happened overnight. Raisa had made plans to join the tour. She had cancelled that night's performance and the remainder of the London run. She had confirmed Boyko as acting creative director.

The one thing she hadn't done was to look at, or speak directly to, Ava.

As Raisa and the undertaker discussed priests and clothes and coffins, Ava's thoughts scurried on their wheel. She knew through Jack, who had promised her it was just the grief talking, that Raisa blamed Nicky's death on the combination of Ava's provocative wink and then her lateness to the party. Both these things had combined to put Nicky in a mood and a place that had made him vulnerable to falling alone. That was unbearable because it was true. Worse was the thing that was not true. Raisa would have been there at the lawyers' meeting where they had discussed taking the company away from Ava, but she didn't know about their argument and she didn't know that Nicky had turned his threat into a decision. As it was, the will had not been amended: Boyko's inheriting the company remained an idea.

If Raisa had known what had been said between Nicky and Ava last night, it would have looked to her as if Ava had a reason to want Nicky gone. The absurd word *motive* might be applied to his death.

This put Ava in the lonely position of not being able to tell anyone what had really happened in case it was misinterpreted. It must remain another secret to squash down in the landfill of things she couldn't talk about.

'White clothes,' Raisa said now. '*I* will shop for him.' She had reverted passionately to the traditions of the motherland. 'The Russian way is three days and three nights in the home of the deceased before the funeral.' She managed to convey the impression of looking at Ava without actually meeting her eye. 'Not the place in the country. He never lived there. I mean the theatre. We lay him out on the stage. Three nights.'

'I do have to advise against it in this circumstance.' The undertaker twirled a screen to face them. A yellow bar graph shone back. 'It's thirty-one degrees outside and hotter tomorrow.'

Ava registered the horror of what he was really saying – the reality of death, the rot and the smell – without emotion. The images she had seen of death, mottled skin and maggots, were as intangible as images on a slideshow, nothing to do with her. Nothing to do with her *father*, for whom death was so ridiculously out of character.

'We can get a portable air machine,' said Raisa, as though she were instructing a techie the night before a show.

Ava felt the undertaker's gaze land on her. Two of the fish in the tank danced a flirty *pas de deux* around a stone castle.

'Miss Kirilov?' he asked gently. Bubbles rose in the tank and popped on the surface.

'Kirilov*a*,' said Raisa. 'In the Russian system, the feminine surname changes. It means she is his daughter.'

Daughter. Ava had sullied the word. As if she could still be his daughter after what she had done. She had given up the right. She did not deserve his name, although she intended to earn it back by making good on her last promise to him. She would dedicate the rest of her life to preserving his work and his methods. She would become his most perfect creature. And if it felt like a betrayal of that emerging self, that wild dancer within? Well, look what that woman had done. Wink murder. Ava had cost Nicky his life. She could not let it cost him his legacy.

'Apologies. Miss Kirilova. But yes, as his daughter, as the next of kin, you really should be involved in these decisions. We do understand how difficult they are, but in my experience people regret it if they aren't.'

Raisa answered for her. 'I looked after him in life. It is my job to do it in death, too. It's the last thing I can do for him.'

'Is this alright with you?' he asked Ava. 'You're absolutely sure?'

She tore her eyes away from the fish tank. 'Yes,' she managed. 'I'm sure.'

Small, safe words, the only ones she seemed able to utter right now. It was as though she were confined to single syllables, tight little words, no overspill possible.

When everything was finalised, the undertaker ushered them into the dazzling street. 'I'll be in touch later,' he said. 'I'm glad you two have each other, at least.'

Ava turned to the woman who had known her since she was a little girl. 'Do we?' she said.

The look Raisa gave her could have frozen fire. This is your doing, said her eyes. You are on your own. Do not come crying to me. I am not your mother.

The grey walls of the theatre rose to meet a perfect blue sky. Ava noted dully that she owned this building now, everything in it and everything it stood for. Outside the main entrance was a bank of flowers, Tesco lilies rotting in plastic. A couple of middle-aged women stood arm in arm before them. She stopped on her way to the stage door, stepping back and pressing herself against a plane tree in the hope that they wouldn't turn around and see her.

'He died in her arms, you know,' one muttered to the other. 'Her face was the last thing he saw.'

They didn't specify whether they were talking about Ava or Raisa. Where did these rumours even come from?

She walked the theatre's perimeter, passing a row of dumpsters, to the stage door, where Boyko was waiting for her.

'Miss Kirilova.' They eyed each other warily, both unsure how their relationship would work without Nicky mediating. Acting creative director Boyko might be, but she was effectively his boss now. She wondered whether he resented Nicky for dying before everything was transferred to him. She had never gleaned any sense of personal ambition from Boyko, just a satisfaction at being Nicky's receptacle.

Whatever he thought, Boyko was a pro, and she knew that any politics would wait until after the funeral, after the tour.

'He's on the stage,' he said. Together they walked through the corridors that looked the same even though everything had changed. 'I just cannot take it in. I've spent the morning with him and it still doesn't feel real. Raisa and I dressed him ourselves. It felt like one last thing we could do for him.' Outside the door to the stalls was a pile of mattresses, a stack of fat rolled-up sleeping bags. 'A few of us thought we'd spend the next couple of nights on the stage. We don't want him to sleep alone.'

She nearly said, 'Really?' Her father was the most fiercely private person she knew, so drained by the intensity of his work that he couldn't bear other people in his space at night. Supper would always end with a dismissal, so he could get ready for sleep alone. It was a running joke, that you had to be as swift leaving Nicky's table as you were crossing his stage. She heard his voice in her head: My last night on planet and I listen to bloody men farting whole time? A mad, sick laugh surged inside her. She buried her face in her hands and Boyko read it as a sob.

'Oh, *Ava*,' he said, and his use of her first name cut the tension. He didn't pull her in for a hug, but he took her hand and squeezed it tight, the way he had on the first night when they were waiting in the wings as Von Rothbart and Odile, dressed to dance in feathers and bones. A warm current passed between them and she knew then that this relationship, at least, would survive. After all, weren't they now working towards the same thing? Heritage, preservation, precision, inheritance? Weren't they both trying to keep Nicky alive?

'Do you want me to come with you, or would you rather say goodbye alone?' he asked.

'Just me.'

'We thought so,' replied Boyko. 'There's only me, Raisa and Jack in the building. You can say anything to him. You will have absolute privacy. Take as long as you need.' He opened the door for her to enter the auditorium and, when she was in the aisle, he closed it softly behind her.

Nikolai Kirilov's white coffin lay on the black stage, framed by the faded red velvet curtain. The image recalled an old Soviet leader, embalmed, waiting for his *politburo* to file past him, an effect marred rather by the four portable air-conditioning machines that surrounded him, the fat white larvae of their flues trailing away to the edges of the stage, throwing hot air into the wings and the stalls. The closer she got, the louder their humming grew.

Approaching the stage from the front felt somehow improper. Ava was nervous, a dark inversion of first-night butterflies. She had never seen a dead body. She climbed the stairs at the side of the stage and entered a bubble of freezing air. As she approached the coffin itself, Ava's eyes involuntarily lost their focus; to regain it she looked at the rest of the room, the coffin a blur of white in her peripheral vision, a sleeping swan.

She might have stayed there forever but her body was brave on her mind's behalf and she found herself standing over the open coffin, hands gripping the wood either side of his shoulders.

He was dressed in his usual roll-neck and slacks, but the clothes were – at Raisa's insistence on the *Russian way* – white, which looked entirely wrong. He looked as though he were about to go fencing.

'You're so *little*,' she breathed. Nicky had always been lean but now he seemed like a child. The muscles of his face had slackened into a repose she had never seen in him in life. He had never relaxed, not even when they were eating supper together in the evenings or travelling. He was always working, even when he wasn't working, preoccupation his default state. He had been in perpetual motion even when old, even when in pain, his head nodding as he beat internal time to a score, his hands waving as he made a dance in his mind. It was the uncanny *stillness* that told Ava he was really gone. It was the stillness that told her that this was not her father but her father's body and now she was in the world without him and who did that make her and how was she supposed to *be*?

'You can't go yet,' she said. 'You haven't finished me.'

Her unthinking words revealed a truth. She *was* his creature after all. The ingratitude she'd shown him sent up a flare of shame inside her.

'I'm so sorry, Papa. You know I didn't mean it – you know that, don't you?'

She tilted her face to the ceiling as though expecting some sign. A spotlight, maybe, to buzz into bright white life and shine down its blessing. But the lights were out. Nothing came. Nothing changed. She would never be forgiven. She did not deserve to be.

51

Ava trod the warren of corridors in search of Boyko, trailing her fingers along the familiar concrete walls. How many times had she done this as a child, the only schoolgirl allowed to roam the complex after hours? Sometimes, waiting for Nicky to come out of a meeting or rehearsal, she had played games with herself, kept her left hand touching the wall and made maps in her head of the routes she walked.

She heard Boyko before she saw him, his voice travelling around an L-bend.

'Between us we can keep things ticking over. But what about when the tour is over? Raisa, we planned for an absence, not a departure. He was *everything*. Ballet master, creative director, production designer . . . financial director.' Boyko leaned hard on those last two words. 'I had a look at the books. His system is impossible to penetrate.'

Ava felt a prickle of fear. Dealing with the money was someone else's problem, but *having* it, or not, was hers now.

Raisa sounded as if someone had taken a cheese-grater to her throat. 'The lawyers have already got the auditors at work.'

'And have they seen Ava yet?'

'Boyko! We can't ask the child to deal with probate in her state.'

Ava had another flashback to her teenage years; Raisa had often referred to her as *the child* when she and Nicky didn't agree on some aspect of her dancing or her upbringing, as though that was any of Raisa's business.

Boyko picked up on it. 'The child! She's a woman in her thirties.'

'None of Nicky's dancers can look after themselves, Ava least of all. He kept them all like children.' She sighed. '*We* did.'

A rush of defensiveness made Ava rise up on her toes: how dared she speak like that of the great Nikolai Kirilov? But she sank to her heels just as quickly. It was true. She couldn't fend for herself: she barely understood this conversation. He had not taught her how to carry on his work.

'Christ, you're right.' Boyko clicked his tongue. 'What a mess. But even so: surely the nature of probate means the person who deals with it is *always* grieving?'

'Grieving, always. Carrying a two-hour ballet, not so often.' She was beginning to sound more like the old Raisa. 'It's complicated. Tangled up. You how know Nicky is.'

Ava caught a sharp in-breath as Raisa realised her mistake with the tense, but she didn't correct herself.

'Well,' she continued. 'Ava has some assets in her name, but the company needs some untangling. We are talking months, not weeks. The lawyers will feed through the details to us and we'll have the conversations with Ava while we are on tour. The most important thing is that we minimise the disruption to *Swan Lake*. Sakurako is holding the fort, but it's not her people pay to see. Nothing must derail Ava's performance. *Nothing*.'

'Oh, I know,' Boyko sighed. 'She is box office. More so than ever, now. And the tour is Mr K's legacy.'

'No,' said Raisa. '*She* is his legacy. As long as she dances, he lives forever.'

52

The funeral was held in the Russian Orthodox Church in Kensington. This place with its incense and icons, its jade greens and lapis blues, its ambers and garnets, was the opposite of Nicky's stripped-back stage aesthetic. The entire company was present, of course.

Gentle organ music played as Ava, hair draped in a black lace scarf, walked up the aisle on Jack Charlton's arm, a horrid parody of a man giving his daughter's hand in marriage. Like a wedding, it had been just the two of them in the car on the way there. Jack had cried his eyes out, the great man-mountain shaking so violently it seemed that he might crumble to a million grey pieces.

Dancers' eyes clicked away from Ava's as though her gaze was radioactive, but they looked at Jack like children to their mothers. Only now, as he handed a tissue to one of the male soloists, did she understand the extent of Jack's caretaking. He was more than just a physio: he loved the dancers in a way that went deeper than muscle and bone. Thank God for Jack.

They claimed their seats next to Raisa in the first pew. She was in full widow's weeds, her face inscrutable behind a black veil. The nave filled up behind them. The church buzzed with low, respectful murmurs. Every time Ava craned to see who had arrived, the voices stopped, as though her head was a dial that turned down the volume. In these lulls, Ava's heightened senses were alert to every sound: high heels clacking on ancient tiles, the organ playing respectfully minor and low.

With no visible cue, the music swelled and the ceremony began, a priest head-to-toe in white swinging incense as the coffin was borne in by Luca, Boyko and four of the male soloists. Grief and guilt built up inside Ava like lactic acid in a muscle. There was only one way to process this and that was on stage. She wished now that she had insisted on performing the night after it had happened. In the ballet *The Red Shoes*, a girl's dancing slippers are enchanted and she is condemned to dance until she dies. That's what I need, thought Ava. I need to move until my feet are bleeding. She felt the urge to get up from the pew and run out of the church through the London traffic to the safety of the stage, but then the space next to her was empty and Raisa was on her feet, climbing the stairs to the pulpit. Suddenly the only sound was the fluttering of a hundred orders of service turned into makeshift fans.

She took a deep inhalation, the jagged after-breath of tears cried over days. 'I first danced with Nikolai Kirilov sixty years ago,' she began. 'We had over half a century together. And it wasn't enough. In Russian folk tradition, we have a "good" death or a "bad" death, and this influences other events. An example of a good death is when a person dies of old age, at a time God has planned for them, surrounded by their loved ones and this brings good harvests. A bad death may be unexpected or violent and after it will come storms, droughts, bad fortunes. Nicky was not a young man and he died in the arms of his beloved daughter. But he had so much left to give. This was a bad death.' She stared a long reproach Ava. 'This was a bad death.'

Ava thought for a wild instant that Raisa had known all along and had only been waiting for her moment in the pulpit to accuse her of killing her father, in front of everyone who would ever matter. Fear amplified her heartbeat to a timpani thump behind her ribs. She closed her eyes so that when every head in the church turned her way she wouldn't have to face it.

But Raisa was talking about their childhoods in Russia now, their first meeting at the Vaganova in the fifties.

She had no idea what had happened in the corridor. No one did. It was something Ava would take to the grave.

53

The wake was at the theatre. Where else? The same figures who had attended the opening night only a few days earlier again mingled, now dressed in black, in the atrium. Strangers paused in their gossip to offload their commiserations on to Ava, grasping her elbow and whispering that they were so sorry, that the ballet world had lost a great, that his spirit would live on through her.

Ava and Luca danced their own eulogy. Everything was distilled to its purest form, stripped back to the work. They wore plain black leotards and shoes broken in and sewn at the last minute, hot tears landing on her fingers and making the needle slip and gouge the skin under her fingernail. Their only accompaniment was the grand piano and a single violin in an arrangement created especially for this one-off performance, the violinist standing alone in a barren forest of empty chairs and music stands.

The last *pas de deux* from *Swan Lake* was four minutes and thirty-three seconds of betrayal, regret and anguished goodbye. From the beginning, she was not Odette but Ava. Through the steps she told her story: not acting, but not telling the whole truth either. She passed through the Kirilovan ideals of shape and speed. She discarded control and prettiness for something wild and true. She was a wild thing, constrained only by her skin. Creating, rather than imitating, for the first time in her life.

The fever infected Luca: the familiar *pas de deux* took on a new force, pure emotion originating from both their cores. This was what it felt like to carry your whole self into a dance and still call it ballet.

When they were finished, the violin's final note hung in the air. Was it that, or shock, that delayed the ovation? The quality of the applause was different in a way that couldn't be explained only by the occasion. If claps could come with question marks, then these would have.

The strength drained from Ava's legs: once in the wings she staggered, slid down the wall until she was sitting cross-legged in the dark. Her feet were burning; she untied her shoes and kicked them off. The ribbons signed autographs on the floor. She buried her face in her knees.

Eventually a heat at her side told her that Luca was sitting beside her.

'What *was* that?' Shock had stripped his voice of its usual playfulness.

'Sacrilege?' she replied.

'It was definitely a departure.'

'Well, look, I won't dance like that on the tour. From now on, I do it his way.'

'You're the boss.' He drummed a little rhythm on his thighs. 'Please don't take this the wrong way. This is in the context of me loving Mr K as much as anyone. But do you think that losing him . . . could it be that it frees you up to be who you really are?'

A tremor passed through her. Luca was as close as anyone had ever been to breaching the omerta of . . . it was buried so deep even she couldn't access it.

'We can talk about it on the plane,' he said, and then, sensing that even that was too close to the bone, 'Or, *or*, I could never mention it again as long as we both shall live?'

Only Luca could make Ava laugh at a time like this. Only Luca really knew her now. If there was anyone she could tell about those minutes in the corridor, if there was anyone who was on her side, it was him. She drew a fortifying breath.

'Luca, I—'

The curtain twitched and Boyko was there, looking terrified in his collar and tie. 'Ava, that was very . . . powerful.' He bounced on his heels, as though warming up. 'Now listen, there are a couple of people I want you to talk to outside.'

'For God's sake, Boyko,' snapped Luca. 'She's just buried her father. Give her a break.'

'Right. Yes,' said Boyko, and then, 'Sorry.'

'Well, that bodes well,' said Luca as Boyko retreated. 'He's hardly ruling with an iron fist, is he? Four days in charge and already he's taking instruction from his principals.'

He rose to standing without using his hands, limber as a snake obeying its charmer's flute. 'I'll go and press the flesh. You just go up and do what you need to do.'

He pulled her up as he always did and followed Boyko off the stage.

The floor was cool beneath her feet. She left her shoes behind on the unattended stage, called the lift, and let it carry her away.

54

Outside Ava's dressing room the lift bing-bonged repeatedly as Sakurako, Tomasin, Boyko and Felicity cleared out their dressing rooms for the last time. In the Gulag, lights winked as the dancers packed for the tour. Tomorrow was a rest day, then came the flight to Madrid.

She couldn't have said how long she'd been staring blindly out of the window when a scuffle outside and low murmured voices broke her trance. The lift scraped its doors together one last time, silence fell, and then there was a knock on the door.

'Miss Kirilova?'

It was Felicity, stepping half in and then half out of the door as though she was dancing with it. 'That was so – I mean completely – just so expressive – well, extraordinary.'

'It was a one-off,' said Ava, and Felicity looked so relieved she knew they'd all been talking about it and what the hell she thought she was doing.

'Well, what a *treat* for those of us who saw it, then.' She glanced backwards over her shoulder. 'Look, I found a couple of girls from the corps skulking outside, all star-struck. I know technically they shouldn't be here, but everything's crated up now and I didn't have the heart to send them packing. Anyway, they brought you these for good luck.'

She disappeared for a second, then returned swinging a flower arrangement in a pink card box. A spray of roses: half white, half dyed black, and interspersed with feathers in the same colours. Tacky as hell, like something you'd find on the buffet table at a three-star hotel. An insult to Ava's taste. Usually her mouth formed a reflexive smile at the sight of flowers – she had known the beam to flick on when passing a florist's window – but today she couldn't muster anything but irritation.

'For God's sake. What's the point of flowers when we're flying in two days' time?'

'Oh, I think it's a lovely gesture, so sweet. Actually, I had thought you might want to say thank you in person?' Felicity jerked her head backwards in a motion Ava didn't immediately understand.

'Why?'

Felicity pursed her lips and Ava wondered if she was about to give her a lecture about manners. Ava felt like screaming until her mirror cracked.

'It might be good for their morale?'

Ava had thought she had danced out all her anger, but now a fresh strain of it blasted through her. 'Their morale? *Their* morale? I'm the principal dancer of this company, Felicity, I'm supposed to carry this show and hold it all together for nine months without my father and you want *me* to boost *their* morale? Forgive me if my priority isn't tending to the feelings of some bloody junior dancer with crappy taste in flowers right now.'

Felicity blinked at her, aghast. 'Right,' she stammered. 'Of course. Sorry. I'd better just . . .' She went back into the corridor and Ava heard her say, 'Sorry, girls, I should've realised it wasn't a good time . . .' before closing the door behind her.

Ava exchanged an appalled glance with her reflection. Felicity hadn't said the girls were still *there*. This was not the person she wanted to be, taking her anger out on Felicity and two junior dancers who must have spent half a week's pay on that bouquet. She was acting like the worst part of him. She was a *bully*.

She yanked open the door to apologise but the corridor was empty. Even the flowers had gone. The only sign they had ever existed was a single black feather on the floor.

55

Ava Kirilova moved like a ghost through the concrete passages of the London Russian Ballet Theatre. In a corridor, a cleaner swept up a pile of white and grey feathers with a wide broom.

In Nicky's room, last-minute tour plans were being finalised. Caterers wheeled trolleys along corridors; cleaners swept litter from floors that had hosted their last ever guests. Every now and then a door would bang, or a blurred silhouette would pass across a door pane of frosted glass. Ava was no longer needed. And yet she was reluctant to leave the theatre, to say goodbye to it in its old incarnation. It felt too final – a ridiculous notion, given that nothing could be more final than a funeral.

A strange, bewitching force drove Ava down to the stage. Her stage. The lights were out, no red marks on the side of the stage. The only illumination was the green glow of the exit signs at the back of the house.

Her shoes lay where she had tossed them, just visible, the ribbons curled pink against the black floor. They still had another show left in them. No point leaving them here and angering the *domovoi*. When she picked them up, an electric charge seemed to pass through them.

That same force that had brought her here made Ava slide her aching feet into the shoes that held her shape and, when she laced them up, to pull a little tighter than usual. The punishment of the ribbon as satin sliced like wire into her skin felt wrong and right at the same time.

She executed a quick *pas de bourrée*, stopping when her right toe knocked against something solid. She leaned forward in a clumsy arabesque to inspect the object and saw the dull glint of a little silver hammer, rather like the one the injured second swan had carried. It must be the new vogue among the younger dancers. She kicked it to one side; it Catherine-wheeled across the stage floor and vanished behind a curtain.

Ava Kirilova began to dance.

No music, no partner, no audience, no choreography, only the steps her body compelled her to make. One last time to use this voice before dedicating the rest of her life to Nicky's work.

Yet his hold on her remained. Even this freestyle, impromptu performance culminated in a series of the *fouettés* that had caused so much trouble. She whirled on stage, dancing for the first time not in character but as herself. With no red light to guide her and no ballet master to correct her, Ava Kirilova travelled a little closer to the edge of the stage with each rotation.

A small voice inside her said calm down, slow down, stop. She held that voice underwater until it drowned.

She was not counting her *fouettés* but it was on the twentieth turn that it went wrong. Something gave at the heel of the right shoe: a rip, a detachment. It was as though a rug had been pulled; she lost her footing and staggered blindly across the stage, the momentum and dizziness of her own turns making her helpless.

When she fell from the edge of the stage, it was not like stepping off a rock into a lake. It was a car crash, not a rollercoaster. The six-foot drop into the orchestra pit was violent and ugly. The bad rhyme of the music stands and chairs broke her fall. There was no mattress, no welcome, no soft landing.

56

The hospital was green and white light.

Her knee was barbed wire and boiling oil.

Pain – not pain, the word wasn't big enough for this – pulsed from bone to skin in waves.

Jack held her hand. 'Oh, my darling,' he said. 'Oh I'm so, so, sorry. For this to happen to you, of all people, now, at all times. My poor, poor girl.'

Ava Kirilova's final curtain fell like a guillotine.

57

'Obviously he never actually got to move in, bless him.' Felicity
waved her hand over her chest in a guess at the sign of the cross.
'So Raisa says all his things won't be there yet. I don't know if
that's a comfort or a torture?'

The only torture was to go on living like this.

They were in the back seat of an Addison Lee, the passenger
seat pushed forward to accommodate Ava's outstretched leg. The
painkillers they had given her in the hospital slowed the doctor's
words, which looped in her head, to a lazy slur. *A tear to the
meniscus, the worst I have ever seen. You need three months' rest
and rehab to let it settle. Surgery will get you walking, but you
will never dance again.*

The decision had been made for her with those words. This
was the last journey she would ever take.

'At least you have something to look forward to. You probably
don't feel like looking forward to anything at the moment but you
know what I mean. You're not just any old injured-out dancer. I
know it's no consolation but honestly I think you'll be a *wonderful* creative director.'

'Thank you,' Ava said, not because she agreed, but to keep
Felicity's breathless monologue going.

Of course she could not take over the company. That complicated aspiration had been cut from her, blunt as final as amputa-
tion. The only way to honour Nicky's legacy was to hand the LRB
over to Boyko. Her ambition, her ego, had cost her first her father's
life and then her own leg. She was tainted, toxic. No one could
live with loss on this scale.

Felicity's prattling let Ava curl inside herself.

'Because it can be hard, can't it, to have constant reminders, although of course it's not as if you can forget, even for a second. Well, for a second, maybe, that first moment when you wake up, and then it all comes rushing back to you, doesn't it?'

'Absolutely.'

If Felicity registered Ava's mechanical, already-dead tone, she didn't remark upon it. 'The thing is, the house was all set up for Raisa to care for him here. It's all on the flat, no steps even between the house and garden. Jack says it's much better for you than your place because you had that one step down to the garden, didn't you, and he didn't want to take any risks. It's in a place called Gabriel's Hill. Mad, isn't it, how you can live in London your whole life and there's still these little pockets you've never even heard of, let alone been to? It's supposed to be very nice.'

'Mmm.' Ava stared blindly at a row of Georgian townhouses, and then at the high-rise estate facing them. Would London *ever* thin out?

'So we've got a lot to get through. I'm on a super early flight tomorrow to get me to Madrid in time for the matinée, but this afternoon I'm all yours. We've got to unpack and also go through – well, we'll deal with that once we're in, and . . .'

Ava let the drone merge with the rumble of the engine. Felicity had packed up her dressing room for her and emptied the wardrobe at her flat. She had loved that place, with her pictures and her privacy and the barre on the bedroom wall. She observed with detachment that it was a shame she would never see it again. That same watching-from-a-distance part of her remembered now that at one point she had thought of offering it to the second swan, but then the cracks in her relationship with Nicky had started to show and she could care only for herself. It was out of her hands now. In a few days the flat would revert to the company, or wherever her property defaulted to after her death, and they could house whoever they liked there.

One word pierced the fog.

'Sorry, what about Luca?' She turned her heavy head to Felicity.

'I said, he'll come around eventually.' Felicity faltered. 'Boyko naturally had to keep Sakurako and Tomasin in the principal roles while we find him a new partner, which is obviously a *nightmare* with no cover for the main roles – oh, God, sorry, I didn't mean – anyway, Luca's doing Benno, for now.'

Benno. A good part for a rising star but really just the prince's sidekick. Luca was in the kind of role he'd been dancing ten years ago. She had derailed her best friend's career.

'He must hate me.' More guilt: another stone for her pocket.

'God, no, how could he hate you? He's just – it's too big for him to know how to say it. He can't hide this behind a joke. We're all dealing with this in our own way.'

Ava registered the dark pouches under Felicity's eyes. 'And how are you dealing with it?'

She squeezed Ava's hand. 'Work. There's so much to do.'

They were in a tree-lined parade now, little designer boutiques and one of those restaurants pretending to be a pub. At a large gate, the driver indicated left.

'Are we here?' she asked in surprise.

'Yes,' said Felicity, as the driver left the car to enter a keycode on a huge iron gate.

'But this isn't countryside at all!' They were still in London-London, barely even suburbia.

'It was Mr K's idea of countryside,' said Felicity fondly. 'A handful of trees and he thought he was stranded in the wilderness.'

The gates gave on to a leafy hill. They were the only car on the road. The driver pulled up outside a bungalow. In its front garden was a sculpture of twisted steel that – like a Kirilov ballerina, like one of his creatures – conjured a world of movement with a few clean lines.

'Oh, how *lovely*,' said Felicity. 'What a wonderful place to get well. So quiet. So private.'

Good. No one to stop her writing her own end to her story.

'And so safe,' she continued, as a black car rolled silently by. 'They've got their own private security force!'

Also good. If they could be the ones to find her . . . dealing with things like that was probably part of their job remit. She imagined a former police officer or soldier, used to such sights.

The driver helped Ava on to her crutches. She winced as she hauled herself step by agonising step towards the house. She was ungainly, unbalanced, unballerina.

'Go through to the back, Ava, while I get your things.'

She stood in a hallway. A pile of unopened bills and junk mail lay on the floor where the door had pushed them aside. White walls hung with art made it feel like a museum or perhaps a hospital waiting area. Bedroom doors were flung open. A third door was closed, a silver key in the lock. The larger bedroom was dominated by a huge canvas that caught her eye and held it. The greeny-grey wash looked abstract at first glance but if you stared through it you fell through time and saw a landscape, the endless steppe of her father's childhood. She kept her eyes on that for a long, long time, as though she expected a little black-and-white boy in vest and knee socks to run at her from the notional horizon as though across a huge stage, and land panting in the room before her. Ava's throat constricted.

The second bedroom was smaller and plainer: the only art a bland silk-screen print in pale pink and yellow. *I make special room for you*, he had said. This was it, was it? It had all the personality of a standard double in the kind of corporate hotel they found themselves in on tour. There was nothing of her here: no proof she had been anything but an extension of him.

When all the bags and cases were piled in the hallway, Felicity stood in the doorway with a bulging Waitrose carrier. 'Go through to the back, go on. I've got some basics in, I'll put the kettle on. Ooh, isn't this nice, Ava? He's got – he *had* – such wonderful taste.' Her brightness sputtered for a second.

In the huge living area, the sun hammered its fists on the huge patio doors. The *Swan Lake* tour poster was propped against the wall, next to an unsettling dark blue painting. Ava turned away from both of them, lowered herself inelegantly on to a black leather sofa, sticky and unpleasant. She drank the weak tea Felicity made, then listened to the xylophone clatter of wooden coat hangers as she unpacked clothes that Ava would never wear.

When Felicity had finished, her face was shiny and pink. 'Scorchio!' she said. 'Now listen. As I was saying in the car, we've got someone to stay with you.'

But that will ruin everything, thought Ava. She bit her tongue until she tasted salt.

'And obviously pretty much the entire staff are on tour or sabbatical because of the revamp. So we thought we'd arrange for Lizanne to be a kind of companion?'

Ava didn't know a Lizanne, which was fine by her. A stranger would be easier to get rid of.

'Right,' she said. 'Good idea.'

'Oh,' said Felicity, clearly having expected more resistance. 'Well. Fabulous. Right, then. She can be here tonight, if you like? I'll get her to call you. Before she comes.' She pulled a printed sheet from her handbag. 'What else? Um, I have to talk you through the security measures and stuff. And also . . . pffff, it's a bit delicate.' Felicity looked over Ava's shoulder at the paintings on the walls as though hoping to find scripts with the right words written on them. 'I didn't tell the others about this but when I was in your dressing room, and then again at your flat, I found rather a lot of cash squirrelled away. I counted it up – hang on.' Felicity pulled a mint-green notebook from her handbag and flipped to a page of scribbled numbers. 'There's actually – well, I stopped counting at around thirty-five thousand pounds?'

The subtext was: Ava, what the hell?

Any other time, Ava would have been stunned to realise how much she had siphoned off. Any other time, to have her fund exposed would have been humiliating. She waited to feel guilt or shame but those words had new meaning now. This secret was so far down the ladder that her cheeks barely burned.

'So I know a little bit about – I've been chatting to your father's solicitor, and . . .' Felicity straightened a perfectly aligned painting. 'Perhaps don't put it in the bank just yet. It might not do you any harm to have some cash around. Apparently the company's finances will take a while to untangle. I'm going to take out some petty cash, Ava, around three thousand, and put the rest in the safe. I've got your passport, too, and all the other documentation for the house and what have you. I'm sorry, we haven't had a chance to go through that. I have the code: you know how to access it when you need it, don't you? It's 19401988: your father's birth year followed by yours. I won't write that down. But once I've locked it behind me, only you can open it again.'

'Sure,' said Ava.

'And what's this?' Felicity opened a checked laundry bag and pulled out a bunch of black rags, the ribbon of a *pointe* shoe. It was Ava's stage gear: the leotard she'd been cut out of in hospital and the shoes she'd been wearing when she fell. Felicity quailed. 'God, sorry, Ava, I thought we'd got rid of all that . . .'

But Ava had already picked up the shoes, her hands finding their way where the feet never would again. The ribbon had gone on the right heel, come clean away from the satin. That would make anyone lose their footing.

Looking down at her fingernail where the needle had gone under the nail bed and pulled the half-moon out of shape, she experienced a lurch of vertigo, an echo of her fall. Of all the things to end her career: her own carelessness with a needle. She felt the shock of the impact, strong as the first time.

Using all the strength she had left, she threw the shoe at the poster. Its blocky toe hit Odile's shoulder, but the 'glass' in the frame was Perspex, and no damage was done.

Felicity bent to retrieve it. 'I tell you what. Let's put it all in the studio, for now. Lizanne can sort through it, if you want her to.'

'What studio?'

Felicity nodded to the door halfway along the corridor with the silver key protruding from its lock. She looked as if she was going to cry. 'Mr K hoped that you might stay with him here, sometimes,' she said. 'And he knew you were more likely to do that if you had somewhere you could dance.'

They got to their feet, Felicity with effortless grace, Ava with effort that left her sweat-drenched and shaking. As they drew closer, the smell of rosin, like incense, filled the air. Felicity opened the door and the smell intensified: she flipped a switch and they blinked into a bright white room. At the far wall stood Felicity and a scrawny old woman, dressed in black and hunched over walking sticks. *Raisa?* Only when Ava stepped back in horror and the old lady copied her did she realise she was looking at her own reflection in a floor-to-ceiling mirror.

There was a barre nailed to the wall: Ava groped her way along it until she came to what could only be described as a shrine.

The photographs of Ava outnumbered the icons in the Russian church. Ava in costume, Ava in rehearsal, Ava on stage. A pair of her first *pointe* shoes, framed – Ava recognised the dark bloom of blood on the right toe, felt again the shock of sudden-onset adult-hood. The notes for every dance he'd ever made on her. A toile from an old costume fitting. A framed review of *Zeus and Athena*. One huge blank space remained, a picture hook patiently hanging high on a wall, and Ava knew that it was waiting for the *Swan Lake* tour poster.

On the other side of that gap, a collection of smaller frames, silver and gold. There she was with her father in Red Square, both wearing fur *ushanka* hats. Next to that, a certificate she had never seen but instantly knew the significance of: some animal instinct made her narrow her eyes to blur the lettering, then cast them down to the floor and along the skirting board. Face-down on the floor in the corner was a frame that clearly hadn't made the cut.

'Ooh, what's this little thing?' Felicity picked the frame up, turned it over and blanched. Ava could see her fishing for the right thing to say but there was no need: she knew from the frame itself, its scrapes and notches, the peeling of the gilt, what it held: an old snapshot, the stark unflattering gloss and flash of a 1990s camera. It had been taken at Ava's first public performance. She was four years old and the parent holding her hand wasn't Nicky, it was—

It was—

Her detachment receded and feeling rushed in. Ava twisted her whole body away from the picture. She couldn't get out of the room fast enough, staggering on her sticks like a malfunctioning robot.

'Lock it up!' The force of her command took them both by surprise. 'Lock the whole room up and put the key in the safe.'

'But what if you—' began Felicity.

Ava's voice soared to a child's pitch. 'Please, Felicity! Please, I can't!'

Felicity dropped the laundry bag and rushed to take Ava's arm. 'Of course,' she said. 'Of course, my love. Whatever you need.' She turned out the light and locked the door behind them. 'You sure?' she asked.

Ava nodded. 'Take it away. I *can't*.'

She stood shaking in the corridor, willing the earlier numbness to return. Her pulse ran a race with itself, only slowing when at last she heard the beep-beep-beep as the safe door closed, the soft click of the painting connecting with the wall.

58

When Felicity had gone, Ava picked up the telephone handset and took a moment to study the unfamiliar interface. It rang in her hand and she almost dropped it. She jabbed the green button, hoping that would receive the call.

'Hi, lovely, it's Lizanne.' *Hi, lovely?* Even if Ava hadn't been intending to get rid of Lizanne, the voice would have prejudiced her against her. Grating and ingratiating, an edge of desperation under the informality. 'I was just calling to let you know I'll be over tonight.'

'Thanks, but I won't be needing you.' Ava stroked the cover of the pale green notebook, then slid it into a drawer. 'I've actually booked someone else for the job. I won't tell anyone; you can keep the money.'

There was a gasp on the line. 'It's not about the *money*. I'm supposed to look after you. Go through, you know, the whole recovery process with you. It was all arranged.'

'Not with me.'

She heard Lizanne swallow. 'But – the medicine, and the post, and – look, I'll keep in touch anyway. I'm in the theatre most days. If you want me, just call. You've got the number? What am I saying? Of course you've got the number.'

'There's really no need. Thank you. I'm going now.'

She let the phone crash into its cradle and she was free.

She sat in the living area, her gaze resting on the dark blue painting until it rippled like water. The tide of her thoughts pulled her back to the ballet. The white swan chose death over living without the person she loved the most. Substitute the prince for ballet itself and Odette's choice now seemed reasonable. Substitute the prince for her father and it seemed inevitable.

The sun bore down like a laser. In the bedroom there were five days' worth of opiate painkillers. By tomorrow, the whole company would be out of the country and there would be no more knocks on the door. Just one more blazing dawn to survive, and she would follow her father.

59

Death came to Ava Kirilova in her sleep that night. Given time, she might have outgrown the guilt; she might have danced out the grief. But one had caused the other, and both came from another loss that was threatening to surface after half a life submerged. And that was more than she could survive.

Muscle memory dies hard: flesh follows its ingrained patterns at the risk of its own destruction. Limbs twitch to perform their old movements even when they are broken. The brain has no such loyalty to the truth: it is plastic, able to reshape reality to protect itself from pain. When life is unliveable, the mind comes to the rescue. It whispers stories so convincing that they become not just a refuge from reality but a new reality.

In the empty stage set of the dreamscape, Ava Kirilova rewrote her own history. Her body was broken beyond repair and reshaped beyond her control, so she changed her story instead. Her mind dashed through her past, scavenging moments and memories, things she had experienced and things she had only seen, from which to construct a safe identity. As she slept, she returned to a time before she was Ava Kirilova at all.

In that space between sleep and reality she thought the sound – an old-fashioned, mechanical trill – was a backstage bell. Ten minutes to curtain: time to check her make-up, secure her head-dress, tame stray feathers, breathe in, breathe out. Then it rang again, and she opened her eyes to blinding sunlight and sweat in soft sheets. She was not napping in a dressing room at the London Russian or on a bunk in the Gulag; and that bell would never sound for her again.

She was in Ava Kirilova's big white bed and the noise was her doorbell.

'I'm coming!' Her voice echoed in the too-big space.

The front door was close by. In this bungalow, the bedrooms were at the front of the house. Still, the journey when she contemplated it felt ten times longer. Gingerly she raised herself to sitting; carefully she grabbed the crutches that had stood sentry while she slept, and began her slow shuffle. Mr K taught them to leap as high as their heads and still land soundlessly. People came to see ballerinas, not to hear them. Every step on crutches was a betrayal of her training.

The front door itself was solid bronze, more suited to the entrance of a museum than a private house. Either side of the door were glass panels the texture of bark, and through one of these she saw a shifting pastel shape. Sliding back the bolt and turning the key was a balancing act. The door swung inwards; heat hit her like she'd opened an oven. The shape revealed itself to be a huge bouquet of flowers, fat pink peonies and heralding lilies, supported by tanned bare legs in gladiator sandals.

'Flowers for Ava Kirilova,' said the voice behind the bouquet.

'Oh, sorry,' said Ava. 'I'm Juliet.'

INTERVAL

NICKY

60

Drizzle. Always the drizzle when the new intake arrived in September. But Nikolai Kirilov did not mind that. If they could love his theatre in rain they would adore it in sunshine. On a damp day in the second week of September, the new intake arrived to begin their careers at the London Russian Ballet Academy. As always, they arrived for registration not at the entrance to the tower block but via the theatre's front door, and gathered in the atrium. Nicky watched them from the second-floor balcony. Each child was accompanied by one or two parents dragging trunks and cases. Some of the girls carried the ballet bags they'd had since they were four: the pastel-pink rucksacks with *Jessica's Ballet Shoes* or *Dancing Princess* in peeling decals on the side. He would soon get rid of those.

The children gravitated towards those they remembered from their auditions, grouping in twos or threes. Even at twelve they were assessing each other as rivals as·well as comrades. The boys and girls, who had not met at the auditions, eyed each other up shyly. Subconsciously Nicky began pairing them. Was there a great partnership here? Every year, a couple of kids stood out for Nicky. From the boys, it had been that cheeky little Italian with the fantastic *ballon* who was currently prising his mother off his arm finger by finger. From the girls, it was Juliet Plunkett. At her audition she had brimmed with an intensity that you just couldn't instil in a dancer. But Plunkett! What sort of name was that? It sounded like a skin complaint.

He scanned the crowds for her. He recognised her from the back by the gait that would have singled her out as a dancer on the street. She walked three paces ahead of a woman absorbed in her flip phone. Scourge of modern life, those things were.

When all the pupils had been ticked off the list, Raisa nodded up at Nicky, who descended the stairs like a prince at a ball. The milling crowd fell silent. Some of the children attempted to form a queue.

'Please.' He smiled and held up his palms. 'Keep talking. Say hello to new friends. I come to you all today.'

Nicky always made a point of greeting every family individually, allowing three minutes per conversation. He praised the child to the parents, mentioned some quality unique to their child and their child alone by rotating the same four or five compliments. This meant that at half-term, when their shell-shocked child returned from their first six weeks at the Academy, the parents would remember how nice Mr Kirilov had been, how kind, how invested in their child. That first half-term holiday was always a flashpoint. The children were institutionalised enough to find home jarring, but not so far under his control that they could maintain their discipline.

He kept Raisa at his side. A man and a woman, an enduring partnership: it helped the parents feel that the company was less an establishment, more a family. The irony of course was that for years Nicky had begged Raisa to give him a child, to play her part in making their union last forever. What a dancer their child could have been! He had even picked out the names: Ava for a girl, after his mother Avelina; Pyotr for a boy, after his father. Or one of each, a partnership! Imagine!

But Raisa would not countenance childbirth, and no other dancer was good enough.

Today, he was relieved to encounter few pushy parents. One father presented a list of vegetables his son wouldn't eat, and a woman gave Raisa the breakdown of her daughter's five-step bedtime routine. Both would go in the trash as soon as the parents had gone. Nicky controlled what they ate now; Nicky rose and sank the sun on their days. His creatures never refused his food, not once they understood that engines as refined as theirs needed premium fuel. And no pupil at the LRBA ever had trouble sleeping. Nicky worked them so hard that they crawled into bed. To begin with, at least, they begged for sleep.

Juliet Plunkett's mother had a small head on a long neck. Her hair was frosted into highlights and the gold in her ears was cheap nine-carat. She wore a crisp white shirt tucked into slim jeans that showcased narrow hips and long legs. She was a little out of shape, but there was a dancer's frame in there somewhere. She even held herself, quite unselfconsciously, in fourth position.

'Mrs Plunkett,' he said. 'Is pleasure to meet.'

'*Ms* Plunkett,' she said. 'Grace. And – you too,' she said, but even as she took his hand she was looking over his shoulder at the theatre with a critical, doubtful eye that told Nicky it didn't have the filter of stardust for her. She didn't see the beauty in austerity, the blank canvas of concrete, just the outdated lighting and the rusting window frames. He saw her brow pucker at the thought of leaving her child here. It was an expression he knew well.

'You dance too?' he asked. 'You look like yes.'

Grace laughed. 'Me? God, no. I don't exercise at all if I can help it,' she said. 'But I keep fit running around after this one.' She placed a hand on Juliet's head. The child rolled her eyes and ducked away. 'I won't know what to do with myself when she's gone. Juggling the diary, Mum's taxi service, the packed lunches, all that.'

Her voice cracked, and Nicky knew there would be tears in the street.

'You have very talented daughter. She is *born* to dance.'

In his peripheral vision, Juliet lit up as if she'd been plugged into the mains.

'Funnily enough, they said that when she was born,' said Grace, not quite crying yet. 'When they moved her legs to check her joints, her hips opened like a book and they just kept going and going. They had to get her checked over by a paediatrician.

But the doctor knew about dancers and he said that's a medical condition known as "perfect turnout" – "You want to get this one on the stage," he said. And twelve years and God knows how much money later, here we are.' Her eyes kept roaming around the atrium, as if hoping to alight on something that would validate the commitment and the expense, justify the imminent separation.

'Please.' Nicky suppressed his irritation. 'Do not judge theatre on walls. Judge on stage. We give Juliet best education dancer can have.'

'Well, what do I know?' said Grace, and then her face crumpled and tears poured, so many and so fast that it seemed her whole head must be filled with water.

'Oh, my God, *Mum*!' Juliet's cheeks blazed with embarrassment.

'Is fine,' he said, a hand on Grace's forearm. 'Is big deal. You trust us with your baby.'

'Sorry.' She brushed her cheek with the inside of her wrist. 'We lost her dad when she was a tiddler, she doesn't even remember him, so it's always been just the two of us. I'm going to miss her so much.' She gave a watery smile. 'I'm going to go now, darling, before I embarrass you any more.'

When Grace opened her arms, Juliet rolled her eyes again, but then her body twitched instinctively into the hug. Mother and child wrapped their arms around each other as if they were drowning. Grace inhaled her daughter's hair.

Juliet was the first to disentangle. Her eyes shone with tears that didn't fall.

'Be a good girl for Mr Kirilov,' sniffed Grace.

'I'll be the *best*,' said Juliet, tilting her chin.

Grace all but ran through the doors, waved once and was swallowed by the street. Juliet breathed in, breathed out, and looked up at him with dry eyes. 'When do we start?' she asked.

He clapped his hands and laughed with delight. The sounds bounced around the atrium, drawing all heads their way. 'Now!' he said. 'We take you to dorms and then we dance!'

At Raisa's signal, the children followed her across the walkway and into the tower block. Juliet was the last in the line. Nikolai Kirilov put his lips to the child's ear.

'Welcome home,' he whispered.

61

The police came two weeks before the end of that first half-term. The uniformed officers, a woman and a man, arrived as Nicky was workshopping a scene from his new ballet. Earlier in the day, Juliet Plunkett's mother had eaten breakfast at her desk. Her takeout breakfast bowl had been labelled without mention of the sesame oil in the topping, a substance to which she was allergic. She had left her EpiPen in the pocket of the wrong jacket, and she had died in the ambulance on the way to hospital.

Nicky did not hear them break the news. By the time he arrived in the boardroom, barely panting even though he'd taken the stairs two at a time, that conversation was over and Raisa had the file ready to go. 'It was just the child and the mother,' she explained for his benefit. 'There's no next of kin. Just some uncle she's never met out in Dubai who doesn't want anything to do with her. He's asked if she can stay at the school while he decides what to do. He'll pay the fees.'

'Of course,' said Nicky. 'Never mind fees. Of *course* she stay.' He tuned out what the police were saying. Let Raisa deal with that. He knew only that he could not lose this dancer. There was more to Juliet than her incredible turnout, her perfect carriage, her acting and her grace, her ability to roll through *demi-pointe* as if her feet were rockers on a chair. There was grit in this oyster. She was attracted to the idea of perfection – that there was a correct way to do that, a correct way to do this – but the submission cost her; she had to fight herself to conform. Nicky had decided a week into this term that harnessing this flame would be the great third act of his career.

When the police were gone, they reverted to Russian. 'She will have finished eating her lunch now,' said Raisa, but when she went to get the girl Nicky grabbed his old partner by the wrist, pulling her body in towards his in a smooth imitation of the way they had moved together when they were young. She pivoted on the ball of her left foot to face him.

'Not so fast,' he said.

They had shared an intuition on stage that carried over into their every interaction. He saw in the flare of her pupils that she knew what he was going to say.

'Raisa, what if our Ava isn't a baby but a girl?'

She took a step back from him and shook her head. 'Don't be *ridiculous*, Kolya.'

They descended the steps together in perfect synchrony even while opposed.

'She is the raw material of perfect,' he said. 'She is so unformed. And all that fire! I can't lose her to someone else. She is still young enough for me to create the best dancer the world has ever seen. We can make her together, Raisa! If we find her the right partner, it's the next best thing to being able to dance together again!' His fingertips tingled at the thought.

'I never wanted to reincarnate myself,' she said. 'That was always your dream. And you can't seriously expect her to take your name. It's all she has left of her family.'

'*I* will become her family. What better family than this? She has never known a father. I can give her that.'

They were in the atrium now. He gestured broadly at the space, his heart thudding the way it had always done moments before a show. He felt the old urge to perform a *grand jeté* but then he was struck by the thought he might lose her to the Royal Ballet or the English National, or, worse, to one of the great international companies, and weights seemed to attach themselves to his feet. No one but he could realise this dancer's potential. No one.

Raisa said, not looking him in the eye, 'You are assuming she will say yes.'

That stopped him in his tracks. 'Why wouldn't she say yes?' Apart from anything else, the child was all but homeless.

Raisa clicked her tongue. 'She has just lost her mother, Kolya! Have you forgotten that? She won't know which way is up!'

He took a moment to reframe the mother's death, not as an opportunity but as a loss.

'Then she needs me in many ways,' he countered. 'Stability. Attention. *Love.*'

Raisa threw up her hands. 'We both know no one can stop you once you have set your heart on a project,' she said. 'I will teach her, of course. I will help you make her the best dancer she can be. But if you think I'm going to be that child's mother – if you think I am going to *bring her up* – then you are insane.'

They broke the news to Juliet in her dormitory. Despite Raisa's insistence that she would not nurture the child, she had one arm around Juliet's shoulder as they sat either side of her on the bed, and it was Raisa who did the talking, saying how sad and sorry they both were about it.

When the facts were delivered, Juliet didn't say anything. She picked up the gilt-framed photograph on her bedside table of her much younger self and her mother at some church hall ballet recital. She clutched the frame so tightly that her fingernails turned a darker shade of pink. After a few minutes, she jerked her head upwards and stared at Nicky with wild, wide eyes.

'What does this mean for me? Will you send me away, without anyone to pay the school fees?'

Nicky shot Raisa a sideways look of triumph. You see? it said. I was right about her. Such dedication to the dance!

Raisa shook her head and stood up: two gestures that said, she's all yours.

Nicky took the photograph from Juliet's hands. She resisted for a second, then let her fingers slacken. He set the frame face-down on her bed, then took both her hands in his. 'Juliet,' he said. 'Dear Juliet. Come. We take tea together.'

62

He led her by the hand, out of the dormitory and past a file of pupils fizzing with curiosity about why they had been forced to wait in the corridor.

'Where's he taking her?' his ears picked out of the whispers, and 'What's so special about *Juliet*?' before Raisa sent them all scuttling back to their rooms. There she would brief them on what had happened, although not on the offer he was about to make. Not yet.

Excited as Nicky was about showing the girl his room, he did not take her there but in a taxi, to the little Russian tea-room three miles from the theatre, where they knew his name and his usual order.

They sat in his favourite booth, set in the corner and garlanded with damask drapes. Juliet remained silent as the samovar steamed between them, and the waiter laid out the blinis and the marinated cucumber and the strawberry jam. She remained focused on her hands in her lap. When the tiny cakes came, she looked to him for permission before taking one, but left it untouched. Every movement she made, even sitting down, marked her out as a dancer, and not just any dancer but a Kirilovan one. The perfect straight line of her back, the long white throat under a tilted chin. Twelve years old, perfectly but not yet fully formed: the vessel into which he could pour his experience, his passion, his *life*.

She mesmerised him; she stole his words. He was not sure he knew how to do this in any language.

'I do not see my mother since I am eleven years old,' he said, to his own surprise.

Juliet raised her head a fraction but didn't meet his eye.

'I am eleven when I go to Vaganova.'

The mention of the world-famous academy jerked her head up, and he had her back.

'Eight, ten hours a day, in studio. Strictest ballet school in world! Makes my little school look like playground. Ha?'

She didn't smile.

'In holidays, I work in kitchens; there is no money to send me home. I work, I train, I dance. I travel Russia, I travel world. I know I must defect to West. Soviet ballet too rigid, always the same, controlling my ideas, no freedom. I know this means I do not see her again. Old life – gone!' He made a puff-of-smoke gesture with his hands. 'She die, five years after.'

'But leaving was your choice,' said Juliet, crimson spots appearing on her cheeks. 'I didn't choose this.'

She spoke without accusation, but anger bubbled in his blood. Only a dancer who'd had the luxury of growing up in the West would assume defection was a *choice*. He had had to leave the motherland to dance freely! It was a compulsion as strong as the need to dance.

But the child could not help where she had grown up, and her brimming eyes cooled his veins.

'I know is not same,' he said. 'But I understand *some*. How it is to miss Mama. And I understand how it is for ballet to save. Find new family. Listen. I have suggestion.'

There were conditions attached, of course, but he sold it to her as if he were pitching to a new patron. A room of her own in his apartment, which more or less meant living in the theatre. He would bring her on tour and she would take class with the company. Private coaching from himself and Raisa would fast-track her to soloist. He would create dance after dance on her, original works, and he would mould the classics to her, too: *Giselle*, *Sleeping Beauty*; and one day, when she was ready, he would create the ultimate dance on her: a Kirilov *Swan Lake*.

When he finished, he found that his mouth had gone very dry. He took a sip of water.

'What you say?'

Juliet's unexpected silence shot an arrow of fear into Nicky. Perhaps Raisa was right. It was too soon. He should have made her sweat a little: threatened her with the uncle in Dubai, pretended the fees would be a problem. But, as the seconds ticked by, he understood that she was absorbing it, rather than considering whether to accept it.

'Will it make things weird with my friends?' she asked him eventually.

God, yes. That was the idea: to pluck her out of the flowerbed and grow her like an orchid under glass.

'Maybe in beginning,' he conceded. 'But where you going, you no need friends. Anyway. There is no friendship in ballet. Partnership, yes. Rivalry, yes. Friendship? Not so much.'

She nodded at this harsh truth as if he had confirmed something she had long suspected.

'I give you some time in corps,' he offered. 'Six months. For experience. For discipline. *And* – ' he felt the familiar rush of a good idea arriving fully formed ' – we ban company from discussing. You are my daughter, is no other story. No one to gossip. Is new rule.'

'Not mention my mum, either, though?'

Nicky was no stranger to being cruel to be kind, but he felt an internal lurch as he ascended to a new plane of tough love. 'Is for best. We do this hundred per cent or we no do at all.'

'Am I allowed to *remember* her?'

He laughed. 'Even *I* cannot control in here.' He tapped his forefinger on her head, not her heart. 'But is not good to only think of past. I give you future. Best future!'

She picked the little cake on her plate apart, sending pink crumbs over the white tablecloth.

'Is problem?' He was so used to uttering the phrase sarcastically that it came out harsher than he'd intended, and he saw her retreat into herself. 'You tell me. We solve,' he said as gently as he could.

'It's just – I feel bad for my mum, changing my name.'

The ungrateful little— He bit back his instinctive reply.

'I understand,' he said. 'But is not name change. Is coronation. This make you ballet royalty. Eh? *Ava Kirilova*.' An electric thrill ran through him as he spoke the name aloud to someone other than Raisa. 'Ultimate ballerina. Big chance. World is waiting.'

She cupped her hand, scraped the crumbs from the tablecloth and scattered them back on the plate, as though she had all the time in the world.

'Is your choice,' were his words, but his tone said *these are my conditions*. If this was to work, his power must be absolute.

A long, fractured breath came out of her. At the end of it, her face was set. Her decision was made.

'OK,' she said. 'I mean, thank you.'

It was the result he wanted, if not the effusive gratitude.

'Thank you, *Papa*,' he said.

'Thank you, *Papa*, she repeated, and the word – the name he knew she had never called anyone before – acted like an incantation. She smiled, and it was like the first snowdrop of the year. The bond between them formed, strong enough that he felt that he might raise his hand into the air between them and feel an invisible cord connecting them. She was his.

After all those years of longing and persuading and giving up. He had his Ava, at last. His little Kirilova.

He could not *wait* to create her.

CERTIFIED COPY OF AN ENTRY OF ADOPTION

NO OF ENTRY   308904

DATE OF BIRTH OF CHILD   22 March 1988

REGISTERING DISTRICT   London

BIRTHPLACE OF CHILD   Loughton, Essex

NAME AND SURNAME OF CHILD   Juliet Plunkett

SEX   Female

NAME AND SURNAME OF   Nikolai Petrovich

ADOPTER   Kirilov

ADDRESS   446 Commercial Road,
      London N1

OCCUPATION   Ballet Director

DATE OF ADOPTION ORDER   4 April 2001

Description of Court or by Whom Effected
London High Court of Justice, Family Division

ACT III

ROMAN

63

Once they had taken the money out of the safe, neither of them could believe what they had done. Juliet sat on the sofa with the money spread around her, almost scared to touch it. Roman rifled through the box of paperwork, words dancing on the pages, not knowing what he was looking for or how he might recognise it when he found it. He took out a silver key from between two folds and dropped it on to the marble worktop with a little chime. Juliet began to shift cash from place to place without seeming to count it. Next, he drew a passport and an airline ticket, opened them both up.

What he saw made his sweat cool on his skin.

He looked at Juliet, then at the photograph of Ava Kirilova, then back again. The story his eyes were telling him couldn't be true, because that would mean that – it *couldn't* be – his mind kept running into a brick wall.

'Juli—' he began, but a shadow caught his eye and the name died on his lips.

Backlit in the doorway, like a bad fairy at a christening, was Katya.

The experienced soldiers had told Roman it was true what people said about time expanding in a crisis: some trick of the brain means that it really is possible to see your life flash before your eyes when violence is imminent. It was not Veronika and Zlata who revisited him now. Rather, in the breath before hell broke loose, he replayed the past fortnight with Katya and Juliet (Juliet?). He had gone from dupe to conspirator to love and back to dupe again. Katya had lied to him; he had lied to Katya; Juliet had been lying to him. Juliet *was* Ava Kirilova, she must be. Unless

289

she was some long-lost twin sister or doppelgänger like something from one of her own ballets, No. 36 Gabriel's Hill was *her* house, that was *her* money, those were *her* paintings. So why call herself by another name? Why pretend the ballerina in the poster was someone else? Why break into her own damn safe?

Why lie to him, or rather – why *this* lie?

'Max?' Her eyes were wide and wet. Was she acting now? The irony only clipped the side of his thoughts: that he, who had lied to her on a gross scale from their first meeting, had no right to the truth from her.

Whatever this is, thought Roman, my job is to resolve it and keep us all safe, but before he could complete the thought Katya was in action, taking Juliet's crutch and bringing it down on her head. Juliet – he could only think of her as Juliet – pitched face-first on to the sofa, her bad leg twisting behind her, and time resumed its normal pace.

'*You fucking liar!*' Katya rained blows upon Juliet's back and legs but Roman knew that her words were meant for him. The same survival instinct that had seen him drive across Ukraine made him slide the passport into his back pocket – Katya must not know about it – then grab the crutch and dash it to the floor. He held Katya's arms by her sides and spoke to her as calmly as he could manage. She wasn't listening. Something had come loose inside her. She looked capable of anything. Whatever crazy long game Juliet was playing, Katya was the emergency here. Everything he did would be to keep Juliet safe. Everything else – and it was a roaring river, accumulating behind a dam – he would deal with when she was safe.

'Max, please!' Juliet didn't *look* scheming. She looked broken and terrified. 'What's happening? Who is this?'

'Are you *sleeping* with her?' asked Katya.

'Of course I'm not!'

To his horror, Katya cupped his balls. Her hands were so close to the passport that he didn't dare buck away. 'Get off! What are you doing that for?'

'Showing the cripple who's in charge,' said Katya, but she took her hand away from his fly. She was listening, even if that attention was the calm before the next storm.

'Right. Well, calm down and listen. I've been working on this for a while.'

'So the story about the footballer and the watch was bullshit?'

'OK, yes. But—'

'I *knew* it. Why didn't you just tell me about this?'

'Because. I knew you'd do something like this. I knew I'd have a better chance working on my own. And I would have, too – I'd have been out of here and on my way to you with a sack of cash if you had waited for me at the Jester like I told you to.'

She nodded once, deciding to believe him. 'So what were you going to do with her?'

'I'd have left her sleeping, then brought all this to you,' he improvised. 'And then we would have had a discussion – *without witnesses*, for God's sake – and we would have counted up the cash and we would have – I don't know, it's hard to say without knowing how much is here. But it's tens of thousands, Katya. It's life-changing money.'

'So now what? She has seen us now.'

'Thanks to you,' he said.

He saw Katya curse her own impulsivity, which meant she believed him. So what did he say now, that would get Katya out of here and make Juliet safe? He was driving a car in thick fog, only able to see a metre ahead and the road bending all the time.

'Max—' interrupted Juliet. Roman wanted more than anything to drop Katya and hold Juliet but he couldn't afford to. 'Max!' Juliet's voice was distorted; her lip was beginning to swell where Katya had hit her. 'Show me that passport and tell me who the hell this person here is!'

Katya turned on her. 'Stupid bitch, shut up!' she said in English, and then switched back to Ukrainian for Max. 'We get rid of her.'

'No,' said Roman. 'That was never in my plan. I'm not having that on my conscience, Katya. I'd rather give us both up to the police.'

Katya looked around at the money on the floor. With all that cash within touching distance, she couldn't afford to call his bluff. 'So what's the new plan?'

'We can lock her in this room.' He pointed at the keys on the table. 'There's no phone in here. She can't raise the alarm. And then we need to get away. Once we're – safe, I'll get a message to Force Patrol, they'll come and free her.' He nodded towards the kitchen area. 'She's got food and water, she can last for days in here.'

'And go where?'

'Well, that's the problem, isn't it? I don't think we should stay in the UK. She doesn't know your name. It's OK for me, I've got documentation: I can get a visa to go to the States or Canada or somewhere. I can work it out from there. If you hadn't turned up here, we'd have been able to buy you a new ID as well. You can leave the UK no problem – they don't really do exit checks – but then you'll have to go on somewhere you won't need a visa. I think there are about ninety countries that Ukrainians can travel to without visas.'

'For a reason,' said Katya. 'They are all shitholes no one wants to go to.'

Rage erupted. 'Well, you should have bloody thought of that before you came charging in here, shouldn't you?' The force of his words burned his throat. 'Katya, there's no other option. We need to get you to Heathrow and on a plane.'

'What, and I can just march through customs with money in my bag?'

Time expanded again, but this time the future rather than the past played out in his mind. He formulated a plan in under a second.

'We can get around that,' he said. 'I know someone who'll swap this cash for a watch – no, I mean it this time. You can go through customs wearing your money.'

She shook her head. 'It's too complicated.' Her gaze returned to Juliet: her eyes narrowed. 'I think we should make her quiet now.'

'No,' he said. 'We had a chance to make this easy, and *you* fucked it up. You want this money, you do it my way. We take what's here and then we go.'

'Or what?'

Roman picked up the discarded crutch and held it between his hands like a crowbar, let his arms flex to show her that he might not be built like her bodyguard fiancé but he was still bigger and stronger than her and meant what he said. Katya couldn't suppress a flinch; for the first time in his life, Roman's physical power over woman carried a sick, undeniable thrill. Her response was instant.

'Yes,' she said. 'Yes, we'll do it your way.'

Did he detect relief in the slump of her shoulders? Was he mad to imagine she had been waiting for him to puff up his chest since they had met, and now it had happened she was glad?

'Come on, then!' he said. Katya began to collect the money. Most of the cash was still bound in bricks but the loose leaves were everywhere and Katya stuffed it in his holdall, in her pockets, even in her bra.

'OK, that's all of it,' she said. 'Let's go before I change my mind.'

With a leaden heart, Roman double-locked the patio doors and the window in the kitchen area. Keeping one hand on the living-room door, he tried to catch Juliet's eye, to send her his apology and reassurance that he would be back for her. But she had turned away.

He turned the key behind her, locking her into the back of the house. He could hear her calling Max's name as he and Katya locked the great front door behind them, and then they were on the driveway, the steel dancer silver under the moonlight.

They began the long walk back to the Jester to wait for the morning, and for the watch-dealer to open and turn this dirty money into gold and then into freedom.

64

At two in the morning, the Jester stank of blueberry vape and fried chicken. Roman escorted Katya through the snoring men to the men's bathroom – he wasn't falling for that one again – and stood outside the door while she used the toilet in the stall and he used the urinal.

His cubicle had never seemed so small. He sat on the floor, back clammy against the plywood partition, hot legs swelling inside trousers he couldn't remove as the passport was still wedged in his back pocket. Katya sat on the bed with her back to him, piling up money into little blocks.

Juliet (he had to keep thinking of her by that name for now) had been alone now for two hours. Hurt, frightened, angry, and possibly even more confused than he was.

He wished again that he'd been able to look her in the eye, just for a second, before they had left. She would have understood that he was trying to protect her.

'Ninety thousand,' whispered Katya. 'So far. Forty-five thousand each.'

He would keep five thousand. That was all they'd planned on taking to begin with. Five thousand to share between him and Juliet, and the rest to pay Katya off.

'I'll give you forty thousand pounds in exchange for my old wallet,' he said.

She looked up sharply. 'What?'

'I want you gone,' he said. 'I want you to go far away and never come back. The more money you have, the more likely you are to stay away. If you give me my wallet back, I can become Roman Pavluk again.' He had the feeling that he wasn't running away so much as downwards: plunging vertically through society, back into the underclass. He was going to lose everything again, and how many times could a man do that before it broke him? 'I can leave here tonight and break off his trail. When Force Patrol let Juliet out, she'll have the police looking for Maxim Shevchenko, but he'll be just another missing person.'

He'd risen out of his whisper. The guy in Sergey's old room – Roman hadn't had a chance to learn his name – rolled over and murmured in his sleep.

'So what do we do now?' she asked.

'We wait for the broker to open. You turn your cash into some-thing shiny, and you take the next train to the airport.'

'Suits me,' Katya said. She pulled Roman's wallet out of her handbag – it had been there all along, in a side pocket. She tossed it to the floor in front of him and scooped the cash towards her in a fluid movement any dancer would have been proud of.

They sat in stalemate for hours: one of the night-shift boys came in; an early-shift worker got up. Katya had her phone to keep her awake – her nails clicked infuriatingly against the screen as she scrolled through Instagram – but she was on the mattress and her sitting position soon gave way to a slump, and by five she was lying on her belly, head resting on her arms. Discomfort gave Roman an edge, the base of his spine grinding against the wooden floor. Eventually Katya's head slackened completely. Not that she could be trusted. He kept himself awake by digging his fingernails into his forearm until he drew blood.

Eventually Katya rolled in her sleep, lips lolling apart, eyes darting beneath closed lids in a way not even she could fake. Her head was only half on the pillow; Roman eased it from under her and flexed it between his hands. Katya's own words came back to him. *No one would notice if that girl was gone.* And who would miss Katya? She had no family, no friends: she had, as far as he knew, loved and been loved by one person only. He shifted on to his knees and held the pillow inches from her face. She couldn't weigh that much more than Juliet, and carrying Juliet was as easy as lifting a child. He could borrow Saleem's car – the keys hung behind the bar – drive her far out of London and still be back to release Juliet before dawn. He plumped the pillow between his fists, felt the density of its foam. Swiftness was the key. A knee on either side of her body, perhaps even pinning down her hands with his legs while he pressed the life out of her—

Roman gagged and dry-heaved: he recoiled from Katya as though invisible hands had pushed him away from her. Of course he couldn't do that; it was not who he was. It was as though a stronger man, maybe his drill sergeant from the army or Shevchenko himself, were behind him, holding his arms.

There had been enough death already. His neglect of Veronika and Zlata had already sent him to the brink of hell; this would topple him into the pit. He dropped the pillow, exhausted as though the tussle had been physical and not moral.

Better to wait it out, wave Katya off on an aeroplane in time for him to get back to Juliet and tell her everything and hope that she forgave him.

He was drenched in sweat, losing water he couldn't afford and the tell-tale passport was growing damp. He took it out and opened it on the photo page, remembered how efficiently Ardem's people had inserted his photograph into Shevchenko's passport. It would be so easy for Katya to find someone to do the same for her. If the blasted thing survived the night in his pocket, that was. He rifled through the black bag. Loose cash had been stuffed into a slim padded envelope. He tipped the money out and slid the passport in before placing it back in his pocket, hoping it didn't look too conspicuous.

5.30am. Roman's gritty eyes stayed open. Dehydration furred his tongue. A coffee, he needed a strong coffee. Katya rolled over and at last her phone fell from her grip. Roman picked up the handset, unlocked it using the code he'd seen her tap out a million times. He combed her photo app for the evidence she'd stolen from him, the wallet with his real ID in it. Nothing.

He did an image search for Ava Kirilova, the ballerina, knowing and not knowing what he was going to find.

The first image was the *Swan Lake* poster he had seen so often. So was the second, and the third, and the fourth. Three pages into the search, though, was a close-up of Ava Kirilova's face, a black-and-white headshot, and it blew away any remnants of his initial theories had about doppelgängers and coincidences. It was her, it was Juliet. He knew that face the way he knew his own in the mirror: the slightly mismatched eyebrows, the long neck that he had kissed so often. I would know you anywhere, he had said to her, I know you all over.

He clicked from one page to another, trying to piece it all together. Ava Kirilova had performed the roles of Odette and Odile just once, to great acclaim; her father – the fabled Mr K! Juliet had never told him *that* – had died in a fall minutes after she had taken her final curtsey, and five days later she had been injured while dancing alone.

Roman grew hotter with every new fact. He pulled at his collar, trying to understand. He eased his trousers over his hips, folded them, with the keys and passport still in them, into a cushion and carried on reading. Then, years-deep into a chat-room thread he found in a grainy scan of an old newspaper, a reference to an unnamed pupil at the London Russian Ballet Academy being adopted by Nikolai Kirilov and changing her name to Ava Kirilova.

Roman cried out in shock, making Katya stir and turn in her sleep. He sifted again through the loose leaves of correspondence they had grabbed from the safe, but there was nothing here to support or confirm that it was her.

He wished he kept a notepad with him so he could make sense of this, scribble a timeline or a spider diagram to help him set the contradictory facts in his head in order, but he didn't even have a pen. There might be paper behind the bar or in the lounge but that would mean leaving Katya, and, since she had rolled over, Roman thought that her sleep looked lighter.

Instead, he pressed the heels of his hands deep into the sockets of his eyes and tried to map what he knew mentally.

He came to what felt like seconds later as a mobile phone alarm sounded a few cubicles away. Grey daylight seeped through the coloured windows, painting the plasterboard at an angle that told him it was at least seven o'clock. Doors banged and voices carried. Katya's bags were gone, and for a moment his heart soared because taking her bags surely meant she was never coming back. She's gone, he thought. She's taken the money, she's gone to the dealer on her own and she's gone. Euphoria flooded him like a drug. He would go to Juliet now, he would run all the way to Gabriel's Hill if he had to and he would tell her how sorry he was and hope that she forgave him.

He staggered to the bar in his T-shirt and underwear and drank two pints of water straight from the tap. He used the toilet and washed his face in the sink. In his cubicle, he shook out his balled trousers from the night before.

They should be heavier. They should have jingled when he shook them.

Roman's euphoria did a handbrake turn. He reached into the pocket even though he knew it would be empty. His wallet was gone again and the key to 36 Gabriel's Hill was missing, along with Ava Kirilova's passport.

For the second time that night, he replayed their earlier conversation. What had Katya said to him? That with Juliet out of the way they could sell the house to a cash buyer. And he had shut down the worst and grandest of her schemes by saying no, they couldn't, because they'd need identification, a bank account.

A passport.

JULIET?

65

The silence after Max and Katya's departure has a finality to it.

They aren't coming back.

I recast every meeting, every conversation we ever had. The day I caught him in the shower – was that a set-up? That time he gave me a lift? Katya had knocked on my door the day before that, I'm sure of it. Who is she? His girlfriend? His *wife*? He must have closed his eyes and pretended I was her. I think of all the times he's touched me and I want to throw up.

The ticket is still there, lying on the floor and overlaid now with a dusty print from Max's work shoe. The passport he had, the one he said was Ava Kirilova's, is gone. The grand scheme of his betrayal makes sense, but that detail doesn't. Or perhaps it does, but pain stops me ordering my thoughts. All I can do is lie here and let it travel through me. I am hollowed out, nothing but a vessel for pain. He has hollowed me out.

After maybe half an hour, the waves of pain lose some of their power. The worst of it localises and then separates itself from my original injury. A hot throbbing at the base of my hamstring sends the message that Katya hit me at the bottom of my thigh, not directly on the knee. Knowing this doesn't lessen the agony but it helps me manage it.

Reflected in the door, I look like something dragged from a ditch. I traverse the living room, lurching from one item of furniture to the other, eventually settling on a high stool that makes a passable Zimmer frame. I try the door handle but of course it doesn't give. If anyone knows how to lock a person in a room, it's a security guard.

I pause to ride another surge of agony, digging my knuckles into the soft leather seat of the stool. When it has released me, I scrabble in drawers, looking for a spare key, even though I know there is none. The room is stifling even in the dark. I feel like a dog trapped in a hot car. When the sun rises the heat will suffocate me. Max wouldn't do that to me. And yet. He planned it down to the last detail, even deactivating the safe so I can't trigger the alarm on it and call Force Patrol to my rescue.

The scale of his deception takes my breath away. I picture the two of them, already heading for an airport, congratulating each other on a job well done. He'll be telling her how horrible it was, feigning desire while I squirmed underneath him. She'll laugh and tell him that it's fine, he can go back to what he's used to. Cheekbones and curves again, as opposed to the hollow eyes and gristle of me.

Was *any* of it genuine? The lift he gave me on the way home from the bank? The shower in the garden? Surely I went after him . . .

I went after *him*. I was wrong too. I was calculating too.

The difference is that I changed. By the end, I meant it.

I deserve to be punished, but not like this.

My head aches with the effort of concentration, and it throbs where Katya hit me. I put my hand in my hair and find an egg-sized lump on my skull, at the back, under my hair.

She wanted to knock me out. She wanted me dead.

And what stopped her? He did. That doesn't make sense either. Better, surely, to do away with me altogether; better to silence the witness.

Unless he saved me for the sake of it. But that opens up the possibility of hope, and hope is the enemy of action.

I open the freezer, wrap the last of the ice Max brought me in a tea towel and hold it against my leg. It doesn't burn if I keep the ice pack moving, cooling myself like machinery in a factory. I remember the moment when he came to my door, grinning like an idiot with his huge bags of ice. I thought I had him and I was so pleased with myself.

I harness that hurt and press it down into a hard little nugget of vengeance. Fuck him and fuck her. I'll find a way out of this room,

I'll call the police and sell the pair of them down the river. I'll tell them Max forced me to open the safe. There's nothing – except maybe Max's word, if they ever catch him – to say that I invited him in. Nothing except his word and his fingerprints on the glasses, the door handles, the taps. The headboard of the bed. Thoughts of wiping it down before the police get here are over-written by remembering everything we did in that bed, how far from a lie it felt at the time. The memory winds me, it bends me in half.

Max and that bitch have taken everything: the keys, all the documents and all but a few euros of the cash. The passport is definitely gone. Why did he get so wound up about that? Not everyone returns their passport; they go missing and get replaced and then found again, and people change their flights all the time. Why was he so *angry* with me about it?

Or was that fake too?

My own passport must be . . . I don't, I realise, actually know where my passport is. The thought stirs something inside me: a gathering force that tugs at the diaphragm and which, for all its power, is shapeless and without name.

I press my face against the patio door, gaze into the garden. The sky is light, it's well past dawn, but clouds have whitewashed the blue. I shake the handle. The action feels good for its own sake even though the glass is as strong as concrete. I wish I could pop the pane like Lego.

Suddenly Max's words come back to me. *They unscrewed the lock from the kitchen window.*

The lock on the long, thin kitchen window is riveted to the frame by uncovered screws, the cross-headed kind that need a tiny Phillips screwdriver. There are no tools in here, but a fingertip search of every drawer in the kitchen eventually yields a paring knife – the one I used to release the vodka from its security tag, what feels like a lifetime ago – that will fit in the tip of the screw. Far from ideal: better than nothing. The ceramic handle is sweaty in my grip and I cut my hand twice, but after about ten minutes and some swearing I have loosened one of the six main screws. Muscle memory kicks in when it's time to repeat the task but the second screw is tighter and takes longer to liberate. I throw it to the floor with a clatter: I can slide the lock a little, see a square hole where I will be able to pull out the mechanism when all three screws are out. When, after nearly an hour, I release the final screw, pop the lock and push open the window, the air is colder than it has been for weeks. I stick my head out and breathe it in.

Dragging my bad leg through the gap has me screaming out loud – no one comes, of course – and there's no way I can pull that bar stool through, so I have nothing to balance on. But I am out, my little knife in my swollen hand. I scream again, with relief this time. The clouds let go a sprinkle of rain; concentric circles appear on the surface of the pool. Using the outer wall for support, I make slow, sore progress around the garden. The side gate is locked but I'm virtually a locksmith now, and if I can't breach the gate perhaps I can make it through the bushes and across the fence into the garden next door. Once I am on the street I will be safe.

A glass bead of water shatters on my forearm, then another. In the time it takes me to tilt my face to the sky, it's really raining. Clear marbles roll off rock-hard earth. Rain rattles the water and drums on the roof. Over its snare, all I can hear is my own breathing.

My own breathing, and the jingle of keys being tossed and caught in a hand.

I pivot on the ball of my good foot and there in the living room is Katya, framed by the door she has opened. In her hands, Ava's keys. At her feet, a wheeled case and Max's black bag. Contempt tugs the corners of her mouth upwards.

'You stupid bitch,' she says.

66

As far as I can tell, the front door is locked behind her and she is alone.

'Where is he?' I ask her. I hope he's fucked her over; I hope he's taken his share out of that black bag and left her behind. I hope she knows how it feels.

Katya's make-up has sweated off, apart from those eyebrows, and the drizzle has slicked her hair. She has no weapon this time but she *is* a weapon, size and good health on her side. I stagger back, then check over my shoulder to gauge my distance from the pool. I'm away from the edge, but when I look back she has moved in on me and I take a reflexive step away from her. Up close, her skin is poreless, as if it's been airbrushed for a poster, but her breath is dehydrated and stale. My fist closes around the knife in my hand.

'You *lie* to me!' she says. Is this about the money she saw on the table? Was *that* the start of all *this*? The bruises she gave me on my legs and shoulders throb a warning. As if I need reminding how dangerous she is. '*What is all the shit with the passport?*'

'I wish I knew!' I shout. 'You tell me!'

'You fucking dumb or you crazy? You lie on your own *name*, on *who you are*! You *lie*, Ava Kirilova.'

Her words produce a physical sensation: a brush of something so cold it burns, like dipping my toe into an ice bath.

She takes another step towards me; I stagger back. My palm is sweaty and I'm starting to lose my grip on the knife. 'My name is *Juliet*,' I say but it feels strange in my mouth, like trying to pronounce a new word in a foreign language.

'You make him lie to me too. Why? When you have everything?' She loosely gestures to the garden, the house, to me.

'It's not mi—'

'For fun? You lie for fun? You make fun of people like me who have *nothing*. It's not funny. It's not *fair*!'

'I promise I'm not making fun of you.'

Katya charges towards me as though she's about to leap into my arms. I raise the hand that's holding the knife but she's too fast: she catches me by the elbow and it flies from my hand. She twists me by the arm so that I'm facing the pool, and pushes. Water rises like a solid blue wall to smack me in the face. I go under on an in-breath so that when I come up for air Katya already has the advantage: her hand is on my head and I'm down again, her nails like metal barbs in my scalp. When she yanks me up again by my hair, it rips out at the root. I go under again. Shapes are black and blue, and it doesn't feel like water in my nose, it feels like fire. I lose my sense of everything: which way is up, which is down, whether I'm breathing in or out. Water floods my lungs, panic floods my veins.

I break the surface, seize a mouthful of air that might have to last me the rest of my life. My hands find Katya's wrists on my shoulders and all those years of training were not for the stage after all but for here, now, a choking, bubbling moment when I hook Katya by the neck and pull her into the water with me. She flaps her arms like a big black bird.

Now *I* have the advantage of surprise, and I'm not going to waste it. My heart and lungs go *bang bang bang*. Lactic acid burns and cramps in my hands as I take a hank of her long hair in each hand and pull downwards. She's scratching me to pieces under the water, my thighs shooting out red liquid threads that instantly dilute to nothing. I watch these threads as Katya struggles, swimming on the spot. I have held these arms above my head for minutes at a time, I have trained them with weights. I am superhuman. Her strokes turn to jerks as she weakens. Red snakes swim through the water then die.

When she stops fighting, I count to fifty. My arms are shaking but my hands are locked on her shoulders.

Ninety-eight, ninety-nine.

One hundred.

My breath is ragged but there's a rhythm to it: inhale for one count, exhale for the next One hundred and forty-eight, one hundred and forty-nine. She is still as a stone but a couple of tiny bubbles remain in the water.

One hundred and fifty.

My sinuses burn. I throw up hot clear water into the pool and still maintain my grip.

One hundred and ninety-nine, two hundred.

The last bubble dies.

I don't know how I know when she has gone, but I *know*. Letting go of her hair, I raise my hands from the water. Long black hair winds around my fingers and I pluck at the strands, flicking them into the water where they float like river weeds. One of Katya's fingertips is torn and red, although no blood pulses from it, and a single purple fingernail swims slowly down to the bottom of the pool.

It takes everything I've got to get to the steps and haul myself on to the flagstones with twitching arms. With nothing to lean on, I lie down on my back in the muggy air, defenceless and spent, ribs rising and falling under sodden clothes.

I feel strangely numb given that I have just crossed a line, the ultimate line: stepped from one world into another, the newest member of the world's most terrible club. I have taken a life, and knowing that I did it to preserve my own doesn't lessen the enormity of it. I will tell the police that—

'Jyulyit!'

I open my eyes.

Max is standing over me, almost as breathless as I am. A line of red dots and dashes on his cheekbone tells me he came in his old way, through the Greek Temple garden.

He's holding the pool rake, brandishing it as a weapon. He looks as if he doesn't know what to do with it. As if he doesn't know whether it was meant for her or for me.

67

Just be quiet, says a sensible voice inside my head. Don't say anything, try to distract him, try to get yourself out of this house and on to the street before he can hurt you. Don't make him angry.

The sensible voice in my head is interrupted by my real one.

'Get away from me,' I scream, loud enough to send a blackbird flying from a tree. 'Get away from me, you *bastard*.'

He drops the rake – it clatters on the flagstones, next to the keys – and holds up his hands. 'I'm not going to hurt you,' he pants, which is exactly what he would say if he meant to harm me.

'Aren't you going to go in after your girlfriend?' I nod towards the pool. If he thinks he can save her he'll go in after her, and while he's giving her the kiss of life I can get the keys and make a bid for the front door. It will take me a full minute to gain ground that Max can cover in seconds, but I have to try.

He stands with his hands on his knees, his breath slowly regulating. Rain rolls off the suede of his head and into his eyes, but he doesn't blink.

Katya has drifted towards us and now floats parallel to the edge, close enough to touch. Max reaches down into the water and flips her on to her back. I inch backwards, shuffling on my bottom like a baby, trying not to wince every time I drag my bad leg along with me. The knife is out of my reach but I grab the keys as I go.

I don't want to look at Katya but I can't look away. She looks like a beautiful waxwork, eyes staring up at the white sky. Max hooks his hands under her arms, pulls her out, lays her on her back, pushes down on her heart once and at last places his ear to her mouth. He stays like that for a full minute, while I progress from the flagstones to the grass.

'She's gone,' he says eventually, and drops his head to his chest.

I haul myself up to standing by the doorframe, shoving down the spike of jealousy that rises in me at the sight of him kneeling over her. Max picks Katya up again. She is limp in his arms and her head lolls back, her sopping hair trailing along the ground. The orchestra in my mind strikes up, crests the final strains, and dies.

He stares blankly into her eyes and for a heart-stopping moment I think he's going to kiss her. 'She's gone,' he says again. He frisks Katya as if he's looking for something; his hands still over her hips, and he wrestles a sodden padded envelope from a pocket on her skirt and lets the pulpy mass slap down on to the stones. And then, with a grunt, he throws her back into the pool. As the displaced water slops over his feet, Max turns to me, expectantly, as though I'm supposed to read – what? – into this gesture. All I see is a man capable of hiding a woman's death. I cling to the doorframe and feel my heartbeat in my fingertips.

'Oh, thank God, Jyulyit, she's gone – no, *please* don't—' he says when he sees me flinch. 'It's OK. I'm not going to hurt you. What did she do to you?'

He moves to thumb away the blood that trickles from the lacerations on my leg. I slap his hand away. 'Don't touch me,' I say. 'Don't touch me or I'll scream.'

'I'm not going to hurt you,' he says, and as if to prove it he picks up my dropped knife and hands it to me, handle first, before resting on his haunches. 'Jyulyit?' He speaks my name carefully, almost doubtfully. 'We have to talk. I have lied to you, I know; we have lied to each other.'

'I haven't lied to you.'

What? It's true. My only deception was the attraction I feigned at the beginning, and that became real. For me, at least.

He draws his chin into his neck in the way that says, *really?*

'I *haven't*!' I insist.

He goes to speak, but instead he studies my face for an uncomfortably long time, searching my eyes, my nose, my mouth as if they're the windows and doors on a property he needs to secure. This silent examination is more unsettling than any violence.

'OK.' There's a nursery-rhyme intonation to his voice, as though he's talking to a child. 'OK. Let us deal with this first. Jyulyit, I know what happened here. I know what she was like; she was coming here to kill you. I know you had no choice.'

'Was she your wife?' I cut in.

His face creases. 'I don't have a wife,' he says. 'Please, there's so much we need to get straight. Firstly, tell me, do you need to go to hospital?'

I probably do. My lip is split from earlier and my legs are bleeding but they are surface wounds. My knee is singing its usual song of agony.

'I don't know,' I say honestly.

'The doctors would need the story of how this happened to you. Many questions would be raised. For both of us.'

Never has a threat been spoken so gently.

I thought I knew what an adrenaline rush felt like, but no performance compares to this. My left leg is shaking uncontrollably and my arms, so powerful just minutes before, are useless strings of rubber. I try to point the little knife at him, but it's not easy when I need one hand for balance. He watches me fumble with what looks like pity.

'I am thinking about these questions for your protection,' he says. 'Always I was acting for your protection. To keep you safe from her. Yesterday. Every day. I have made a big mess of it, but I was trying to keep you safe. Eh – why should you believe me? I have given you no reason,' he admits. 'Maybe this convinces you.'

Without ever turning his back to me, he winds out the pool cover until all that's left of Katya is a shadow under canvas.

A sign that he is telling the truth?

Or one inconvenience out of the way, one remaining?

68

'Go for it,' he says. 'Ask me anything.'

I move so he can only see my profile. 'You say she wasn't your wife. But she was here before you were. You have a relationship with her.'

He holds up his hands. 'I wasn't—' he begins, then drops the lie along with his hands. 'Not in the way you think. Do you want to sit down for this?'

I shake my head and grip the doorframe tighter.

'OK. Katya was from *Ukraina* but I met her here in London. She'd had some bad luck, to say the least. The life she thought she was coming over here for – it didn't work out. She lost her relationship, then her work, then her home. When she found out about my job, she wanted me to help her get her hands on some cash. To steal from one of the clients.'

'That's why you made . . .' Shame shoves the word *love* back down my throat. 'That's why you made friends with me?'

He looks away. 'At first. Yes. I wanted to see what I could get from the house. I didn't want to, Jyulyit, I was sick about it; I couldn't sleep. But I let it slip about my past, and she was blackmailing me.' He swallows hard. 'She was blackmailing me about—' His words catch in his throat.

'Because of the reason you left home?' I supply, then kick myself for making this easier for him. He hesitates before nodding, a vestige of macho pride even in the middle of all this. 'But Max, you said they wouldn't come after you here.'

His laugh is joy's opposite. 'It wasn't the British police she was going to inform, if I didn't help her get back on her feet. It would have taken one phone call; anonymous. And I told you, didn't I, what they do to men like me at home? I thought I could put her off but as the days went on she became more desperate. And more crazy. And I was deeper in the shit. Lying to you more and more. When you told me about opening that safe, my God. I thought I could pay her off. I thought it was a gift. I should have been honest with you from the start.'

'I wouldn't have trusted you,' I tell him. 'You were a stranger.'

'We still are strangers.' He shakes his head again, gives that laugh that's not a laugh.

The vast, crazy truth of the statement halts the conversation for a moment. The rain is relentless; my arms and legs are goose-fleshed. I would have expected the heatwave to have made me more tolerant of being cold and wet or even to welcome it, but it's as miserable as rain ever was.

'But you *took* the money,' I say. 'She had money, tens of thou-sands of pounds. Why did she come back?'

His eyes bore through to a part of me so deep, so locked-down, so *private*, even I'm not allowed in.

'Because she wanted more. She wanted everything you have.'

That makes no sense. I had nothing except— 'You? It doesn't look like I *ever* had you.'

He tries to shrug but it comes out as a wince. 'You did have me. You still do, if you want me.'

I'm starting to thaw. I fight it.

'But I am not what she wanted. Katya wanted money, yes, but she wanted more than that. She wanted a life. To take an identity. She wanted to steal your name and all that you own.'

I snort at the irony. 'But you know I haven't got anything! That was the point of borrowing from the safe. Didn't she know that?'

There he is again, trying to decipher me. 'You really don't know, do you?'

'Jesus Christ, Max. Know *what*?'

He examines my face so intently there's nothing for me to read on his. Instead of answering, he picks up the envelope he fished from Katya's corpse. The brown paper layer of the envelope disintegrates, leaving bubble wrap behind. He looks at the pass-port again and says, 'I need more. There is another room inside, yes? A . . .' He clicks his fingers while he searches for the word. 'Dancing room?'

The little hairs on my arms stand to attention. Drizzle clings to them like dew on grass. 'There's a studio,' I say. 'But it's locked.'

He has the silver key in his pocket. 'I think this?'

'Don't come near me,' I say, but he's edged past me into the living room. He pauses for a second in front of the *Swan Lake* poster, shakes his head, and then he's opening the living room door, he's halfway along the corridor, he's letting himself into Ava's studio.

I make special room for you.

'What?' I ask Max.

He looks at me strangely. 'I didn't say anything.'

There's a moment or two I can't account for. A peeling away from the present.

He leaves the studio door open, screening off the front of the house, my only way out. I can hear his footsteps. There's a strip of yellow light beneath the door and the floor: occasionally his shadow passes through it.

I don't realise my teeth are beginning to chatter until I call, 'I think you've probably had everything worth stealing,' and chop up the words.

His reply is muffled. 'I am not going to steal anything. I think, I hope, I am going to restore something.'

'What the hell's that supposed to mean?'

The sound of running water is the reply. He emerges a minute or two later and takes a large bag of sea salt from the kitchen cupboard. When he turns back to me, his eyes are like two bruises and exhaustion drags his voice down into a new, subterranean register. What has he seen in there?

'I have what I need to explain it to you. But I need time to organise the things. I have started you a salt bath, to get you warm. And for your legs.'

I look down: they are streaked with what looks like rusty water. Some of the cuts are already beginning to clot. Max spreads his arm, like an usher in a theatre. I press my back against the cold glass.

'If you think I'm going in there with you, you can forget it,' I tell him.

He responds by closing up the studio, opening the front door and handing me the phone.

'You can call 999 whenever you want,' he says. 'You can walk into the street and do it. I would prefer to talk to you first so we can understand. I will be in the studio, trying to make sense. Take the bath or do not. Take the phone or do not. Trust me or do not.'

A wave of something passes between us but it gets lost in translation.

He returns to the studio and shuts himself in.

The wind changes direction, flinging hard rain at my back, and I tell myself that's why I cross the threshold. But really, what choice do I have? I am falling far from myself, and the only person who can catch me is him.

69

The salt in the water stings my legs but soothes my eyes. I go right under, as if to prove my lungs still work. The pressure builds in my chest. There's a knock on the door but only his hand appears, dropping a clean towel on the bathroom chair and leaning my crutches against the wall. This demonstration that our licence for intimacy has been revoked drags me dangerously back towards trusting him.

When I limp back out into the living room, in shorts and a long-sleeved top, Max has not only tidied up but he's arranged Ava's things into little piles on the coffee table. Documents and objects are ordered formally, as though he is presenting evidence. I lower myself on to the sofa, joint by swollen joint.

He's watching my eyes, to see where I'm looking, to see what I make of it. I oblige him. There's a sheaf of squared-off documents, a stack of framed pictures and, at the far end, some torn black fabric which my eyes land on then skitter off again.

A black feather, floating upwards
Pricking my finger and tasting blood

'I made you some tea,' he says. 'The English cure for everything.' But he's serving it the Russian way, black and in glasses. I wrap my palms around it, enjoying the burn. 'And I put all the money back in the safe.'

'Thanks,' I say.

He leans forward. 'Have you anything you want to tell me, Jyulyit?'

I shake my head. I can't form thoughts, let alone the words. Over his shoulder, the garden glitters. Without the blazing sun it doesn't look like Los Angeles any more. I train my gaze on the trees in the distance, the pool a blue mass at the base of my sightline.

He closes his eyes, as if drawing on deep reserves of patience. 'How to begin?' he asks himself. He lets his hand hover over the piles, like a kid choosing a cake from a buffet. He reaches for something at the far end of the line then thinks better of it, and lets his hands fall back into his lap. 'So. You know it is said that you are not supposed to wake up a person who is sleepwalking, so I hope I am doing the right thing here.' Max rises to pull closed the window: rain makes streamers on the glass, forcing my attention on to what's in front of me, what's between us. 'Shit. I am so out of my depth here. Maybe we can start with what was in the safe. The things you have already seen. To lessen the shock.'

He slides the passport across the table to me. 'Look at this.'

'I can't touch it.'

'I cleaned it.'

He has misunderstood me. It's not just the ickiness of touching something that's been so close to a corpse: I physically can't make myself do it. The cold wet dread is back. It creeps up my body. My eyes slam shut without my permission.

> In the black, a single red light like a devil's wink

I snap them wide again.

'Please,' he says. 'Just look at it.'

It is harder to pick it up than it was to hold Katya down. There are bite marks on the cover, where the owner has held it in her teeth while she rummaged through her bag for her boarding pass or purse.

I do that, I think.

The cold water rises.

I leaf through the stamped pages. US immigration, China, India. Every time I look up, he is studying my face.

'Picture page,' he says.

I can't bring myself to do it. Gently, softly, he turns to the final page, where her name is printed next to a face. The laminate has gone wavy and the photograph has blurred: it looks like a face that's been held underwater.

I drop it on the floor.

The smell of the oil in the lift shaft
Pressing a button, down, down, down
Up, up, up, up

'Jyulyit,' he says, and then, very softly, '*Ava*. It's you. She's you.'
He turns my shoulders to face the poster on the wall.

Hands on my waist, lifting me high in the air
A girl dancing in a window

'The whole time, the whole summer. You saw that plane ticket.
Ava Kirilova never caught her plane because she was here all along.'

'*That* is not me.'

The cold water rises.

'This is your house. Your money.' He rustles more papers.
'Look. Hospital letters, to Ava Kirilova, describing *your* injury.
Medication *you've* taken.' Headed paper, green hospital crest.

A white room, green glass and boiling oil
I'm so sorry

'And then there's this.'

A picture frame. The parchment-coloured paper of an official
certificate. Black ink and a red crest. The letters dance as though
I'm reading them through water but my ears can't block out his
words.

'You're the same person. You just changed your name. Here you are
when you were a little girl. With – this must be your mother, right?'

He shows me a photograph of me at my first ever ballet
performance. A raftered church hall. Elasticated slippers, frilly
pink leotard.

The ballet teacher saying, This one's got the bug alright
I don't know where she gets it from

The parent beside me is a woman: short skirt, highlighted hair,
dangly earrings. She looks a lot like someone I know, only I have
never looked at anyone with the raw, dumb love that blooms on
her face.

Oh, my God, Mum!
Be a good girl for Mr Kirilov
Ty moyo luchsheye tvoreniye

Max takes my leg gently by the ankle. His grip is loose but firm: there is no wriggling out. In his other hand is a pink *pointe* shoe. The ribbon is ragged, coming away at the piping. He turns it upside down so I can see the initials AK embossed in the leather.

'You said that all ballerinas have shoes that fit them and no one else.'

Before I can stop him, he slides it on to my foot. It feels right. It fits better than any man, better than any hand I have ever held. It feels so right it might kill me.

> *Her hips just kept going and going.*
> *Who do you like dancing best, Odette or Odile?*
> *The church with its icons, its saints and crosses*
> *The angle of his leg when he fell*

'Jyulyit?' He drops to kneel at my feet. 'Jyulyit, try to *remember*.'

> *A silver hammer*
> *A white tablecloth*
> *The silver samovar*
> *The white coffin*
> *Ava, you are* thirty
> *She wasn't carrying her EpiPen*
> *I'll be the* best
> *Welcome home*
> *Oh, my God,* Mum!
> *Mum*

Memories order themselves suddenly and the film of my life plays on fast-forward. The icy water rushes up my spinal cord and closes over my head and I remember everything. Give me broken and twisted limbs, give me the barbed wire and boiling oil for the rest of my life rather than another second of this.

70

Pain commands my body as strictly as any ballet master; it folds me in on myself like invisible hands, forcing me into the foetal position, which my bad knee can't accommodate. I feel awkward and ugly and everything hurts to touch. The sounds I make come from somewhere beyond language: high at first, until my voice cracks and the noise sinks into a kind of lowing. It seems impossible that this great grey sound should come from something as small and pink as lungs and a throat. It should issue from a crack in the earth, a well, a cave.

Over time, words return to me, and I throw them up like water, fast and formless.

'This girl from the corps, this second swan, she kept *staring* at me—

'Everyone gets replaced but I thought I was—

'Named after his mother—

'I was just trying to stop him getting in the lift—

'Just wanted to dance that way *one more time*—

'They all wanted to be me but even *I* didn't get to be me—

'And I said something like, just dance through the pain—

'And she screamed like an *animal*—

'How can I have been so—

'Didn't know it was me in the poster—

'I've never known guilt like it—

'If I had only danced *his* way I would never have fallen—

'Promised him I would devote the rest of my life—

'Silver hammer, just lying there and—

'Rather be dead—

'Can't remember the moment I—

'After my mum died he—

'Just *knew* my name was Juliet—

I keep going, strangely lucid as the two halves of me, Juliet and Ava pass the narrative chaotically back and forth between them. It's as though they are in conversation, while some other person, who must be me, slowly begins to understand what has been happening in my head: that these two selves have been lashed together with ribbon but unable to communicate for half my life.

By the time I finish, the sky has changed; a weak sun rims the clouds with gold. The shards of my past are laid out for us to piece together. Max goes straight for the sharpest one, the jagged heart shape in the middle.

'You lost your mother,' is all he says, softly spoken words that sink a barb into the rawest part of me.

I want my mum.

My instinct is not to cry out but to sleep: to escape cruel clarity and slide back into comfort. My limbs and eyelids become heavy. To reset. To unknow. I flop sideways, my ligaments loosening to welcome oblivion.

He cups my jaw in loosely his hands. 'No,' he says, calm but insistent. 'Not again. Stay here. Tell me about your mother. What was she like, Jyulyit?'

What was she like? She was my world. Kind. Patient. She liked fizzy wine and Capital FM. She was clueless about ballet and yet from the moment I mimicked the dancers in a Christmas TV showing of *The Nutcracker* her life revolved around it, driving me to classes and auditions, finding the money for shoes and costumes and fees.

And then, when I was twelve, she loved me enough to let me go.

'Her name was – her name was – her – she was called Grace.' When the sky doesn't fall, I relax all over, as if some vital stitch has at last been unpicked. 'Her name was Grace. I haven't been allowed to talk about her for so long, I don't really know how to start.'

'What do you mean, not allowed?'

'None of us were allowed to mention her. Or the adoption, at all. The other dancers. The staff. It was a condition of . . . well, it was a condition of being part of the company, I suppose.'

'You weren't allowed to mention your *mother*? But how were you supposed to grieve her? It is bad enough for an adult to mourn—' His voice breaks for a second here, and I guess he's thinking about his own parents. 'But for a *child*. All this, and the way he called you his creature. You cannot create another person. You can only control them.'

Carefully, Max moves around to face me. His voice is on tiptoe.

'Living on the contact line, you get to know about trauma. Something that happens to you so big your mind cannot process it. It knocks you off course. Leaving home is a trauma, then your mother dies suddenly and you don't get to say goodbye. And her name becomes a dirty word? And you are only twelve? My God, Jyulyit, you were a *baby*. He took your *mother* away from you. Or at least he tried. But clinging to the name she gave you . . . doesn't it prove she was always in there?'

He taps the skin over my heart and the well of tears spills again. The skin between his eyebrows folds deeper than ever.

'I wish I could unravel this for you,' he says. 'You need to talk to a professional. To understand what, exactly, has been happening to you. Why your . . .' When he casts about for the right word, I can tell he's doing so from kindness rather than a lapse in translation. 'Why your delusion took the shape it did.'

'How can I?' I wail. 'From what I know about counselling, it doesn't work unless you're honest with the therapist, and how can I ever have an honest conversation that doesn't lead to . . .' I nod towards the door: he follows my thought down the corridor, through the picture window and into the pool.

'I guess all that can wait,' he says. 'I don't want to push you, in case . . .' He trails off, but it's clear what he's thinking. In case it happens again.

He breaks away from me, yawns and palms his eyes. When he

looks back at me, the rims are so red he looks like he's been crying blood. 'We both need to rest. But can I ask you one more question first?'

Knowing sleep is on the other side makes it easier to nod.

'What do I call you from now on?' he asks. 'Do you feel like Ava, or Juliet?'

The first answer on my lips is neither; that I will never be a whole person again. Then the twelve-year-old girl holds the thirty-year-old woman's hand, and from somewhere another hand, cold for years, encloses them both, offering a comfort warm as sunshine.

'Both of them,' I say.

71

In bed, we lie on our backs, fully clothed. We've slept a little; it's mid-afternoon. When I move my leg, one cut that won't heal, a crescent in the shape of Katya's fingernail, makes a little red comet on the white sheets.

'If only I had looked you up at the beginning,' he tells the light fitting. 'There was a time when I had a working phone and I knew the name Ava Kirilova but I didn't care enough to look you up. Everything would have been different. There would be no body in the pool. God knows I hated Katya, but she would still have her life. And we would not be in this fucking mess.'

I press against him – for solace, not from desire – and we both stare at the ceiling. 'No,' I say. 'The opposite. From what you've told me, if she had known who I really was, she would have tried to kill me. The body in the pool could have been mine.'

The same shiver passes through both of us.

'There are probably enough wounds on your body to prove self-defence,' he says, but hesitantly, handing the what-next over to me. The weight of the decision we have to make sinks through me so quickly I know the next few seconds are critical if it is not to pull me under for good.

'Even if we call them now, they'll know she spent time under the cover; forensics can find out that sort of thing. She didn't put herself there and there's clearly no way I did it on my own. Even taking panic into account, it doesn't look good.'

Who's going to say it first? Max does, although not in so many words. 'The ground at the end of the garden, where the water comes in from next door – it's soft enough to dig.'

We are really going to do this. Everything comes into sharp focus: the lines of the furniture in the room seem to sharpen their edges and I swear I can hear individual blades of grass on the lawn outside rub up against each other.

'There are tools in the shed,' I answer, surprised by the conviction in my voice.

'You'd have to live here forever,' he says. 'You'd never be able to leave.'

You, not we. Is he asking what happens to him now, asking my permission – because it's my house, and I am the one with the money – or is he saying that in the long term this is *my* problem? Either way, the decision is mine.

If he stays, I am known, in all my madness and history.

If he goes, I am alone with it.

A hollow minute passes.

My next words, when they come, are a blind leap into a black water.

'It's too big a house for me to live in alone,' I say. 'It's too big a secret for one person to keep.'

His face is grave. 'If it is ever found out, I will say you knew nothing.'

'But look what happens to me when I'm under pressure. How can you live with that – knowing I might not have control over what I say, who I believe I am?'

His face tightens as he takes in the scale of this, and then he seems to grow an inch all over, to swell, as if he has decided to absorb my share of it.

'We can't be sure of anything,' he concedes. 'We never could. It's just that we know it now.'

'No more secrets, then. Either of us. If we're going to lie to the world, we have to be honest with each other.'

'I promise.' His swimming-pool eyes lock on to mine. 'No more secrets.'

ACT IV

ROMAN

72

Juliet's struggle had exhausted her. Less than an hour after waking, she had fallen asleep again on the living room sofa. He draped a throw over her and wondered what her reality would be when she woke up.

Once, a few weeks and a million years ago, Roman had asked himself if he could love a woman he barely knew. Now he asked himself if he could love a woman who barely knew herself.

He took a spade from the tool shed and sliced a weak smile into the waterlogged earth at the end of the garden. Under the soft topsoil was sticky London clay, yellow and unyielding. Digging stilled his shaking arms and reawoke the muscles in his back that he'd honed at the car wash. He made the pit too wide at first, basing it on a burial plot, until it hit him that of course it did not need to accommodate a casket, just a slim woman and the things she had carried. When he had dug as deep as his chest, and blisters began to slow his progress, he let himself stop.

Into the churned-up ground went the tiny bottles of nail polish, the cheap flip-flops, Katya's make-up bag, her purse and her passport. The money was already back in the safe. He set aside two things: his own yellow wallet and Katya's phone, which he had found in the black bag, and which still had nineteen per cent left on the battery. As soon as he had done what was needed here, he would send it on a journey inspired by a crime novel he'd read on the flight from Ukraine to London. He'd get to a big car park and wedge the handset in the tarpaulin of a long-distance lorry, so that if anyone ever tried to trace her, the signal would show her travelling far away from London. In the meantime, he would delete everything he could find that connected her to Juliet. Her most recent search history was actually his: Ava Kirilova and the London Russian Ballet Company. He cleared the all-time history, then tapped into her messages.

An old thread caught his eye – a name that had become more familiar than his own, a name that had become his own. It looked like a one-way conversation, Katya firing off ten messages a day asking Shevchenko where he was, why wasn't he calling her, if he had left her then please at least tell her.

Oh, *Katya*, he thought, registering the loss of love as well as the loss of life. She had made his life hell but her tragedy had begun, as so many of them did, with a broken heart.

Roman slid the screen up until he got to Shevchenko's last communication.

Max: *I know what I'm doing. Sweet dreams princess.*

Katya: *Be careful.*

Max: *The big job has been brought forward to tomorrow. This time next week, I'll have enough for the deposit on this.*

The property Shevchenko had shared images of was heart-breakingly modest. Their little piece of England was a one-bed flat, barely bigger than a hotel room. Roman scrolled back through their love story, from the property websites to heart emojis. When he got to the dick pics and the nudes, he turned off the phone.

Checking that Juliet wasn't watching, he opened his wallet. Everything was there: his driving licence, the international passport that had been the cause of so much trouble. He slid a dirty forefinger into the slit in the fabric and felt the ragged paper of the only family photo he had left. He looked at his watch. 3.32pm. He freed the picture from its hiding place.

Veronika's cousin's wedding. He wore a suit and a bad haircut, Veronika was in a red dress that flared at the shoulders and hem and fitted at the waist and had made him want to pull at the belt and unwrap her like candy, a desire intensified by the fact that he was sleeping on the sofa. Zlata was five years old and dressed – after a last-minute call to the bride to check it was OK – as Elsa from *Frozen*, a plasticky blonde plait clipped into her black curls. They had made her a little nest of coats so she could sleep by the dance floor, but she had outpartied the lot of them, being dragged home only when Roman and Veronika had started to flag.

She had had six months left to live.

Roman looked the length of the garden to where Juliet was now framed in the doorway. She looked impossibly delicate on her crutches. That quality that he had recognised in her in the beginning, that secret sadness that reminded him of his own? This was it. She too had been instrumental in the death of the person she loved most in the world. And he could never tell her that he understood. Never share her burden. The shock and betrayal of finding out he had been married and had a child might send Juliet back into that dangerous safe place in her head.

3.37pm. He folded the photograph in half and dropped it into the pit. As he shovelled dirt over them it felt like a loss but an ending, too. He was burying Veronika and Zlata at last. He was priest, sexton and chief mourner at the funeral he had never been able to give them at home. '*Do pobachennya, moya malenka rodyna,*' he murmured, 'Goodbye, little family,' when they were safe under a thick layer of earth. The word *family* finished him off. He dropped to his knees and wept. Not for Katya, not even for Juliet but at last for his girls and the lives they would all still be living if he had been a better man.

'Max?' Juliet called to him from the open patio doors.

The need to share his truth was a pressure in his chest that threatened to stop his heart. But that same pain gave Roman a foretaste of how much it would hurt if he told Juliet and lost her, too. No more secrets, she had said, and so he must keep this. It was better that he be loved as a man he was not than despised for who he really was. His fantasies of her whispering his name, of knowing who he was, his boyhood dreams, his life as a teacher, shrivelled to nothing. Veronika and Zlata would never live again in their conversation. Losing his name was his punishment and his reward, and Juliet would be his atonement for Veronika and

Zlata – and yes, even Katya. He would glove his own hands with the blood that was on Juliet's, and he would stay by her and nurse her back to health. By the time she reached him at the end of the garden, Roman Pavluk, his wife and his child were all under a layer of soil.

'Oh, Max,' she said, when she saw his face. 'Please don't cry.'

'I'm fine.' The skin on her bad knee was reddening, as though lava boiled beneath. How bad should they let it get before they took her to a hospital and risked the questions?

'We should – you know, the pool,' she said, with a backward nod. 'Easy for me to say, when I'm not the one doing it.'

'No, it's OK. Let's get it done.'

He cranked the handle that retracted the pool cover. The rain had made the cover's mechanism stick and it squeaked unpleasantly as the tarpaulin rolled up into a fat cylinder. Katya was still face-down, thank God, the youthful, feminine curve of her back now a bloated, sexless, ageless torso bobbing above the surface. As if to make up for her stopped heart, his own began to pound fiercely. Her tanned flesh was already taking on a greenish tinge. He felt his gorge rise. I can't do it, he thought, I can't touch her. Calling the police now and giving himself in, letting both of them be questioned, seemed a small price to pay if he could be excused from touching her skin.

Juliet seemed to sense what he needed. 'There are spare sheets in a cupboard on top of our bed. So you don't have to . . . you know.'

Our bed. He clung to that phrase on the way to the bedroom. When the horror of everything wore off, all this would still be Juliet's, and she was going to share it with him. He was determined that it would never feel like a prison for either of them.

'Let's do it, then.' Juliet shook out the sheet, laid it on the ground like a shroud. 'Oh, I can't believe we're doing this. I can't believe it, Max!'

The rising hysteria in her voice frightened him. How easily would she flip back into her alter ego? He had talked her out of it once, but would he be able to do the same again? The thought prompted an unexpected pang of missing Veronika and her straightforward, entirely sane and predictable contempt.

'We can't do this,' said Juliet.

'She would have killed you,' Roman reminded her.

Free of the tarpaulin, Katya's body had washed up near the pool steps. She was close enough for him to reach out and reel her in by the hair. He fought the urge to vomit as he prepared himself to drag her by the hands on to the flagstones and then to the sheet.

I'm doing this for us, he told himself. I'm doing this so we can be free from a crazy bitch who wants one thing so badly she would do anything, hurt anyone, to get her way.

The doorbell shrilled, loud and long, a nerve-jangling sound immediately followed by the rattling of the letterbox and a woman's voice calling, 'Hello?'

LIZANNE

73

When Mr K holds Lizanne's face in his slim hands, tells her she's going to replace Jennifer as the second swan and says, 'You are perfect creature,' *well*. It's not an exaggeration to say that it feels like she has been born again, that this is the beginning of her real life. Just moments before, when it looked like Céline was going to be the chosen one, disappointment had plunged her into the deepest, darkest part of herself, and now she is soaring. The ups and downs of this career are wild. Moods can turn on a penny; careers can be made or broken by the placement of a little finger.

'Sorry,' she says to Céline afterwards. It confirms that she was right to befriend Céline. She looks like star material, with her green eyes and her shiny hair, but she's too uncontrolled to be a true Kirilovan. To be a true *rival*.

'Like fuck you are,' replies Céline. But nothing can dent Lizanne's euphoria.

Since she was a schoolgirl, with Ava Kirilova's picture tacked above the bed in her dorm in the Gulag, she has wanted to be her. And now, for half a minute, on stage, every night, she gets to be. It's not quite a leap into Ava Kirilova's shoes, it'll be a while before those are empty, but a leap in the right direction. And Ava's star won't hang this high for ever. In the next three, four years it will start to descend.

In her most reckless fantasies Lizanne dreams of replacing Ava, not just as Mr K's prima ballerina but also as his daughter. Not literally, not the full adoption: Lizanne is an adult with two living parents. But emotionally and professionally – and they are the same thing, in ballet – she knows she would be the perfect successor.

When Delia in wardrobe measures her and they turn out to be exactly the same size, Lizanne takes it as a sign that this was meant to be. But, when she plucks up the courage to approach Ava, it all goes wrong. She gushes like an amateur, like a fan at the stage door. Worse still, she forgets the 'Miss Kirilova' in the heat of the moment and the resulting snub happens in front of half the company.

It takes an hour for her cheeks to go down, but, when they do, she's forced to reflect that maybe it was for the best. That little setback will keep the brake on. Ambition is taken for granted in ballet, but if anyone saw the true scale of Lizanne's, how hot it burns, they would recoil.

That night, in the sweltering privacy of her Gulag bedsit, she WhatsApps the news to her mum on the smartphone she's had for two years now because it's the twenty-first century and what else are you supposed to do? Contrary to Mr K's beliefs, the phone has never distracted her or impeded her dancing. It's an insult to a ballet dancer really to think that all those years of training, ambition, love, will be undone just because you can hail an Uber and browse Instagram. To be discovered in possession of a mobile phone would be a sackable offence, but Lizanne isn't the kind of girl who gets found out. She's the kind of girl who gets *on*.

Lizanne needs not just to become Odette but to become *Ava Kirilova*'s Odette. She begins to follow Ava around the theatre, watches her through the studio door, one eye on the corridor so that she can act casual at the sound of footsteps. She wishes there were some kind of secret window so that she could watch Ava's rehearsals in full, take notes, even film her.

Lizanne has actually learned a lot of the role of Odile this way. She knows all the solos. She can't practise with a partner: she doesn't trust any of the male dancers at her rank to keep it quiet. Ideally she'd like someone like Luca, but he is Ava's. So she goes over the variations in secret whenever she gets the chance. She knows it's just a fantasy but she likes the idea that she could take over the part at a day's notice. She sneaks into Studio 4 when she's supposed to be resting and dances Odile's *coda* from Act III again and again and again. It's taking a toll on her body, especially her right knee, but she doesn't care.

She creeps into the stalls when Ava and Luca are rehearsing this scene with Mr K. When Mr K tears strips off Ava for travelling during her *fouettés* she sees the problem instantly. The problem is not the *fouettés*, it's Ava's attitude. With this production, Ava has started, not to question Mr K's methods exactly, but to bring in her own interpretations.

There are better dancers than Lizanne in the company, with better alignment and turnout, but they don't listen the way she does. You have to not just obey Mr K but make a *show* of that obedience. You have to surrender to him and be *seen* to surrender. That's what makes you stand out. Lizanne honestly doesn't know why the others can't see it. It's so simple! Not that she's going to let on.

She wants to say something like this to Ava but how can she, when all these rigid hierarchies are in place and she's supposed to scuttle past *Miss Kirilova* with downcast eyes like a Victorian scullery maid on the main staircase? It's a one-sided relationship, but Lizanne feels that her side of it is big and strong and heartfelt enough for both of them. All Lizanne wants is to *be* with Ava, sit at her feet so she might dispense what's left of that incredible talent. Ava's magic was a dropped thing, a discarded shoe that she could pick up. A magic dress. Something from a legend, a prop from a ballet.

74

She has Luca to thank for granting her access to the principals' floor. He mouths the numbers of the keycode while Lizanne watches through the wire-hatched glass of a fire door. Another manifestation of how Mr K's rigid hierarchies breed not respect but carelessness. They've got complacent, the principals. It doesn't occur to them that a junior dancer would dare infiltrate their space: so much so that they don't even bother to lock their doors.

At Lizanne's most recent wardrobe fitting, she noticed that there was a gap where Ava's Odette and Odile costumes usually hung. She asked Delia where they were, and Delia's stammered 'I don't know' gave Lizanne her answer. Typical of Ava to keep her costumes in her dressing room so that Wardrobe comes to her rather than the other way around. God forbid she should have to return a friendly hello.

That black swan dress beckons Lizanne through the layers of floors and walls. She knows it will fit her and, having tasted Odette, she is desperate to see herself as Odile. She picks a day when all four principals are rehearsing with Boyko and Felicity and makes her way into Ava's dressing room. It is twice as big as Lizanne's bedsit and trees dance outside the window. Lizanne smooths down the hair that she's twisted into a coronet on top of her head. It doesn't look right on her: nothing looks as good as it does on Ava.

The wardrobe key is in a pot on the dressing table. Lizanne opens the door to see white swan and black swan side by side on their dressmaker's dummies.

This is a terrible idea.

She can't stop herself.

Her ambition overrides her common sense. The urge to be the best dancer, to get to the top quicker than the others, was always stronger almost than the compulsion to dance. Sometimes she is scared of it. Like it could make her do terrible things.

She tells herself that Ava Kirilova will understand this.

She stands before the mirror, strips, admires herself this way and that, before gently removing Odile's dress from its manne-quin. It looks heavier than the white dress. 'This is *insane*,' whis-pers Lizanne, as she steps into the tutu, slides the bodice up and over her shoulders; but right now, just under two weeks before first night, there is a collective madness in the theatre, a sense that the company as a whole is marching towards an eighty-strong nervous breakdown, some terrible event; and that that mass hysteria has infected her. It's as though they are all cells in Mr K's body and whatever affects him strikes them down too.

Lizanne looks in the mirror: Odile sparkles back at her. This feels so right it's almost painful. She knows that one day she will wear this dress on the stage below. She marks the steps of Odile's Act III solo but, when she finds that she is not marking the steps but dancing for real, something just within the bounds of sanity warns her not to get carried away.

She stops. She takes a selfie. A forbidden act caught in a forbid-den image on a forbidden device.

When she removes the dress, to her horror a feather on the bodice catches on her bracelet. When she tries to jab it back into its bed, a handful more come loose. The more she tries, the more feathers fall out, and her fingertips become smeared with purple glitter. The floor is awash with feathers, someone's plucked the magic bird right there on the dressing-room floor. She hears the lift begin to clank its way up the shaft. In a panic she hangs the dress with its bald bodice back on the dummy, shoves the spare feathers under her arm and makes it out of Ava's room, along the corridor and through the fire doors just as the lift arrives.

There is no one else in the corps dressing room, thank God. Lizanne bundles the feathers into a cropped sweatshirt and stuffs it into her locker, along with a pair of Ava Kirilova's discarded shoes, which she rescued from the bin weeks ago. She tries them on, as she has before. They wear the same size shoe but there the similarity ends. Ava Kirilova's arches are a genetic blessing, the feet you would design if you were an engineer trying to create the ideal ballerina. Lizanne's feet are wider and a little flatter. Not that that will stop her; it just means she has to work twice as hard just to reach Ava's starting line.

As she kneels, the nagging pain in her right knee flares. It's just the extra sessions she's putting in with Mr K. It's not *supposed* to be easy. If it doesn't hurt, you're not doing it right.

Those one-on-one sessions are the greatest intimacy Lizanne has ever known. She gives herself over to him: she is his servant. Lizanne has never really dated but she imagines this is what love must be like. Working alone with Mr K like this, you don't focus on the dancer in the mirror, you become the mirror and it's him you're reflecting. She aches not just because of the extra steps she's doing but with the effort of not blurting out I love you or, worse, do you love me? He calls her his second swan, and on their last session together this breaks her.

'Mr K, do you think I could ever become the *first* swan? Do you think I have what it takes to dance Odette and Odile?' As soon as the words are out, she feels lighter, but not in a good way: more like she might pass out.

He looks her up and down, this body he knows better than she does, the muscles he has reprogrammed, the bones he controls. Then he chucks her under the chin.

'One day I think yes,' he says. 'One day.'

She is fucking immortal.

75

The next day, Lizanne is passing Studio 3, boiling to actual death in her black leotard and an ill-chosen cropped sweatshirt. She swings the little silver hammer her parents gave her, had made for her in fact, when she got into the LRB Academy aged twelve. She carries it with her wherever she goes. It's more than just a tool, it's a talisman and a comforter. Passing Studio 3, she sees Ava Kirilova cross-legged on the floor, roughing up the *pointes* of her shoes. She even does *this* elegantly. Everyone hates sewing their shoes and Lizanne thinks that maybe if she offers to do something so – *humble*, is the word she's looking for – then that will somehow re-set their relationship. Show Miss Kirilova that Lizanne isn't a threat. Not yet, anyway.

The offer backfires. It feels as though Ava stops just short of spitting at her.

Lizanne is sure that when she is a principal dancer she won't be such a stuck-up bitch. She nearly says something along these lines, so it's for the best when Sakurako Sato comes to steer her away. As they leave the studio, Lizanne notices in horror that there's a black feather from Odile's costume caught in the fine knit of her sweatshirt, and it's hanging by a couple of spines. If it falls off now, while Ava's watching their retreating backs, Lizanne has *had* it. Thinking quickly, if not logically, Lizanne plucks the feather from her sleeve, but it settles on Sakurako's hood. That's OK. It's not as if Ava will notice, and if she does she'll assume Sakurako's had a costume fitting.

'She's really best left alone when she's like this,' consoles Sakurako as they leave the studio behind them. 'She's carrying the show, and she's worried about Mr K. Well, we all are.'

When I'm principal, I'm going to be like Sakurako, thinks Lizanne, gracious and generous. She acknowledges that nothing in her behaviour so far, ever, has pointed towards this, but that's because she's never been where she wants to be. Once she is principal, her ambition will be sated. Physically of course being principal must be incredibly draining, but emotionally Ava Kirilova must be so secure. She has nothing to worry about! Nothing to prove! She has no excuse not to be sweetness and light.

'Sure,' says Lizanne, and decides to quit while she's ahead. She will focus first on dancing her way so deep into Mr K's heart that Ava will have no choice but to accept her.

76

Dance through the pain, says Ava Kirilova, and so Lizanne does, even if it means she fluffs the last step as Odette in the window on the dress rehearsal. Not that it matters. She realised when she was in the wings that no one in that audience of ballet students would be looking at her anyway. All eyes are on the black swan. The white swan is little more than part of the set. It's an anticlimax to realise that actually her movements matter more when she's just a normal swan and she has to move in formation with the other ballerinas.

But Mr K's secret promise keeps her going. She knows he's watching her even more closely. She cannot put a foot wrong.

By the end of Act IV, when Odette and Siegfried have jumped from their rock and the swans are tearing Von Rothbart feather from limb, her knee is really starting to burn. She tells herself that if Ava hadn't told her to push through the pain she would have sat this out. She will never take advice from anyone except Jack ever again. But she has to keep going. If she leaves the stage now she will fuck up the rehearsal and Mr K might never forgive her.

The irony is that it happens when she's at rest. The knee doesn't give out when she's *en pointe* or even in *plié* but when both her feet are flat on the ground. She feels the ligament tear like a sheet of paper but she goes down heavily, like a felled tree.

77

She's lucky. The man across the desk from Lizanne is telling her she's *lucky*. It's the day before the *Swan Lake* première and, in a green glass box of a hospital, Mr Sandhu, her consultant orthopaedic surgeon, is giving her the shape of her recovery. She's lucky that the tear in her meniscus is lateral and shallow. Three months' rest and some hardcore physio to build up the surrounding muscles, followed by surgery to reconstruct her knee. If her luck holds she'll be back on stage within a year. She focuses on the surgeon's hands with their long, elegant fingers – they remind her of a pianist's – that land precisely on his keyboard as he types her notes into his computer. Those hands will cut her open and stitch her back together again.

'You'll certainly never ignore a twinge again after this, will you?' asks Mr Sandhu.

'God, no.'

'I see this a lot with Kirilov's dancers,' he says, shaking his head. 'Too bloody scared to say anything in case they get excommunicated.'

Lizanne isn't about to tell him it wasn't fear that made her dance on a knee she knew wasn't right, it was ambition. And she was right about it making her do terrible things.

'They don't expect you to negotiate the stairs in that tower block they put you all in, do they?'

'Ah, no. They're going to put me in a flat.'

Mr Sandhu rolls his eyes at the vastness of Mr K's property empire.

Even if the lifts in the Gulag were reliable, Lizanne couldn't have stayed in there, not with all the work going on. They've given her the address of her temporary home and she's looked it up on Google maps. It's an ex-local authority maisonette on a shitty estate and the only thing to recommend it is that it's on the ground floor. She'd been hoping for one of the mansion flats or Victorian conversions, close to the theatre, like the ones all the principals live in. She'd even dared hope they'd put her up in Ava's own flat, which is supposed to be beautiful, and has its own garden and is, after all, going to be empty for the next six months. No such luck. But then it's all been very last-minute and she mustn't see it as a measure of her standing in Mr K's eyes.

Céline helps to move her in. 'It's not that bad,' she says, looking around the magnolia box full of orange pine furniture. 'I mean it's better than the Gulag. You're going to be so bored, though.'

'No I'm not,' says Lizanne. 'I've got a plan. I might be out of action for the summer. But I've got one advantage the rest of you don't.'

Céline regards Lizanne's crutches disbelievingly.

'I'm going to be *here*,' she says. 'In London. I'm going to be here for Mr K. Really get to know him.'

'Has he been in touch, then?'

'Not yet.' Lizanne doesn't let that deflate her. 'But I wouldn't expect him to be, before first night. He's got another swan to coach, for one thing.'

A shared envy sits in the room with Lizanne and with Céline, who once again failed the second swan selection process. 'But yeah. I'm going to wait until he's in his own recovery and then he'll be bored and he'll be desperate for a dancer to visit him.'

Céline smirks. 'Good luck getting past Raisa.'

'You don't understand,' says Lizanne. 'We have a different relationship now, me and Mr K.'

'If you say so,' says Céline.

Lizanne doesn't elaborate further. Céline can't be expected to understand what their bond was like. She will get to that house in the country and she'll listen to his stories and never contradict him on anything. She will make sure that by the time the tour is over he will love her like a daughter.

When the theatre is reborn and the next season is under way, Ava will have no choice but to work with Lizanne. She'll win her over, she knows she will. They'll be like sisters.

And if she doesn't – well, Lizanne has youth on her side. She has time. And soon she will have Mr K more or less to herself.

There isn't a suitable seat for Lizanne and her crutches on the first night of *Swan Lake* and anyway she isn't sure she's ready to see her replacement dancing in the window. She goes to bed early and watches trash TV with her phone switched off. She finds out about Mr K's death the following morning when she's brushing her teeth, pulling off a balancing act with a crutch and her tooth-brush. She's got a mouthful of toothpaste when her phone flashes up the number of the payphone in the Gulag, which means it's probably Céline.

'Are you sitting down?' asks Céline, her own voice thick, as though she too has something in her mouth.

Lizanne spits minty suds into this sink. 'Why, what's the scandal? Did Ava mess up the *fouettés*?' She half wants the answer to be yes, so that Mr K is steered ever-closer to a younger alternative, but before she can develop that fancy any further she realises that Céline is crying and also there must be something wrong with the connection because it sounds as though she is telling her that Mr K is dead.

'Slow down, say that again,' says Lizanne.

'He died, last night,' says Céline. 'He had a fall in the corridor and he died. Mr K is dead, Lizanne. We're never going to see him again.'

Lizanne's future evaporates, dry ice rolling off a stage.

Her good leg goes from under her.

78

Lizanne skips the church service – too far away, too formal, too bloody *much* – but she meets Céline outside the theatre for the wake. Céline is pink-cheeked above her black dress and her freckles are starting to come out.

'Help me with these,' Lizanne says, nodding down at the bouquet in her arms. It's an arrangement of roses, half white and half dyed black. There are black and white feathers in there too – that was her idea. The cost made her eyes water but it'll be worth it.

'Are they for Mr K? Because people are laying flowers on the pavement outside the—'

'No,' says Lizanne. 'They're for Ava.'

'That's really thoughtful of you,' says Céline.

'Well, if I don't get to talk to her today, explain what Mr K promised me, it'll be another six months.'

Céline looks at her evenly. 'You really are something,' she says.

At the wake, Lizanne can see – perhaps only Lizanne can see, from her strange new viewpoint between ballet and the real world – that everything has fallen apart. Felicity is smiling manically. Raisa is thinner than ever and looks like a raisin. Boyko is withdrawn and wild-eyed. Even the dancers seem to have lost their posture, spines bowing, necks shortening, faces slack. Jack is keeping it together but there is not enough Jack to go around. Ava is moving through the crowd like a wind-up toy, trapped in a handshake-greet-smile-repeat loop. Lizanne doesn't doubt it's a mask for the grief Ava is feeling inside. She knows what Ava is going through because she too had a special, close relationship with Mr K.

Actually in some ways it's worse for Lizanne than for Ava, because at least Ava still has the tour.

The atrium is a forest of dance-world dignitaries, newspaper critics (she stands behind the legendary Ian Bayer at one point), bloggers Lizanne recognises from Twitter, dancers she recognises from Instagram. On crutches, even with Céline holding the bouquet for her, she can't penetrate the crowd. She gets within touching distance of Ava just as it's time for the performance.

The performance is one of the greatest pieces of dance Lizanne has ever seen. It breaks her heart and makes her jealous and inspires her. It unsettles her too: there is a new quality to Ava's performance. Her steps are faultless but there's a freewheeling element to her transitions, as though something has come loose inside her.

Afterwards Lizanne hangs around to tell her this but word soon spreads that Miss Kirilova will not be coming out of her dressing room. Phrases like *Of course she must* and *Completely understandable* pass through the crowd and the theatre begins to empty.

'I've got to pack,' says Céline, and transfers the bouquet to the crook of her other arm. 'Maybe you should leave these on the pavement after all?'

Lizanne did not spend all that money to dump this bouquet in the street with a load of yellow chrysanthemums; and she did not dance eight hours a day for a decade to walk away from Ava Kirilova now.

'No, let's give them to her,' she says. 'It's fine. I know the codes to the principals' corridor.'

'Lizanne!' Céline's hands fly to her mouth. 'We can't!'

'There's no one else around,' says Lizanne. 'Please. I can't manage crutches and the flowers *and* the keypad.'

'For God's sake,' says Céline. 'If we get into trouble, I'm blaming you.'

The lift lurches to the principals' corridor and Lizanne dictates the code to Céline. But before they can knock on Ava's door Felicity emerges from her room, black-clad and pink-eyed.

'What on earth are you two doing up here?' she says.

'I got these for Miss Kirilova,' says Lizanne.

'I mean, how did you get in here?'

'The door was open,' improvises Lizanne.

'Oh, *Luca*,' concludes Felicity. 'Well, I don't suppose it matters now. This is the last we'll see of it like this. Look, it's very sweet of you both but Miss Kirilova's travelling the day after tomorrow. Why don't you take them back to your place, hmm? I'm sure they'll brighten it up no end.'

Brighten is hardly the word to describe these flowers: black and white, dark and light, life and death; and as she looks at them Felicity seems to sense that, and also the effort and cost that must have gone into them, because she changes her mind and says, 'Tell you what, let me try. She can only say no.'

Ava Kirilova doesn't so much say no as throw her rejection like a dagger, landing it between Lizanne's ribs. 'Forgive me if my priority isn't tending the feelings of some bloody junior dancer with crappy taste in flowers right now.'

Felicity and Céline cringe so hard they appear to shrink. Maybe they need to make space for Lizanne's mortification, which feels as if it might actually be lethal. Her cheeks are so hot they sting. It takes all her composure not to cry.

'Sorry, girls, I should've realised it wasn't a good time,' says Felicity. 'My fault, I shouldn't have knocked. She doesn't mean it. I don't think any of us are quite thinking straight at the moment, are we? I wouldn't take it to heart, Lizanne. Why don't you go home and get some rest? We hear you're going to be rehabbed back to rude health, once you've had the surgery.'

With great concentration, Lizanne turns the boil down to a simmer and says, 'Absolutely!' mirroring Felicity's super-duper demeanour.

The piece-of-junk lift pulls Lizanne down, away from her last chance to tell Ava Kirilova who she is, who she is destined to be.

She and Céline hug their goodbyes in the atrium.

'I'll miss you,' says Céline. 'Be good. Do your physio.'

'Buy a fucking phone,' says Lizanne.

No one's guarding the door to stage – standards are already slipping – and Lizanne spends a moment taking in the auditorium in its present form, for the last time. She gathers strength just from being here. *She* will be rebuilt along with the theatre and they will both be better than new and one day she will fulfil Mr K's prophecy and dance Odette and Odile right here on the stage where she fell and to do this she must impress Ava Kirilova and why is this all so bloody hard?

Something catches her eye, stage right, at the front, within reach. She uses the torch on her phone to investigate. The ribbon of a ballet shoe, as pale as pink can be without being white. It curls like peeled-off skin. She picks it up: her torch picks out the letters AK on the sole. The injustice of everything suddenly takes control of Lizanne and, with a Herculean effort, she stretches down to grab the ribbon and the shoe it's attached to, and then its twin.

Her fingers slide into her bag and close around her silver hammer. She bashes the shoes but they're broken in already. She wants to hear something break. She drops the hammer and uses her hands, pulling at ribbons, twisting and tearing. She takes out all her anger and frustration at the injustice of it all on satin and leather and wool. She is angry at Mr K for dying, she is angry at Ava Kirilova for encouraging her to dance on a sore knee, and when she calms down she will understand that above all she is angry at herself for her own dumb persistence, and her belief that injury would never happen to her. She pulls at the ribbons, she twists and she tears them. She feels a rip and then stops: not because she is satisfied but because of a rumble in the floor that travels up the lengths of her crutches and vibrates in her arms. The lift is on its way down. Someone is coming. She drops the shoes back where she found them and scoots across the black ice of the dance floor, to hide in the wings, stage right.

Lizanne's eyes adapt quickly to the near-dark and she identifies at first glance the figure emerging stage right. She watches Ava pick up her sabotaged shoes and turn them over in her hands and then, with mounting horror, she watches her lace the ribbons up.

She pulls them tight, using the kind of force that would surely reveal any real damage, and Lizanne lets out a breath she wasn't aware she'd been holding. Ava has made it pretty clear that a dancer's shoes are her own responsibility. Ava breaks into an effortless *pas de bourrée* that makes Lizanne ache with longing to dance again, and as she does so she kicks against something on the floor.

As Ava tips forward to examine the obstacle, Lizanne instinctively gropes for the hammer in her bag. She waits for Ava to make the connection. To pick it up, point it in her direction and say, *I know it's you*, because even if the shoes are safe to dance in, which they will be because it's not like anything actually came apart, this is really not a good look for Lizanne. But Ava kicks the hammer away like a piece of crap. It spins across the stage and comes to a halt somewhere in the black velvet recess of the far wings.

Ava Kirilova begins to move. Lizanne's own heartbeat is so loud that it must be audible: she imagines that Ava is dancing to it. Even in the dark, those beautiful lines, those loose new shapes could only be made by this body. Lizanne is so transfixed that she doesn't notice that Ava is dancing too close to the edge until the second she teeters.

The noise as she crashes into the pit brings Jack running, then Boyko, then a couple of techies. The house lights come up; a spotlight blazes on the broken swan. When the paramedics arrive, their green overalls look all wrong in this space of black, white and red. No one thinks to look to the left; no one knows Lizanne is there. No one notices the silver hammer on the side of the stage; even a dying star outshines precious metal.

When they have all gone, Lizanne waits a long time before retrieving her hammer. The stage door is unlocked and she opens it on to the street, astonished to find that it is still light, that it is still summer, that London is still there.

What has she done? What the *hell* has she done?

79

The irony.

Lizanne will dance again while Ava's career is over. It's horrific, of course it is, and she wishes she hadn't done it, but it's not as if this was her intention, and wringing her hands won't change anything.

In fact, it kind of presents her with an opportunity.

Ava will need someone to look after her. A companion, if you will, or even a live-in PA, Lizanne doesn't mind getting her hands dirty. She's meant to be resting, she's still on crutches, but she's got used to getting around on them. She trembles as she calls the theatre and puts the suggestion to a frazzled Boyko. He says he'll have to consult Raisa, but the relief in his voice tells her this role is hers for the taking.

Just the two of them! She can direct the charm offensive she had planned for Mr K on to Ava with no interference. It almost makes tearing her knee worthwhile.

She's going to drop the formalities, the 'Miss Kirilova' stuff that keeps them apart. Everything has changed and it's time the company moved on to a more modern, fluid, inclusive way of communicating. This is the kind of thing they'll discuss into the night, over endless cups of tea.

They've given her a little office space, if you can call it that, in the theatre. It's being gutted and rewired but they're doing the Gulag first so she can work without disruption for a while yet. They've put her up in the sweltering boardroom as it's one of the last places to be redone. Up here, amid the hammering and the banging and the dust, she will spend an hour a day sorting out post. She still has the bunch of black feathers with violet tips that she tore from the bodice of Odile's dress that time and she keeps them in a little vase, like spiky flowers, to remind her of the role she must one day dance.

It's from this room that Lizanne calls Ava, saying she'll be moving in. To her horror she finds herself adopting this dreadful sing-song how-can-I-help-you? voice rather than addressing her like an equal. Ava basically sacks her before she's even had a chance to start the job. She's got her own people in.

Of *course* she has.

Lizanne forces herself to stay cool. She might not be able to get her feet under the table at the house but she can look after Ava from afar. She messes up her first job, which is to divert Ava's delivery of prescription drugs from her old flat to the new place in Gabriel's Hill, and instead sends them to the theatre. You can't redirect a redirection so she's got to hand-deliver them. And that's no bad thing. It's almost as though her subconscious was finding ways to bring them closer.

There's no rush. They have all summer.

The early days are clearly really hard for Ava. At one point she even calls and asks Lizanne if there's any chance she can have her job back. Lizanne stutters; she doesn't know what to say. The poor girl, of course she wants to dance again, and her asking Lizanne for help is surely a sign that there's a thawing between them. In the next breath, she forgets herself and talks as though Mr K is still alive, a slip of tenses that breaks Lizanne's heart. But then Ava cuts the conversation stone dead as she always does and at least Lizanne is spared the awkwardness of having to correct her.

She never mentions her job again. In fact she never mentions Mr K again, full stop. Lizanne's been reading about grief online, she knows it comes in waves and that denial is one of the stages, and that must be where Ava is right now. She'll pass through it and into the other stages, and when she does, Lizanne will be here for her.

*   *   *

These sudden hang-ups are a regular feature of their conversations. Half the time she doesn't pick up at all. Spite flares in Lizanne. She now wants to *flaunt* her own recovery in front of Ava, if anything.

But no. That will not bring her closer to her goal.

She checks in most days, either with a call or a visit. If there's more than two days' silence she goes up there. She drops off either Ava's pain relief or her fan mail, depending on what's come into the theatre that day. There's a heart-stopping moment when one of the black feathers finds its way into that day's stack of post. There's keeping in touch and then there's taking the piss. Lizanne slides the feather out from between the envelopes and lets it fall to the pavement.

Other days, she doesn't go in. She stays in her Uber, or her Addison Lee if she's making the company pay, checks for a bit of movement in the house, or at least to see that the previous package has been taken in, then tells the bemused driver to keep going. She's seen the girl Ava's got in to look after her; she saw her leaving the house on one of her earliest drive-bys, a very pretty girl who manages to make her black nurse's tunic look impossibly chic; and once she saw another guy in black, maybe a physio, ring on the doorbell with a big bag of ice. When Lizanne is sure that at least Ava Kirilova is being taken care of, she scales back her visits.

One day, Lizanne calls the Gabriel's Hill house to find that Ava is not there. The phone rings for so long she hits a recording of a voice inviting her to check the voicemail. Thinking nothing of it, she keys in 1234 which is the default passcode for idiots everywhere and hears a message from Jack, expressing concern that she isn't calling her back, worried that Lizanne isn't looking after her properly, and leaving his number.

The next time she tries this, she intercepts a message from Luca – pissed off his face – and another from Jack, his tone insistent this time. Lizanne *says* things are fine but he needs hear it from the horse's mouth, and Juliet must say if she's not happy with the arrangement. Lizanne wipes them both and diverts the house phone to her desk at the theatre. Now they literally can't get through to her without coming via Lizanne and it looks like she's at Gabriel's Hill as well, which is win-win. The only problem is that the phone on her desk goes, there's no way to tell if they're calling the theatre direct or ringing the house. She has to work that out by the tone of whoever's calling. The stories she feeds back to the company, who still think she's living at Gabriel's Hill, say that Ava's very withdrawn and she doesn't want to come to the phone but that they're getting on well and really they mustn't worry, she needs to focus on the tour.

Jack or Felicity speak in the future tense, saying it *will* get better, they'll find their feet *soon*, as though they aren't already two weeks into it and halfway across the world. Thank God for you, Lizanne, they say. Thank God Ava has you, looking after her and talking to her and keeping her sane. But, could you ask her to return our calls?

A band of rebels go rogue and buy themselves smartphones, including Céline, and from her Lizanne gets the fuller picture. Raisa has stopped eating. Luca is out clubbing every night and turning up to shows hungover or still drunk. Discipline among the corps has completely broken down. Money is a problem. In Prague, the hotel wouldn't let them stay because a credit card bounced. *Send us a selfie of you and AK!* Céline texts. Lizanne panics and switches off her phone.

80

After a couple of weeks of this dance of approach and rejection, something inside Lizanne dies. It's as though someone has cut out her drive and ambition, all the things that make her *her*. Is this . . . depression? She leaves Ava her mobile number in case of emergencies, and then, with the curtains closed against the blazing city sun, she watches twelve hours of *Love Island* in one sitting.

After four days of sweaty unwashed misery, the weather breaks. The rain wakes London up. People come out and dance in the street. She wonders how Ava Kirilova spent this rainy night. Probably being tended to by her team of staff. But that night Lizanne sleeps better than she has in weeks and the following morning she gets up early. When there's a break in the rainfall and the sun comes out, mist fizzes from pavements and she feels inspired to move again.

Outside the theatre there's a giant skip filled with the old red seats from the auditorium, but her little office is still intact. She collects a week's worth of post, noting with alarm that there's a letter addressed to Mr K from a debt-collection agency, but she doesn't have time to dwell on that because the phone is already ringing as she unlocks the door.

It's Luca again. It's mid-morning but he's drunk and hysterical.

'I miss her so fucking much,' he keeps repeating. 'I miss her so fucking much. Why isn't she calling me back?'

Because I wiped your message, thinks Lizanne, because I didn't want you to know she wouldn't let me in, because I still, if you will leave me alone, have time to make a success of this. She is furious with Ava for putting her in this position.

'She has good days and bad days,' says Lizanne, not really knowing what she means by that.

Luca takes a long sniff. 'Fucking . . . put her on the phone. Get her, now.'

'She's just in the bathroom right now,' says Lizanne.

His tone hardens. 'I'm on to you,' he says.

Her thoughts leapfrog to the shoes, the hammer, the fall. She realises that she has squared her shoulders as though to front out an accusation.

'What do you mean?' she asks.

'*Why* can't we talk to her?' There's a noise which might be Luca belching, or retching. 'Is it – has she killed herself, and no one will tell me?'

'Luca, don't be ridiculous,' says Lizanne, but now the possibility leaks down her spine like cold sweat. They have been out of touch for days and days. For all Lizanne knows, Ava Kirilova *could* have done something drastic. She pictures a flock of blowfly swirling over her body. She suppresses a swell of nausea.

'Look, I'll get her to talk to you as soon as I can. Where can I reach you?'

'Look it up on the sodding poster!' he shouts. 'We're not exactly hard to find!'

The line goes dead.

Breathe in, breathe out. Lizanne's skin is damp.

According to the tour itinerary they are currently in Schiphol airport and she can hardly put out a call. She considers calling Jack or even Céline but no. They will only insist on talking to Ava too.

She takes the phone off divert and calls the Gabriel's Hill house but hangs up before it connects. She can't keep hiding behind voicemails and missed calls. She needs to confront whatever's there. *Whatever* is there.

Once the decision is made, she feels a kind of elation. Whatever else happens today, even if Ava is decomposing in a bed or she's alive and she throws Lizanne off the property or they all find out she's been lying and she loses her job, and she *never* gets to dance Odette and Odile, she will at least be free of the dread of the future. Of not knowing what she has set in motion. Of not knowing where it will end.

81

London rolls past. Lizanne's dread builds as the Uber driver bleats on about the heatwave of 1976. She mentally lists her objectives, in order. First she must ascertain – because for some reason she is thinking in the language of a police procedural – she must *ascertain* that Ava is alive. Then, presuming the news is good, she must obtain some kind of evidence to this effect. Persuade Ava to call Jack, ideally. It is probably not the time to ask for a selfie to show Céline.

Once the practicalities are out of the way they can talk. *Really* talk. About what it feels like to fall, about Mr K, about the tour; and eventually, when the mood is right, the conversation will naturally turn to Lizanne and her future.

It's half-past twelve by the time they get to Gabriel's Hill. Yummy mummies drink outsize coffees and dandle babies outside the Wheatsheaf.

The gates to the estate take forever to part.

She's brought her umbrella but at No. 36 Gabriel's Hill only a faint lingering haze tells of last night's rain. The windows at the front of the house are open. Someone is in. It might just be a cleaner or a housekeeper or another member of that black-clad army that look after her. Well. Perhaps they will be easier to sweet-talk.

She usually tells her driver to wait but this time she sends him away to remove the option of losing her nerve. When the car has gone, an eerie quiet remains. Lizanne walks on the lawn so she's soundless even on crutches. She strains her ears: there are voices coming from inside, or maybe from the garden, faint enough that it could just be a radio. The dread releases its grip by one finger.

She presses the doorbell for a count of five. Afterwards, there's a ringing in her ears and it's hard to tell whether the voices have stopped. She hinges awkwardly at the waist to peer through the letterbox. It's got some kind of sprung mechanism in it that threatens to slice her fingers off, so she uses her silver hammer to prop it open. She can see nothing but white walls, paintings and closed doors.

'Hello?' Lizanne's voice echoes in the corridor. 'Hello?

There's a muffled thud – the closing of a door, maybe.

When no answer comes, the old anger is back; it is redoubled. Anger that Ava hasn't been taking her calls; anger that the rejection, that haughtiness she showed the whole time they were dancing together has been extended into this, her servitude. Getting her into trouble.

'Hello?' She finds herself using that customer-service tone again. 'Miss Kirilova? It's me, Lizanne.' She's starting to ache with the effort of stooping, a pain that starts in her knee but spreads rapidly to her hip, from where it is further relayed up her back, one bone at a time. 'I really, really, really need you to let me in this time. Everyone's really worried about you and I'm worried they're going to sack me or something for not looking after you.' The only sound is the distant whoosh of cars on the main road. '*I'm* worried about you. If you don't let me see you I'm going to have to—' She stalls for a second because really what can she threaten Ava with? She has no power. The last weeks have shown her that. 'I'm going to have to call the police or something?'

The door at the end of the corridor opens to reveal, in silhouette, the long lines and thwarted grace of Ava Kirilova. Lizanne has been a student of that body long enough to recognise it in any condition. She's *alive*, she thinks, relief diffusing through her veins. The worst-case scenario can be discarded like a sandbag.

Ava pulls the door behind her and approaches in an ungainly gait that resembles Lizanne's own. As she gets closer Lizanne realises that there's something wrong with the skin on her legs: they are slashed and bruised. Is she cutting? It's not the kind of thing you'd expect from a dancer at her level, it's more—

The heavy front door swings open. Quickly, Lizanne pulls the hammer from the letterbox, loops the cord around her wrist and tucks it into her palm.

Ava Kirilova leans almost drunkenly on one crutch, her face a chalky base for livid pink blotches that spread down under the neck of her sloppy joe sweater. Her bottom lip is swollen like she's had bad filler. Her legs have been carved up into deep welts, at least one of which is still bleeding.

For all this, it is she who staggers at the sight of Lizanne.

'Oh, my God, what's *happened* to you?' says Lizanne, at the same time as Ava says,

'Lizanne? *You're* Lizanne? It's *you*.'

It's confusion rather than her usual contempt. Surely she can't have forgotten Lizanne, but just in case she prompts, 'I was the second swan?'

Ava barks a laugh. 'I know *that*,' she says. 'I just didn't make the connection with . . .' She gestures at the telephone on the table beside her, the medium for almost all their conversations.

Lizanne seizes the break in Ava's attention to advance another metre into the house. If she really hadn't understood, then it was nothing personal. This is still salvageable.

'So who did you think was calling you?' she says. 'No wonder you didn't make my job easy for me!'

'Your job?' She realises that Ava might be farther gone than she thought.

'Not my day job, obviously. I mean the whole thing of being, like, your companion. Making sure you were OK. And you've kept me at arm's length the whole time.'

'Well, you can see I'm fine,' she lisps. If it weren't so horrific Lizanne would want to laugh. She flashes back to the time Ava spoke about Mr K as though he were still alive. She has clearly had some kind of breakdown, which would explain *a lot*. Has someone done this to her or has she done it to herself – and which is worse?

'I'm not being funny, but you don't look fine.'

Ava doesn't engage, just glances at the door behind her. Lizanne draws closer again. It's like a game of Grandmother's Footsteps. Ava steps sideways to block the corridor, and then it feels more like fencing.

'You've got to start calling people back,' says Lizanne. 'Not just me. I had Luca on the phone, and Jack's really worried.'

Ava looks at the telephone and says, '*Luca*,' like some mystery's been solved.

Lizanne wonders now if Ava might be drunk. She edges forward until she's close enough to sniff the air. There's no trace of alcohol, just the sweet apple smell of soap or shampoo.

'No, he called *me*. From the airport. They're on an aeroplane right now. I'll wait and you can call him, yeah?'

'I'd actually really like you to go.' Ava throws another glance over her shoulder, as if she's thinking about darting into the living area and barricading herself in. A now-or-never feeling overtakes Lizanne. She has nothing to lose and also everything.

'I'm not happy leaving you alone,' she says. 'I think you need someone to talk to. I want to be a friend to you, Miss Kirilova. We're the only ones left in London. And we've got so much in common.'

This would usually be Ava's cue to scornfully tell her they have nothing in common but instead she continues to stare blankly, and this emboldens Lizanne.

'More than you know,' she continues. 'I understand what you're going through. Not just the injury. I understand how you feel about Mr K because so did I; I was close to him too.'

Ava screws up her face and turns it to the wall. In this gesture Lizanne sees how alone she must have been in her grief. She needs to show her that that's not the case.

'He said I reminded him of you. He said that just a couple of days before he died. He said I had what it takes to dance Odette and Odile, Miss Kirilova, and that's because of you: because I modelled myself on you. I want to learn from you, I want to be the next link in that chain. I want to honour his last wish.'

It was supposed to offer comfort but she can tell from the way Ava Kirilova shakes her head that the question of now-or-never has been answered and it's gone the wrong way.

'*Go*,' she orders, and Lizanne wishes she could spool her little speech back into her mouth and swallow it.

'I'm sorry if I upset you.' She stretches out her hand, forgetting about the silver hammer looped around her wrist. It swings back and forth like a little pendulum.

Ava's eyes blow wide, the whites ringing the irises. Lizanne can almost see the memories flipping across her face like a series of glossy photographs thrown on a detective's table.

'You,' she says again, her tone stripped of doubt. 'It was *you*.'

82

Ava is half-laughing, the way people do when they don't believe what they're hearing. 'I *knew* my ribbons would never have come loose.' She examines a fingernail and nods, as if something has been proved. 'What did you do?'

Lizanne shakes the silver hammer off her wrist and drops it into her bag, as though it can be unseen. 'It's not what you think,' she says to buy herself time while she struggles to concoct a plausible alternative. A counter-accusation leaps to mind: she can remind Ava that if she hadn't advised Lizanne to dance through the pain they would both be on tour right now. But, even as the thought forms, she understands that the two acts aren't comparable. One is a careless remark that Lizanne was – it is suddenly, blindingly clear – under no obligation to heed. The other was a spiteful act of sabotage that cut short a career.

Or, rather, two careers. Because now Ava knows that Lizanne is at least partly responsible for her fall, any chance she had of dancing Odette and Odile has gone for good. There's not much cross-pollination between the London Russian and other ballet companies, but something like this . . . this news will travel.

She is over.

If only, she thinks with a clawing desperation, she had some dirt on Ava that would force her to take her back into the company and thrust her to stardom. Some *leverage* that would redress the balance of power.

'Please just go,' Ava repeats. 'Or I'll have to call the security guards.'

Lizanne should turn around and go but something stops her. It's ambition, the force that's bigger and dumber and stronger than she is. *Don't give up*, it whispers in her ear. Ambition has its hands on Lizanne's shoulder blades and it's pushing her forward even though she doesn't know what it expects to achieve. Ambition puts the words, 'I'm sure we can talk this through,' into Lizanne's mouth. Ambition pitches Lizanne forwards on her crutches and swings her body forwards, bypassing Ava Kirilova and reaching the connecting door.

The door swings open and she's in the living room.

She sees it in colours.

The white bedsheet laid out on the grey flagstones.

The bright blue pool where a woman's bloated body floats face-down, long black hair and greying limbs.

Yellow grass leading to a sweep of green grass with brown earth piled in hillocks around a, around a – there's only one word for a hole like that.

There's a slamming feeling inside Lizanne. 'No,' she says, backing away. 'Oh, my God, what is this?'

'I had to let her in,' says Ava, desperation wrestling with apology on her face and in her voice. 'I couldn't stop her.'

Who is she, this unstoppable woman she had to let in, thinks Lizanne, and what did she do that was so bad *this* was the result? But then, as she follows Ava's gaze, she understands that Ava is not addressing her, but talking about her. *She* is the one who just came in, and Ava is explaining this to another person in the garden.

Edging towards them both is a man holding a shovel, someone Lizanne has seen before. It's the physio guy, the one she saw with the ice that time. His T-shirt is filthy and so are his hands, his nails and cuticles outlined with black dirt.

This explains Ava's split lip and her refusal to let her in. This man, this *bastard*, has been holding her hostage or something; he's some kind of abuser. Lizanne is afraid, but she knows a chance for redemption when she sees it. She will be Ava Kirilova's saviour. 'It's OK. It's alright, I'm going to call the police,' she says. But before she can hit the first 9 Ava raises the end of her crutch and flips it from her grasp. It lands with a thwack on the wooden floor.

Not the guy. *Ava.*

Lizanne recalls how it was her threat to call the police that persuaded Ava to let her in.

Ava doesn't *want* the police. She opened the door to stop Lizanne calling them.

The couple lock eyes in a wordless exchange: Lizanne sees them make the decision. Then they take a collective step towards her, moving in perfect unison, like dancers.

'Stay where you are,' says the man as he puts himself between Lizanne and the way out.

ENCORE

JULIET KIRILOVA

83

Eighteen months later

'So the trick with this step is *lean* into it,' says Boyko, twisting his torso to demonstrate. 'Bring your whole body in, not just the feet.'

'Got it,' says Femi, and copies him instantly. Chloe takes a beat longer to pick it up, but then the three of them are swooping their breasts in a move that owes more to Fred Astaire than anything you'd expect to see in a classical ballet. They are rehearsing the Neopolitan dance from Act III, tambourines with coloured ribbons in their hands. This *pas de deux* is not a lovers' dance: if they're trying to seduce anyone it's the audience. They dance at, rather than with, each other. Femi and Chloe are both compact and athletic dancers; they are made for each other. Although I have them dance with others: there is no such thing as monogamy in my company. I encourage a kind of promiscuity. My dancers learn to lift, and be lifted by, different bodies. I will never be left in a position where I have no one to cover a role.

'I like that,' says Boyko. 'It's playful, cute.'

When the 2018 *Swan Lake* tour, with its nervous breakdowns and its absconding dancers and its shambolic performances and, dear God, its bill, came to an end, Boyko was overjoyed to cast off the creative director role. He is now senior ballet master and he was born to it. He is not an originator but an interpreter. It turns out that he wasn't married to my father's style after all: he just loves to take direction. His genius is in bringing someone else's vision, someone else's shapes and stories, to life.

Femi and Chloe look through the glass to me and I smile the approval that will make them better dancers. I'm in what I still think of as my father's room. I took away the mirror and replaced it with a wall of glass. Now the dancers can see me as I work, as I take calls, sketch ideas, or just watch them do their beautiful thing.

I sent his chair and some of his paintings to Raisa for her *dacha* in the mountains near Sochi. I kept his samovar and the rugs and the photographs, although I added the one of me holding my mother's hand. For these days, I am proud of both my parents. It's part of my story, no longer a secret, that they only met once, twelve years after I was born. They loved me in different ways, each imperfectly because there is no other way to love. To reconcile the two halves of me, I reclaimed the birth name she gave me, and the stage name he did.

This is the creative hub of the company now. There's a boardroom upstairs for big meetings, and I gave that to the men and women with suits and finance degrees whom I hired from outside, first to audit the business, then to save it, and now to run it. The more I learn about how a business works, the more I am astonished that my father thought he could run this side of things as well as make dances. It turns out he was not a financial genius at all; his business practice was slapdash to the point of criminality. The cash-in-hand system he insisted on was nothing to do with teaching us discipline and everything to do with failing to declare income.

We do everything properly now. We were forced to sell all of the properties apart from the theatre itself and the adjoining tower block, which, despite its conversion into state-of-the-art studio apartments, the kids still call the Gulag.

And of course there is a third property that can never be sold.

'Let's try again from the beginning,' says Boyko. The pianist takes it from the top, music I never thought I'd be able to tolerate again in any context but which I've listened to every day for the last half-year. In two weeks, the London Russian Ballet Company will première my reworking of my father's reworking of *Swan Lake*. These steps are based on the greats: Ivanov and Petipa, Ashton, Kirilov. And now it's my turn. Just as once I wore the swans' headdress and took my place in that long line of ballerinas, now I make dances and follow different footsteps.

Femi and Chloe are as in tune as reflections. Under my direction Boyko has cajoled from them a performance as precise as my father demanded but more fluid, their acting more instinctive. They are the same steps, danced the way I wish I had been allowed to. As they bang their tambourines, I experience one of the moments of joy that keep catching me by surprise, edging through the grief without my permission. One day I hope that enough of these moments will string themselves together that I can forget about my past for whole minutes at a time. I miss dancing and I miss my father and the two losses remain indivisible. And of course any pride in my new work – and I am proud; I think we're creating something special – will always be tainted by Lizanne's arrival in my garden, and what I was forced to do next.

Femi and Chloe break for water. I love to watch my dancers chat, stretch, *be*, almost as much as I love watching them dance. Chloe picks up her phone and together she and Femi pout for a selfie. The company has a proper online presence now and I encourage my dancers to share their lives online, to chase sponsorship. Why should they live like church mice? How does that make them better dancers? I encourage them to have individual brands. Some of them do modelling work on the side. Instagram helps my dancers reach a new generation of fans. I use a career redevelopment consultant to help ageing dancers decide what to do with the rest of their lives, and she says that the more connection a ballet dancer has with the outside world – even if it's just through a screen – the better equipped they are to thrive on the other side.

I've let colour into the building. Studio 1 is now a summer-sky blue. The new paint smell has gone and there are scuff marks all over the walls; arcing tracks of *pointe* shoes at head height, the occasional handprint. I could repaint it but I like it this way. I want the place broken in like ballet shoes. My dancers are making their marks on the new LRB. I want the place to feel not like mine but *ours*.

'Back we come,' says Boyko, 'no rest for the wicked,' and his dancers line up, eager to learn.

The door opens behind me and because he didn't knock I know it's him. I don't turn around; I lean back into the strong arms that have always felt made for me.

Luca rests his chin on the top of my head. Platonic: *right*. My Prince Siegfried, my best friend.

'How's it going?' He nods at the rehearsal.

'I'm happy with it. They're both exactly on the music; you can tell they're hearing the same thing. I've got high hopes for this partnership.'

I feel him shift on the word *partnership*. It's such a loaded word for us. We were stupidly lucky; our chemistry was a once-in-a-career thing that we could never hope to replicate. And it's hard for me to watch him dance with his new partner, not just because it should be me but because even an objective eye can see it's not the same. I had to cast them together for this production. Whether they will last beyond it depends on how the show is received, and other factors beyond my control.

Chloe reaches out her hand and Femi is there to receive it. He spins her in a pirouette.

Then Boyko shouts the name 'Katya!' and the ground tilts beneath my feet.

I stagger despite Luca's support; he grabs me around the waist and doesn't recoil from my new loose body. You can keep yourself in shape and I've tried to, but nothing feels like being a dancer, the slings of muscle that hold everything in tight. That still do, in his case.

The vertigo builds and builds. Katya. Katya. Katya.

'Let me get you a chair,' says Luca. Without his support I reach for my cane, the black one topped with a swan's head, for the first time in weeks. But then Boyko repeats his instruction and this time I hear him properly – 'Catch her!' – and the world rights itself.

'If you just catch her by the elbow here, spin her in? See the difference.'

'Got it,' says Femi. He repeats the movement, this time to perfection.

'Sorry, I'm fine,' I tell Luca.

I'm not fine, but I will be. I repeat mantras to myself, the way I used to say *up, up, up,* during *fouettés*. Words have always looped in my head; I need to make sure they are the right ones.

You killed her in self-defence, I begin, and the other words flow like steps I've danced a hundred times. Your father's death was an accident. You have lost two parents. You are allowed to grieve. You must grieve. You are a dancer who cannot dance. Just as my old life began every day with company class, performing the same movements until I had internalised them completely, I now begin each day by narrating my history to myself, strengthening not muscle memory but the memory muscle.

I have spent the last year and a half sifting through my subconscious, trying to get to the bottom of what happened to my brain when it broke. I regard that summer now with a kind of baffled awe at my subconscious mind's attention to detail. Why did it choose to write the story it did; why did I conspire to steal my own money? I hid in my childhood name, desperate to return to the comfort of being mothered, but I didn't think I was a twelve-year-old. Maybe I 'returned' to the corps simply because I could build that story around what I saw in the mirror. Maybe I wanted to return to a time of camaraderie, before I was catapulted out. Or perhaps some protective part of my brain decided it was easier to mourn the loss of a budding career than a great one. Or was it my fixation on a certain member of the corps, a younger dancer who crouched in my shadow and wore my clothes? Without the professional help I can never seek, I'll never know. Nor can I know if I would have tipped into delusion without the double punch of losing Nicky and my career in the same week.

I do know, though, that something would have had to give. I was growing apart from him and beginning to create myself. I had come to despise my own complicity in disowning my mother. At some point, I would have had to step outside Ava Kirilova so that I could be free to hate her.

84

I don't feel Luca move away from me; don't hear the door open. Don't hear Max come in. But when I open my eyes, there he is, next to me.

'The guy from *The Sunday Times* is here to talk to us,' he says. 'He's waiting in the atrium. I said to give us fifteen minutes, I think she needs feeding first.'

He unclips the sling he wears across his body and gently lifts Gracie out. 'Mama's here,' he tells her, swinging her above his head until she shrieks with delight. He's so good with her, such an instinctive dad that it's hard to believe he's never been around a baby before. 'Here you go, sweetheart,' he says.

I kiss the urgent pulse of our daughter's fontanelle. She smells of cream and hay, an English garden in the heatwave. 'You *are* hungry, aren't you?' I say as her rosebud mouth roots around for my breast, and with the ease born of practice I pull down my top. She latches on the missing piece as the heart of me falls into place.

Luca studies the rehearsal with renewed concentration and Max places his hand on the small of my back. After five minutes, Gracie is done, head lolling like a drunkard, a sucking bubble on her top lip.

'Give her to Uncle Luca,' he says.

Max shrugs off the sling and hands it to Luca. When I pass Gracie into his arms, she throws out her arms and legs in a startle reflex.

'She's going to have perfect turnout,' says Luca, gently guiding her into the sling, then holding his hand out for the nappy bag. 'I'll take her for a walk. Show her the stage where she'll dance one day.' He whispers in Gracie's ear. 'I can cope with anything but the really runny ones, OK?'

'Thanks, Luca,' says Max. They like each other: not quite friends, not yet. But it will come.

'What are you thinking?' Max asks, as we wait for Ian Bayer to arrive.

'I'm thinking about the interview we *should* have faced.'

I mean the police: he knows it. He always knows. He runs his hands through his hair, scratches his scalp. 'In the interview,' he says, 'are we going to give away which ending we chose?'

I think he means us for a minute, but then realise that of course he's talking about the ballet. Because there's another version of *Swan Lake*, preferred by the Soviets and popular in China, a happily-ever-after in which Odette is restored to human form and she and Siegfried are reunited. Max means that Bayer might ask if we went for the 'Hollywood' ending, as Papa used scathingly to call it, or embraced the tragic original.

'No way,' I say. 'Let's save that for the first night.'

He nods. There's something else on his mind.

'What are you thinking?'

'Do you think he'll ask about Lizanne?'

I go cold. 'He might,' I say. 'And if he does we just answer as honestly as we can, without giving ourselves away.'

He picks up my hand and kisses the knuckles and says, 'We will be OK. I'll take my cue from you.'

Love in a ballet is magic. It comes out of nowhere: a look, a mime, and everyone watching knows. These people were meant to be together. They are the other half of one another. And it's going to be perfect, and it can be because it only has to last for another hour or two, expressed in bodies moving to music on a stage, before it ends in either tragedy or triumph. That's the real reason lovers die in tragedies. It's the only way their love can remain immaculate.

Love in real life is different. Ours was born in deception and moved through desire to death before we even knew each other.

And then, before we could get used to that, it was antenatal appointments, him holding my hand through childbirth, broken nights and dirty nappies and joy that neither of us feel we deserve. This is us, now: enmeshed, indebted, pooled, committed. Even in real life, you can't pull Cupid's arrow out of your heart without tearing the tissue around it.

In the ballet the heroine often has to die.

We did what we had to do.

Katya.

Lizanne.

THE SUNDAY TIMES

A Star Is Reborn

Ian Bayer

I last met Juliet Kirilova in the sweltering summer of 2018. It was the eve of her debut as Odette/Odile in one of the most anticipated productions of *Swan Lake* in a generation, an extraordinarily dark and daring interpretation of the ballet and that rarest of beasts, a five-star evening for every critic present.

It has, of course, since become infamous as Kirilova's last public performance, as her last use of her stage name, Ava, and as her adopted father Nikolai Kirilov's last night on earth.

Since that summer, both Kirilova and the London Russian Ballet have been to hell and back. The lightning of bad luck struck the iconic theatre twice in a week. After a fall, Kirilova retreated from public life while the company almost collapsed amid allegations of tax fraud and poor management.

So it's a pleasant surprise to be greeted by a smiling, relaxed Kirilova in the newly made-over theatre. The building's iconic brutalist exoskeleton remains the same but, inside, the starkness that at times felt designed to exclude all but the most devoted balletomane has been replaced by a light, fresh space designed to lure the ballet-curious in from the street.

Kirilova's office overlooks the cavernous Studio 1, visible through a plate-glass wall. It's important that she can watch the rehearsals, says Kirilova, but it's more important that her dancers can see her. 'My father had many gifts, but transparency wasn't one of them,' she says. 'He did things the old-fashioned way: for his generation, the ballet master was a god who couldn't be contradicted. I want the work

I do with my dancers to be a conversation. There are so many exciting ideas bubbling up through our new performers.'

We are here to discuss yet another production of *Swan Lake*, Kirilova's reimagining of her father's reimagining. 'I wanted to do something radical,' she says. 'And, for some purists, the most radical thing you can do is tell a story.'

The show is a creative *pas de deux*, the vision of two people. The ballet was developed with Kirilova's creative partner and new-minted husband, Ukrainian-born Maxim Shevchenko. The couple are tactile, an easy flow of conversation between them. All Shevchenko knows of his wife's career is video performances, and he says it's one of the greatest regrets of his life that he never got to see her dance.

'Once we'd decided to revisit *Swan Lake*, Max and I talked for weeks about what it *meant,*' says Kirilova, and Shevchenko nods. 'We took it apart and examined it from every angle before deciding it was about being able to trust your own mind. It's about questioning Prince Siegfried's grip on reality. Is the swan real, or just something he's conjured up?'

Shevchenko was in the Ukrainian military before the conflict brought him to the UK. 'I don't have a background in dance, and that's a strength,' he says of his role as Kirilova's dramaturg. 'My job is pure storytelling: I want people who don't know anything about *Swan Lake* to understand it on first viewing. The problem with *Swan Lake* is that a lot of it's just dancing.'

I raise my eyebrows. And that's a problem because . . .

'*Swan Lake* is a dancer's dance. Audiences – big audiences, the numbers we want to attract to our theatre – love *plot.*' The big numbers he mentions are the only allusion in our conversation to the company's financial difficulties. Kirilov left debt and chaos in his wake: the London Russian has no choice but to sell out every night. 'I'm influenced by story, by the fiction I grew up reading. Our *Swan Lake* is a thriller.'

As well as shaping the ballet's storyline, Kirilova credits Shevchenko with the fact that she is helming the ballet at all. 'There was a period where I thought I'd never leave the house again, let alone return to the world of dance, and Max got me through that. And of course now he's getting me through my nerves about the opening night. Will anyone want to see what I do?'

She needn't worry about that. The twelve-night run sold out within three days; a world tour is scheduled to include the Bolshoi Theatre in Moscow, the Metropolitan Opera House in New York and the Shanghai Grand Theatre. The details of the show are closely guarded but one of Kirilova's casting choices is the elephant in the room. The new principal was plucked from the corps: a name unknown outside the company and, if the bitchiest rumours are true, barely known within it.

'Everyone wants to know . . .' I begin. Kirilova and Shevchenko shift in their seats, sensing what's coming next. 'People are wondering why you cast someone so . . . fresh?'

As if on cue, the studio door opens and in walks Lizanne Livry, the new Odette/Odile. She waves through the glass. To say that Livry was a surprise choice is to be generous. She is not only inexperienced but also vulnerable as a dancer. In 2018, Livry suffered from a similar injury to the one that ended Kirilova's own career. The two women became close during their recoveries and whispers at court suggest that it is friendship, rather than talent, behind the promotion. That, despite her claims of meritocracy, Kirilova is doing exactly what her father did: picking a favourite and then shaping the ballet around them.

'I can come back later?' says Livry, even as she's making her way across the room, nodding a hello to me. She picks up a little silver hammer from a window ledge and raps it into her palm. 'Been looking for this everywhere.'

I ask if it's OK for Livry to answer some questions. Kirilova beckons her protégée into the office and makes room on the sofa for her. She is keen to pre-empt my questions. 'Lizanne has put in a hell of a lot of work. And she has an instinct for story that's very rare.'

It's a tactful way of skirting the issue of technical ability.

Is there a degree of her dancing vicariously through Livry? Kirilova considers her answer for an uncomfortably long time.

'You know what – maybe there is. Perhaps in Lizanne I see a version of myself who recovered. In the same way that my father saw me as an extension of, or a replacement for, his own performing days. I think it's probably inevitable. We know from the first day we go *en pointe* that our days as dancers are numbered, and making new dances is one way to come to terms with that death.'

Kirilova's voice cracks on the last word and I'm reminded of everything she has lost. Livry reaches across the sofa for Kirilova's hand. 'I really have worked for it, and in Av— in *Juliet*, I've had the best mentor anyone could hope for. And besides,' she says, winking, 'I know where all the bodies are buried.'

It's an odd joke that falls a little flat: Shevchenko frowns, and Kirilova's laughter feels forced.

'Well,' says Livry, 'I'd better go. I'm down to my last pair of shoes and the pile in my dressing room won't break themselves in.' She crosses the room on the diagonal: halfway to the door, she leaps in a spontaneous *grand jeté* and I see it: star quality, suspended in mid-air for a moment. She lands lightly and waves over her shoulder on the way out of the studio, her little silver hammer swinging from her hand and the world at her elegant feet.

Juliet Kirilova's Swan Lake *premieres at the London Russian Ballet Theatre, March 23, 2020, with a 30-city world tour to follow.*

ACKNOWLEDGEMENTS

Thank you to my brilliant and beloved agent Sarah Ballard. Thank you Eli Keren for absolutely bringing it. Thank you Jane Willis, Amy Mitchell, Georgina le Grice, Alex Stephens, Lucy Joyce and Fatima Amin and all at United Agents.

Thank you to everyone at Hodder & Stoughton: my fabulous new editor Jo Dickinson, and my fabulous not-new publicist Leni Lawrence. Thank you Carolyn Mays, Sorcha Rose, Kate Keehan, Alice Morley, Dom Gribben, Iman Khabl, Catherine Worsley, Sarah Clay and Richard Peters. Thank you to Ruth Tross for reading an early synopsis of this book some time in the late Jurassic period and to Kate Howard for her caretaking during the interregnum. Thank you Linda McQueen for a brilliant copy edit.

Thank you Tetyana Denford (whose novel *Motherland* I can't recommend enough) for translating Roman's words into Ukrainian. Thank you Valeriy Akimenko of the Conflict Studies Research centre for insight into the Ukrainian conscription process. *Spasibo* Viv Groskop for the masterclass in the Russian patronymic system.

Huge thanks and bottomless apologies to the orthopaedic surgeon Mr Simon Thompson who gave generously of his time to explain *exactly* how he would fix Ava's knee so that she could dance again, and whose advice I ignored because it didn't suit my plot. I know that if you had operated on her, she would have lived to twirl another day.

Thank you to all the early readers of *Watch Her Fall*. Helen Treacy, my novels only start to feel like proper books once you have set eyes on them. Emma Mitchell, your feedback was invaluable. And my dear friends in the crime-writing community, Michelle Davies, Sarah Hilary and Paddy Magrane: thank you, not just for reading but also for listening.

Thank you to Ellen Chambers from the charity Dancers' Career Development for putting me in touch with the two brilliant ballet dancers who helped shape this novel, Mariana Rodriguez of the Northern Ballet and Matthew Broadbent of the Scottish National Ballet. Thank you, both, for answering my relentless questions and giving me such detailed responses to my manuscript. Any faithful portrayal of the ballet world is down to Mariana and Matthew: any inauthentic details are all mine.

Thank you Magda Charlton, who won an auction in aid of the Sobell House Hospice in Oxford, to name a character in this book. Magda, I hope you and your husband Jack Charlton are happy with his fictional namesake.

Thank you, too, to two ballet dancers I have never met, Natalia Osipova and Reece Clarke of The Royal Ballet, who brought me to tears as Odette/Odile and Siegfried in Swan Lake at the Royal Opera House in London in March 2020. Watching that performance was the last 'normal' thing I did before the COVID-19 pandemic halted the world on its axis. I was inspired too by the scores of dancers who shared their lockdown online. I watched, awe-struck, as they used kitchen worktops as barres, turned pirouettes on squares of lino in tiny flats and, as the summer progressed, performed on rooftops, on canal banks and rooftops.

Finally, thank you to my family. My parents, for always being there. Michael, for everything, as always. And thank you to the dedicatees of this book, our daughters, Marnie and Sadie, my constant companions through the strange, sad year of 2020. For every still, sunny day we spent together there seemed to be two when I had to close my study door in your faces and write. You bore the stress and uncertainty with grace and humour and I could not be prouder of you. *Moyi lyubimiye devushki*, my most beloved girls.

READING LIST

The ballet world is full of remarkable people, many of whom write as beautifully as they move, and extraordinary true stories, as gripping and dark as anything you'd find in a thriller. I could not have written *Watch Her Fall* without the following sources of inspiration.

Dancing on my Grave by Gelsey Kirkland
Life in Motion by Misty Copeland
A Body of Work by David Hallberg
Blood Memory by Martha Graham
Dancing Through It by Jenifer Ringer
Ballerina by Dierdre Kelly
Rudolph Nureyev: The Life by Julie Kavanagh
Swans of the Kremlin: Ballet and Power in Soviet Russia by
    Christina Ezrahi
Bolshoi Confidential by Simon Morrison
Hope in a Ballet Shoe by Michaela dePrince

Order the new utterly gripping thriller from Erin Kelly . . .

THE SKELETON KEY

THIS REUNION WILL TEAR A FAMILY APART . . .

Summer, 2021. Nell has come home at her family's insistence
to celebrate an anniversary. Fifty years ago, her father wrote
The Golden Bones. Part picture book, part treasure hunt, Sir
Frank Churcher created a fairy story about Elinore, a murdered
woman whose skeleton was scattered all over England. Clues
and puzzles in the pages of *The Golden Bones* led readers to
seven sites where jewels were buried – gold and precious stones,
each a different part of a skeleton. One by one, the tiny golden
bones were dug up until only Elinore's pelvis remained hidden.

The book was a sensation. A community of treasure hunters
called the Bonehunters formed, in frenzied competition,
obsessed to a dangerous degree. People sold their homes to
travel to England and search for Elinore. Marriages broke
down as the quest consumed people. A man died. The book
made Frank a rich man. His daughter, Nell, became a recluse.

But now the Churchers must be reunited. The book is being
reissued along with a new treasure hunt and a documentary
crew are charting everything that follows. Nell is appalled, and
terrified. During the filming, Frank finally reveals the whereabouts
of the missing golden bone. And then all hell breaks loose.

From the bestselling author of *He Said/She Said* and
Watch Her Fall, this is a taut, mesmerising novel about
a daughter haunted by her father's legacy . . .

HODDER

WE KNOW YOU KNOW

This novel was previously published as
Stone Mothers in hardback.

A lifetime ago, a patient escaped Nazareth mental asylum.
They covered their tracks carefully. Or so they thought.

Thirty years ago, Marianne Smy committed a crime then fled
from her home to leave the past behind. Or so she thought.

Now, Marianne has been forced to return. Nazareth asylum has
been converted to luxury flats, but its terrible hold on her is still
strong. A successful academic, a loving mother and a loyal wife,
she fears her secret being revealed and her world shattering.

She is right to be scared.

Read on for an extract . . .

HODDER

PART ONE
PARK ROYAL MANOR
2018

1

The blindfold hurts. His inexperience shows in the knot. It's tight but crude, and has captured a hank of my hair. Every time he takes a corner too fast, I rock to the side, the seatbelt slicing my shoulder and the tiny needlepoint pain in my scalp intensifying. He brakes without warning: I'm thrown forward. A loosening of the purple silk near my right temple lets in a little light but no information.

He has gone for full sensory deprivation. There is no music, only the rhythm of my breath and his, the bassline of the engine, the key changes of the shifting gears. The radio would help. An accumulation of three-minute pop songs would let me measure time. If forced to guess, I would say that we have been travelling for an hour but it could be half an hour or it could be two. I know that we drove out of London, not deeper into it, and that we must be far out of town now. For the first couple of miles I could track our route by the stop-start of traffic lights and speedbumps. It takes ten minutes to escape Islington's 20-mile-an-hour zone in any direction. I'm sure I smelled the barbecue restaurant on City Road but I think he circled the Old Street roundabout twice to confuse me and after that I was lost.

Once we were out of the city and moving fast, my nose caught a couple of bonfires – it's that time of year – but they had the woodsy feel of a domestic pile rather than anything agricultural or industrial. Sometimes it feels like we're in the middle of nowhere, winding through lanes, then he'll go smooth and fast again, and the rush of passing traffic will tell me we're back on an A-road. If we were heading for an airport, I would have expected the boom as the jets graze the motorway. I will not get on an aeroplane.

'Shit,' he mutters and brakes again. The last few strands of caught hair spring loose from their moorings. I can feel him shift in the seat, his breath skimming my cheek as he reverses slowly. I take the opportunity to put my hand up to my head, but he's watching me as well as the road.

'Marianne! You *promised*!'

'Sorry,' I say. 'It's really getting on my nerves now. What if I close my eyes while I re-tie it? Or while *you* re-tie it.'

'Nice try,' he says. 'Look, it's not far now.'

How near is not far? Another minute? Another thirty? If I twitch my cheek I can see a little more. What light I can sense starts to flicker rapidly through the violet gauze. Sunlight through a fence? The pattern is liminal, more irregular than that. We're in a tree tunnel, which means a country lane, which means—

'Sam! Have you booked us into a spa?'

I can hear the smile in his voice. 'I think I've done better than *that*.'

My shoulders relax, as though the masseur's hands are already on them. I can't think of anything better than two days being pummelled floppy by muscular young women in white tunics. It must be that organic place on the Essex coast I've been longing to try. I could relax in Essex. I could get to Mum in an hour and to Honor in two. Maybe, when Sam says he's done better than that, he's even arranged for Honor to *be* here.

The road is uneven now, all potholes and gravel, and I put my hands up, ready to unwind the scarf.

'Two more minutes!' Sam's voice vaults an octave. 'I want to see you see it.' The tyres crunch. I wait patiently with my hands in my lap as the parking sensors quicken their beep. 'OK, now,' he says, undoing the knot with a flourish. 'Welcome to Park Royal Manor.'

The name is familiar from the brochures and so is the image but shock delays its formation.

I see it as a series of architectural features – crenellations and gables, fussy grey stonework, tall forbidding windows – but I can't take in its breadth.

'I'm too near,' I try to say, but it comes out in a whisper.

Nazareth Hospital, or The East Anglia Pauper Lunatic Asylum as it originally was, wasn't designed to be viewed up close like this but as a whole, from a distance, whether you were being admitted to it or whether it was one last haunted look over your shoulder as you left or ran away. The last time I saw the place, and the way I still see it in my dreams, was from afar. It seemed to fill the horizon. It is perched on what counts for a hill around here, its width a warning to the flat country around it. Built to serve three counties, it is too big for modest Suffolk, its soaring Victorian dimensions all wrong.

I can drive from London to Nusstead almost on autopilot so how did I not recognise the journey?

Sam rubs his hands together in glee. 'How much d'you love me right now? Come on, let's have a proper look at the place.' He reaches across me and thumbs my seatbelt unlocked. I cannot get out of the car. A scream claws its way up the sides of my throat.

The pictures in the brochure didn't do the changes justice. The floor-to-ceiling panelled windows have been unbarred, hundreds of uncracked panes in new frames. The ivy and buddleia that sprouted impossibly from tilting chimney pots and rotting lintels has gone, replaced by a Virginia creeper whose remaining deep red leaves are neatly trimmed to expose silver brick. The vast double doors have been replaced by sheets of sliding glass with 'Park Royal Manor' etched in opaque curlicue. My eyes refuse to go any higher.

'What . . .' I begin. 'What are we doing here, Sam? What are we *doing* here?'

He mistakes panic for surprise. 'I got you a little pied-à-terre. No more crashing on Colette's sofa or shelling out for a hotel.'

I look down but that's even worse. No, I can't see the renovated clocktower but I can see its shadow, like the cast of a giant sundial, a dark grey finger pointing right at me. For all the fancy ironwork of its clock face the tower was only ever a lookout post in disguise – Nazareth ran on its own time – and I feel watched now. I pull the blindfold clumsily back down over my eyes, the hem of the scarf catching in my mouth.

'Marianne?' says Sam, staring at me. 'Marianne, what's the matter?'

It isn't a scream after all but its opposite, a dry desperate sucking in of air that contains no oxygen, only dust. 'I can't go in,' I manage. 'Please, Sam, don't make me go back.'